George R. Fitz-Roy Cole

The Peruvians at Home

George R. Fitz-Roy Cole

The Peruvians at Home

ISBN/EAN: 9783337378141

Printed in Europe, USA, Canada, Australia, Japan

Cover: Foto ©Andreas Hilbeck / pixelio.de

More available books at **www.hansebooks.com**

THE PERUVIANS AT HOME

BY

GEORGE R. FITZ-ROY COLE

LONDON

KEGAN PAUL, TRENCH & CO., 1, PATERNOSTER SQUARE

1884

I DEDICATE THIS WORK

TO MY MOTHER,

SOPHIA FRANCES COLE,

AS A SMALL TOKEN OF MY LOVE AND ESTEEM

FOR ONE WHOSE CONSTANT LOVE AND ENCOURAGEMENT

HAVE BEEN THE LIGHT AND GUIDE

OF MY LIFE.

b

PREFACE.

IN the spring of 1873, I had occasion to visit Peru on private business. I resided in that country for upwards of two years, during which time I had opportunities of seeing its most important towns and sights. The objects of my visit, together with the introductions I carried with me, brought me into contact with all classes of Peruvians, from the politicians and merchants of Lima, to the farmers and labourers in the province, the fishermen on the coast, and the miners among the hills; in fact with men who, differing from each other in habits of life as much as in colour and character, form a mixed society, both strange and novel. Peru is perhaps of all countries in the known world (excepting the Caucasus) unparalleled for the number and variety of races comprising its people. But to the ordinary European traveller the country is chiefly known as the great guano-producer; unfortunately also of late years it has attained a less enviable reputation as a kind of political quicksand, in which large sums of good money have been lost without return. I do not propose to discuss in this volume the gross mismanagement of Peruvian finance by men, some of whom are now no more; much less the terrible penalty which the nation has had to pay, owing to the misapplication of the funds intended for its advancement, and which, better distributed, so rich a country and so intelligent a race were entitled to expect. It is of the inner life of Peruvians that this book treats—the peculiar traits of character, domestic customs and usages, the description of men and manners, and of the soil and scenery, all of which subjects deeply interested and amused me. Since my visit, the country has experienced all the horrors of a disastrous war, continued over several years and on both sides with a spirit of determination and rancour not usually shown by modern belligerents. The character and habits of a people who thus voluntarily sacrificed all that man holds dear, for the sake of preserving their nationality, cannot but be of general interest and, to some extent, instructive.

The chapter headed " John Chinaman Abroad " was written for *Fraser's Magazine* in October, 1878, and is reproduced with the kind permission of Messrs.

Longmans, Green, and Co. I think also that the articles entitled, "The Saltpetre Deposits of Peru," and "A Railroad across the Andes," which I contributed respectively to the *Journal of the Society of Arts* on September 10, 1875, and to *The Alpine Journal* of May, 1878, and which describe routes and places but little known to the public, will add to the interest of this volume.

Among the readers of the following pages, perhaps there may be some who, knowing me personally, will ask how it is that I have at last been induced to write and publish a more or less complete account of one section of my travels. But it is a fact that I have never been able to give a satisfactory reason for not complying with the often-repeated suggestions of friends to publish, in the collective form of a book, my impressions of Russia, Peru, and of other countries which I have visited. I have invariably replied to all such suggestions that my travels commenced at a time when I was very young, though, it is true, at an age when the mind is generally very ready to receive impressions, and that I did not think my observations could prove of any great public interest, nor did I feel inclined to give the time and labour which writing a book involves. I responded, however, to the friendly pressure laid upon me, so far as to write several separate articles, which, on being sent to the magazines, were, with one exception, accepted by the respective editors. With this I thought I had paid the dues usually expected from him who goes to foreign parts and sees new and strange things, and I hoped that with these my literary labours had come to an end. Comforted with this feeling, " I went my way," while old Father Time went *his*, and having many genuine interests in life, one year succeeded another in rapid succession.

At last the war (just ended) between Chili and Peru sharply revived public attention once again with regard to these distant countries. The sudden notoriety acquired by Peru as a combatant, gave her enemies the opportunity to repeat in contributions to the press the old expressions of abuse which have been so unjustly heaped on the Peruvians. I, for one, cannot stand by inactive and watch the weak man oppressed by the strong, or witness without emotion the rich and arrogant trample on the feelings of the humble and innocent. If we hear a man accused wrongfully, while we know something which, being told, may affect the verdict, should not conscience compel us to come forward as witness to the truth? So at least my conscience has counselled me. I knew that great untruths had been written about Peru and the Peruvians in contributions to the public press by persons who had never seen that country, but who felt keenly the losses they had sustained in Peruvian loans. Added to this, but few serious works of impartial criticism on the country and its people have been published of late; in fact, if we exclude the one-idead pamphlets dealing with the loan business, the number of books written on Peru during the last ten years is limited to two or three.

Briefly, I felt it to some extent my duty to publish my experiences, hoping that they might help to dissipate the misconceptions which were fast becoming rooted in the public mind, and accepted as truths. I knew this self-imposed task would prove a long one, but many have undertaken tasks whose only payment has been the satisfaction of having fulfilled them worthily, difficult and hard though they might often be. Suffice it to say, that on this occasion I welcomed the prospect of an absorbing occupation like that of writing a book, involving as it does months of toil and unremitting attention, with feelings of pleasurable anticipation, mingled with a sense of responsibility. The journal which I had regularly kept during my residence in Peru, my unfinished sketches, and memoranda of the correspondence maintained ever since my return home with the friends made in that country, were all at hand; and with these materials the present work was commenced at the end of February last.

Now that my task is completed, I feel at times like a schoolboy when class is over and recreation begins ; at other times I miss the habitual occupation as the presence of a friend, whose companionship has become dear. But besides this feeling of regret, I confess to experiencing a supreme sensation, which is a mixture of satisfaction, fear, and thankfulness, something akin to what a parent is said to feel on the birth of his child. All this I feel, excepting that I am not vain enough to be elated before the verdict of public opinion has been pronounced on this the first (and probably the last) important literary offspring of my brain. Public opinion is often compared to a fair goddess, whose favours are hard to win. Novice as I am in the art of wooing her, my courtship may not prove successful. The favour of this goddess is said to be more readily extended to those who have already made their names known in the field of literature, or have attained some place in the aristocracy of letters. I have no such credentials. The merits of truth and sincerity are the only claims I can urge, for I have not attempted to give fictitious value to my descriptions of life in Peru by any high colouring, or by relating anything which is not strictly consistent with truth. I have written a simple, truthful account of what I saw in the language habitual to me, without attempting to court favour

by imitating the possibly more attractive style of
contemporary sensational writers. Whether this will
ensure success, Time, the great solver of many
enigmas, can only prove. With the consciousness of
having worthily exerted myself to please, and occasionally to instruct, I wait the verdict of public opinion,
which I have symbolized as a goddess, whose favours,
though difficult to win, are of a quality which lead
one to run the risk of experiencing only the chilling
disappointment of unrequited courtship, in the hope
that honest work may gain honest meed.

G. FITZ-ROY COLE.

54, QUEEN ANNE'S GATE, S.W.,
    July 31*st*, 1884.

CONTENTS.

CHAPTER III.

LIMA.

PAGE

The Plaza—Private Houses—A Mansion—A Reception—Peruvian Beauty—Peruvian Gentlemen—Convents—Retreats—Theatres —Bull-fights—The Matador 39

CHAPTER IV.

CHICLAYO AND THE CHICLAYANOS.

The Plaza at Night—The Cathedral—Mixed Races—Religious Ceremonies—Miraculous Images—Pizarro—Inca Government —Inca Land Laws—Natural Religion—Spanish Christianity— Spaniards and Peruvians—Social Customs—Musical Talent— Mixed Beverages — Domestic Qualities — *Esprit de Corps*— Petty Quarrels—Chiclayo—Early Morning—Objects of Interest —" Tell me Something New " 53

CHAPTER V.

PROVINCIAL LIFE.

Foreigners in Peru—Settlers—Adventurers—Annual Fête—Native Industries—Eten—Straw-plaiters — Social Customs—Chilca— Santa Rosa—" Oiling the Waves "—Sociability of the Peruvians—Cock-fighting—Monsefu Fête 73

CHAPTER VI.

NATIVE CUSTOMS.

Railways—Eten—Balsas—Cholos—Simple Food—Fingers *versus* Forks—Provincial Life—The Ethiopian Eye—The Panuela— Riot in Chiclayo — Local Government — Vultures — Huacas —Pottery—The Picci Skull 87

CHAPTER VII.

IN THE SOUTH.

CHAPTER VIII.

PICA AND TARAPACA.

CHAPTER IX.

THE NORTH AGAIN.

CHAPTER X.

PAST AND PRESENT.

CHAPTER XI.

PERUVIAN ANTIQUITIES.

CHAPTER XII.

JOHN CHINAMAN ABROAD.

CHAPTER XIII.

A RAILROAD ACROSS THE ANDES.

THE PERUVIANS AT HOME.

———o◇o———

CHAPTER I.

WESTWARD HO!

Routes—Starting—H.M. Mails—Farewell—" Life on the Ocean
Wave "—Social Influences—First Sight of the West Indies
—St. Thomas—Coaling—Jackmel—Kingston—Mr. Bagot
Smith — Home-welcoming — Necessities — Black Labour—
View from Mr. Smith's Villa—Road to Newcastle—Life on
a Sugar Estate—Cane *versus* Beetroot Sugar.

IN 1872, the writer went out on board one of the
Royal Mail steamers, which leave Southampton fortnightly for the West Indies.   His destination was
Peru, in which country he resided for over two years.
But his knowledge of the country and of its people
is not limited to the experiences gained during his
residence, for he has maintained a continuous correspondence with the friends he made there ever since
he returned home.   Arriving at St. Thomas, after
fifteen days' steaming, he changed into another

B

steamer, which landed him at Colon, or "Aspinwall," as it has been renamed in these latter days. It is of little use describing a voyage which has already been so often described. The name Aspinwall was given to the port originally named Colon, after Columbus, by the American speculator who "promoted" and carried out the Panama Railway. He covered that narrow and singular strip of country, which, as the maps show, unites the large continents of North and South America by a narrow neck of land. Mere thread as it is, it is at present causing a sufficient amount of difficulty to M. de Lesseps and his shareholders, now that the question of cutting it has come prominently forward.

From the other side of the isthmus the writer took ship for Peru; the cost of the single journey from London to Lima, including incidental expenses, was little under £100, and took a month to accomplish, facts which make one realize the distance, and the fact that Peru, interesting country as it is and full of unexplored beauties, lies somewhat beyond the range of the ordinary British tourist.

Time, to the writer, was an object, otherwise those who enjoy the sea, and much of it, would prefer the longer and slower route, which, touching at more than one point the coast of Brazil, takes the traveller through the Straits of Magellan, bordered on either side by high snow-clad mountains, and thence along the whole length of the beautiful coasts of Patagonia and Chili, affording glimpses of fine scenery, and a brief acquaintance with many different countries and varying types of humanity. As to the cost of this route, it is much the same as the other, but the difference in time is considerable, the Straits route taking about six weeks, as against a month by the isthmus.

Peru may be reached by yet a third route, namely, by crossing the Atlantic from Liverpool to New York, and then taking one of the steamers which ply between that place and the Gulf of Mexico, going on to Aspinwall. The writer returned home by this route, and the pleasant and instructive society he met on board, consisting of Californian families returning to the States from Aspinwall, caused him to rejoice in his decision. This route involves a stoppage for a few days in New York, giving an opportunity of seeing the sights in that interesting city, also the beauties of the Hudson River.

Of the three routes, the West Indian is to be preferred, on account of the shorter time and superior conveniences.

On embarking at Southampton on board the Royal Mail Steamship Company's ship *Nile*, the deck was a scene of bustle and excitement. " St. Thomas," " Vera Cruz," " Jamaica," " Panama," " Colon," " Callao," " Mexillones," " St. Kitts," " Antigua," are a few of the names shouted out as the mail-bags are tossed up from the quay, for stowing away in their respective places on board the huge and crowded boat just starting for the West Indies. These English mail-bags, generally the latest arrivals at all departures, whether of steamers or trains, how numerous they are, and how indicative of the multiplicity of "British interests," and also of the many relatives and friends who must be living far away from all they love and revere in their native land! In honourable banishment and not forgotten, as these ponderous mail-bags show, and most of them with the hope, more or less well founded, of "making their fortune" and "coming home to spend it," in some cases to be realized, in others—well, perhaps there are some "whose mind to them a kingdom is," and who can make themselves as happy and contented in the land of their adoption, with the interests they create for themselves, as they would be at home. More so indeed in many cases, we may reflect as we look round on the struggle for bread in this overstocked old country, as witness the dozens of eligible applicants called forth by the announcement of one small poorly paid vacancy in almost any department.

After the mail-bags follow a number of boxes of "specie," which are carefully slid along the bridge and thence taken to the safe room. At length the bitter "parting hour" has arrived, the bell rings for visitors to leave, hands are pressed and tears shed, and a never-to-be-forgotten epoch is marked in the lives of many, some of whom are now bidding each other farewell for ever, happier that they know it not. In this case the old adage may be true, "Where ignorance is bliss, 'twere folly to be wise." Ah! life, with all its intricacies, uncertainties, and deep mysteries, and its many sorrows, does it contain for any one of us anything so bitter or which saddens the heart so completely as the act of bidding farewell to one we love, with the consciousness that we may never meet again alive?

But the sad episode is over, and now the engines commence to move, at first slowly (something like a wrestler who cautiously feels the strength of his adversary before putting forth his whole might), and with a brisk south-south-west breeze on her bow, the *Nile* clears out of Southampton Water, and makes for the open Channel. In this age of much travelling, there are few who have not had some experience of these Atlantic liners, which are considered of no account unless they are fitted and provided with all the comforts and conveniences of a first-class hotel on shore. In the writer's experience, life on the open sea always follows much the same monotonous routine, and this *ennui* is only regulated in proportion to the state of our own health, our capability of falling back on our own resources, or on a due appreciation of the society of our fellow-travellers. To most, it is to be feared, "the tocsin of the soul, the dinner-bell," marks the great event of the day. The writer was once advised by a " globe-trotter " and author, who has long ago made his mark, never to publish the *ménu* of any meal he might have consumed during his travels, unless it contained something quite out of the common. The ordinary itinerary of life at sea for most of us does not merit more record than the *ménu;* but to the sympathetic mind there is to be found an exhaustless field of study among the various characters of our fellow-travellers. Perhaps no other situation affords quite so good an opportunity for reading the character and disposition of a fellow-creature as that of a long sea-voyage. Withdrawn from his habitual associations and occupations, a person's character becomes as it were unmasked; official duties which impose an artificial restraint and often induce an air of repellant formality are thrown on one side; the presence of wife, husband, or child, which unconsciously influences our conduct, is missed; and under these circumstances, the most chary and unsociable human being unbends, sinks differences, and falls into conversation with his neighbour. In a few days on board ship we get to know more of our neighbours' thoughts and character than in years of casual meeting "in society." And thus is the tedium of a long voyage beguiled, for "the proper study of mankind is man."

Perhaps there is no more wonderful and pleasing sight to be seen anywhere by an Englishman than the very first glimpse of the West Indian Islands. Accustomed all his life to the heavy atmosphere and dark days of an English winter, the bright sunshine and brilliant colours of the West suddenly burst on his view, and at first the sight seems too gorgeous to be real, and as if our fancy had conjured up some highly wrought brain-picture of an enchanted land. It is difficult to believe that those pink objects, golden-tipped by the rising sun, which appear to float on the surface of the dark blue line where sea and sky meet, are *real* islands, or that the beautiful blue liquid, smooth as a lake, through which we are piercing our way, is the same element and composed of exactly the same substances as the brown, angry-looking waves which we left behind not long ago in the English Channel. Then the sight of porpoises rolling and racing astern, as if their very lives depended on their arriving at St. Thomas before the ship, and the flying-fish darting high up in the air, their bright scales flashing in the sunshine like bits of highly polished silver, increases the bewilderment and favours the idea of unreality and enchantment.

> " The flying-fish leap
> From the Indian deep,
> And mix with the sea-birds half asleep."
>
> SHELLEY.

Beautiful isles of the West! If bright colours, clear sunshine, and a warm but genial atmosphere, together with a fruitful soil, producing abundant and varied growth, were the only requisite elements to form an earthly paradise, how fitting would be that designation for you!

The first land touched in the New World was

St. Thomas, one of the Virgin Islands, formerly the central depôt for all West Indian produce and trade. A natural bay, shaped like a horse-shoe, but of moderate size, with entrance to the south, forms a harbour, sheltered on all sides from the wind by high hills clothed with verdure. The violence of the hurricanes, which from time to time sweep round the bay and carry everything afloat before them to destruction, is by many attributed to the height of the surrounding hills, which offer no escape to the wind. It is asserted that the hurricane rotates round the bay again and again, like the water in a whirlpool, gaining strength at each rotation.

The agencies of the various shipping companies are situated in the front of the anchorage ground, and behind them runs the principal street, with shops full of a variety of articles, principally of apparel. There are also several hotels, the best of which was the Hôtel de France, where visitors on shore obtained some excellent cream ices, which were rendered doubly acceptable by the excessive heat of the weather.

It was a relief to get on shore and escape the noise and dust of "coaling," which commenced in right earnest soon after the anchor had dropped—in fact, our ship soon became the prey of the coalers. A huge barge was moored on either side, loaded to the top with coal, and an army of sturdy blacks, naked to the waist, set to work shovelling coal into baskets, which were then carried by women to the shoot, and their contents discharged into the hold of the steamer. The women were as rough and uncouth as the men. But the labour was carried on under a continuous stream of jokes and songs ; for the negro is a careless, jovial fellow, under whatever circumstances he may be found. Compared with his more serious brother, the white man, he is thoughtless as a child. Now and then the coalers would stop working, and the whole gang join in some such chorus as the following :—

> " He is a hang-dog, Johnny,
>   Aha ! aha ! aha ! aha !
> But him don't hang the *old man* "—

the " old man " possibly meaning the stern arm of law and justice.

The noise of coaling, varied by the songs of the coalers, continued all night and all the following day, which was Sunday.

The passage from St. Thomas to Colon was made in the steamship *Corsica,* a ship of smaller tonnage than the *Nile,* and offering less comfort and convenience to passengers. Touching at Jackmel, the port of Hayti—whose inhabitants are said to live in a chronic state of revolution, but were fortunately at that time unusually quiet—to put down the mails and a single passenger, the *Corsica* steamed on to Port Royal in Jamaica, where she was overhauled by the health inspector. Kingston Harbour lies three miles

further up the Straits ; it is formed by a narrow strip
of land projecting straight out from the mainland, and
then curving round and running parallel for some
length, thus providing one of the safest of the many
natural harbours to be found in the West Indies.

A fellow-passenger, Mr. Bagot Smith, paymaster
in her Majesty's forces, now returning to his duties at
Kingston, offered the hospitalities of his temporary
home, by which the writer profited, for so good an
opportunity of seeing something of Jamaica and West
Indian life was not to be lost.

The town of Kingston is well laid out, especially
the western portion, where the houses are well built
and spacious, with a wide balcony running all round
the ground floor, providing a shady cool resting-place
during the hot hours of the day. Most of these
dwellings have large gardens, in which grow magnolia
and banana trees, whose delicious fruit and beautiful
foliage add not inconsiderably to the pleasures of
West Indian life. Leaving the town, the road to Mr.
Smith's house passed over the wide even plain, which
intervenes between the coast and the range of hills
rising several thousand feet above sea level, and which,
in consequence, are said to afford every imaginable
variety of climate. The house is some six miles distant from Kingston, and at its elevation, one thousand
feet above the sea, the air is cool and pleasant, even
in the summer months. On the way up, a long level
tract of ground was pointed out as the local race-

course; for even here in the West Indies, the sporting proclivities of the English race find an outlet. The "turf" looked brown and baked by the sun, and the grass was thin and weedy, which the driver of Mr. Smith's buggy accounted for by saying that no rain had fallen for two months, and the country was suffering from the prolonged drought.

The tall cacti, which formed a thick picturesque hedge some twelve feet in height on either side of the road, seemed alone among the vegetable world not to suffer from the want of water. Here and there groups of cocoa trees, their tall smooth trunks like the masts of a ship, surmounted with magnificent heads of huge fan-like palm leaves, offered tempting oases of shade from the sun's heat. These were, however, quite inaccessible, owing to the low brushwood which generally clothed the hillside.

Several nigger huts were passed along the road, and many a hearty welcome was shouted to Mr. Smith by their occupants, who were generally seated in front of their dwellings. One fat old lady, beaming with smiles and good-nature, inquired tenderly after his family and children (whom she had never seen), and put all manner of questions about England, Queen Victoria, Mr. Gladstone, and the expected comet! "Me so glad to see you back, Massa Smith; and you do look so well, you do, sir. You look quite bloomy, dat you do, sir!" she cried, as the buggy moved on. A male nigger, who together with his cordiality had evidently an eye to the main chance, shouted, " Hey, Massa Smith, you come back? Yes. Well, me hope you brought me hun'red pound!" These Jamaican blacks appear to be a happy, good-humoured, lazy race, asking nothing but to be allowed to earn the simplest of food with the least possible expenditure of physical exertion. A rough cabin is easily formed of boughs and twigs interlaced, the roof plastered over and made watertight with mud ; a small plot of ground behind is dug over and planted with the thrice blessed yam ; and, hey presto! here is a home and means of providing in plenty for husband, wife, and numerous progeny.

The yam, or West Indian potato, is the universal and frequently the sole article of diet used among the Jamaica negroes, who seldom eat meat of any kind. More often than not, the humble garden is also planted with banana, fig, and orange trees, the fruit of which is taken down to Kingston market to be sold, the proceeds supplying clothing and other small household needs of the family. In a climate so genial and so suited to the negro race, the necessities of life (as they understand it) are few and easily obtained, the pressing need for fuel to soften the rigours of the climate, which taxes our own poor so heavily, being unknown in Jamaica; for there, at least on the coast, the inhabitants can, if they like, sleep out of doors nearly all the year round, without danger of catching cold. Thus the ambition of the Jamaica black is limited to the power of purchasing a small plot of ground on which to form his homestead as described, and to be able to lead a life of comparative idleness, interrupted only by the days' labour he may think fit to give to others, with the view of gaining sufficient to supply the deficiency of income which his own plot of land fails in doing. It is a fact generally admitted in Jamaica, that the negro will only offer himself for hire under extreme pressure; for as long as he has a crust of brown bread and a yam for dinner, he feels himself quite independent of all men. "A crust of bread and liberty" is his motto, and to bask idly in the sun his ideal of happiness. It is owing to this characteristic idleness, which is probably constitutional in the negro, that the larger employers of labour in the West Indies are turning their attention to the useful and industrious Chinaman, who may already be found employed in large numbers in several of the islands belonging to the British, as well as in Hayti and Cuba.

The view from Mr. Smith's house, built as it is on the slope of the hill, is very picturesque. Immediately beneath lies Kingston, with its white-washed buildings peeping through the rich tropical foliage; and beyond that the blue sea, stretching away to Port Royal (which we had passed that morning), with ships sporting the bunting of nearly all nations, anchored off land; beyond this, the darker blue of the broad Atlantic in the far distance, marking a scarcely perceptible line where it meets the sky, which rivals it in pureness and density of colouring. To right and left spread the hills in gentle undulations, their slopes covered with verdure, wild flowers, and cactus in full bloom, and the masses of low green shrubs which characterize this part of the country. Towards evening, when all nature seemed to be preparing for rest, the scene was most impressive, one to touch even a traveller of world-wide experience with feelings of pleasure. The red and golden hues of the setting sun were reflected on the water beneath, while they tipped the hill-tops with golden gleams, as if loth to quit the lovely scene of tropical luxuriance. It was a glorious new experience to the travellers recently arrived from the dark and chilly North.

No visitor to Kingston should neglect to drive up the beautiful valley which gives access to the interior, and to the military sanitarium at Newcastle, situated high up among the hills. This valley is the chosen place of residence for the richer Kingston merchants and government officials, who build themselves charming villas on either side of the stream which runs down the centre. The ground all round is well wooded and clothed with beautiful flowers and plants, and one can well understand how glad the business men must be to reach such an agreeable retreat after the day's work has been done in hot, dusty Kingston.

Perhaps the most enjoyable mode of existence in the West Indies is that led by the farmer, or, more properly speaking, the landed proprietor, since there is no regular class of tenant-farmers in Jamaica as at home, the land being invariably cultivated by the owner himself. Mr. Rose, one of our fellow-passengers on the *Nile*, who was returning from a short visit, described in words which amounted to ecstasy the life he had led in Barbadoes, where his father had purchased for him an estate. Rising at five a.m., he used to ride round his property, and, to quote his own words, "talk sugar-stick" with his manager or factor until ten, when he breakfasted. This "talking sugar-stick" included, as may be imagined, a great variety of subjects, such as the planting and watering of the cane, labour, machinery, and all the numerous arrangements which have to be made daily on a sugar estate, be its size large or small. During the heat of the day, correspondence and accounts were got through, and at five p.m. either another visit would be paid to the plantations or a call made upon a neighbour. Occasional balls and parties vary the routine of a life which is nearly always an industrious and simple one, removed as it is from the constant temptations and excitements so easy of attainment in busy, restless Europe. "But to be really happy in Barbadoes, a man should be married," said Mr. Rose. Most young men living alone in the country (ay me, even in a town !), and surrounded with plenty and luxury, must naturally yearn for the companionship of the gentler sex, and they will probably agree with the speaker,

who, in fact, did not long delay acting up to his opinion
—we will hope with all the success he expected.

Unfortunately, sugar-growing in the West Indies
is not so prosperous a business now as it was in former
years, and especially in the old slave-dealing days,
when labour was cheap and plentiful. But besides the
greater cost of labour, planters have to contend with
severe competition from the beetroot industry of
France, which has been extensively developed under
the encouraging protective laws of that country. Notwithstanding the large proportion of saccharine matter
produced by a given quantity of beet, its cultivation
and treatment in France have been found to be relatively less remunerative than that of sugar-cane in
the West Indies, Peru, and other tropical countries,
which are entirely unsubsidized by the State, and
where manual labour is both difficult to obtain and
expensive. Perhaps the quality of the different sugars
—as they are sold in the market—may have something to say to this, double quantities of beetroot
sugar being required to produce the effect of half the
amount when that manufactured from the cane is
used.* This may be one encouragement to our
colonists. Let us hope that the novel experiment of

* A fashionable French lady informed the writer the other
day in Paris that she always ordered her sugar from London.
She explained that the best quality of English crystallized sugar
is superior to French sugar of the same description in sweetness
and clearness, and is therefore more acceptable at the "five
o'clock teas" which have lately become fashionable at Paris.

introducing cheap Chinese labour may bring them better fortune and prove the means of restoring at least partial prosperity to these beautiful islands, the possession of which has always been a source of pride and also profit to Englishmen.

But we must not linger too long by the way. Jamaica and its interesting associations are at last left behind, and after three days' very rough tossing on the Caribbean Sea, we reach the port of Colon, or Aspinwall, and, for the first time, the writer sets foot on American soil.

CHAPTER II.

ISTHMUS OF PANAMA AND THE PERUVIAN LITTORAL.

Colon—Panama Railway—Luxuriant Vegetation—Native Fruits —Mulatto Labour—Panama—City of Panama—American Enterprise—Streets of Panama—Poorer Population—M. de Lesseps and the Panama Canal—Dredges—The Canal—Quantity of Material—Harbours—Contracts — Expected Time of Completion—Estimated Benefits—Coast of the Pacific—Alligator Hunting—Guayaquil—The Sea-coast—The Littoral—Rainless Districts—Cultivation of Rice—Rice—Abstemious Habits.

SOON after landing at Colon, the traveller finds himself confronted by a colossal bronze statue of Christopher Columbus, the gift of the late Emperor of the French to the State of Columbia. Columbus stands in an upright position, clothed in a loose robe, and stretching out his right hand in a protecting attitude over the form of a female Indian, who kneels at his feet and whose features are apparently moved by emotions of astonishment and fear. Altogether it is a striking and suggestive object which greets the traveller straight from European shores.

The foreshore round Colon is flat and marshy, and is said to be very unhealthy during the wet seasons, when yellow fever often prevails. The town itself contains few objects of interest, consisting as it does simply of the usual miscellaneous assortment of stores, provision and drinking houses, which are always to be found in the less civilized South American seaports. The lack of good hotel accommodation is explained by the fact that passengers on landing proceed immediately across to Panama, where every necessity is supplied. The distance across, from Colon to Panama, is about forty-five miles, but the fares charged for the transit by the American Railway Company, in 1872, would bear comparison as to extortion with those of any civilized European country. We were charged £5 per passenger, and at the rate of five cents for every pound of luggage exceeding one hundred and fifty.

After leaving the terminus, which is situated on the Island of Manzanillo, the railway crosses the narrow strait separating the island from the mainland, and enters a level country which is in places submerged by the overflow of the River Chagrès; the line touches the river itself at a point about five miles from Aspinwall. On either side of the road a dense impenetrable forest of bright green luxuriant vegetation flourishes to a height of thirty or forty feet, forming an effectual but undesirable shelter from the breeze which blows every afternoon from the sea.

Trees, shrubs, and tendrils in endless combinations of colour entwine together, sometimes joining, sometimes stifling each other. From the rich leaf-mould produced by the decay of all this rich vegetation after the fall of the leaf, fresh plants rise, apparently more vigorous and richer, owing to the manure produced and added to each season.

Ten miles further on, and the Chagrès is crossed, and the rise to the Andes begins. This mountain chain is here at its lowest. The view from the summit, situate half-way between two mighty oceans, is perhaps unique of its kind. Here and there the tops of tall palm trees and bananas overlook the dense forest of fir, birch, olive, and orange trees, which spreads nearly all over the country. But this luxuriance of vegetation proved a serious obstacle to the completion of the railway. When the ground was cleared, vegetation quickly sprang up again as strongly as ever, if the surface was left untouched even for a few days.

About half-way across the isthmus, the train stopped at a small station, where a number of native Columbians came to offer for sale to the passengers fruit and flowers and cooling drinks of their own preparation. Among the baskets of bananas, prickly pears, and oranges, we noticed the *chirimoya*, perhaps the most delicious of all tropical fruits. Its fruit is round, the largest about the size of a small cocoa-nut ; externally it is green, the skin being rather thick and tough. The fruit is snow-white and juicy, and provided with numerous small black seeds covered with a delicate substance resembling ice-cream. Both fruit and flower of the *chirimoya* emit a fine fragrance, which, when the tree is in full blossom, is very strong. It is difficult to describe the flavour of this fruit, unique and delicious as it is.

The vendors of these delicacies, chiefly women, all belonged to the native Columbian creoles, with perhaps more of the native Indian than Spanish blood in their veins. Some of the younger ones would have been reckoned "pretty" anywhere, their regular features, olive complexion, and dark eyes beaming with a somewhat subdued and sad expression, and their lithe graceful figures forming a type of female beauty which must be admired whenever seen. As is customary among all South American women, the hair, which is dark and grows straight and not curling, is worn in two long plaits falling over the shoulders They seemed to know but a few words of Spanish, which words, however, they used freely to press their wares on their customers.

Work on the railway is done almost entirely by mulattoes, overlooked by Americans, it having been found impossible to induce the natives to leave their farms and accept regular service under the company. As a rule, these mulattoes are big burly fellows, apparently endued with great physical strength ; they are coarse-featured, and as to their characters, lazy and untrustworthy to a degree. The writer has closely observed the Ethiopian eye, which expresses, as a rule, the character of its possessor. When stirred by anger, the native savagery of the aborigine shows itself—a savagery which has not been tamed by the restraints of civilization, and therefore closely resembles that of the beast—it burns through these coal-black optics, and tells of the devilish spirit which lurks within. At other times, these same eyes are capable of expressing the deepest pathos and affection, or greed and avarice with equal intensity, when love or selfishness becomes the motive power.

Panama, which is the western terminus of the railway, used to be an important military and commercial centre during the long period Spain ruled over those vast countries of South America. The place was at one time considered a kind of capital or centre of government, whence troops and instructions were sent to the governors and viceroys of the Spanish colonies situate on the west coast of America, which comprised in the aggregate an immense territory, extending from the Straits of Magellan to what is now called British Columbia. The royal mails, starting from the coast of Spain, were sent in a direction as straight as the winds would allow to Colon, and from thence carried across the isthmus over a paved causeway, the remains of which the writer observed still traceable in the vicinity of Panama. This city now contains a cathedral and several smaller churches and convents; these are frequently built of cut stone and present a most habitable and substantial appearance. The ruins of one church specially attracted attention, on account of the apparent unsuitability of the design in a country where earthquakes are of such frequent occurrence. The roof of this church had been supported by a series of wide-spanning arches, the remains of which were scattered on the ground in all directions.

Panama boasts of its grand hotel, besides several smaller ones. "The Grand" is due to the enterprising spirit of certain Americans. As it stands, it is an actual proof that the Monroe doctrine, by right of which the United States Government claims the exclusive right of interfering in the political affairs of the South American countries, is not looked upon as a dead letter by its citizens, but acted upon in real earnest. The remarkable interest taken by the citizens of the United States in the affairs of the southern continent and its inhabitants is apparent in the number of North Americans to be found in all the larger towns of Peru, Chili, Ecuador, Costa Rica, and other states, bringing with them their "notions" of improvement, and assisting the natives to develop the natural resources of the soil. Indeed, the destiny of a great number of these small republics (not to mention the bigger ones) is probably to be absorbed by the greater power of the North, which is continually, like the octopus on the sea-shore, or like Russia in the northern hemisphere, stretching out its encroaching arms. Here they extend in a southerly direction. However this may be, the fact that the Americans regard with eyes of extreme jealousy any Europeans who may visit the west coast was patent to the writer. It seems an idea common to all great and powerful nations that the proximity of countries inhabited by new or weaker races calls for a special and singular "protection" to be extended over them. As in Europe, so in America, the "mission of Holy Russia," has it not resulted in the annexation, "at the earnest request of the Khans," of an immense and valuable tract of land extending to the much-talked-of Merv? Is American enterprise likely to be behind-hand in the rich sparsely inhabited countries joining them? The advantages promised by such special protection consist of the exclusive right of educating the native to wear clothes, and of supplying him therewith, together with other luxuries, the desire for which is induced by his introduction to civilization. Obviously, this system has given birth to doctrines analogous to the "Monroe" before now.

The streets of Panama, with their shops well furnished with the various products of South America, alongside of the more artistic manufactures of Paris and Vienna, and the quaint figures and faces met with on the trottoirs, are interesting to see; but the high temperature must make Panama a very undesirable residence for any length of time. The centre of the town, and that portion facing the beautiful Bay of Panama, dotted with its picturesque islands, and the suburbs which lie on the eastern side, are the most favoured places for a stroll in the early morning or in the cool of the evening. Like most cities, Panama has its poor (or rather its poorer) population ; for in South America no one who is fit for any kind of work need remain for long in want of food. They live in rows of cottages built of bamboo in the outskirts ; they are chiefly mulattoes, and belong to the labouring class. They are employed about the shipping in the bay, the town buildings, or as porters in the carriage of goods to and from the country or the railway. It was quite distressing to observe how prevalent among them was that frightful and unsightly disease *elephantisis*, in which one leg swells and swells till it assumes elephantine proportions. This disease is attributed to impoverishment of blood brought about by fever—it seems almost entirely confined to mulattoes, or to those having some trace of negro blood in their veins.

Public interest in the Isthmus of Panama has enormously increased since M. de Lesseps commenced the cutting of the canal by which it is intended to connect the Atlantic with the Pacific Ocean. M. de Lesseps, who is Président-directeur of the "Compagnie Universelle du Canal Interocéanique," the society charged with this important undertaking, has recently been so good as to forward to the author particulars of the scheme. Although the object aimed at is well understood, and has been discussed in many places and by many men, the precise means by which, as it is hoped, the object may be attained do not appear to have been yet published in English, either by the press or in any private work. A brief description of the scheme may therefore perhaps be of interest, now that public attention is directed that way.

The general plan of the canal is easily described, but the methods prepared for overcoming the difficulties which may be expected *en route* are far too numerous and complicated to elucidate here. It is proposed to cut a trench, measuring twenty-two mètres at the bottom (the surface of the water will measure fifty mètres in breadth), from one side of the isthmus to the other, at a sufficient depth to provide eight and a half mètres of water throughout. The total length of the canal, measured from the Bay of Limon in the Atlantic to a point opposite the island of Périco in the Bay of Panama, these being the two entrances, is seventy-five kilomètres. On the Panama side, for a length of fourteen kilomètres, and on the Colon side for about twenty kilomètres, the canal will be, in great measure, excavated with the help of steam dredges. These dredges, the largest and most efficient of which are those manufactured in the United States, are destined to be of incalculable use in excavating the enormous quantity of material which must be removed to form the canal. The average daily work performed by one of the largest of these dredges, in marshy or soft ground, is stated to be 3800 cubic mètres; but when beds of coral are met with, the quantity diminishes to 1200 mètres. The smaller dredges excavate about 800 mètres per diem, under the most favourable circumstances.

The difficulties to be overcome in cutting the central portion of the canal, where it will have to be cut through the Cordillera for a length of forty kilomètres, are of much greater magnitude than those found in the two preceding sections. From the twentieth kilomètre (on the Atlantic side), where the surface of the ground is about eight mètres above sea level, the ground rises gradually to the summit, where it attains an altitude of 160 mètres. From the summit, the ground falls abruptly towards the Pacific, being at the sixtieth kilomètre only eight mètres above sea level, and from that point it slopes gradually to the level of the sea.

It will be understood that in order to cut a canal, which shall have no locks, wide enough to allow of two ships passing each other, through ground which rises to this considerable altitude, the removal of an enormous quantity of earth and rock is necessary. In fact, at the meeting of the shareholders of the company, held in Paris, on the 28th of September last, M. Dingler, managing engineer of the canal works, stated that "the great difficulty of the undertaking was the enormous quantity of material which has to be removed, and which is estimated at 100,000,000 cubic mètres."

Taking the easiest attainable route across the isthmus, the canal will intersect and, in many cases, occupy the beds of existing rivers, the largest and most important of which is the Chagrès, which discharges into the Bay of Limon. For obvious reasons it was thought unadvisable to discharge the water of this river into the canal. The line of the Chagrès is therefore to be diverted, and its waters will empty themselves into the ocean through a number of new channels, which will be cut separately but parallel to each other. To reduce these new drainage canals to as small dimensions as possible, it is proposed to accumulate the flood waters inundating the Upper Chagrès in the winter months into an immense artificial reservoir, which will be capable of storing a milliard of cubic mètres of water. This reservoir is to be formed by throwing an embankment (the materials for which will be excavated from the canal) across a deep and wide valley at the point where the Obispo and Santa Cruz hills face each other at no great distance. The quantity of material which will be absorbed by this embankment will be no less than seven million cubic mètres. M. Dingler, while admitting that to form a similar embankment in France would cost no less than four francs per cubic yard, thinks that on the isthmus one franc per mètre will cover the cost ; so that in his opinion the whole embankment and the works accessory to it will cost only eight millions of francs.

The formation of suitable harbours will be an inconsiderable work, in comparison with the cutting of the canal proper. At Colon, it is thought that ample shelter will be provided by throwing out two breakwaters—indeed, perhaps one will suffice ; while at Panama it will be sufficient simply to cut a deep channel through the shallow waters of the bay, which is already naturally protected.

With 100,000,000 cubic mètres of earth and rock to be removed before the canal can be made, the estimated cost of the undertaking, put by M. de Lesseps at 600,000,000 francs, has naturally excited some criticism. The accounts of the company show that about one-third of this capital sum has already been exhausted in acquiring a large interest in the Panama railroad, in the purchase of materials, the construction of edifices, and the removal of 4,555,534 cubic mètres of earthworks, which is the total quantity excavated up to March 31, 1884, according to the official returns.

The contract price of the dredging at Panama, which is being done by the Franco-American Trading Company of New York, is 1 fr. 50 c. per cubic mètre ; and at Colon, where the American Contracting and Dredging Company are the contractors, it varies from 1 fr. 29 c. to 1 fr. 50 c. per cubic mètre. The work of excavation in the central portion of the isthmus is nearly all being done by blacks belonging to Jamaica and other West Indian Islands, who have been induced to come over by the offer of unlimited employment on the canal. The excavation is all done by piecework, and, according to the report of Lieutenant Rodgers, of the U.S.N., to his Government, dated January 27, 1884, the actual price paid for work performed on the Culebra or summit section ranges from three to eight francs per cubic mètre.

The date fixed for opening the canal, according to M. de Lesseps, is the year 1888.

In so interesting a work as this, which, when completed, will influence the maritime commerce of the whole world, and facilitate and cheapen the means of communication between nations hitherto separated by natural barriers, M. de Lesseps and his supporters are entitled to the best wishes of every one for their success. Twenty-four millions sterling looks a large price to pay for the benefit of the canal, but no doubt it can be shown that this expenditure is justified by the large receipts which the canal may be expected to earn in the shape of tolls from the ships which may use this new route to the East. The questions as to whether the canal can be made for the sum estimated, or if, when made, it will but create competition with the canal at Suez, are too broad and deep to answer here. As to such possibilities, it is hoped that the reader may be assisted in forming an opinion by the data here given. The one important fact remains, that the work has at last been actually begun in earnest, and the probability is that it will be completed in due time, though it may possibly cost more than the sum estimated at first. It is curious to learn who the enterprising persons really are who lend their money on this venture. At the meeting of the shareholders of the company, when M. Dingler explained the engineering features of the scheme, M. de Lesseps declared that he looked for his supporters among that class of men whom Lord Palmerston has dubbed "les petits gens," and he ended by saying, " Eh bien, ces petits gens ont fait les plus grandes œuvres du siècle." (Bravos ! Applaudissements répétés.)

The journey southwards from Panama is one of the pleasantest sea trips that could be chosen in any part of the globe. The Pacific keeps up the good character given to it by the early Spanish navigators, for its surface is seldom troubled by storm or tempest. Notwithstanding, this sea is not a favourite voyage among sailors, their dislike to it arising mainly from the dense fogs (known by the name of *guara*) which frequently prevail along the coast during the winter months, and, secondly, to the peculiar sweeping motion of the rollers which break on the shore, and render landing often a task of danger and difficulty. But in its normal condition, the Pacific is smooth as a lake ; and the pleasant warmth-giving sunshine glorifies the magnificent scenery of the chain of the Andes.

Proceeding southwards, the first port touched by the Pacific Company's steamers is Payta, which lies to the extreme north of Peruvian territory; but on the return northwards, they run up the Guayaquil river as far as the town of that name, which is the seaport of Ecuador. The "experiences" of a trip up the Guayaquil give a very fair idea of the life one would expect to lead in Peru, of its many interests, which can be made so real and absorbing, and also of. the complete absence of those public entertainments, games, etc., the frequenting of which has become almost a necessity to the Londoner and Parisian.

Mr. Smith, British Consul at Guayaquil, proved to be a great sportsman, his "happy hunting-ground" being the mud-banks of the river, and his quarry the alligators which frequent these places. So keen was the consul on this peculiar kind of *chasse* that he was able proudly to show his visitors many scores of skeleton alligators, of all sizes and ages, which he had killed during his residence. Some of these skeletons measured nearly ten feet in length ; and the *manner* of killing the creatures was as bold as it was surprising. Mr. Smith explained that it was the habit of these omnivorous beasts to bury themselves in the soft mud as the tide receded, and to stay there in a comatose state, warming themselves and resting, till the rising waters brought back the fish and reptiles on which they feed. Armed with a sharp-edged axe, Mr. Smith would wade in top-boots across the mud, and approaching the sleeping beast unawares, jump on his shoulders and proceed to hack away at his neck till the head was severed from the trunk. Quite vainly would the awaking alligator strike out right and left with his long fan-like tail, or gyrate round and round in the futile hope of unseating his assailant, who, like the Old Man of the Sea, was from his position placed beyond reach of attack whether by tooth, claws, or tail.

Guayaquil possesses many good-sized houses, some of which were originally built by the early Spanish settlers, who loved to live within sound of their church bells, preferring to trust the management of their country estates to an overseer rather than live *en campagne* all the year round themselves. This custom of fixing his permanent residence in the nearest provincial town is to this day nearly universal among the proprietors on the West Coast. The advantages obtained from the society of our fellow-creatures are duly appreciated in regions thinly populated, and where country sports are unknown.

The principal residences surround the public Plaza or square, and are fronted with a covered arcade, like the Rue de Rivoli in Paris, only on a smaller and less magnificent scale. The walls are built of sun-dried brick, plastered over with mud and whitewashed; being of great thickness, an equable temperature is maintained within throughout the year. An air of stillness, which almost amounts to stagnation during the hottest hours of the day, seems to pervade the whole town, the inhabitants of which live an apparently inactive life, and one suggestive of no wish for self-improvement.

Soon after leaving the mouth of the Guayaquil, the appearance of the coast undergoes complete transformation. Instead of the exuberant foliage of Ecuador, a waste of sand on shore and hill strikes the eye everywhere. At last, Peru is sighted, that country of strange contrasts, in some places most luxuriantly fertile, in others barren and worthless, a country possessing natural resources unequalled by any other country in the world within the same area.

Previous to the recent war, ending with the conclusion of peace with Chili, which has deprived Peru of the province of Tarapaca, the Peruvian littoral extended over 1500 miles in length. The lofty chain of the Cordillera runs for nearly the whole length parallel with this coast line, leaving a strip of comparatively level country, varying from fifty to one hundred miles in width, between the foot of the mountains and the sea. This strip is cut up and divided into valleys, of which Payta is the most northerly, and stretches of high barren ground by the spurs of the great mountain, which shoot out laterally, like the ribs from the human spine. These wide intervening valleys are filled with rich soil, and are well suited for the cultivation of rice, sugar, maize, potatoes, lucerne, and a score of other edibles for man and beast. Where the

land has remained fallow for a short time, it is found
clothed with thick brush, or as it is locally called,
monté, generally consisting of a number of various
kinds of trees, bushes, and creepers. Chief among the
forest is to be distinguished the algarova, one of the
most valuable trees in South America. The commonest
shrub is the *chilko*, which grows very rapidly, and often
attains a height of thirty feet or more, making it very
suitable for fencing purposes. The shoots are round
and slender, and grow round the parent stem in twisted
and contorted branches, which soon become covered
with small round green leaves. Among the creepers, the
espina, or thorn, is chiefly noticeable. It would appear
to be an aftergrowth of rice, for it is invariably found on
all grounds where rice has been grown the year before.
It derives its name from the number of exceedingly
sharp-pointed thorns which cluster upon its shoots and
tendrils; and such is its vitality, that it frequently grows
quite independent of support to a height of thirty feet.

It is a fact, that along the whole of the Peruvian
littoral rain never falls; one of the many reasons
assigned being the general barrenness of the coast,
the inference being that so dry an atmosphere contains insufficient moisture to form many rainclouds—
those that are formed, gathering at an unusual elevation, are attracted laterally to the thickly wooded
heights of the Andes, where they shed their burden.
Hence cultivation is exclusively dependent upon irrigation; the importance therefore of each valley de-

pends upon the size of its river, which again is relatively proportioned to the height of the adjacent mountain chain. A glance at the map will suffice to explain the configuration of the Peruvian littoral and the physical conditions which influence its climate. It will be seen that the coast does not follow a straight line; but from Payta it trends in a south-easterly direction as far as Arica, at which point it turns due south, and follows a line nearly parallel with 70° long. W. of Greenwich. One of the results of this configuration is that the northern portion, from Arica to Payta, is much better watered than the southern, from Arica to Iquique. The northern portion is partly confronted with, and to a certain extent arrests and taps, the south-west tradewinds, which come heavily charged with rain from the Antarctic Ocean; while the southern, offering no opposing front, catches less of the moisture borne to it by the clouds.

In the valleys of Payta, Piura, Lambayeque, Trujillo, and others, which must be passed before the capital Lima is reached, rice and sugar are most cultivated. Rice, indeed, is a daily article of food alike among rich and poor. At the table of the rich it is served separately as a vegetable, or in the *plat de resistance*—a stewed duck smothered in rice, highly seasoned with red Chili pepper. The humble peon,*

* Literally, "footman," a day labourer—he who travels on foot, as distinguished from *cavallero*, a gentleman—he who rides on horseback.

oɪ labourer, is content with a simple dinner of rice boiled till it is soft, when it is well drained from the water, a handful of small beans added, a little Chili pepper, and often, but not always, a few pieces of goats' flesh or mutton. Unlike the English labourer, the Peruvian invariably prepares his own dinner, which he requires no one to cook or to bring to him. Before starting for work in the very early morning, he buys the simple provisions already named, and carries them with him in a small iron pot, which subsequently serves as a kettle to cook his dinner in, all that he needs to seek at the place of his daily labour being a few sticks and some water. Sometimes a few *camotes*, a delicious kind of sweet potato, are placed among the burning wood ashes under the kettle ; and on high days and holidays a gourd filled with chicha (beer made from maize) completes the feast which the peon considers fit to be placed before the king, much more the president of the Peruvian Republic !

General abstemiousness in matters of eating and drinking is a remarkable characteristic of all classes in Peru. Very few, even of the wealthy, indulge in rich cookery ; they are content with the most simple articles of diet, served in the plainest possible manner. As a general rule no wine or spirits of any kind are taken at meals, the beverage being plain water. Sometimes there is *chasse-café*, or a post-prandial cup. Indeed, the European and North American is freely accused of introducing the custom of alcohol drinking among the people of Peru, and the sight of numerous saloons or bars, "fixed up" on the Yankee system, which had already (in 1872) been opened in the capital, goes far to justify this assertion.

Notwithstanding this bad example, drinking among the Peruvians is chiefly confined to *dias de fiesta*, or the appointed days of religious festivals, and to the occasions of family rejoicing, such as a marriage or christening festivity. The fact that the cholo, or native labourer, is fond of his *chicha*, does not prove that he is a drunkard, although the same cannot be said of the zambo or Peruvian mulatto, a curious specimen of humanity, who frequently shows, beside his marked African nature, a mixture of Indian and Spanish blood in his veins. He is certainly addicted to strong drinks. *Chicha*, the favourite beverage of the natives, as mentioned before, is made from maize, the liquor being only half fermented. It is of a yellow colour, and has a "sharp" flavour, which does not at first please most palates, but is generally better liked upon further acquaintance. It contains a very small percentage of alcohol, and a great deal of farinaceous nourishment, and undoubtedly goes far to account for the fat, strong appearance of those who consume it habitually. The liquor is certainly well suited to the climate, and if not indulged in to excess must be considered a valuable article of nourishment for those engaged in arduous labours under a tropical sun which exhausts the strength and promotes thirst.

CHAPTER III.

LIMA.

LIMA is the political as well as the commercial capital of the Republic. It is there that the great mercantile houses transact their business, and there that the rich haciendados, leaving their estates, perhaps hundreds of miles distant, to be managed by an overseer, love to live and spend their means. Previous to the last war with Chili, the conveniences and comforts to be had in Lima were far superior to any found in the provincial towns of Peru—indeed, among the capitals of South America this city ranked first. Since the war it has somewhat suffered in reputation, and old *habitués* miss the former neat appearance of its streets, and the various signs of wealth which were then exhibited everywhere—the display of costly European wares in the shop windows, and the lavish expenditure of the richer inhabitants at their entertainments. With these exceptions, Lima and its suburbs remain unaltered, the public buildings and monuments having all escaped the wholesale destruction which is so often the fate of European cities when captured in war. The public buildings, streets, and squares, with their rows of private dwellings and convents, probably bear much the same appearance as they did at the commencement of the present century, when the Peruvians threw off the Spanish yoke. As to their architecture, it is partly Moorish, but owes more to Spanish additions. Like Guayaquil, the streets of Lima are laid out at right angles to each other, the principal square, or Plaza Mayor, where stand the cathedral and public offices, being in the centre of the town. Of how many important events in Peruvian history, of how many sanguinary scenes, has this Plaza been the scene? How often have the insurgent citizens and the soldiers of the president of the day fought out their quarrels on its till recently unpaved surface? How many unpopular presidents have been sacrificed to public vengeance, and hung from the top of one of the round towers which stand on each side of the cathedral door, it would take long to enumerate.

The larger and more important quarter is situated on the left bank of the river Rimac, which divides the town into two districts, the northern one consisting of the suburb of San Lazaro. Most of the houses in Lima are only one story high; some of the smaller ones consist only of the ground-floor. The larger class of houses resemble those of the richer inhabitants of Guayaquil, which have already been partly described. On either side of the entrance leading into the *patio*, or inner courtyard, there are little rooms which are sometimes used as shops, or, as is frequently the case when protected by an iron railing, as sitting-rooms for the ladies of the family. Here, as elsewhere, the fair sex love to watch the passers-by, and, no doubt, comment freely on their personal appearance. Directly facing the main entrance are the principal rooms of the dwelling-house, the smaller and less important ones being built on the other two sides of the *patio*. From the large size of the rooms, the luxury of the decorations, and the richness of the furniture, which is often imported at great expense from London or Paris, many of the private dwellings might be called palaces.

In particular, the large house belonging to Señor L——, which stands in a street running off the Plaza de la Constitucion, from its size and the good taste shown in the choice of its contents, rivals in splendour many a mansion in Belgrave Square or in the Avenue des Champs Elysées. In contains, on the first floor, three spacious drawing-rooms *en suite ;* the floors and ceilings are all of carved oak, brought at immense expense from Europe, and the walls and doors are artistically decorated in distinctive styles and various colours, the first room being on the " Old English " pattern, ceiling and walls panelled with richly carved oak, and partly lined with dark red

velvet tapestry, the furniture made of the same materials. The furniture and decorations of the second
room are blue satin, walls painted blue, and the carv-
ings Grecian in style. The colours chosen for the
third and last room are amber and gold. On entering
from the street, we notice that the *patio* is inlaid with
Roman tiles. There is a fountain in the centre, of richly
carved white marble, its spacious bowl filled at the
time of the writer's visit by a mass of tropical plants
and flowers. The staircase leading from the *patio* to
the reception-rooms is all of white marble also, and
forms a fitting approach to the many costly objects to
be seen in this truly palatial abode. .

An invitation from Señor L—— gave the writer an
opportunity of "assisting" at a Peruvian dinner-party.
Dinner was served in a side room, entered through
the " red " drawing-room. With respect to the meal
itself, there was nothing special to note ; the *plats*
were prepared by a French cook, who, it was said,
had resided long enough in Lima to have added to
his Parisian art some knowledge of Peruvian cookery.
The wines and liqueurs were rare and choice, and of
the most celebrated European vintages. After dinner,
the host, who was a widower, held a reception in the
three drawing-rooms, all of which were brilliantly
lighted up with wax candles. Many accustomed to
the good taste in dress and manners which distinguish London society, might have been surprised to
note the tone of good breeding pervading the Peruvian

assembly.   Many of the ladies' dresses had been ordered from Paris, and were quite in the fashion of the old world, or, rather, the fashion which reigned when these things were sent out.   But if the ladies' dresses passed muster, what shall we say of the wearers ?   The Peruvian belle, when she is really beautiful, may well rank on an equality with the fairest specimens of female loveliness which the world produces.   Her complexion can scarcely be called dark, although her eyes and hair are so ; for her skin is often very fair and transparent.   She seldom has much colour.   Her features are small and delicately formed, the nose straight and particularly well-shaped, and the ear small and delicately curved, lying quite flat to the head—a rare beauty.   The mouth is small, and the lines of the lips straight, and, as with all great beauties, the lips themselves would be called too full by an artistic eye.   The teeth are straight and regular, and as white as newly fallen snow. In manner and conversation she is like the Spanish doñas, quiet and reserved, but soon becoming vivacious and mirthful, when excited by humour or the sense of the ridiculous.   In stature she is of medium height ; the figure is light and gracefully moulded, but given to develop rapidly after the age of sixteen, when the more mature charms of womanhood are quickly acquired.   Her movements are full of grace, and have ere now been the theme of travellers' special admiration.   Unaccustomed to much exercise on foot, the paces of the Limeña are unusually short, even for a woman, the feet moving so as to cause but a slight vertical motion to the figure. The high-born señoras, with head erect, appear rather to glide than walk, such is the even manner of their progress.

The polite manner, powers of perception, and ready repartee of the Peruvian gentleman cannot fail to be noticed by a stranger. His intellect, especially among the well-born and well-educated, belongs to no mean order, misapplied as it may have been by many of their statesmen in decisions which involved the prosperity of their country. It is impossible to converse for five minutes with a well-educated Peruvian of the upper class without being surprised at the apparent ease with which he masters questions in which he might reasonably be supposed to take but little interest, such as the ever-shifting panorama of European politics. The late Don Manuel Pardo, at one time president of the Republic, was a noticeable example of this remarkable power of adaptation of mind. Immediately applying his quick and ready reasoning to facts and conditions presented to him for the first time, by analogy he generally arrived at correct conclusions.

The conversation on the present occasion was chiefly confined to subjects of local interest, the politics and social gossip of the hour, and the reciprocal courtesies usually exchanged at any large gathering of people in any part of the globe.

Of the numerous churches and convents founded in Lima whilst Peru was yet a Spanish colony, two or three are deserving of special notice. The largest of the monastic establishments is the convent of *San Francisco*, situated in the vicinity of the Plaza Mayor. Mass is read daily every half-hour in this convent, from five in the morning till noon. A curious superstitious tradition attaches to the small chapel within the convent, which is called the *Capilla de los Milagros*, or the " Chapel of Miracles." It is recorded that, during the great earthquake of 1630, the image of the Madonna, which is placed above the entrance door, turned towards the grand altar, and, with outstretched arms, invoked the divine grace in favour of the city. It is believed that by this intervention the capital was saved from total destruction. The monks' cells, though simple, are quite comfortable to live in ; and the spacious and well-arranged gardens within the walls seemed to be well attended to.

The convent of *Los Descalzos*, situated on the other side of the river in the suburb of San Lazaro, also belongs to the Franciscan monks. This convent is approached by a broad avenue planted with six rows of trees, and it stands at the foot of a sterile hill. The situation is unhealthy, and, in consequence, the monks suffer a good deal from intermittent fever.

Among the other convents may be mentioned the *Recolita de San Diego*, and that of *Santo Domingo*, which is very richly endowed, *San Pedro, Nuestra*

Señora de la Merced, and *San Augustin*. Besides these monastic establishments, there are smaller convents for friars, and sixteen nunneries. Of the latter, the *Monasterio de la Concepcion* is the largest, and it is said to be very rich. *Santa Clara*, the *Encarnacion*, the *Capuchinas de Jesus Maria*, the *Nazarenes*, and *Trinitanas descalzas* are some of the other nunneries, which go far to prove to what a great extent the religious feelings which prevail among all Peruvian women, indulged in to excess, tempt them to take the veil. Besides these regular nunneries, there are a few other religious establishments called *beaterios*, or the bigots, which may be entered and quitted at pleasure by extremely religious women, who wish to lead a cloistered life without taking the veil. There is also an institution, the *Refugio de San José*, which is a place for the reception of married women who wish to withdraw from the ill-treatment of bad husbands. This institution also admits wives whose husbands have arbitrarily obtained permission of the archbishop to send them to the Refugio, with the hope that a little temporary seclusion and quiet meditation may improve their characters.

The public places of entertainment in Lima would be considered very few in comparison with those in a European city. As in all Roman Catholic countries, the festivals of the Church are marked days in the calendar, and the proceedings of each day include, besides the religious observances, a great deal of holiday-making. Perhaps the most popular way of spending the afternoon is to drive out to one of the numerous "tea-gardens," which are generally to be found in some picturesque spot within easy distance of the town, and to pass away the time with music and dancing, while enjoying the fresh air and fine scenery.

The principal place of public amusement (next to the arena for bull-fights) is the theatre, a building erected as long ago as the year 1662. The internal arrangements are far from commodious, and contain none of the comforts and conveniences which modern theatrical opinion considers necessary for the comfort of the playgoers. As to the performances, they are for the most part wretched, both as regards the merit of the pieces and the actors' talent. Commonplace intrigues form the subject of the pieces, and the dialogue consists of vulgar jokes. Occasionally an opera company from Europe, on their South American tour, will visit Lima and gratify its inhabitants with their performances ; but the occasions of such visits being rare and the stay brief, the opera can hardly be counted among the amusements of Lima.

But the announcement of a bull-fight fills all classes of the inhabitants with unconstrained joy. The female population takes even more interest therein than the male. The ladies prepare their finest dresses for the occasion ; and the boxes and seats at the *corrida* are often bespoken weeks before the event is to take place. While bull-fights have been excluded from the category of public amusements in all the other South American states, Peru adheres with tenacity to the customs of the mother country, and even endeavours to surpass her in what is called the " magnificence " of the performance—indeed, the cruelties which are practised at the bull-fights of Madrid are excelled at Lima. The writer saw his first (and only) bull-fight, at Lima, in company with a fellow-countryman, whose feelings were so overcome by the sight of bloodshed and cruelties that he left before the performance was half over. On the other hand, it is asserted that these exhibitions are far nobler and more humanitarian than any which may be seen to-day at Madrid, or in any other part of Spain. At Madrid, says the Peruvian sportsman, the victims are old and decrepit cab-horses, which have been bought at a low price on purpose to be killed by the bull, with the intention of providing sanguinary scenes *ad lib.* for the benefit of the spectators. At the Lima bull-fights, on the contrary, it is urged that all the horses permitted to enter the arena must be of pure Arab breed, and, owing to their sagacity and the agility of their riders, they seldom fail to escape the bulls' horns. If there must be a victim, is it not just that it should be one of the men who provide the sport (for which service they are well paid), and voluntarily risk their lives, instead of the poor horses, which have no voice in the matter?

On this occasion, as usual, the *torrero* (bull-slayer) and his *picadores* (literally, "prickers") were all Spaniards by birth, and a more blood-thirsty, villanous crew the writer has seldom seen assembled. Each man was bedecked in the faded velvet jacket, knee-breeches, and white socks, which form part of the attire of the professional bull-fighter. The bulls, which it must in justice be admitted, were fine well-fed wild-looking creatures, were admitted singly into the arena at a signal given by blowing a trumpet; and as the animal was led forward, the sport began. A mounted *pica-dore* approaching, endeavoured to fix in the neck of the beast a small steel dart, one end of which was sharply pointed and washed with brimstone, a strip of coloured ribbon being attached to the other. The usual proceedings are as follows. If the bull turns and charges, the rider causes his horse to whirl round and approach the quarry on his other side, when frequently the dart becomes fixed in the spot aimed at. The sharp pain resulting from the prick and the brimstone combined infuriates the animal, and he rushes blindly forward straight ahead, as if "making for" the people sitting on the lower tiers of seats which occasionally encircle the amphitheatre. But before many paces are made, a red flag is waved before his eyes by one of the foot *picadores*, which causes him to turn and face his new assailant. Pierced with another small dart, as sharp and as burning as the first, the bull roars and becomes mad with rage, and, with eyes

E

flashing fire, he tears round the arena, pawing the sandy floor with his feet and turning his head right and left at each object presented to him. The game grows fast and furious ; the music plays some stirring galop ; the *picadores* cross and recross the arena, as if possessing charmed lives, planting their darts in all parts of the infuriated animal ; the spectators clap their hands in excitement, some of the ladies even tearing off their black mantillas to wave them in the air, until upon a given signal the music ceases, the voices of the audience sink into silence, the *picadores* retire behind wooden screens placed for their protection at the ends of the arena, and the bull, decked in gay ribbons of many colours, is left alone on the battle-field, triumphant. But his triumph is imaginary, for the cessation of the attack signifies nothing more than a reprieve of his sentence. The clear notes of the trumpet sound again, heralding in the *matador*, who is the hero of the day. His dress is somewhat richer in quality than that of his companions. He is armed with a short dagger-shaped sword, which is generally carried in his right hand, hidden under a small shawl, brilliant red in colour, thrown over his left arm. A cheer bursts from the audience, and the *matador* advances boldly to face the bull. The agility and quickness shown by the *matador* on this occasion in evading the charges of the bull, whose strength was only partly spent by previous exertion, were marvellous to behold. The importance of the red shawl was soon shown in the way in which it was extended at arm's length to attract the bull's attention. But in one of his final charges, the noble beast received his death-stroke. At the first good opportunity the sharp-pointed sword was thrust with unerring aim through the nape of his neck, reaching the very centre of his heart, and with a gasp, amid the cheers of the audience, the band meanwhile playing the National Anthem, the creature fell on his knees and, rolling over, expired.

There can be no doubt that bull-fights are barbarous and disgusting diversions. But "prize-fighting" at home, where the combatants are incited to mark each other's faces out of recognition for love of gold, and at the instigation of so-called "sportsmen," may, as far as regards cruelty, be ranked on a level with bull-fighting. The comparison does not, however, lessen the barbarity, or excuse the continuance of the latter diversion in the minds of all right-thinking people. Both are relics of the past, and the legacies of ancestors who looked complacently upon the shedding of human blood for the gratification of their passions, or of revenge, or simply to provide them with the means of excitement, in days when healthy pastimes and recreations were but little known. It must be allowed on behalf of the Peruvians that they are accustomed to these diversions from early childhood, and they regard them with perfect indifference, custom, no doubt, blinding them to the cruelties they witness in the bull-ring.

"If a Pizarro of any other European nationality than the Spanish had overrun and conquered our country," said the mayor of a provincial town one day, "we South Americans would at this time have been rivalling in prosperity our contemporaries, the citizens of the United States." This speech is typical of that old feeling of hatred felt for the Spanish yoke by the creole. The modern Peruvian, even if he has more Spanish than Indian blood in his veins, when in a facetious mood, is wont to say that the Spaniard took away everything from his ancestors that they held dear, and gave them nothing worth having in exchange; that he has inherited from the Spaniard all the vices of the old world and of an old form of civilization, without retaining the virtues of the simple aborigines of the soil. The Spaniard gave him a language and a religion, it is true; but the Inca possessed both, and he was no idolater, since he worshipped the same Supreme Being, only in another way, through the medium of the Sun, instead of the intercession of the Virgin and of Christ.

CHAPTER IV.

CHICLAYO AND THE CHICLAYANOS.

IT is evening on the 8th of April, 1873. The Plaza, or principal square of Chiclayo, is filled with a mixed multitude, waiting for the religious procession announced as shortly to take place, while at the same time they enjoy the delightful coolness of a tropical evening. Among the crowd we perceive the Arbulus, Arizolas, Aguirries, and many others of the *gente descente*, or notables of the place. Let us stroll round the Plaza, before joining these new but already sympathetic acquaintances grouped along the trottoir.

Huge piles of algarova wood (carob-tree) are burning on the open space in front of the unfinished cathedral, whose massive brick-built walls and towers

illumined by the flames are relieved against the back-
ground of the dark blue sky beyond. In shape a
cross, the cathedral is designed to hold some two
thousand worshippers, and the immensely thick outer
walls have already reached no mean height. In
imitation of the Italian style, a square tower, whose
summit is reached by an inside staircase, flanks either
side of the wide western portal.

Entering the building, the visitor may question
the stability of the brick arches which span the centre
aisle and are destined to support the roof, in apparent
defiance of the volcanic tremblings which are of such
frequent occurrence on the coast of Peru. These
arches spring from Ionic columns, built up with large
bricks, which divide the centre from the side aisles,
wherein niches for the side chapels are already
hollowed out. The walls of chancel and transept are
finished and ready to receive the dome which is to
crown the magnificent gift made by President Balta
to his compatriots of Chiclayo, in gratitude for the
support received when he successfully contested the
Presidency of the Republic. It would scarcely be
fair to criticise the details of this half-finished building. In its present condition it forms a strange contrast to the humble dwellings surrounding it ; and
now that its founder is dead (President Balta was
murdered in prison by Gutierrez, who took his place),
it seems likely that a long time will pass before it will
answer any further purpose than that of a landmark to

travellers, who exclaim " Dios mio!" at its size, but as good Catholics wish it finished and well filled with worshippers.

Turning towards the Plaza, we behold a crowd composed of very varied types of humanity. Twenty-two different races have been counted as composing the modern Peruvian people, and by the light of fresh fagots which are now heaped on the bonfires, we can discern every shade of brown and black skins varying from the intense black of the Congo negro, whose big heavy frame contrasts with the slight tall figure of the white creole, as with the intermediate link, the mulatto. All shades of brown and brownish-yellow are there, ending in the white complexion of European settlers. Nor are the differences confined to appearance; they extend to religion and language. Were it really a picture, exception might be taken to the want of unity and common interest, for the gestures and indications of character among these groups are as distinct as their faces; but taken in detail they form a curious study of humanity. The black races have not yet reached southern Peru, with its mining works and barren sands, but in the rich easy-going provinces of the north, they have prospered. Their African progenitors were brought to cultivate the extensive and fertile sugar and rice plantations. The more gentle and manageable cholo stands alongside his darker brother, speaking Spanish it is true with a better accent, but with scarcely more accuracy.

Whatever their colour, all wear the *poncho*, or bright-coloured shawl, white cotton trousers, and white straw hat which constitute the picturesque male attire of the country. The women who keep the booths where *chicha* (beer made from maize, partly fermented, but innocent of hops), lemonade, and sweet cakes are to be bought, are dressed modestly in black serge, their dark hair plaited and thrown back over the shoulder in two or more long plaits.

Now a murmur breaks from the crowd, and all eyes turn in the direction of the church on the north side of the square, whence slowly issues the procession of white-robed priests, preceding the " chapel " borne on the shoulders of twelve zambos and followed by the town musicians playing solemn music. Images of our Saviour and of six of the apostles are seen within the " chapel," which is decorated with flowers and lighted by numerous wax candles.

On approaching the cathedral the music ceases, the musicians lower their brass instruments, and the priest heading the procession chants the Te Deum, joined by the musicians' voices and those of a crowd of both sexes following and carrying lamps and torches. As the procession nears the centre of the square, laughter and talking ceases among the gay throng, . and no sound breaks the stillness of night but the solemn chant. The cholo reverently bares his head, and falling on his knees, remains in that attitude of humility with arms crossed on his breast, till the procession has passed. The profound respect, we may say awe, with which these religious ceremonies are regarded by the native seems to corroborate the idea that till lately this simple race were much imposed on by priestly craft; and many are the stories of imposture practised, by means of which the cholo was terrified into obedience, and his contributions towards the *camarico* (recess behind the altar where the images are dressed) extorted. Some of these contrivances may remind the historical reader of the trickeries performed in pagan times and by the Egyptian priests. In South America their success was aided by the people's credulity as a race, exceeding, it is said, even that of the worshippers of Busterick the German divinity, whose temple stands on the Weser. This image was cast in metal, and the head served as a boiler for the generation of steam, which at the fitting moment was discharged in the worshippers' faces, simply by withdrawing plugs from the eye holes by means of secret wires. The noise accompanying this discharge, and the volumes of steam which speedily filled the temple, added to the effect, and may well have seemed miraculous in an age when the knowledge of steam power was almost exclusively confined to the priesthood. Here in Chiclayo it is said that not many years since a telling effect was produced in the Easter processions, by the figure of our Saviour being made to stumble at intervals under the weight of the cross, symbolizing

His progress to Golgotha. The figure regained its position by means of concealed wires worked by the chapel-bearers. The ignorant cholo mind being incapable of understanding the simple mechanical contrivance by which this was effected, attributed the movement to supernatural agency. This credulity is but the natural outcome of the child-like faith fostered for centuries under the fatherly rule of the Inca, just as we often see ancient creeds and customs long since obsolete reappearing in modern times under different conditions, the names only being changed while the principles are identical.

It suited the ambitious schemes of the adventurer Pizarro and his band of needy followers to paint the Inca as an infidel, steeped in the blackest vices of paganism. The golden visage, set in a frame of shooting sun-rays of the same metal, facing eastwards in the Temple of the Sun at Cuzco, was taken as evidence of his idolatry, and Cuzco was called the Peruvian Mecca, the Inca taking the place of the Prophet. The human sacrifices on the death of the king were exaggerated—it was said that hundreds of his wives and concubines were buried alive on such occasions. Tales of the miseries endured by the natives through the forced labour exacted by the State were wafted across the seas to Vice-regent Philip's ears, describing the condition of the Peruvians as worse and more pitiable than that of the Egyptians under the remorseless Pharaohs.

Pizarro demanded fighting men in the name of humanity and to free an enslaved race, and when this plea failed, he touched the keynote of Philip's mind by bribing him with some of the golden images and vessels torn from the walls of the Temple of the Sun.

It was not till long after the spoliation had been made, and civil war, combined with treachery and an irresistible will, had wrested his empire from the Inca, that disinterested inquiries elicited the truth and brought to light a system of government which Prescott has described as "the mildest but most searching of despotisms." Then for the first time the unique and provident system by which land was cultivated under the Incas, one-third of its produce being allotted to the people, another third towards supporting the Church, and the remainder to the State, was submitted to impartial criticism.

Then arose the question—how were those immense piles of quarried stone, still to be seen in the temple walls at Cuzco and only comparable in size to the Pyramids of Egypt, raised, unless by organized slavery on a very large scale? The answer is obvious. The despotism of the Incas was acknowledged, but it is maintained that its advantages counterbalanced its interference with individual liberty; that the equal distribution of the land's produce between Church, State, and people gave to each their due and provided for the support of the population, including the aged and those unable to work for their living; and that it also maintained right rule and supremacy in matters of civil and religious government throughout the Inca's domains. Want and misery were unknown, for the labour of the able-bodied provided sufficient for the support of the sick and aged. No one could become so impoverished as to be in danger of starvation. On the other hand, no one could become wealthier than his neighbour, as the land was held by yearly tenure from the State, each family being allotted a share calculated, in proportion to their numbers, to yield sufficient for their support. In fact this system was the ideal of communism; but one only possible under an enlightened " Paternal Despotism." The hours of the working day were likewise divided into three, one portion being spent on the " Home Farm," the other two on Church lands and the Inca's lands respectively, the produce of these last being employed partly in support of Church and State, the remainder forming a reserve fund on which to draw for the support of the sick and aged. When a crown tenant fell ill, the Inca sent labourers to cultivate his fields, and provided food for his family till he was able to resume his labour. The work of supervision, and care that the law was duly observed, fell chiefly on the clergy, who, according to the most reliable Spanish historians,* exercised complete control over

* Solozano, the Abate de Pradt, Lafuente, Oliver, and others.

the people, being authorized emissaries of the " Child of the Sun," the name by which the Inca was best known. Religion was the chief, if not the only means, by which the State maintained control over its vassals. Great national movements, as well as the petty details of daily life, were alike regulated by the priesthood. If an outlying infidel tribe along the tributaries of the Amazon were proceeded against and conquered, the warriors were urged on by religious fanaticism, much in the same spirit that " Holy Russia " turns to account the blind faith of her subjects in their Czar, as an incentive against the followers of the Crescent. So did our own Crusaders a few centuries ago. In Peru the "Sun " was the emblem, for the "Cross " had not arisen ; but the spirit was the same.

This abject submission to laws clothed in religious guise, is of course distinct from the faith founded on conviction, but it is an admirable political engine. It is an outcome of man's natural need of a Deity to reverence and obey, whatever form his differing idiosyncracy or surroundings may cause it to take. The Peruvians believed in an invisible God dwelling in the Sun ; the Inca was His child, sent to be His representative, prophet, and oracle on earth. Pizarro slew this Oracle, denouncing him as an impostor incapable of summoning to his aid the supernatural power of which he had boasted. At sight of the lifeless body of Atahualpa the Indian lost heart ; his

hereditary leader and spiritual guide was gone ; he
threw up the contest, and abandoned the Temple of
the Sun.   Christianity was then carried by the swords
of the conquerors into this newly acquired portion of
the New World.   Religion and conquest joined their
forces to subjugate the Peruvians to Spanish control.
The crowd of missionaries and monks of all denomi-
nations, following in the wake of Pizarro, made use of
the most ingenious stratagems to enlighten the deep
ignorance in which they considered the nations to be
be steeped.   But if history is to be believed, these
adventurous priests were not always impelled onward
by the disinterested desire of improving the moral
condition of the natives, since their well-known greed
for gold brought upon them the satire of the great
Spanish poet, who wrote—

> " Su color de religion,
>   Van a buscar plata y oro
>   Del encuvierto tesoro."
>   LOPE DE VEGA.

Religious education given to the children was
found to be the surest means of converting the
parents, aided by solemn ceremonies illustrated by
arrangements and contrivances within and without
the church walls, which appealed to their most
vulnerable point, the imagination.

It is said by Solozano, in his " Politica Indiana,"
that laws were passed prescribing the occasions and
the manner in which these " tricks " should be carried

out. Baron de Humboldt* asserts that the Spanish
missionaries, in order to convert the natives, showed
them paintings on canvas drawn on a large scale and
representing the disobedient condemned to the flames
of hell. The horrible sufferings were so skilfully
portrayed as to frighten the natives into begging the
priests to cease even from describing the agonies
which *might* happen to any of them after death.
Thus the "religious" education consisted of certain
illustrated dogmas, coupled with a few precepts calculated to engender fanaticism among a people incapable
of reasoning out the moral and elevating truths of
Christianity. The Inquisition preached the inhuman
doctrine that it was right to slay the heretic, and right
for the proselyte son to raise his arm against his
infidel father. When fair means failed, foul were tried,
and the work of conversion advanced by rapid strides.

The pages of history relating the conquest of Peru
and the conversion of the aborigines to Christianity,
is stained with records of the worst extravagances
conceived by humanity. The dissensions among the
conquerors, their treachery towards their leaders, the
gross manner in which the latter frequently attempted
to throw off their allegiance to Spain, their ill-treatment of the natives, and the impostures and licentious-
ness practised among the missionary priests, detract
largely from the glory which so great a success would
otherwise merit. In proof of the influence of individual

* "Political Essay on the Kingdom of New Spain."

character on such lawless society as that existing in Peru when Gonzalo Pizarro (brother of the conqueror) traitorously assumed the independent sovereignty of the empire, the success of Pedro de la Gasca, a member of the Inquisition, may be mentioned. Leaving Spain by order of the Vice-regent Philip, but without either money or troops, he arrived at Panama, and by sheer force of persuasion gained over a number of Pizarro's followers, by whose aid he suppressed the rebellion in Peru, captured and caused to be executed the rebel leader, and, as President of the Audiencia or Council of Lima, brought the government into shape and form. This may be read in detail in Busk's History of Spain.

But it is with the inner life of the Peruvian people that this book has most to do, as evidenced in their social customs. They are a hospitable and sociable people. For instance—

"You will join our *tertulia*," exclaims a friendly voice, as we prepare to leave the Plaza. "Willingly," is the reply, for the *tertulia* implies a pleasant evening gathering, where both sexes join in sociability. The Peruvian's love of home is proverbial, and the early age at which the young Republican seeks to form a home of his own by marriage, is a remarkable trait of national character.

The Peruvian Benedict is certainly a more respectable personage than the capricious being who figures as the "young man" of South American society.

Occasionally, though, improvident marriages occur ; a consequence of the nightly serenades. Where young ladies reside, the presence of one or more impassioned Romeos under the *reja*, or iron grating of the window, may generally be predicted, and these occasionally lead to rencontres as disastrous as the one between Don Baltazar and Don Rafael in Toledo, so graphically described in the humorous pages of Gil Blas.

It is at the *tertulia* that Peruvian women chiefly show their claims to the attention and praise so commonly awarded them. Throwing aside the reserve, partly assumed and partly real, which characterises their bearing out of doors, both on the Plaza and at Mass, their natural amiability leads them to exert themselves in entertaining their guests, becoming animated in conversation, showing both in questions and repartee great quickness of perception. Often indeed they increase the number of their personal attractions by the fascinating accomplishment of singing to a guitar accompaniment, reminding one of Moore's words—

> " She who but feathers the dart when she speaks,
> At once sends it home to the heart when she sings."

The refreshments handed round on these occasions are chiefly of the liquid order, and to any one recollecting the sage advice of a celebrated physician, " Drink what you like, but never mix your liquor," it seemed strange to be offered first English stout in tiny glasses, followed by curaçoa, and afterwards champagne, port, and sherry. In Russia the same variety is observed, but *there* less is left to the guests' choice, all these incongruous liquids being mixed together in a huge bowl and called punch.

The señoritas do not disdain to join, and few refuse their polite " Una copita con V. Señor " (Your health, sir). Spirits are also taken, and Italia, a white spirit, distilled from a musk grape, originally imported from Italy but now largely cultivated for this purpose, is a delicately flavoured liqueur. Mr. Henry Swayne, one of the most successful settlers in Peru, informed the writer that he had lately commenced its cultivation on his estates at Cañete and San Jacente, with the view of supplying the English market. Italia may now be found in many of the London clubs.

Intemperance, however, is here chiefly confined to the mulattoes and other races sharing African blood ; the white creole of Spanish descent is sparing in his use of intoxicating beverages, frequently drinking only water himself, though he sets wine before his guests. The extent of his indulgence consists in a *petit verre* of Italia as *chasse-café*. Yet over most of South America the cultivation of the vine is neglected, a regrettable fact, as that section of the population addicted to intemperance are thereby driven to the more hurtful use of spirits.

It is a truism that to know a man thoroughly you must see him at home. The Peruvians would well stand this test. Their love of home and domestic affections are proverbial, and their gregarious nature leads them to prefer the life of cities to that of making their homes on their estates. Thus in Chiclayo most of the proprietors have their residence *en ville*, their estates lying perhaps ten or twenty miles distant. They like to live within sound of the church bells, and they take a pride in the beauty of their native town, akin to that of the Roman patricians when they extolled their "ancestral Tiber." This sometimes produces a jealousy between the towns, for which a stranger is at a loss to account. "Soy Chiclayano, y no hombre para eseuchar talês cosas" (I am of Chiclayo, and not a man to listen to such tales) is the reply to a patriotic Lambayequano. The two towns are but six miles apart, yet the Chiclayano considers the men of Lambayeque some degrees beneath him both in the moral and social scale. Perhaps the narrowness of mind so often seen where little interchange of thought takes place between town and town, or country and country, may account for these prejudices ; cosmopolitans get their angles rubbed off. It is not so long since a somewhat similar feeling divided the rival towns of our own country, Liverpool and Manchester. Since the crossing of Chat Moss by a railway has opened the way to more frequent communication, mutual interests have operated to destroy the hostility. But in Chiclayo and Lambayeque the interests clash, chiefly on the irrigation question, a doubly important one in this rainless country.   In dry seasons, the river supply is insufficient for the agricultural wants.   The Rio de Lambayeque divides into two branches, one ending north of the port San José, the other some ten miles south, and near the Caleta or port of Eten.   This delta is owned by residents of Chiclayo, Reque, Monsefu, and Eten, all towns and villages lying on the southern arm of the river, a small portion only being owned by Lambayequanos, whose town lies on the northern arm, six miles from the coast.   The laws regulating the water supply, despite their simple construction, invariably give rise to disputes, sometimes ending in bloodshed, between the commissioners severally appointed by the towns to meet at the *toma*, or partition-weir.   Attached to the fee-simple of each estate are certain rights, entitling the holder to so many *regaderos*, or irrigations, the number of which, originally regulated in proportion to the area cultivated, is complicated by purchased rights, custom, etc.   Sometimes a cultivator will buy an estate lying above his own, simply that he may use the water-rights appertaining thereto on his own land.   The commissioner's duty is to calculate the amount yielded by the river, and apportion it accordingly by raising or lowering the rough stone weir stretched across the deepest branch of the river.   Occasionally parties, made desperate by the prospect of drought, threaten to demolish the weir.   In fact, the commissioner's duty is at all times an arduous and ungrateful task. These quarrels, and also hereditary feuds between the principal families, sadly mar the harmony which apparently ought to reign where Nature has showered her blessings so freely, where the sun daily pours his beams over fields of golden sugar-cane and maize, while at night the breeze is soft and mild enough to permit of sleeping in the open air without danger.

The towns in this valley are all built after the same model—one prevailing throughout the Two Americas. A large square Plaza, surrounded by government buildings, municipal courts, the gaol and the church, with some private houses and shops, forms the centre or nucleus of the settlement, from which radiate streets in all directions.

The houses are invariably planned on the Moorish pattern, *i.e.* having in the centre a courtyard, the four sides of which are formed by the various rooms. The welcome shade and coolness generally to be found in these courtyards are a boon duly appreciated in a hot country like Peru, and prove the fitness of this mode of construction. All the walls are built of sun-dried bricks, which, when plastered over with mud and whitewashed, present a neat and clean appearance. The streets are sometimes paved with cobble-stones, but more generally left in their natural state, and their surfaces much pulverized and broken up by the continuous traffic of years—possibly centuries.

At Chiclayo there are no public water or gas-works; the supply of these two wants is therefore left to individual effort. It is quite a remarkable sight to see the water-mules, with a full bucket of water slung on either side, trooping into town from the neighbouring brook in the early morning. "Agua fresca, agua, esta mañana, Señora" (Fresh water, water for you this morning, lady) cries the dealer as he hurries his mule down the street, selling his article at a price which would make the hearts of share-holders in London water companies sore with envy. Nearly all provisions and necessaries of life are brought to town on horse or mule back, the soft unpaved roads of the country being quite unsuited for the passage of vehicles. Beside the water-carriers, troops of ponies and mules and donkeys—some laden with bundles of green *alfafa*, or lucerne, huge enough to leave nothing visible of the beast except head and legs; others laden with pigs, kids, meat, vegetables, and all kinds of market produce—may be met in all directions.

A Spanish-American town is always seen at its best in the early morning, soon after sunrise, when the air is fresh and cool, and not yet heated by the sun. At that hour the partly veiled señora trips to early matins, or perhaps to bathe in the river; the *chacrero* goes to his farm; presently the shop-shutters are taken down, and the buzz and movement of human life begins much after the same fashion as at home, only several hours earlier.

It would seem, however, that all the activity of most inhabitants of South America is worked off in the first half of the day, in the hours between sunrise and breakfast, which meal is usually taken at eleven or twelve o'clock. After that hour, the great heat begins, and the *siesta* is almost universally indulged in, so that if any more out-door work has to be done that day, the few hours before sunset, when the air is cooled by the sea-breeze, are alone available.

Life in Chiclayo moves but slowly, and is seldom varied by public amusements of any kind. It would be thought very monotonous by a new-comer from busy quickly-moving Europe. Indeed the chief "distractions" are the religious ceremonies and processions already described, which naturally do not convey the same meaning to the mind of the Protestant as to the Roman Catholic.

Work of some kind is the only panacea for the dreadful ennui which would be experienced by a visitor having no special occupation or luxuries. But indeed there is no excuse for any one remaining unoccupied in these fertile valleys of Peru, which teem with interesting curiosities of the animal and vegetable world, the study and description of which would well repay research and might tempt a lover of natural history to contribute his mite to the general amount of knowledge. The strange and beautiful tropical plants and fruits, the trees so unlike those left at home, the latter filled with beautiful birds of brilliant plumage and varying song to be found in Peru, excite the beholder's curiosity, and might well awake in the dullest mind that desire for fresh glimpses of knowledge which is said to be man's common inheritance. "*Give* me something new," says the child already tired of the toys received on his birthday. "*Tell* me something new," says the child of larger growth, his learned and cultured parent ; possibly the *enfant gâté* of European luxury and ease, with skilled hands near to supply his every want, even to the desires born of an artificial existence in which nature and the beautiful works of the Creator are perhaps only seen in their native habitat, at long intervals.

The writer ventures to hope that "something new, something true" may perhaps be found in these pages.

CHAPTER V.

PROVINCIAL LIFE.

Foreigners in Peru — Settlers—Adventurers—Annual Fête—
Native Industries—Eten—Straw-plaiters—Social Customs
—Chilca—Santa Rosa—"Oiling the Waves"—Sociability
of the Peruvians—Cock-fighting—Monsefu Fête.

THE visitor from busy Europe whom chance may
lead to remain for any length of time in a Peruvian
valley, must not expect to find the numerous distractions which at home are provided by the numbers
whose business it is to cater for the public amusement.
Should he prefer a life of continual gaiety, he will
sorely miss the various attractions of the turf, theatres,
shooting, hunting, and the numerous town and
country pastimes to which he is accustomed. It is
even worse for a follower of studious pursuits. The
absence of all libraries and societies for the cultivation of knowledge restrict his resources even more
than those of the pleasure-seeker. Both, it is true,
shortly become absorbed in the special business which
may have brought them to the country; but when

once the road or railway has been made, or the land cleared and prepared for cultivation, things drop back into their old narrow grooves. Should circumstances induce the visitor to stay on from year to year, he gradually becomes more used to the ways of the place, as his interests therein multiply. Such a one is sure to find encouragement at every step, and a ready welcome to the houses of the best families. If he shows average abilities and energy, he will soon find himself trusted with the management of affairs, and the reward of his opinion and assistance is generally marriage with a daughter of his patron. Here in the north, and especially in the valleys of Chiclayo and Lambayeque, this ready road to success has resulted in the well-to-do position of many foreigners, and a well-intentioned stranger is welcomed with kindness and hospitality, though he may be penniless and friendless on arriving.

Be it well understood, however, that the native employer understands how to discriminate between the intelligent and steady craftsman and the large class of indolent *mauvais sujets* who go to Peru, thinking to find a better field for the quaint notions of freedom picked up in the gin palaces of New York and "'Frisco." This is a very numerous class; they are full of "tall talk," and to judge from the certificates of their abilities (delivered verbally, to reduce their travelling impedimenta), are capable of making anything, from a sewing-machine to a railway. If necessary, they could discourse learnedly on politics, and even deliver the true principles of republicanism from the presidential chair. They are great at "guessing," but very decided in their opinions as to the exact number of grains of nutmeg which a brandy cocktail should contain, and in the mysteries of "gin slings," "pick-me-ups," "eye-openers," "Angostura bitters," and similar horrible compounds, which they assiduously concoct for the benefit of the first among them who buys a shanty and sets up a "bar." What with the German-English talk, the nasal twang, roaring laughter, and often, when under the influence of drink, the loud curses followed by blows, the milder-tempered native may often ask himself, like John Chinaman, "Is not our barbarism better than their civilization?" At all events, the Peruvians are gentle-mannered and warm-hearted. In "Cuzco and Lima," Mr. Clement Markham justly eulogizes the existence of these good qualities in all the people he visited among the heights of the Andes, and such the present writer found them in the north and the south, on the seaboard, and up among the mountains. There is one great difference in the habits of daily life prevailing here. In no parts, north, south, or on the seaboard, are games and out-door sports, so universal all over Europe, practised here. In fact, except in Lima itself, these seem totally unknown. On *dias de fiesta*, or fête-days of the Church, some attempt is made towards amusing the public, with the usual routine of ecclesiastical processions and ceremonies which take up the greater part of the day.

On one occasion we attended the annual fête at Monsefu, a town of Spanish origin, lying between Chiclayo and the port of Eten. The fête took place in the latter days of September. We had been invited six months earlier, with the understanding that it would be a sight worth any sacrifice to behold.

Entering on the western side, we passed under a tumble-down triumphal arch, and found the Plaza and streets of the town crowded with people of the same type as those we had seen in Chiclayo on the occasion of the Easter procession. Among the crowd were some who had come from distant parts of the Sierra, Indians in name as well as in appearance, and easily distinguished by the long black matted hair hanging over their shoulders and sometimes plaited like a woman's. They brought *alfojas* (saddle-bags), *ponchos*, and skins of the Vicuna, bark and other products of the Sierra for sale, and would take back in exchange salt, spirits, and foreign goods.

The chief articles for sale were, however, straw hats, brought from Guayaquil, and those manufactured in the adjoining town of Eten, distant only two miles, of which mention will shortly be made. Corn, fruits, *chicha*, spirits, and the usual catalogue of articles were also to be purchased. The inevitable brass band played in one corner of the square, and the business of the day began by following the crowd first round the square, then into the side streets, stopping now and then to salute a friend, who never took leave of you without offering his *chicha* gourd or bottle of spirits. There was much talk, much drinking, and much smoking, but no games of "kiss in the ring" among the young folk, though among the crowd were many pretty girls well worth kissing, and also robust youths who must have thought so! An air of staid formality appears to constrain this Spanish-American race in all they do, which is all the more conspicuous when the shovel is thrown aside and the holiday *poncho* donned. In the field the labourer overlooks the abruptness of his overseer's "Melchior, be alive with that axe!" But in the Plaza at Monsefu on a fête-day he will have nothing less than, "Don Melchior, how are you, my friend?" And why not? Are we not all brothers? At least in South America. "Omnes homines naturâ æquales sunt."

Two miles south of Monsefu, the small native town of Eten claims mention, from the fact that its inhabitants are said to have preserved the unmixed purity of their race since the conquest. Dr. Hutchinson, in whose company the writer visited Eten, in November, 1872, suspects the Etenites to be of Inca descent, giving as his reasons their resemblance in face and form to the figures in Montero's great picture of the obsequies of Atahualpa.* During our visit we entered several dwellings, in all of which the

* "Two Years in Peru," vol. ii. p. 205.

owners, with their wives and daughters, were grouped tailor-fashion on the floor, busily engaged in plaiting straw into hats, mats, and cigar-cases, or in weaving woollen quilts. Quite young children, apparently under five years of age, were entrusted with the coarser and easier kind of workmanship required for the cheap hats, while the elderly members of the group worked the fine straw into cigar-cases and other small articles, some of which were beautiful specimens of plaiting, made of fine white straw, the ornamental designs of figures and flowers being worked in with green or red. Some plaiters are clever enough to be able to copy any figure of which you may give them a model, be it fish, fowl, or human being. One dark-haired Eten maid showed us a piece of work which had occupied her incessantly for six weeks, and she only asked fifteen dollars for this ; but some are said to sell for as much as a hundred dollars. The roughly plaited sombreros sell at one or one and a half dollars each.

The women were all dressed in black serge gowns, over which a white shawl is thrown on the rare occasions of their going out of doors. This costume has been worn for three centuries, and is said to be a sign of mourning for Atahualpa. In Eten, brothers and sisters are allowed to marry; this, we are told, was customary among the Incas. For the last twenty years the curé of the town has tried to induce his parishioners to abandon the evil custom, but has met with only partial success. Their personal appearance confirms the suspicion; for their small stature and weak childish limbs denote a physique which has deteriorated from other causes than sedentary and indoor habits, and total abstinence from field-work. In one particular Dr. Hutchinson's description of Eten errs. The Etenites do *not* cultivate the ground themselves, but rely for their support exclusively upon their straw and cotton manufactures. They buy their meat, vegetables, and provisions chiefly from the neighbouring towns of Monsefu and Requé, and the close proximity to Eten of the chacras, cultivated by the people of Monsefu, probably led the doctor into error.

One day we called on the parish priest, and endeavoured to obtain some further information respecting his parishioners; but for all our urging we got little. An air of mystery hung over the Etenites, which the priest had apparently failed to pierce, though he had lived among them for a great many years. We were told that they were good Christians; that they attended church regularly on holydays, and gave freely towards its support; that they worked all the week at their plaiting and mat-weaving, and that as we had seen them grouped on the floor of their cottages, so they might be seen any day of the week all the year round, working away, and holding little communion with any one outside their own doors; that they intermarried among themselves, and that no

Etenite had been known to contract marriage with a *forastero*, or stranger. The doctor did not like to be beaten; so to gratify his thirst for information we walked round the dusty Plaza and peered into the cottages again and again. But it was all to no purpose. We were shown the mats, the hats, and the straw ware; we were told in bad Spanish the prices thereof; but nothing could we extract about the social relations of the vendors, or their traditions and beliefs. Mr. Stevenson, Señor Paz-Soldan, and Mr. Spence, in their writings, speak of the same reticence among the Etenites concerning their probable origin. But they are no exceptions to the general rule. It would be nearly impossible to extract similar information from the inhabitants of any village in the Indian Sierra; for the double reason that the traditional instincts of the race forbid the divulgence of such secrets to foreigners, and, what is more probable, that in their ignorance of the art of writing they have gradually forgotten whatever there might have been to tell.

In many respects, the village of Chilca, lying to the south of Lima beyond Lurin, bears close resemblance to Eten. Both villages are built on a barren plain, whose soil produces nothing to support its inhabitants, who occupy themselves likewise in plaiting and weaving. The Chilcans are stated to have carefully avoided mixing with people of other races, and in this respect resemble the Etenites. The feeling of strong local attachment, so strongly developed in the Peruvians, and the reluctance to leave the place where their ancestors first settled, no doubt account for the anomaly which maintains villages in the same spots, though they were once cultivated gardens, and now, deprived of water, have deteriorated into waste lands. But in the case of the Etenites, this may perhaps be traced to the dispersion of the great united Incarial family effected by the Spaniards. Driven from their ancient cities in the mountains by the sword and the ruthless exactions of their insatiable conquerors, and feeling incapable of serving as bondsmen those whose libertine excesses and inordinate greed they soon learned to despise, they seem to have fled to arid wastes which offered no temptation to Spanish pursuit, and where, undisturbed, they could condole together on their misfortunes.

Another isolated community, similar in many respects to that of Eten, may be found at a few miles' distance to the north of the latter town, at Santa Rosa. Lying on the coast, its sole industry is fishing ; the village huts are built on the low sand-hills fringing the coast, which here, as all along the north Peruvian seaboard, slopes with a gradual incline into the sea. Santa Rosa lies half-way between Eten and Pimentel. Here the tide falls only four feet, excepting at spring-tides. Long land-nets are laid down at high tide along the front, which, when raised at the ebb, are generally well filled with mazarilla or bream, of which a considerable haul is often made. For reaching the fishing ground and gathering in the catch, the Santa Rosan fishermen use small canoes made of plaited rushes, measuring from eight to twelve feet in length. The pointed ends are covered in like an ordinary canoe, while the paddler sits in the open, uncovered space in the centre, which also holds the fish caught. The canoes are propelled by means of wooden paddles with knife-shaped blades, and the fishermen exhibit considerable skill when passing through the heavy surf which constantly prevails along the coast.

Should any enterprising philanthropist establish a system of "oiling the waves" along this coast, it would indeed be a blessing to the canoeists. Fancy being borne in calmly on the smooth long roller and safely landed high and dry on the beach, instead of fighting one's way with difficulty through the cresting breakers, eye and hand both having their work to do, spite of the spray dashing into the face. In the experiments made at Peterhead, Aberdeenshire, in 1883, it was clearly proved that a few drops of common oil had the effect of spreading a thin film over the cresting waves (one drop spread to a circle three feet in diameter), which quite prevented their "breaking;" and then the "ground swell" acted as a lever, and bore small craft unresistingly to land. Those interested in the subject will find valuable statistics as to the efficacy of this process in an article by Miss

Gordon Cumming in the volume of the *Nineteenth Century* for 1882. Failing such valuable aid, one cannot but admire the skill of the Peruvian fishermen in guiding their well-filled canoes safely through the breaking surf.

To return from this digression to the fête at Monsefu. It is perhaps difficult for a stranger, with European ideas of active enjoyment, to understand the South American notion of complete idleness as happiness, these people apparently recognizing no intermediate stage between that *dolce far niente* and industrious labour. Active recreation, such as is afforded by the greater number of English sports, is here unknown. The principal pleasure in South America consists in the interchange of visits between neighbouring families, a proof of the sociability reigning throughout. And they appear to love each other's society, though, as is often the case, when they meet they have little to communicate. Thus, while some went to Monsefu to mix among their friends and see new faces, many others were there with the sole object of selling their wares or buying new ones. Whether business were done or no, all would make merry, and go home determined to come again next year.

Among them were "sportsmen," and these assembled in a cockpit, where their favourites were advertised to fight during the day. The cockpits are circular in shape, the floor of the arena being levelled and spread with sand, while the seats are raised all round, like an amphitheatre, in tiers one above the other, for the accommodation of the spectators. The fighting birds are all of the English breed known as game-cocks; and here it is the custom to arm the birds with *cuchillos*, or knives of four inches in length, which are strapped on to the left leg. These *cuchillos* are much sharpened at the points, and are curved in form of a scythe. When the day's sport is over they are carefully cleaned and put away in small cases, with much the same care as a gentleman bestows on his razors. As may be imagined, with the use of such formidable weapons, the combat is soon over; a stab or two from the stronger or more skilful cock settles the affair, and the murdered " birdie " falls without uttering a cry, but with open mouth, as if gasping for the life which he feels is fast leaving his body.

On one occasion, we were present at a match in which five celebrated cocks, who had won their laurels by fighting knifeless, were backed against an equal number, destined this time to engage in fatal conflict. At first they fought single matches, and a sum of one hundred dollars was laid on each match, with two hundred extra for the winner of the greatest number. The conqueror in one round fought with a new adversary; and one brave fellow killed his two birds. Twice it happened that both combatants were so badly wounded that they were unable to stand up, and the judges had to watch closely which of the two first dropped his head in death, in order to name the victor. The betting raged briskly all the time the two birds were dying, and the odds were influenced by the twitching of a limb, the closing of an eye, the droop of the head, or by such signs as to connoisseurs denoted a speedy collapse. The scene was disgusting, scarcely less so than the national bull-fight, in which men share the risk with the bull.

Bull-fights are not included in the list of diversions practised in the provinces; they are confined exclusively to Lima, where they still form, as in the "good old times" of the Spanish viceroys, the most popular amusement. Occasionally a bull may be driven into the Plaza at Chiclayo or Monsefu, to endure the harmless worrying of a dozen amateur *picadores;* but in the absence of trained skill, the animal is let off none the worse, save for disturbance of mind.

A good business was done at Monsefu at the *picanterias*, or small restaurants, where *chicha* and *picantes* of fish, meat, and vegetables are sold. *Chicha* is a beer made from Indian corn, and is of a dark yellow colour, possessing an agreeably sharp and slightly bitter taste. There are scores of *picantes*, among which the zango, lagua, the charquican, catapulcra, and adobe are the favourites. Zango and lagua are made of pork and flour, catapulcra of beef or mutton and potatoes baked and pounded, adobe consists of fried pork. All the dishes are highly seasoned with cayenne and achote grains, which give them a red tint. So there was choice of dishes; and

we could observe certain epicures visiting each restau-
rant in turn, tasting a small cup of *picante* at each,
till they found the one which took their fancy. Gor-
mandism is by no means exceptional. The *correct*
answer to an offer of refreshment is "Yes;" and *picantes*
and *dulces* mark the divisions of the day for many of
the Peruvians.

CHAPTER VI.

Railways — Eten — Balsas — Cholos— Simple Food — Fingers *versus* Forks—Provincial Life—The Ethiopian Eye—The Panuela—Riot in Chiclayo—Local Government—Vultures —Huacas—Pottery—The Picci Skull.

THE provinces of Chiclayo and Lambayeque are better off for railways than any of the other valleys in the north of Peru. They rejoice in both a broad and a narrow gauge line, which, to a certain extent, compete with each other in carrying sugar to the coast from the haciendas near Chiclayo and those along the road to Saña, also the rich rice crops from Ferenafé. The broad gauge (4 ft. 8½ in.) starts from the port of Eten, at a point two miles from the town. The description "port" must be taken in the sense in which it is understood on this part of the coast, for Eten is nothing more than an open roadstead, where such large-sized steamers as those of the Pacific Steam Navigation Company can only find anchorage at a distance of not less than three miles from shore. The Eten Railway Company have done much towards mitigating the dangers and inconveniences of landing on a coast whereon the mighty "rollers" of the Pacific break with considerable violence. They have thrown out a jetty, or iron mole, nearly half a mile in length. The line connects Eten with Chiclayo, at which point it divides into two branches, one proceeding northwards and passing Lambayeque *en route*, and the other eastwards towards Pomalca, Combo, and Patapo. Dr. Hutchinson, in "Two Years in Peru," has enumerated the government decrees under which the Eten and Pimentel lines were constructed, and here, as in other cases, the "Railway War" which naturally took place is only of local interest. Suffice it to say, that a second party of capitalists put their faith in the superior advantages of the small Bay of Pimentel, lying between San José and Eten, only six and a half miles north of the latter place.

The narrow guage (three feet) leaves the port of Pimentel in a more direct easterly direction, and consequently forms a shorter route to Chiclayo, where it likewise divides, one branch going to Picci and Ferenafé, and the other to Lambayeque, whence it is intended to proceed further north, on to the Jayanca, Motupe, and the broad grass lands of Olmos. On this portion of the seaboard of South America, the coast bends in a north-westerly direction, and shelves into the sea at so slight an angle that at Pimentel a depth of four fathoms is only reached at a distance of three-quarters of a mile from the shore, and at San

José and Eten the distance is greater still. In this respect the shore line resembles the foreshore of North Holland, where a similar discussion arose as to the best way of providing a suitable harbour for the Hague, off Scheveningen in the North Sea. The question has occasioned much debate among Dutch engineers, and a parallel question arose in 1872, when it was proposed to establish a great port of refuge and commerce in the north of Peru at Pimentel.

On such a coast, the only safe means of landing is in the *balsa*, or raft, formed of perhaps a dozen trunks of the Guayaquil cabbage tree, lashed side by side. This raft is propelled by means of a large lugger sail, and steered by cholos using long paddles aft. These cholos are by far the hardiest and most healthy race of men in the province. At the proper season, they take long trips of several days' duration out to sea in search of fish, and seldom come back without a good boatful. They are square-built, sturdy-looking, sunburnt men, with splendid constitutions, a proof of which is that they can imbibe large quantities of the *vitriol* which is sold in the villages under the name of *aguardiente*, without suffering very severely from its "after effects." To their credit be it said that signs of intemperance are rare, and, taken all the year round, the cholo is a sober, hard-working man. Rice boiled with small scraps of meat forms the basis of his daily food, and as it is extensively cultivated in the province, it is an inexpensive form of nourishment. Beans and potatoes are much esteemed, and the Peruvian cholo stands as living evidence of the strength and health obtainable from a nearly exclusively vegetable diet. Another example of this is the Scottish Highlander, whose food consists mainly of oatmeal porridge, as simply prepared as rice in Peru, or even more so. Here the rice is boiled in a little water and then strained off as best may be, then strips of Chili pepperpods are mixed with it, imparting a sharp and agreeable taste. Water is the usual beverage; when *chicha* can be procured it is considered a great treat.

A foreigner is at first surprised at the abstemiousness of the people and the simplicity of their food—habits not confined to the humbler classes, but prevailing among the rich as well. Even in these days of cheap cutlery, knives and forks are by no means in general use. A wooden spoon is the only thing used among the poorer classes, and with food for which that implement is unfit, such as roast meat, fingers do the work of knives and forks. An unpleasant piece of politeness consists in picking out a tit-bit from the cooking-pot with the fingers, and offering it to the guest. This is a habit even among the higher class, who might know better; but it is as much a mark of civility as the same habit among the Persian *haute aristocracie*, who tear off the wing of a fowl with their hands, and offer it to a guest out of respect to ancient usages—much as the very old-fashioned Highlander spits in his hand before offering it to a guest in hospitable welcome.

One cannot expect to find in these up-country districts the manners or the delicacy of thought to which we are accustomed at home. In the family circle, whether strangers are present or not, the conversation is of the most "free" description, and matters which with us are scarcely even alluded to are discussed in the most open manner, and this among the first families in Chiclayo.

In provincial drawing-rooms, the conversation is, as a rule, restricted to subjects of local interest, the sayings and doings of the neighbours forming its staple. Human nature is alike all the world over, and "Little Pedlington" has its parallel even under Peruvian skies. Still, the contrast between republican and national feeling strikes one's observation. In the dullest of English provincial towns, the conversation turns at least occasionally upon Government and its doings, on the national relations with other governments, etc. A Republic is split up into sectional communities, and local affairs are paramount. Here the provincials seem very little to care what may be happening in Lima, their political capital. The cholo, for instance, takes but little interest in national events ; he has more pride in saying, " I am a Chiclayano," than in proclaiming his nationality. They cannot be called a *united* nation ; for they are cut up into factions and parties, which are often brought into collision through the private interests of their leaders.

In Chiclayan society, traces of Ethiopian origin more or less diluted are very prevalent; but one is not supposed to notice the various indications of "black blood" which the practised eye very soon learns to detect. There are several signs, but, as in the case of passions or character, the eye is the best indicator of descent. There is something in the eye of an Ethiopian which differs entirely from any other; it seems to change more quickly and remarkably at every change of thought and feeling. The eye of the Hindoo is *intense* in its expression, but far less susceptible of the many variations between anger and love which may influence the individual. The very soul of the mulatto and mestizo may be read in their eyes, and with practice one really seems to read the thoughts passing through their brains, as if they were printed in a book. Just now it is fashionable to hunt for the "divining rod." Messrs. Cumberland and Bishop declare that the *real* impediment to the success of their thought-reading experiments is the difficulty of finding "proper subjects." The writer thinks that the much-desired *medium* (if he really exists in the flesh) is more likely to be found among the warm-blooded mulattoes and mestizos of Peru than the less emotional races of Northern Europe. The mulattoes are the restless members of Peruvian society. If anything is on the tapis, either in the way of amusement or fighting, they are sure to be foremost among the leaders. At night, in the hacienda and in the villages, they form "fandango rings," in which much consumption of *chicha* takes place, and not a little noise.

The *panuela*, performed by two persons (of opposite sex) to the music of the guitar, is the favourite dance. The dancers stand *vis-à-vis*, the step is a "shuffle," and each performer waves in the air a handkerchief (*panuela*) in time with the movements of the dance. At first the performers stand at a distance from each other; but as the dance proceeds, the music becomes quicker, and consequently the steps more rapid, and they approach nearer and nearer. The spectators clap their hands as accompaniment to the guitar, shouting "Aha! aha!" and a song with some such words as—

> "And I winked at her, did I, did I ;
> Aha ! aha ! aha ! aha !
> And she smiled, and then looked shy ;
> Oho ! oho ! oho ! oho !"

and so on *ad nauseam*. This chorus is a necessary accompaniment to the dance. Then the couple whirl round each other, the man waving his handkerchief once over the lady's head ; and then they part, the music growing slower and more slow as the dancers recede from each other. Repetitions of these movements follow, varying in character according to the skill of the performers, and eliciting corresponding applause from the spectators, the consumption of *chicha* and *aguardiente* not being forgotten, and perhaps contributing to the general hilarity which prevails.

But the sports are not always harmless; they sometimes leave behind, as a remembrance, something worse than sore heads. A nice little affair which occurred in Chiclayo on March 16, 1873, gives some idea of the excesses to which the national character may be driven under provocation, and the prompt measures resorted to by the self-constituted authorities. The matter was, that about a dozen prisoners, either undergoing or awaiting sentence in the *carcel*, or prison, attempted to escape, and got so far as to succeed in disarming their gaolers before the affair got wind. Then quickly seizing their carbines and revolvers, the townsmen rushed to the *carcel*. The prisoners thinking that they could brave the mob, fired on them and wounded several. Then the cry resounded in all parts, " Han escapado! " (They have escaped!) People rushed to their homes, and, fearing some serious riot, put the shutters up to their windows and double-barred the doors. We foreigners took refuge in an apothecary's shop, awaiting the end of the tumult. Presently came a knock at the door, and a chola woman came to beg some lint with which to bind up her husband's wounds, he having received a musket ball in the throat. The firing continued for half an hour, then it ceased. Another knock was heard at the door, and a voice cried, " La ordèn esta ya establicido ; estan muertos "

(Order is now restored ; they are dead). We afterwards heard the summary mode in which this was accomplished. The *carcel* consists of one room in the municipal building, on the north side of the Plaza ; towards the side of the street it is closed by a simple grating formed of iron bars. The townsmen advanced in line to this grille, and levelling their carbines deliberately shot down the prisoners, no attempt to interfere being made on the side of the Government authorities.

The sanitary arrangements in provincial towns are of the most primitive nature. Those of Chiclayo may be taken as an example. Cesspools are made for the inhabitants' use in the *corral*, or open yard which is found behind all the dwellings ; these pits, which are shallow, are very seldom emptied, their contents being left to be absorbed by the dry sandy soil in which they are dug. When filled, a few feet of earth thrown on hide them from view, and new ones are dug alongside the old. Water is brought in buckets on donkey-back every morning, and its carriage making it dear to purchase, but little is wasted. The house-refuse is thrown out into the streets at night, and collected early in the morning by carts which convey it to the refuse-heaps on the outskirts of the town. These same refuse-heaps strike a stranger with disgust, for some of the oldest of them rise to sixty feet in height, and contain the "waste" of more than one generation of Chiclayanos. They are made doubly disagreeable by the presence of the red and black *gallinagos* (*Cathartes aura, Cathartes fœteus*), which play much the same part at Chiclayo that the hungry lean dogs do at Constantinople, being general scavengers. Both these species of vulture are brownish black in colour; in the one (the Turkey vulture proper) the head and throat are red, and in the other black. They are about the size of a turkeycock, but lanky and bony in appearance. They hop about over the ground with short jerky springs, seeking their food, which however filthy, they devour in greedy gulps—truly "unclean birds." They roost on the housetops, where also they take a noontide *siesta*, like their protectors. "Protectors" is the right word, for these birds belong to no one; but the public services they render as unregistered scavengers are sufficiently appreciated to admit of their presence being tolerated, and to throw a stone at a *gallinago* would be to court unenviable popularity. The red-headed vulture especially leads a lazy, foul life on the dungheap, from which he can only be tempted by the scent of carrion from afar. On these occasions, they evidence extraordinary powers of perception; for no sooner does some unfortunate overladen donkey or beast of burden succumb to his fate in the distant *monté*, than his carcase is surrounded by scores of these horrid ugly carrion birds, which very soon leave only his bare bones to bleach in the sun.

Dr. Hutchinson, whose researches in Northern

Peru have been previously referred to in these pages, has, in his work "Two Years in Peru," sought not unsuccessfully to muffle that peal of bells on which changes in praise of the interesting race of the Incas have been so persistently rung by Prescott, Markham, and a host of other writers, both English and Spanish. That the fine architecture and other marks of pre-Spanish civilization date from a period long antecedent to that in which the Incas flourished, and that this race was in fact a *de*structive rather than a *con*structive one, form the key-notes of his book. His opinion is, that the real history of the Peruvian race has still to be written, and that the only materials from which it can be compiled lie buried in the thousands of *huacas* or burial mounds, and under the ruins of temples and fortifications everywhere to be seen along the coast. In this opinion the writer concurs, and he thinks that few will dissent who know the country. Every new *huaca* opened may be said to do the work of the stone thrown on the wayside cairn by the passing traveller, just as in Scandinavian fashion, the "Old Man" is built up by degrees by the constant contributions of passing wayfarers, who thus help to benefit "those who come after," by raising a pile which points the way onward, in the right direction.

In making the Chiclayo-Ferenafé section of the Pimentel Railway, the constructors had occasion to cut through one of these *huacas* at Picci, a small village lying half-way on the road between these towns. The output was rich in skeletons and in pottery vessels. The pottery consisted chiefly of the black ware, common in the country. One fine specimen was a kind of jug, with two globes joining, a neck rising from each, the two necks connected by a handle. The head of a nondescript animal formed the top of one neck (the other having no ornamental head), and the liquid poured from either mouth. The globular body was ornamented with a simple scroll pattern, rather like those found on Egyptian pottery at Kennah. The sketch of this water jug, made on the covering of this book, will give some idea of its peculiar appearance.

The skeletons are interesting, as proving the existence of a dwarfish race, among which the tallest measured scarcely more than four feet in height, while the rest were considerably shorter. The skulls belonged to the pure American type known in craniology as *brachycephalic*. The characteristics are broad heads with flattened forehead ; most when ex-humed were partly covered with long black hair, and measured six inches and a half in length by five inches and a half broad. The hinder part of the Picci skull is flattened in an upward direction, and, as will be seen from the measurements, their form approaches to a circle. The forehead is low and receding, and the nose seems to commence its curve at the upper part ; the eye-holes are small. The bodies were clothed in matting, and some few copper tools and ornaments were found on opening the bags. The tools were chiefly spades, hoes, and knives, and were made of an alloy of copper and tin. Among the ornaments found were little tweezers, no doubt used by the men for pulling out hairs from beard and eyebrows—a custom of self-torment which we are told these people thought acceptable to their idols, and which very probably accounts for the present beardless state of the modern Peruvian race.

The valley of Chiclayo is literally strewn with *huacas*, some of which were evidently used as tumuli, and others as fortifications and residences. Most of the natural sandhills which dot the plain here and there are crowned with terraces formed of rubble work and adobes, rising in steps from the base upwards, and generally having a broad level plateau on the summit. The earthworks have been scantily examined, and they offer an immense field for the researches of antiquarians and treasure-seekers, the few that have been opened yielding a rich harvest of pottery ware and copper tools. But hitherto the excavations have not been carried far below the surface.

CHAPTER VII.

IN THE SOUTH.

An American Pampa—Clouds—Stones—Nitrate Fields—The
Desert—Great Heat—Trade Winds—Nueva Carolina—Life
in the Pampa—Pampa Society—Loneliness—New-comers
—Woman's Occupations—Religion—Tirana—Bolivian Gip-
sies—Tent-life—Canchoñes—A Sea of Sand—Matilla—Pica
—Baths—Chacras—Tarapaca.

LET us now bid a brief farewell to Chiclayo and its
pleasant surroundings, and pay a visit to the southern
provinces of Peru, where life is carried on under very
different conditions. "Nueva Carolina" is one of
several nitrate establishments, lying at the foot of the
low range of hills which form the western border of
the great Pampa de Tamarugal. Eastwards, beyond
the smooth sandy plain, rises in the far distance the
range of the Andes, raising on high their clear blue
peaks. To paint them we should require a wash of
chrome-yellow at the base, blending with ultramarine
blue, which pales into sky-blue at the peaks. On still
days, there is nothing to break the sharp outline
except an occasional puff of smoke from Misti, the

volcano behind Arequipa. Here and there the west-ward horizon is broken by clumps of algarova trees, their forms reflected in what appears to be water, but is only the mirage, and as in other desert countries, these apparent sheets of water recede as one advances. In places appear dark patches of alluvial soil, in which are still to be traced signs of former cultiva-tion. In early morning, "desert stillness" reigns supreme over the pampa, a silence unbroken till by-and-by a gentle breeze sets in from the sea, raising curious conical-shaped clouds, which travel slowly along the level surface till they are lost to view in the distance. A similar appearance in the Himalayas gave rise to the native legend of "the cows of the gods" going up the mountain peaks to their pasturage on the inaccessible heights, the highest of which, an immense snow-covered cone, is said to be the abode of "the Great Spirit." The appearance of these clouds on the pampa is the signal for the miners setting to work to extract the rich ore which lies on the slope of the western hills.

Seen from the pampa, the low range of nitrate hills resembles the shore as seen from the ocean, and as if to perfect the illusion, now and then a puff of wind raises clouds of white dust, which really look like breakers dashing on the coast. Layers of clink-stone, by some supposed to be aerolites, thickly cover the tops of the hills, reflecting from their bright, flat surfaces the scorching rays of the rising sun. These stones are seldom met with on the plain; they seem to lie only on the higher grounds. If, as seems probable, they are particles of disintegrated trachytic rock, washed down from the mountains and deposited by floods, their present resting-place on the hill-tops must result from the subsequent upheaval of this range of hills. Their absence anywhere on the plains is doubtless due to the deep sand-drifts, which must long ago have buried them deep under the present surface. They are found again in large quantities, but more rounded in shape, on the opposite side of the pampas, in the dry beds of pre-historic rivers, which formerly poured down the deep ravines indenting the face of the Andes. A column of black smoke may be seen at intervals rising above the nitrate hills, speaking alike of the treasures hidden there, and of man's industry in searching them out and converting them to his own use. Before English coal was obtainable, the algarova roots, dug up from the pampa, formed the only fuel used by the natives in the elaboration of nitrate of soda. These beds of lignite are practically inexhaustible, but owing to the great consumption in former times of the material lying nearest, they are now at too great a distance from the mines to make its collection very profitable.

One mile south of Nueva Carolina, the nitrate hills throw out a spur into the pampa, forming a recess known by the name of Pozo de Almonté, or the "Well of Almonté," which is justly celebrated for the abundant supply of brackish water which it yields. For a distance of some three miles, the slope of this spur is rich in nitrate. "El Rincon," "Santa Rosa," and "Dolores," are the names of some of the *fabriques* in which these minerals are refined. For some space in front of the ridge, the surface of the pampa consists of a crust of siliceous mud, which after being baked by the sun splits into cakes, which bear very much the appearance of a lava field in Iceland. For colour, a brush well-filled with sepia and another of chrome-yellow would serve for the pampa and the hills ; the sky would need Prussian blue for its darker parts, toned off into lighter shades and with fleeting white clouds drifting over it. It is a weird prospect ; the sense of vastness and utter loneliness strikes one with awe, and the total absence of any means of supporting life gives a feeling of desolation to the barren expanse of sand and sand-covered rocks, bold as the landscape is. The Pampa de Tamarugal is an immense plateau, raised 3400 feet above sea-level, stretching for a length of a hundred miles or more, the breadth varying from twenty-five to sixty miles, and sand, perpetual sand, over the barren brown hills, seeming as if it would baffle any search after the riches concealed beneath. From the sublime to the ridiculous there is but a step, and the author of "Alice in Wonderland" must have had this sort of landscape in his mind's eye when he made his heroine "weep like anything to see such quantities of sand." But for the miners, not very picturesque objects, the landscape is a desert as solitary and forsaken as that of Sahara, or the waste plains of Palestine and Egypt when untrodden by caravans.

In these latitudes, the sun glows in the early morning like a red-hot fireball, very quickly absorbing whatever little moisture may have been left behind by the night dews. Heat reigns supreme until noon, man and beast alike groaning under the heat, which often reaches ninety degrees Fahr. and more in the shade. After noon this great heat is somewhat moderated by the wind, which on this coast sets in regularly from the southwest at nearly the same hour every day. Then the desert stillness is suddenly destroyed, and confusion succeeds the undisturbed repose of early morning. The wind, at first a gentle breeze, soon develops into a gale, when it raises huge clouds of sand which it sends whirling across the desert to join others beyond, completely shutting out all view of the Andes and of the sky above them. As the gale drives the sand clouds before it, sweeping down the hillsides and breaking on the broad plain, it gives out a roaring sound, as if triumphant at finding elbow-room and material on which to work its will. At times the wind exerts a force equal to a pressure of forty pounds per square foot, and its velocity is such that a rider at full gallop will fail to overtake an object which the wind is bearing to the other side of the pampa. There is nothing to arrest its course, so on it sweeps resistlessly, gathering at each yard more and more sand till these clouds become too heavy to remain suspended, and gradually deposit themselves on the pampa, again to be disturbed by succeeding gales. Heavy rain-clouds are seen scudding aloft on their way to the Andes, on whose western slopes they will presently pour their contents.

Such is the appearance of the pampa in summer. In winter, which season corresponds to our summer, the nights are marked by the arrival of *camenchacas*, or sea-fogs, which hang over the plain till late in the day when they are dispersed by the broiling sun. On these nights the thermometer goes down below freezing-point, and the fogs condense, making the ground very damp and coating with salt both the rocks and buildings against which they are driven by the wind.

Let us now glance at the home-life of intelligent beings whose lot is cast in this barren desert. The buildings of Nueva Carolina are laid out in oblong form, the machinery for refining the nitrate of soda being at the northern end, and the entrance gate at the southern, while the longer sides are formed by dwelling-rooms and offices. The enclosed area is occupied by cooling or precipitating tanks, from which the nitrate, when crystallized, is thrown out on the side roads, and there packed in bags for transport to Iquique, the port whence it is shipped to foreign parts.

Don Fernando Lopez, who is part owner of the establishment, manages its working. His life in this desert region is solaced by the society of his wife, her sisters, and their mother, otherwise life in the intervals of "work" would be dull indeed on the pampa, with its very limited sources of amusement or distraction. The men are, perhaps, least to be pitied, for their day is filled up in the performance of their various duties ; but most English ladies of the writer's acquaintance would speedily grow weary of such a life as that led by Signora Lopez and her sisters.

The limits of pampa society are narrow indeed. When the writer took up his residence for a time with Señor Lopez, there were no other ladies residing within reach, and the domestic day wore itself away in the following fashion. Early rising is the custom, coffee and biscuits are partaken of, say at seven, in the long refectory; then, *sometimes* but not often, comes a short walk or ride on the pampa—more often the ladies beat a precipitate retreat into their private apartments, out of which they do not reappear till towards eleven o'clock, the breakfast-hour. At this meal, the head *employés* at the *fabrique* are seated at the lower end of the table "below the salt," in the order of rank according with their respective functions. After this, the *least* pleasant part of a South American day has to be got over, or through. Those who have leisure wear through the hot hours in a siesta, taken in the gently swinging hammock ; in reading or writing ; those who have not such leisure to spare—well, they work on as well as may be under the discomforts of an oppressive climate, with the thermometer at ninety-two or more. By the aid of reading, working, etc., the ladies of Nueva Carolina manage to kill time, in the companionship of each other, until the dinner-hour at five. The evening is passed in playing games of cards or chess, varied with conversation and music. Sometimes, but seldom, a guest's arrival may vary the even tenour of this life. These are generally travellers on their way to Tarapaca, or to the *fabriques* in the north ; but known or unknown, they are always sure of meeting with hearty hospitality from the owner of Nueva Carolina. And rightly so ; for should not strangers always be welcomed in such remote places ? They may turn into friends ; and what is life worth after all, if it is to be passed alone, separated from the companionship of those of our own kind, from the fellow-creatures from whose congenial society we draw our chief enjoyment, chequered though it may be like all earthly joys, by the bitter pangs of sorrow? It is true, there are those who, disgusted with their experience of the world, resort to seclusion as a panacea for their disappointments, and seem to prefer the meditations of their own minds to contributing anything to the whirlwind of thought, which is day by day wreathing a new girdle round the globe, and urging the human race on the road to improvement.

This seclusion is encouraged by the teachings of Rome, which perhaps found it an easy way of occupying turbulent spirits, by setting them to feed on themselves instead of hatching conspiracies which might prove inconvenient and difficult to manage.

" Millstones and the human heart are driven ever round and
    round ;
  If they have nothing else to grind, they must themselves be
    ground."

Unless the hermit carry with him a rich store of corn, gathered among men, to be ground or distilled into a form which may be handed down for the benefit of posterity, it is surely but a form of selfishness, after all, to ignore the instincts of humanity which would lead us to help each other, rather than devote our energies to personal gratification of the momentary whim. Surely it is flying in the face of that natural instinct which makes us all, rich and poor, small and great, dependent in some sort for our well-being on the daily co-operation each of the other.

In the middle of this desert, life is of necessity carried on under the simplest of simple rules. Nueva Carolina is like "the shadow of a great rock in a thirsty land ;" but yet it is not without a natural beauty of its own. " Barren and ugly as the country is," said Señor Lopez frequently to the writer, " I love it as the country of my adoption and as the place where I found my wife and formed my home." Lopez is by birth a Chilian, who, beginning life as a clerk in the thriving town of Iquique, soon rose by dint of his talents and energy to the position of one of the leading merchants in the province. He received a merchant's education at Valparaiso, and is well read in classics as well as in the history of his own race and contemporary events. He converses fluently both in English and French; but unlike the majority of his countrymen, shows no great longing to visit the Old World, and see for himself the great cities of Europe, and the manners and customs of the dwellers in the crowded squares and thoroughfares of the Old World. "I have read of them," he says, "and that suffices. I should feel bored to death gazing at the lions in Trafalgar Square, or at the palaces of the Rue de Rivoli. In London or Paris I should find no friends with whom to associate, no interests to attract me. Leave me my home on the pampa and its simple life, and constant occupation, and I will gladly leave to others the privileged *entrée* into European society, however grand and luxurious it may be." In short, Señor Lopez prefers being king in his own little court to being a unit in the crowd of strangers. Every one to their taste; and after all, is it not the true secret of a happy life to be in harmony with one's surroundings?

After a time came an addition to this pampa society, by the arrival of a Scotch family, who came to reside at "La Palma," an adjoining factory recently established by some merchants at Leith. An iron house, sent out from Scotland in pieces, had been erected for their accommodation on the rising ground of their property, in front of the factory, which was at that time in process of construction. This iron house could be seen from a long distance, and served as a landmark for many tired travellers crossing the pampa, many of whom have reason gratefully to remember the generous hospitality of its master, Mr. John Moir, manager of La Palma. He had brought with him to these wilds his newly married wife and an infant child, to lead a life which, by reason of its nearly complete isolation from all society of her own sex, must surely signify an enviable depth of conjugal devotion.

Viewing the life led in these wastes, we are bound to recognize, with a sigh, the advantage possessed by Spanish Catholic women over their Protestant sisterhood. The strict seclusion and monastic training of their early youth enable them to view with resignation a home in the sterile desert, and to feel less acutely the want of friends of their own sex. Such a life in the case of a Protestant Englishwoman, accustomed to greater freedom of intercourse with her kind, implies a series of self-denials which must rob her life of much of its natural happiness, unless her home interests are strong and deep enough to compensate for the want of everything else. The Peruvian, on the other hand, reared under the strict *régime* of the Catholic Church, makes herself contented anywhere. Does she not, here as elsewhere, look on the ritual of the Church as the light which guides her footsteps? Religion is to her a familiar friend, as sincere and encouraging on the desert as in the crowded city. Her constancy in religious observances keeps pace with that of the Mussulman. At every step something reminds her of her faith, from the ivory crucifix in her room to the names of the surrounding hills, which the Spanish settlers named after their patron saints. Thus in the desert, where there are no convents or churches, the Roman Catholic woman appears to be strengthened by the constant occupation brought by her numerous religious observances; while the Protestant one, deprived of these landmarks, too often surrenders herself a prey to loneliness and indolence. This, of course, does not apply to women of strong character, whose religion, being a part of themselves, is not dependent solely on outward observances, but teaches them to find or make cheerful occupation for themselves, even in the desert.

Not far out in the pampa, only some six miles distant from Nueva Carolina, the small village of Tirana has sprung again into prominent notice, through the building of a church, subscriptions for which were collected in the province. Tirana was well known in former times as a smelting ground for the silver ores yielded by the adjacent mines, and straggling rows of deserted adobe huts testify to the considerable population once contained in the desert town. The algarova forests, the remnants of which still exist, and the inexhaustible supply of fresh water lying at a shallow depth beneath the surface, induced the Spaniards to make this a smelting station for the crude silver ores of Huantaya, a specimen of which, showing their richness, may be seen in the museum at Madrid. One of these smelteries still remains, and is actively worked by its owner, an elderly spinster lady, who still makes use of the primitive "rocking-stone and bar" for crushing the ores.

The church consists of a light framework of wood, on which are fastened sheets of corrugated iron. Two small belfries on either side of the entrance give the structure a neat and suitable appearance. The building is certainly large enough to accommodate the Tiranians, some hundred souls; but it is expected that the congregation may be increased by the nitrate refiners, who may not object to riding a few miles to church.

The algarova tree prospers at Tirana, and in the adjacent woods we saw some measuring ten feet in circumference at the base, and which could not have been less than fifty feet in height. Their foliage offers a delightful shade to travellers at all seasons, indeed Tirana is an oasis in this desert, and serves as a resting-station between the nitrate fields and the baths of Pica, which lie at the foot of the Cordillera. It is here that the Bolivian emigrants encamp, when on their way from Cochabamba to

seek employment at the *fabriques.* These emigrants
are the gipsies of Southern Peru, and they supply a
large portion of the labour requisite for the production of nitrate. They are a strong, hardy, and not
unhandsome race. Great numbers annually cross the
Andes, taking with them their wives and children,
and after a wearisome journey on foot, extending
sometimes to a length of three hundred miles, they
offer themselves for hire at the nitrate establishments.
Their pay is about two dollars a day—good wages
as compared with their class of labourers in England
—and they are housed by their employers in rough
tents made of coarse sail-cloth, supported by poles
of all sorts and sizes. Every *fabrique* of any consequence owns one or more of these Bolivian
encampments, the inhabitants of which, without
exception, present the most ragged and miserable
appearance of anything of the kind to be seen
anywhere else. The camp is usually built on the
bare plain, and the Bolivians, who have to cut out
their own tents from the rolls of canvas provided
by their employers, shape them to suit their own
somewhat eccentric notions of comfort and style.
There is some resemblance to be traced more or less
in the habits and doings of all tent-dwellers, however far from each other the countries may lie in
which their canvas is spread. The uncouth appearance and frosty atmosphere of the interior of
the Kurdish tent at the foot of Mount Ararat has

I

been made familiar by the accounts of many travellers;
and Captain Burnaby has graphically described the
domestic horrors of the Khivan in his home on the
Steppe, and the atrocities committed therein. Conceive the worst of both united and some notion
may be formed of the wretched appearance of the
Bolivian's home on the pampa. A few old sacks,
too old and rotten to be used again for nitrate, are
spread on the sandy floor of their tent, and serve
alternately as dinner-table and bedding. A pack
of wolfish, starving dogs of mongrel breed prowl or
lie about the tents, only moved to activity by the
sight of a traveller, who is welcomed with angry
growls and a *sortie en masse* of the town garrison.
Often they exhibit their wolfish nature by attacking
stray mules and horses, which fall an easy prey to
their ferocious appetites. Yet, notwithstanding these
unsavoury surroundings, the Bolivian nomad appears
contented with his lot. In the matter of climate, he
is better off than his contemporary in Asia; and a
steady worker may look to returning home after a
year's absence, the better by one or two hundred
dollars.

CHAPTER VIII.

PICA AND TARAPACA.

Route to Pica—Cultivation—Rich Soil—Desert Travelling—
Matilla — Pica — Baths of Pica — Bolivian Gipsies — Pica
Wine—Life at Pica—Tarapaca—Doña Martinez—Con-
tentment.

WE may now leave Tirana, and continue our journey
to the baths of Pica, in response to kind invitations
to visit that much-esteemed spot. The topography
of the country continues much the same. As before,
the same level plain spreads in front, broken here and
there by patches of poor, parched-looking trees. But
the loose sand we had traversed in approaching Tirana
from Nueva Carolina is now replaced by a hard
coating of lime and sand, which renders our horses'
progress difficult, by affording such hard and uneven
footing. A few miles further on, the ground is thickly
covered with low brushwood, till on arriving at the
district known as " Canchoñes," we are welcomed by
the signs of extensive cultivation. Agriculture is here
carried on under a somewhat singular system, but one

which was formerly extensively employed by the Incas and their Spanish successors.

On removing the upper crust of hardened earth, a rich alluvial soil is found at a depth of about four feet from the surface. In this a trench is dug about fifty feet wide and several hundred feet in length. These trenches or *canchoñes* give the name to the district, and the capillary attraction characterizing the alfafa (lucern), maize, and other plants, enables them to suck up moisture through the several feet of soil intervening between the bottom of the trench and the subsoil water beneath. The success attending this first attempt at cultivation in this part of the pampa induced the government to establish an agency, with the power of allotting plots of land to settlers, who are encouraged by being offered the farms on easy terms. At present the mining population of the pampa, as well as the residents in Iquique, depend for their supply of vegetables partly on Tacna, a valley some forty miles to the north, and partly on the Republic of Chili; so if vegetables and grain were well cultivated at Canchoñes, they would find a good market for their produce within easy distance. In this place, water is reached at a depth of twelve feet from the surface, and this, with the rich bed of black alluvial soil, offers great advantages to the intending settler and encourages the hope that at no distant date this district may be under cultivation.

The earth which is dug out of the trenches is

thrown up on each side, and thus serves as additional shelter to the plant from the violent and often cold winds which sweep across the pampa in the afternoon. At the time of our visit, the government agent was busy in erecting a pump, to be worked by a windmill, with a view of utilizing the wind in raising water for irrigation purposes. The supply of water is practically inexhaustible ; for in fact the pampa covers a subterranean reservoir, fed from the rainy districts of the Cordillera, the rainfall filtering through the porous strata which intervenes.

Leaving Canchoñes, with its refreshing glimpse of verdant nature, we again plunged into a weary sea of deep sand, the heat made well-nigh intolerable by a hot glowing sun overhead. At every step the horses' feet sank deeply into the yielding surface, and their slackening pace and evident signs of fatigue made their riders cast longing eyes towards the black speck, visible on the face of the distant yellow mountain in front, which indicated the buildings of Matilla, the first village we should reach. This black speck was the only relief to the eye afforded by the ocean of sand spreading before our view. The heat was intense and the distressed horses seldom moved out of the walking pace they had fallen into on entering the desert. For ten long miles this exhausting tramp continued, and then, as we ascended the mountain slope, the ground became harder. On nearing Matilla, fresh signs of cultivation became visible, and with

common accord we made our way to the brook which
skirts the village on the south, and refreshed ourselves and cattle with its delicious water.

Matilla lies at the foot of the ravine of Chintaguay,
which is irrigated from springs situated higher up the
valley. A fair-sized brook wends its way along the
bottom of the valley, watering the fields of maize and
the vine trees on either bank. After passing Matilla,
the stream becomes absorbed in the dry thirsty pampa
within a very short distance. The inhabitants of
Matilla support themselves by cultivating the usual
products of the country, and by working the silver
and lead mines in the neighbourhood, some of which
are reported to be very rich. The place is also much
frequented by the nitrate manufacturers, who go there
to bathe and enjoy the glimpse of verdure it affords,
so doubly refreshing after a long spell of pampa
barrenness.

When we had seen all that was considered worth
seeing, we pricked on to Pica, resting on the way at a
perquio or farm, belonging to a nice homely widow who
treated us with great hospitality. We were received
in a well-furnished room, opening at one side on a
vinery, and the adornments showed much taste and
an appreciation of comfort very unusual in these
distant parts.

Several similar "farms," mere green patches on
the broad expanse of yellow sand, are scattered along
the hillside hereabouts. They are kept alive by the

rainfall of the Cordillera, which, percolating through porous strata, empties itself into the natural reservoir beneath the surface of the pampa. These underground currents are intercepted at Pica by driving horizontal tunnels into the soft yellow sandstone of which the hill-slope is here composed. These tunnels are sometimes of considerable length, and their drainage area is augmented by making driftways to the right and left, the water being ultimately collected into a basin built at the outfall of the works.

Pica itself is a small native village, boasting of some three or four hundred inhabitants, who both in appearance and habits betray their nearly pure Indian origin. A principal tunnel, driven on the line of a natural hollow in the hill-slope, pours the water into two large basins, from which it is drawn to irrigate the adjacent chacras. The entire cultivated area is encircled by a thick ha-ha of chilka shrub. Within this enclosure, the space is green with beds of alfafa and maize; these are overhung with vines trained on light wooden frames. At the time of our visit, they were covered with rich black and white grapes. Each plot is bordered with luxuriant granadilla, fig and orange trees, their green and yellow fruit glistening between the dark foliage. Here and there the imperial azalea spreads its branches far and wide, heavy with bright crimson blossoms; while beds of violets, primroses, and sunflowers testify to the natural taste of the cultivators. Thus the chacra is a lovely spot, rendered all the more attractive by the forbidding aspect of the sterile sand on the other side of the hedge.

The water at these springs is pure and sweet, as it issues from the soft sandstone through which it has filtered and which has served as its carrier from the distant heights. The basins are two in number and are excavated out of the solid rock, the first being some feet higher than the second, owing to the natural slope of the ground; and a sluice is placed in the partition which divides them, by means of which the water-level can be regulated to that of the higher and lower plantations. The Picanians come to bathe in the water in the early morning, at which time the balmy air, the luxuriant tropical foliage, and the delicious water combine to enhance the delights of this charming oasis. The water, when it issues from the rock, is of moderate temperature; thus the sense of touch is soothed by it, as the sight is by the bright tropical flowers, and a tranquillizing air of repose characterizes the spot. Picanians make the baths a morning rendezvous, where they discuss local gossips and chacra scandal, with such rare items of news as may occasionally flit across the pampa from the great outside world. It was pleasant to note the good manners which prevailed in these aquatic gatherings, in which both sexes take their "dip" in company, the ladies appearing on the scene ready prepared for the water, dressed in the *bata*, or morning-gown of black serge. Nothing occurred at the baths which would have been thought unbecoming on the *plage* at Dieppe, Brighton, or Toulouse.

Visitors to Pica spend the day in the chacras under the shade of the vine groves, listening to the songs of the birds, and enjoying the verdure, which they miss in their homes on the pampa or at Iquique. With few exceptions, the houses do not offer much accommodation ; but then the climate is so mild that people prefer living out of doors, and the shady coolness of the verandah is more thought of than Turkey carpets and damask-covered chairs. It is a life in which artificial luxuries are unknown, but at the same time it is an existence so natural and enjoyable, that what are thought necessities elsewhere would here be looked on more in the light of nuisances.

Apart from its character as a "spa," Pica is used, like Tirana, as a resting-station by the Bolivians on their way to the nitrate fields. The camping-ground set apart for them is a stone's throw from the village, on the hillside facing north. A row of ragged tents made of sail-cloth forms the accommodation offered to the travellers, who in return become good customers to the Picanians in the article of vegetables and other provisions. As aforesaid, the Bolivian needs little to make him happy. The men are short and square-built, with strong arms and legs ; straightforward enough in their dealings but not over-ready to learn unaccustomed duties. Their features are thick-set and heavy, much resembling the Tartar physiognomy ; and while chin and cheeks are nearly bare, a thick shock of dark or black hair covers the head and fore-head, and reaches below the ears. The women are but modified copies of the men, and, judging by the hard day's work they perform in tramping across the desert, laden with a baby slung on the back, then pitching the tents and cooking the food, they cannot be far behind the sterner sex in physical strength. Indeed, their physique must be extrordinary, for many have been known to give birth to an infant during the day's march, without causing a stoppage of more than an hour or so in all. They exemplify the lines—

> " Here down beneath the dusty trees,
> At this lank edge of haggard wood,
> Women with labour-loosened knees,
> With gaunt backs bowed by servitude,
> Stop, shift their loads, and pray, and fare
> Forth with souls easier for the prayer."

An excellent wine is produced from the Pica grape, the cultivation of which is particularly favoured by the soil and climate. This wine, when new, possesses a peculiarly sweet and rich flavour. It is darker in colour than the darkest Madeira. Like most wine, it improves by keeping, and some was given us which had been in bottle ten years. All pronounced it exceedingly good. Its high reputation has led to its being sent to Lima, where it is much appreciated by the connoisseurs of the capital.

The Picanians, who are more Indian than Spanish, are taller than their countrymen of the sea-coast, but they are less stalwart and strong. They cultivate their chacras with great industry, and possess that strong attachment to their native village which is observable throughout Peru, in town and country alike. Chiclayo is the one earthly paradise of the Chiclayano; and the conditions of life at Pica are not to be improved upon, in the mind of the Picanian. "When you come to Chiclayo, I will take you round our Plaza, and show you our grand cathedral; and then I will present you to our *bonitas mozas*" (pretty girls), says the one. "If you will *only* visit Pica, I will take you to my chacra, and give you such fruit and such good rich wine; and in the morning we will all go together to the baths," temptingly urges the Picanian. Is not the well-known saying, "Vedi Napoli, e poi mori," a case in point? The Picanian is one of a simple, happy group of villagers, who rely fearlessly on their industry and the fertility of their soil to satisfy their small requirements. In this serene atmosphere, the seasons never overstep the mild variations which mark their periods, and the seed sown in winter yields its crops in summer as regularly as the sun reaches the meridian at noon. But little is known of what happens in the big world "beyond the pampa," and the life of the Picanian creeps on from days to years, he being apparently as little concerned with events which may transpire outside his district, as the events are capable of disturbing his repose.

. The foot of the Cordillera, which forms the eastern boundary of Tamarugal Pampa, is crossed at intervals by ravines, some of which are but mere ruts in the hillside, providing a water-way for a streamlet discharged from springs above, while others are deep gorges, piercing far into the heart of the mountain, whose water-worn sides show unmistakable traces of the course taken by prehistoric rivers. Such a one is the *quevrada*, or ravine of Tarapaca, in which lies, about two leagues' distance from its mouth, the "city" of Tarapaca, the former capital of the province of that name. The entrance to the ravine is about ten leagues north of Pica ; and for a space of six miles in front, the pampa is strewn with masses of boulders of all shapes and sizes, through which a deep gully marks the course formerly traversed by the river. The sides of the *quevrada* are lined with compact beds of water-rolled stones separated by layers of sand, marking the order in which they were successively deposited. The uppermost of these beds is raised more than a hundred feet above the bottom of the valley along which we rode, beside the stream which unlike those of temperate climes increases in bulk the nearer we approach its source. The ravine was evidently once the channel of a mighty stream, which rolling from the mountain heights, watered the extensive pastures and woodlands of the great

Tamarugal plain. The record of this is clearly written on its water-worn sides, in which the channels can be traced, and in the layers of gravel and sand lying one over the other, as well as on the broad sheet of boulders spreading over several square miles at the mouth of the *quevrada.* This plain also shows evidence of the luxuriant vegetation which must once have clothed it, in the roots of algarova and other trees, still to be dug up in all directions in the bed of rich black soil which still remains.

Tarapaca has nestled itself in a bend of the ravine, at a point three miles from its mouth, where its sides separate, leaving between them a tolerably broad level space, on which now grows maize and other plants similar to those cultivated at Pica. The inhabitants of the town and its outskirts number some two thousand, all told, and are lodged in houses built after the same pattern and with the same materials as those in northern Peru. A small square forms the centre of the town. On one side is the church, surmounted by a single belfry ; the other sides consist of shops and dwelling-houses, with verandahs in front.

We were hospitably entertained by Doña Teresa Martinez, who owned the best house in the square, where she lived with a nephew and niece.

The latter, being a native of Arequipa, was wont to dilate at length on the beauty and wealth of her native town, and the stirring incidents in its frequent revolutions, also the yet more fearful ravages made by earthquakes. Neither these nor the display of revolutionary passions appeared to have diminished her fondness for the place; and her powers of conversation were as great as they were varied. After the story had been told of cruel bloodshed and heartless pillage of gold and silver in troublous times, she would take her guitar, and charm her listeners with songs of love and romance, which sound doubly touching in the beautiful language of Castile. Her aunt, Doña Teresa, was a worthy example of the noblehearted elderly matron, a type of humanity which it is always a pleasure to meet. Though past eighty years of age, she rose at five every morning, and after partaking of maté (a substitute for tea), would usually ride to her chacra, which lies about a mile further down the valley. Her intellect was clear and quick, and she took a lively part in all conversation, showing much knowledge of many subjects, some of which one might have supposed could scarcely have come within range of her experience, passed as the greater portion of her life had been in this secluded nook. She kept the accounts of her estate—incidentally it appeared, if one may judge from the standpoint taken by her nephew, that she was "close" in financial matters.

It may be remarked that thrifty habits are general in these out-of-the way places as indeed everywhere where the absence of public investments and banks foster the instinct of hoarding. Profits made at

Tarapaca, either by the agriculturist or the merchant, can only be disposed of in two ways, either in purchasing more land or stock, or by being buried in the ground, and handed down thus to posterity, a barren heirloom. Those who have already as much income as they require, prefer the latter alternative as the least troublesome ; and the name of those who hoard their savings in stockings, in Peru, is legion.

In all Peruvian towns, the habits and customs of the inhabitants are very much the same. Society is represented by the alcalde (mayor), the principal merchants and landowners, and their families, who frequently meet at social reunions, and amuse themselves in the ways already described. One distinctive feature to be remarked among all classes, is that however rich a man may be, he almost invariably manages his own affairs, instead of employing a deputy or steward. Thus, the owner of land farms it himself—the complicated system prevailing in England, and the class of tenantry resulting therefrom, do not exist in Peru ; the merchant sells his own articles, and keeps his own store. So one of the great characteristics of our own race, this incessant striving to rise above the class into which we were born, and despising the work which our fathers cheerfully fulfilled, which in this nineteenth century so often results in debt and difficulty, is unknown there. The Peruvian takes life more easily, and is content to fill his own niche in life without striving to enlarge it.

CHAPTER IX.

THE NORTH AGAIN.

The Haciendas—Pumalca—Parrots—El Combo—Cleaning the Water-courses — Combo — The Jesuits — Patapo—Native Sugar-mills — Sugar-making — The Coolies — The Coolie Question—Native Labour—Government Inspection.

ONCE again we find ourselves amidst our old friends in the north, and perhaps some account of the haciendas in that part of the country may be interesting. In July, 1873, the writer made an expedition, or *paseo*, towards Saña, in company with Señor Isaga, the owner of Percala, and M. Legrandt, a native of Alsace. Saña is a town said to have been founded by the Incas.

Crossing the Plaza early one morning, mounted on sturdy ambling nags, the party passed over the timber bridge which spans the acequia of Chiclayo, after passing the rice-mill which works for Santa Lucia, and proceeded in an easterly direction towards Combo, an estate belonging to Señor Arbulu, sous-préfet of the province. The road is but a bridle-path cut through the *chilka*, or brushwood, and the roots, which are in many places left protruding from the ground, often cause the fall of a careless or badly mounted rider. The light alluvial soil, worn to powder by years of constant traffic, rises in clouds at each step of the cavalcade, testing the usefulness of the *poncho*—a large square shawl with a hole in its centre to allow of its being passed over the head; the drapery then falls in folds over the body, coming below the saddle, and thus completely protecting the rider from the clouds of dust through which he is passing. The broad-brimmed *sombrero* guards the head from the direct heat of the sun, whose rays pour down in burning heat as he approaches the zenith.

After about half an hour's ride, we passed the buildings of Pumalca on the left; these, we were told, would cease to be used when the new factory was finished which was then being constructed three miles further on, in a more central part of the estate. On reaching the new site, we made a short halt to observe the buildings rising from the ground under the hands of numerous workmen. As in the planning of towns so in haciendas, the quadrangular model is followed and to each building is allotted a square open space. The walls, both of factory and dwelling-house, are built of adobes, which are laid in a mortar consisting chiefly of wet mud. When finished, the outside will be washed over with lime; the dryness of the climate and total absence of rainfall render it possible for this kind of building to last much longer than might be expected.

The algarova tree, which grows plentifully in the neighbourhood, furnishes rafters for the roof. The algarova, a species of carob, is, as it has been observed before, one of the most valuable indigenous trees of the country, under the special conditions of whose climate it finds the moisture which its leaves absorb from the night atmosphere, sufficient for its subsistence. In form, it is not unlike the English apple tree. It sometimes reaches a height of forty feet, but is usually shrunk and dwarfish in appearance, with crooked arms and branches spreading from its trunk like the arms of an octopus. It is an evergreen, and its succulent leaves are round in shape, rough to the touch when baked by the noonday sun, but if touched in the evening when the air is full of moisture, smooth and porous. The fruit comes in April, and even in the most sterile and parched-looking soil, a rich crop of tares may be expected ; these provide food for horses and mules, by which they are greedily devoured. The tare is a bean sometimes six inches long, holding several seeds ; when ripe it is yellow, or dark brown in places where it is toasted by the sun. The quantity of saccharine matter it contains makes it a favourite food with cattle, and even dogs gather under the tree to feed on its fruit when the shedding season arrives. The wood is of a mahogany colour, and very hard to cut ; its cleavage being distorted, the crooked and knotted branches are used chiefly in fences and for rafters to roofs. As this wood retains its resinous properties after years of exposure to the weather, and will take a good polish, it is employed largely in machine-making. Among other purposes it is greatly in request for piston-rod bearers in steam-engines. At Pumalca, and on the high ground of Combo, and indeed generally where the land is too elevated to permit of its irrigation, forests of this tree occur, representing an abundant and cheap supply of fuel for the inhabitants of the towns, and for the working of the sugar-mills.

Before leaving Pumalca, our attention was drawn to a huge mound, some five hundred yards in length and sixty yards in height, which was looked upon by many as a *huaca*, or Inca tumulus.

Past Pumalca, the road winds through a part of the forest just named, which is destined shortly to be cut down, and the clearing planted with canes or sown with corn. All the woods in the neighbourhood of grain-sown land are well stocked with the beautiful birds indigenous to Peru. Flocks of pigeons are seen flying above the tree-tops, hurrying on their way to some neighbouring cornfield ; while parrots with brilliant plumage chatter among the boughs, as if in consultation before attempting another raid on the maize. The largest of the parrot tribe (*Conurus tumultuosus*) is green all over, except his head, which is scarlet, and a few red feathers growing on his breast ; another (*Conurus rupicola*) is smaller in size and has more red in his plumage. The third (*Conurus sitophaga*) is bright green on the back, its wings being fringed with blue, and the breast and forehead of a deep yellow colour. They are all very good eating, a fact of which the writer became aware in a somewhat unexpected manner. Having commissioned a sportsman of local celebrity to bring him some of the best specimens, with a view to having them stuffed, he found on returning home in the evening, the " bag " duly spread on the kitchen-table, but—plucked and ready for cooking ! So the stuffing was of a more transitory nature than he had intended, the sole result being a very savoury supper.

Another common bird is *El Carpentero*, or "the carpenter," a kind of woodpecker, so-called from the hammering noise he makes by rapping his bill against the trunks of trees, to drive out the insects on which he feeds. He is a pretty constant companion to the traveller about here. His body is black, the breast patched with white. Another, the *Saca-ta-real* ("draw out your *real*"), the brown fly-king, deep red all over except the wings and back of very dark brown, whirls in the air, repeating his extortionate summons. These are but a few among the beautiful birds to be seen exulting in their liberty in this, to them, Elysian climate.

Emerging at last from the forest, our path wound

round the base of a cone-shaped hill, called El Combo, standing isolated on the level plain. Its apex, some four hundred feet in height, is crowned by the wooden cross which is so often placed in a prominent position in Catholic countries, as if to take advantage of the moment when the mind is elevated by the beauties of Nature to direct it "through Nature up to Nature's God," and remind us of the God-Man, our great Exemplar.

Skirting the volcanic cone, the *tapia*, or exterior mud-wall, of the Hacienda del Combo is shortly passed on the right, and the shelving ground denotes that we are nearing the Rio de Lambayeque, at a point where it is spanned by a bridge resting on algarova piles. The banks here are steep, and the rude bridge, measuring only one hundred and fifty feet, provides a safe transit at all times, except when the river level is raised above its platform by extraordinary flushes, caused by heavy rainfalls in the Sierra. Dense masses of *caña brava*, or wild cane, line both sides of the river, and are apparently only kept from joining by the rapidity of the current. The quickness with which this plant spreads, and reappears after being cut, entails a vast amount of labour on the cultivators to prevent the flooding of their lands through the choking-up of the river-bed. Sometimes the only effectual method is to burn the canes, a course always resorted to with reluctance, the wood being of value for building purposes.

An ancient custom provides for the clearing of the river and irrigation canals adjoining, at least once during the year, by labour contributed from each hacienda and small chacra, in numbers proportioned to their size and to the quantity of water they respectively consume.

At the appointed time, the *peones* assemble at the head of the acequia of their district, and divide themselves into two bands, the first of which clears away canes, rushes, and other tropical weeds, with the help of long curved hatchets furnished to them. The task of the second party, closely following in the rear of the first, is to deepen and make even the banks of the watercourse. The whole party proceed with their work, stimulated by the music of the drum and fife, the strokes of axes and shovels keeping time with the musicians. They work quickly and eagerly, naturally anxious to get over unpaid work ; and it is indeed surprising to watch with what speed a party of *limpiadores* (literally, cleaners) will descend a watercourse, clearing away all obstructions and leaving its bed and sides clean and smooth as if newly cut. All the *acequias*, whether of ancient or modern construction, are traced in irregular lines across the country, thus taking advantage of the fact that, at each bend of the stream, the water is forced to a higher level on the off-bank than it would attain if running in a straight line. This enables it to spread itself over higher ground.

One short mile further, beyond the bridge, and we pass the gates of the Hacienda del Combo to the left. Combo is said formerly to have belonged to the Society of Jesuits, being one of the many rich estates held by that society before their persecution by the Crown, which has ended in the expulsion of the order from every South American state, with the exception of Ecuador. In 1773, the King of Spain, urged by the "Bull" of June 21st in the same year, despatched an order to the viceroys of his South American provinces, directing them to arrest all the Jesuits simultaneously in one night, and to ship them off to Spain, confiscating their accumulated wealth. With regard to the convent of San Pedro in Lima, this design was defeated by the activity of the vicar-general in Lima. San Pedro was known to contain enormous treasures, but the vicar-general having received private intelligence from his superior in Madrid by the same ship which bore the king's despatch, when the viceroy's officers knocked for admission at the convent door, they found the brethren grouped in the hall *en costume de voyage*, with their baggage ready to embark, and of the treasures not a trace to be found. Nor to this day has any been discovered.

To give some idea of the enormous wealth once possessed in South America by the Society of Jesus, acknowledged as the most moral, but at the same time the most covetous of religious orders, it may be stated that when an edict of another King of

Spain was passed in 1816, less than fifty years after their expulsion, to re-establish them in their former colleges, an inventory was made of what remained of their former possessions, and it appeared that the value of the haciendas available for restoration to the order amounted to 4,000,000 dollars in Paraguay alone. This represented the intrinsic value of estates on which the Crown had realized as much as it was possible to turn into money. A curious carrying out of their precept, "Nolite possidere aurum neque argentem, neque pecuniam in Zonis vestris" (St. Matt. ch. x. ver. 9).

To return to the estate of Combo as it appears now. For many years it has remained uncultivated. At the period of our visit it was overgrown with algarova trees and the thick brushwood which springs up so quickly in this fertile soil when left to itself. It had recently been purchased by M. M. Solff and Co., the proprietors of Patapo, a sugar-factory lying some six miles further in the interior, and justly ranked as one of the most important sugar-plantations in the country.

Less than an hour's ride brings us to the beginning of the *alameda*, or avenue, leading to Patapo. Lofty poplar trees planted on each side of the roadway form a delightful shade, while through the opening between the trees the rider sees with admiration endless waves of the bright sugar-cane, covering the earth as with a golden fleece under the bright reflection of a tropical sun.

On nearing the factory, we observe the details of sugar-making on a large scale. Numerous two-mule carts bring the freshly cut canes to the huge rollers of the steam-mill, which will squeeze away the sweet juice, leaving the cane crushed and dry, suitable for firewood. At Patapo, the sugar is refined; and the machinery brought from Europe is in great perfection and well managed by foreign hands, contrasting favourably with the rude apparatus used by the *chacrareros*, or small cultivators, of whom we shall see more in these pages.

The native *trapiche*, or sugar-mill, is usually worked by a yoke of oxen, which tramp monotonously round and round. Large stones, or more usually a piece of rock, serves to counterbalance the weight of the collar-pole; this gives circular rotation to the centre roller, at a speed regulated by the pace of the oxen. By means of tooth-gearing, the rollers on either side are turned in contrary directions, and the narrow open space between the stones serves for the crushing of the cane, which is inserted by hand. The saccharine liquid is drawn off into kettles; after boiling for six hours it is poured into moulds, and when cooled, is thrown out as *camchacha*, or brown crystallized blocks of sugar. With this simple machinery, a small *chacrero*, boiling five kettles per day, will make three blocks of sugar of two hundredweight each, value about £2 per block.

The scarcity of labour throughout the valley has

forced the proprietors of Patapo to imitate their neighbours in employing Chinese coolies. Don Christian — a partner in the firm, is manager of the factory.

An outcry has lately been raised against the alleged inhuman treatment which the Asiatic coolies receive at the hands of their taskmasters in Peru, and Mr. March, H.B.M.'s Consul at Callao, reported at length to his government upon the traffic in 1876. The writer's experience tallies with many of the charges of cruelty advanced by Mr. March, and which may be taken as based upon his own practical knowledge, or on reliable data. Yet the deductions to be drawn from Mr. March's earlier reports scarcely justify the allegations made by the London *Examiner* (January 13, 1873) in an article entitled, "How some People are killed," which among other reflections contains this passage. "We have, then, to declare that very much of the sugar which comes to this country from Peru is the fruit of the labour of kidnapped men; of men who are kept in loathsome isolation from all the sympathies which make human life differ from that of the brute; of men who for years at a time never see the face of woman, who die of despair, are killed by infernal cruelties, and left to rot like carrion, and to become food for carrion birds. This sugar we English Christians eat; this sugar we allow to compete with that produced by our own planters; and we think that no more anxiety to be consistent in our belief of a political doctrine should stand in the way of our putting a stop to that state of things."

It is difficult to say whether this overdrawn picture served to modify the treatment which the contract coolie receives in Peru, yet it may have evoked sympathy for his condition in the quarters most likely to help him. " Efforts," writes Consul March, " have been made by the Peruvian government to afford protection to these people ; but, notwithstanding, their condition, as a rule, is far from satisfactory. In the first place, the isolation of some of the haciendas is such that the coolie is entirely at the mercy of the master. This master, or his overseer, may be a conscientious and humane person, or he may be the contrary. In the later case, if the coolie runs away, he will either starve in the surrounding wilderness, or—which may be considered quite as bad—be recaptured and punished in a way which he may not survive to tell."

The father of one of the writer's companions in this expedition was killed by his own Chinamen in an outburst of vindictive passion, when the coolies conspired together to revenge the harsh treatment they had received, and breaking into the house, beat their master to death with their farm tools. This was after long endurance ; for one of the punishments this man had imposed on any coolie whom he had caught in the act of escaping was to hobble him with an iron chain, forcing him to work as usual with this heavy weight added, until he considered his punishment sufficient. For lighter offences he used to beat them unmercifully, and curtail their rations to starvation point. This went on till even the long-suffering Chinaman's patience was exhausted, and, rousing himself one morning, he avenged himself in the summary fashion already related.

According to the writer's experience, the treatment of the coolie depends almost entirely upon the disposition and character of the managers of the estate, who, in many instances, are foreigners by birth, the wealthier class of land proprietors preferring the comparative comfort of the provincial towns to the discomfort consequent on a residence in the monté. So they gladly entrust the management of their property to a *mayordomo*, for which situation Europeans are thought best adapted, as they are found to be more competent to exact obedience, and more fertile in resources than their own easy-going countrymen. A crowd of adventurers of all nationalities, coming from the United States and Europe, are attracted to Peru by the golden pictures so freely circulated of its wealth; and both honest and unscrupulous scramble into places of trust apparently with equal facility. An unscrupulous *mayordomo*, incited by the promise of a share of the profits on the working of the hacienda, thinks little of the comfort or even the lives of his coolies. His duty and his private interests, untrammelled by restraint of any kind, compulsory or moral, make him look upon them as so many machines, out of which the object is to extract a value in manual labour out of all proportion to the cost of their maintenance. The more work they can grind out of this human machine, the greater is the satisfaction of the employers and the larger become his own profits.

One of these adventurers, a worthy specimen of the West Indian slave-drivers, a class of men now legally extinct, had the audacity to boast that he had shot a refractory coolie with his own hand, and "got off," paying the value (400 dollars) on the grounds that he had received justifiable provocation. In these estates, remote from towns, and therefore removed from the moral restrictions which public opinion exercises "where men do congregate," the *mayordomo* is completely his own master, and recognizes no law but his own will; so, as in other absolute despotisms, the well-being of those under his sway depends on the amount of justice existing in his own character. There are no government officials whose duty it is to inquire how the Asiatic coolie is treated, and, if there were, they would lack means to *enforce* their decrees. In fact, the military and civil force now maintained by government in the provinces is everywhere inadequate to compel obedience to the laws of the country. So notorious is this fact, that no attempt is made to conceal the motive for the sudden departure of the regiment from a native town, should there be reason to anticipate a rising of its citizens with which the government forces feel themselves incompetent to cope. To avoid unsuccessful collision, they retire to a distance and await reinforcements, whose arrival seldom fails in causing the would-be disturbers of public peace to relinquish their enterprise. In like manner, a large Peruvian sugar-estate forms a little republic in itself, its members form a numerical force superior to any which government is able to maintain, perhaps in the whole province. To maintain order among his own people, the haciendado relies solely upon his own resources, and the means he employs to secure internal harmony are those which long experience has proved to be most effectual. He follows the time-honoured motto, "Divide et impera." To establish an equilibrium of force, he uses the national antipathy of race, held by the zambo and cholo against the coolie, as a counterpoise to any united action of the Asiatics ; and so well is the balance maintained, that at any time the small number of his overseers can control the scales by throwing their weight on one side or the other. Every hacienda which boasts a " Hong-kong," also contains a row of zambo huts. These lie some distance apart, and frequently a water-course divides Black Christian from Yellow Heathen.

Consul Marsh justly credits government with having made efforts " to afford protection to these people," the coolies ; but, he adds, " notwithstanding,

their condition, as a rule, is far from satisfactory."
There can be no doubt that the government of Peru
finds itself much embarrassed as to providing all the
additional labour required by the many sugar-estates
recently established in the most fertile valleys of the
country. This difficulty does not rise solely from the
increased demand for manual labour, or from an
unusual deficiency in the population, but partially from
the continued influence of ancient customs, which
place the able-bodied cholo in the position of bond-
servant to the local landowner—not by reason of
conquest, this state of things dates from the period
when the poorer native's position was analogous to that
of the serfs in the Middle-Ages—or of the Russian
moujik previous to his emancipation by the Emperor
Alexander. The cholo's position resembles most that
of the *moujik*, inasmuch as in the agricultural districts
of Peru every labourer *belongs* to some one whose
debtor he is for sums of money advanced to him on
the prospective security of what labour he may be
capable of rendering. This debt is never repaid in
kind, but by its equivalent in manual toil, a method
which seldom liquidates the accounts, as the poor
man's daily necessities are more apt to increase the
burden in at least an equal proportion. The improvident character of the peon, his love of amusement and of launching out on feast-days, his idleness
on working days, coupled with perfect indifference to
everything but the pleasure of the moment, render him

an easy prey to the calculating master who advances him loans, thus securing his labour for *years* in advance. Should he manage to escape from his creditor, in the hope of earning elsewhere the money which would purchase his liberty, he is quickly traced, and compelled by law to resume work on his patron's land. It is a revival of the Inca system of serfdom, but robbed of its just compensations by the introduction of that baneful Spanish institution called " patronage."

Under these circumstances, it is easy to conceive the difficulty found by a newly established sugar-planter in engaging the requisite labour, and nothing appears more convenient and natural than to borrow help from densely populated China. By throwing out illusive promises, he succeeds in diverting southwards some portion of that yellow stream of humanity, which in 1873 began to flow steadily in a direct course from Canton to San Francisco, threatening to overwhelm California with Mongolian blood, and, as some whisper, the Western States also. Like them the Peruvian sugar-planter cannot resist the temptation of utilizing the valuable commodity, though the advisability of the step taken on such a large scale may be open to question. The present need induces indifference to future consequences, which in California have come to mean possession. In Peru, it adds one more to the numerous shades of colour consequent on the great mixture of races from both worlds. But whatever may be the future effect of so great an immigration, there is no doubt of the responsibility incurred by the planter, and the ugly rumours afloat as to the ill-treatment of coolies point out the necessity for State interference. In the author's opinion (which has been often solicited) the estate proprietor, and not his agent, should be made personally responsible to government for his treatment of the coolies, and be made to furnish quarterly returns as to his human property ; for such it is *de facto* for the time being. If these returns gave the name, age, and state of health and condition of every coolie engaged, to-gether with the date of his contract and name of the agent who " imported " him from China, and in case of death, authentic reports showing how it occurred, each individual would be in a manner under State protection, and the stories of wanton ill-usage would disappear with the fact of irresponsibility which exists under the present system.

These particulars should be entered in a register kept by a special department under government. A certain number of efficient officers would be required to test the veracity of the returns made, and also from time to time inspect the haciendas, and inquire into the treatment the coolies receive. Publication of these returns, with the penalties imposed on defaulting land proprietors, would ensure to the coolie the protection of that all-powerful public opinion, which, founded on sympathy and justice, is seldom wanting in the masses, though often, alas ! failing in individual cases.

L

CHAPTER X.

PAST AND PRESENT.

To return to our journey. Leaving Patapo next
morning, we first visited the hacienda of our travelling
companion, Señor Isaga. This is called Percala, and
lies at that part of the Lambayeque where the
river divides into two branches. Its level is low, well
adapted for irrigation ; and a slightly raised knoll has
been chosen as the site of the house, labourers'
dwellings, and stables.

These knolls, or earth mounds, occurring where
least expected on the level plains, were often used by
the Incas as a foundation for their *huacas*, or tumuli,
though the mounds themselves are of earlier origin and
are generally supposed to date from the time the
land was first brought under cultivation. They are
chiefly composed of the invaluable volcanic sand and

other extraneous matter, which, it is supposed, once covered the whole surface of these valleys. Some of these raised earthworks spread over a large area, and reach to a considerable height, leading the traveller to marvel how the immense quantity of material represented by their cubic contents could have been collected so as to form a level plain, with a surface unbroken by pits or quarries. Whenever the *huacas* erected on these mounds are opened, human bones are invariably found, with some of the utensils and ornaments used by their possessors during life, such as earthen water-jars, copper tools, trinkets, and ornaments of various shapes and colours.

If the local belief is correct, and these mounds were constructed by the Incas, one can easily imagine that the same ingenuity which devised and the perseverance which executed the roads and canals was brought to bear in reducing the naturally uneven surface of the ground to a lower level than the water channels, thus bringing a wider area under irrigation. The material thus cut away was possibly used to form the mounds, and also the adobe bricks with which the *huacas* are built.

The next estate visited was the Hacienda de Sipan, where we found its proprietor, El Viego (the old) Arbulu, as he is termed, awaiting our arrival, seated under the shaded verandah of his house. Don Pedro Arbulu was in his eightieth year. He possessed at least one of the usual attributes of a patriarch, having thirty odd children and an unknown number of grandchildren, all claiming to belong to the house of Sipan. Such is the licence allowed in this country, that a rich haciendado often owns as many wives as a Mussulman, with this difference, that he only recognizes one in general society. It might have been expected that some one of his numerous offspring would have been seen round the old man, but no such gladdening sound as the merry laugh of youth relieved the stern monotony of the place. Arbulu's numerous family were distributed about the mud-built houses of Chiclayo, while he, whose old age would in a northern clime have been solaced by "woman's tender care," here sat desolate under his verandah, his solitude only broken by the rough companionship of the men of the monté.

There was nothing exceptional about Señor Arbulu's house. The same groves of orange and citron trees, showing between dark foliage their orange and green fruit, lined the chacra; beds filled with rich crops of lucern, or with the taller and stronger maize, whose leaves, rustling in the wind, appeared to sing the praises of the balmy air and rich soil to which it owed its fecundity; the same alameda shaded by the familiar poplar trees, led through the home *potreros*, or pasture-grounds, filled with mares and colts, mules, goats, and sheep, and dotted here and there by clusters of lofty bananas; and beyond, Indian corn waving in graceful undulations, stretching away to the horizon in most places, but here at Sipan where little is grown, ending at a hedgerow of bush-wood, or the skirts of a primitive forest. The same dusty sun-burnt, dried-up appearance, characteristic of the flat-roofed farmhouse with its shady verandah and general air of desertion, meets the traveller's eye as he crosses the open space leading to the Peruvian hacienda. If the houses and surroundings closely resemble each other, so does the mode of life followed by the occupants. "Cæsar and Pompey am berry much alike, specially Pompey."

The itinerary of old Arbulu's daily life, if written, would read like hundreds of other Peruvian haciendados who personally manage their own farms. The haciendado rises at daybreak, and after partaking of tea or coffee, goes his rounds on horseback, visiting each work in progress on his estate. For instance, the work of a band of *peones* clearing away monté will detain him, and he will give minute instructions to the superintending *mayordomo* as to the limits of the clearance, pointing out the part to be cut away by hatchets, what may be set fire to without danger, etc., etc. Next comes, perhaps, the ploughing of a cleared space, preparatory to the planting of cane; and matters relating to the team of oxen, the sharpness of the plough, and the management of the work will have to be settled before he continues his rounds. At another point, the tracing of an *acequia* calls for his superior skill and knowledge in the varying of its lines, so as to command the highest ground without wasting labour in experiments, or interfering with the existing plantations. By the time his tour is finished and its several duties performed, it is nearly noon, and he will dismount from his cob at his house-door. Breakfast is served, and the haciendado passes the heat of the day in the cool shelter of his sala, scoring accounts, attending to correspondence, or in conversation. Then comes the siesta, spent in the inviting hammock slung across the sala, or in the verandah. In the evening, he will make a second inspection of his estate, and criticize the result of his morning's instructions ; then the day's work is brought to a close by his retiring to rest soon after supper.

Leaving Señor Arbulu to the quiet enjoyment of this peaceful life, untroubled by the uncertain seasons which in other latitudes render the farmer's prosperity a game of chance, but which here only threatens a scarcity of water—a calamity affecting chiefly the larger cultivators—we continue our ride in the direction of Cayalti, distant some seven miles to the south of Sipan. Here the country is more open and less burdened with monté, and the light soil, disturbed by the horses' feet, being parched to powder, rises in clouds of fine dust, at times hiding our route. On our left towers the Cordillera, apparently to an inaccessible height ; and so powerful is the glare of the tropical sun, that the *quevradas*, or ravines, appear indistinct and undefined as if they had been roughly washed in with neutral tint on the yellowish-grey sides of the mountain.

It was only an hour past noon, yet the heat was intense, registering over eighty degrees in the shade ; this severely tried the horses, whose pace seldom exceeded a walk. The oppression was general and the movement of the air was insufficient even to rustle the leaves of the scattered groups of trees we passed here and there on the route. The stillness of Nature was only disturbed by the weary tread of the horses' hoofs, as they sank deep into the yielding soil. It was like the silence which often precedes a storm, when the voice of Nature is hushed, and birds and beasts seem to await with bated breath the miraculous display of an overwhelming force which they fear without comprehending. Drowsiness steals unconsciously over both rider and pedestrian exposed to the heat at the usual hour of the siesta. This weary march continues for over one hour. Suddenly relief is felt. The rider rejoices in the refreshing seaborne breeze which begins to play on his face, the horse snorts, tosses his head, and endued with renewed activity, breaks from his sluggish pace, the stronger for his late repose, and the party break into a sharp gallop, soon leaving the Hacienda de Sipan far in the rear.

About half-way between Sipan and Cayalti, we came across a sample of the Incas' handicraft, being the remains of the causeway which at one time served as a thoroughfare between Cuzco and Quito. The roadway was raised on an embankment of earth, and measured some twenty-four feet between its walls of crumbled adobe. The pavement was at this time buried in sand-drift, but as far as could be ascertained, consisted of small round stones, which must have been collected from the beds of distant mountain streams, as no stones are found in the rivers which traverse the valley. Standing on the top of the embankment, we traced the causeway running in a straight line mathematically correct, in the direction of Saña for a distance of over one mile, when it became lost in the monté. Professor A. Raimondi, of Lima, published a map of Peru, showing the Inca roads, as described by Cieza de Leon in his " Cronica del Peru," dated 1553, in which the present road is shown as stretching beyond Saña, across the Lambayeque valley and the extensive plain of Olmos, on the way to Piura. When close to the latter town, it mounts the Cordillera, and passing through the towns of Huanabamba, Loga, and Cuença, terminates at Quito. On the map, Saña stands at the junction of two highways from the south, both starting from Cuzco, which was the capital of the Inca's empire. One dips directly towards the coast, to a point south of Yca, and keeping near the sea, cuts the site of the modern Lima, and thence viâ Trujillo reaches Saña ; the other passes over higher ground throughout its course, and winding about the mountain chain, unites Cajamarca with the ancient capital, subsequently meeting the coast route at Saña. On a map published later by Mr. Clements Markham, hon. secretary to the Royal Geographical Society, the war-routes taken by the different Inca conquerors are delineated. It may be worth noting that Huanca Capac does not according to this map appear to have followed the line of the Inca road described by Professor Raimondi (and verified by our own observations) in his march from Chimu (Trujillo) to Tumpi Tumpez (Tumbez) ; for he is made to travel from Pacasmayo directly through Eten and Chiclayo, leaving Saña far to eastward.

The important service rendered to the peculiar government system of the Incas by these stupendous roads, traversing the empire lengthwise from end to end, with numerous cross-branches to the sea-coast, is graphically described by Mr. Prescott, the learned historian of " The Conquest of Peru."

Following the embankment for some distance, we came to an old *acequia,* which, judging from its level, must have carried its waters under the causeway, thus suggesting that both these works were in use at the same date. The slopes and trough of the water-course are sufficiently well preserved to show the use which was made of it, but all traces of a viaduct which may have carried the road across the water have long disappeared, and we could find none of the materials by probing in the sand. These relics of industrial works, which serve to show the extent of civilization reached by a people whose history is all but lost in the mist of conjecture, show also the materials available by the present population, should they desire to improve their condition. To see the colossal works expressing the magnificent ideas of this by-gone race, such as canals conducting water from the dizzy elevations of the Cordillera to the distant valleys along the coast, and roads stretching for hundreds of leagues over a mountainous country, and the ingenuity displayed in devising and constructing them at a time when steam power was to them as unknown as iron tools, leads one to draw a mental comparison between this pagan race and their Peruvian successors of the present day, considerably to the disadvantage of the latter. Uncouth and superstitious as the former inhabitants were, we cannot but give them credit for recognizing the sure road to man's prosperity in the capabilities of the fertile soil. Having power to command the labour of a teeming population, they employed it in making roads and canals. "In our days," says Señor Isaga, "we should require unlimited supplies of gold in order to assemble a sufficient number of workmen to renew these crumbled ruins and draw water from the rain-attracting heights on to our parched plains."

It is deplorable to think that when the needed gold arrived—in the shape of Peruvian loans—no portion of it *was* laid out in such purposes, the whole amount being spent on railways. In that country, irrigation works promise a *certain* return, as the conditions of climate along the seaboard oblige the cultivator to seek his supply of water from a distance. Means for properly irrigating the naturally rich valleys, which only ask moisture to spring into gardens, should naturally have been the first care of a provident ruler. It is no fallacy to say that had hydraulic works been carried to a successful issue with the money lavished on railways, the latter, so to speak, would have made themselves, for the great and immediate increase in the produce of the land which must have followed would naturally have induced the cultivators to supply at their own expense new and improved methods of transport. Demand creates supply. Governments *will* occasionally make the mistake of thinking that what has answered admirably in certain climates and under certain conditions must necessarily apply equally where climate and conditions are different, and where different means might have more readily attained the same ultimate end—the country's improvement and advancement.

Towards evening, the indications of recent cultivation, contrasting with the sandy monté-covered country we had traversed since leaving the Inca causeway, showed us that we must be reaching Cayalti. For more than a mile our track led across an abandoned cotton-field, and the tufts of down which still hung about the dry forsaken bushes seemed to reproach the passers-by for neglecting a useful commodity. The experiment of cotton cultivation was tried in the North of Peru not many years since; it has hitherto proved a failure, the plant not taking kindly to the soil, and therefore frustrating a praiseworthy attempt to add to the national industries. Its planting has been tried experimentally each month of the twelve, and in different parts of the country; but in no case has it been found to yield a profitable annual crop sufficient to warrant its promoters in competing with the North American growers. The atmospheric changes, slight as they are, are still too terrible for this exceedingly sensitive plant to flourish under, and the low night temperature sounded the knell of its cultivation. Yet, strange to say, the seed dropped casually by birds in the hedgerows often develops into a fine creeper, and climbs over the hedges and bushes, yielding a crop every year in its wild state. Here it is protected from the cold winds by the sturdier *chilka*, and in summer its beautiful white and yellow flowers repay the friendly shelter by adorning the plain-looking thickets. In the open plantations, isolated and unprotected, it does not produce sufficient to repay even the cost of planting.

Cayalti rivals Patapo in the extent of its cultivated land and in its annual output of sugar. It is the property of some Lima merchants, and at the time of our visit, the estate was managed by a son of one of the partners, a youth who had but recently finished his studies at San Carlos, the university of the capital. To reach the hacienda, we first passed along lines of cane, then through alfafa meadows, named La Vina, Oyotten, Ohabanda, Sultrapan, Mocupe, and Ocupe. We crossed the river over a bridge built upon algarova piles, at a point just below Saña, and eventually arrived back at Chiclayo by a different but less interesting road than the one described. We had spent on this occasion something like one week very enjoyably and to our advantage in visiting this beautiful Peruvian valley, the associations connected with which still remain vivid and fresh in the author's memory.

CHAPTER XI.

PERUVIAN ANTIQUITIES.

Mr. Squier's Explorations — Pachacamac — Convents — Rope Bridges—Buried Relics—Ancient Cities—The Dragon Myth —Indian Worship—Rough Travelling—Large Stones— Sculptured Monolith—Ancient Gateways—Indians guarding Ruins — Sacred Islands — Chulpas — Peruvian Pottery — Water-coolers — Black Earthen Jars—Curiously shaped Jars —Ancient Figure in Pottery—Ornamented Pottery—Jars of Strange Shape—Relics from Aymara Graves—Dr. Marcedo's Collection.

BUT few visitors to Peru have either leisure or opportunity to explore the interesting monuments and relics which evidence the former existence of races which, as the remains of their works show, must have made great progress both in art and science. Nearly everywhere throughout the country, these ancient buildings are to be found buried deeply under the surface. Their discovery is in consequence both a laborious and expensive work. Added to this, few indeed of the travellers to Peru go with any idea of a purely scientific expedition. As a question of money, the cost of the journey alone is a serious item for consideration. The country is, in fact, a difficult one to explore, excepting by those who carry long purses and have plenty of leisure time to dispose of.

The land of the Incas is certainly for the student of history a fascinating field, but his researches should be undertaken as a labour of love, for unless persevered in with more than ordinary patience, the value of the results will scarcely correspond to the labour bestowed, so many are the disappointments he must expect to encounter. The conqueror's hand fell heavily on the venerable antiquities and monuments of Peru. As Mr. Prescott well observed, " In their blind and superstitious search for hidden treasures, they caused infinitely more ruin than either time or the earthquakes. Yet enough monuments of the Incas remain to invite the researches of the antiquary." Only those in the most conspicuous situations have hitherto been examined. The force of Mr. Prescott's words applies fully as well to the present time as to the period when they were written. The most exhaustive and interesting researches perhaps ever made among the ancient monuments of the country are those recorded by M. Vena, and latterly, within the last ten years, by Mr. E. George Squier. Many of the ruins described by these explorers have been visited by the author, who was thus enabled to verify their accounts. Mr. Squier, imbued with a spirit of research not unworthy of comparison with that of his distinguished countryman, Mr. Prescott, supplemented with no small success the work of his illustrious predecessor in exploring the mysterious recesses of Central America and Yucatan. His investigations ranged over the greater part of the territory at one time occupied by the great "Andean family," which included the Aymaras of Bolivia, who became eventually incorporated with the Quichuan or Inca Empire. With the aid of tape-line and theodolite, he measured the ruins (or to speak correctly, those portions of ruins which remain still exposed to view)* of Pachacamac, the Grand Chimu, Tiahuanuco and those of the sacred isles of Lake Titicaca, besides many score watch- and burial-towers and earth-mounds, which he came across in the course of his journeyings. In addition to this, he describes also the great roads and aqueducts which, as we know, formed such important factors in the Incarial system of government, a system called by Prescott "the mildest but most searching of despotisms."

At Pachacamac, the only edifices traceable are "El Castillo," or the temple which supported the shrine of Pachacamac, and Mamacuna, the convent of the Virgins, which, it is thought, was built by the native Yungas of the coast prior to their conquest by the Incas of the mountains. The shrine is poised on a hill encircled by a series of adobes, or sun-dried brick walls, which are painted red. The edifice,

* "Peru," by E. George Squier.

which is square in shape and greatly injured by excavation, bears on its sides the traces of figures of men, and in places the original stucco and painting can be made out. Mamacuna belongs to the Inca type. It lies on low ground, near a small lake, a mile and a half distant from El Castillo. Both on the hill as well as around its base, the lines of half-buried walls (running always at right angles to each other) mark the site of an extensive town. Concerning the town, it appears that separate "apartments," or flats, consisting of from one to three rooms, were assigned to each family. These three-roomed tenements contain one front room fifteen feet square, a small sleeping-room, and a kitchen.

Perhaps one of the most remarkable works contained in these rooms is an arch, the principle of which was thought to be unknown to the aborigines of Central and South America. Mr. Squier considers the presence of this arch to be entirely enigmatical, as he can scarcely conceive that the knowledge and skill of which it gives evidence could have existed among the ancient Peruvians, wonderful architects though they were, unless it had been found in other places besides. Had the arch been known to the Incas, it does certainly seem strange that the principle upon which it is based received no wider application, for instance, to bridges.

The rope suspension bridges found by the Spaniards on their arrival were the only means employed by the Incas for crossing the deep ravines and rivers of the Andes. The long bridge which spans the Apurimac is one of the oldest, and its approach on one side through an ancient tunnel cut in the rock, fixes the spot as the identical point at which the Incas crossed the river. The suspended roadway on this bridge measures, from fastening to fastening, 148 feet, and its height above the river is 118 feet. The cables, five in number, are made from the twisted fibres of the *cabuya*, or maguey plant, and are about four inches thick.

Among the findings at Pachacamac were a pair of small bronze tweezers, used probably for picking out the beard ; some pieces of alpaca blanket, finely spun and woven in the style known as three-ply, in two colours, a soft chestnut brown and pure white ; a sheet of fine cotton cloth, sixty-two threads to the inch ; a comb made of fishes' fins, set in a slip of wood ; the remains of a fan with cane handle, from which radiated the feathers of parrots and humming-birds ; a necklace of shells ; an ancient spindle ; a wallet, containing beans and pods of cotton ; some fragments of silver ornaments ; and beads of chalcedony. Besides these, there were numbers of utensils and earthen jars, like those to be seen in the British Museum.

The writer unearthed from some of the *huacas* or earth mounds in the province of Lambayeque and Chiclayo, in the extreme north of Peru, relics corresponding precisely in description with those found at Pachacamac, thus proving the enormous area of country over which the Incas ruled. According to Mr. Clements Markham's observation, which tallies with that of the writer, the town of Chimu, as well as others in many parts of Peru, is built on the same plan as Pachacamac. These towns are invariably laid out in rectangular sections, which in turn are divided into smaller blocks of dwelling-houses. A reservoir supplied with water by an open acequia, or small canal, stands in the centre of each section of buildings, and a thick wall surrounds the whole settlement. A series of similar sections and squares, occupying a space some 1600 feet long by 1100 feet broad, is classed as a "palace," and is supposed to have been the residence of a Chimu prince and his retainers, before the Chimus were succeeded by the Incas. But all information that can be gathered by historians about the subjugation of the Chimus by the Incas is vague and scanty. Garcilasso de la Vega, one of the most reliable among the early chroniclers, says that during the reign of Pachacamac, the ninth Inca or king, the Chimu territory which extended along the entire sea-shore from Chançay to Trujillo, was ruled over by Chimu-Cancha, who became subject to Yupanqui, the son of Pachacutec. Pachacutec is remembered as having induced the Chimus to give up the worship of fishes and animals in favour of that of the sun.

Peru is not without her form of the " Dragon

Myth," but, like the Japanese, Cingalese, and many other nations of very ancient origin, the Peruvians can boast of their own special dragon and of the independent part he played in their history. Among the mythological illustrations which Mr. Squier gives in his book, is one of a contest between the gods of the earth and those of the sea. The man of the earth is crowned with a serpent or lizard, the man of the sea is clad in armour made from the shells of crabs, lobsters, and turtles. It is interesting to compare these woodcuts with descriptions of other dragon forms found in the countries mentioned, as well as in Hindostan, Scotland, Germany, and in fact nearly every known country, with variations occasioned by the different customs and modes of thought of the inhabitants.

It is reasonably conjectured that among the Chimus there existed a popular form of worship which was but little removed from fetichism, and was marked by all the extravagances of a degraded superstition. Arriaga, a Jesuit priest, who was commissioned by the Spanish viceroy to inquire into the worship of the Indians in 1621, reported that "In many parts, particularly among the mountains, the natives, perhaps following the teachings of the Inca conquerors, worshipped the sun under his proper name, *Inti ;* and also *Punchao*, or the day ; *Quilla*, the moon ; certain stars, especially *Oncoy*, the Pleiades ; *Libac*, the lightning ; *Mamacocha*, the sea ;

Mamapacha, the earth ; *Puquias*, springs ; and *Razu*, the snowy mountains." As the Hindoo races worship, besides their celestial gods and their representatives, three classes of divinities—the *Grâma Devetâ*, a village god ; the *Kula Deveta*, or household god ; and the *Ishta Devetâ*, or personal or patron god ; so too, the Chimus and the whole Yunga and Chincha family had their village or communal deities, their household *huacas* (their lares and penates), and their patrons or personal *huacas*. It was to these that their principal worship was paid.

Besides these interesting monuments in the north, the south of Peru affords some celebrated ruins, among which the most famous is perhaps Tiahuanuco, or, as it has been christened, the American Stonehenge. To reach Tiahuanuco, the traveller starts from the port of Arica, goes by rail to Tacna, and thence plunges into the heart of the Cordillera. The hardships and privations incident to a journey across the Cordillera will not soon be forgotten by any one who has undergone them. The wretched *tambos*, where the only available provisions consist of a little *chupe* (a weak stew of llama flesh), and whose only sleeping accommodation is a bare bench to lie on, with an armful of fodder for the mules, are the only resting-places to be found in the country. Passing over these difficulties of the road, which is the necessary price paid by the explorer for the satisfaction of his curiosity, we proceed towards the ruins of Tiahuanuco, to reach which the Orsaquadero river must be crossed. This river, which drains Lake Titicaca, is crossed over a floating bridge made by joining together many bundles of dried reeds, on which the roadway is formed. The river is one hundred and fifty yards wide here ; and when it becomes swollen and the current is strong, it is usual to cut the cables at one end and let the bridge swing down the stream, so as to avoid its being swept away entirely.

The ruins of Tiahuanuco lie nearly in the centre of the great terrestrial basin in which are situated Lakes Titicaca and Aullayas. Here blocks of stone, mouldings, cornices, vast masses of sandstone, trachyte and basalt, great monolithic doorways, bearing symbolical ornaments in relief, are some of the objects which lie scattered over the level sandy plain. Here, in this Baalbec of the New World, as at Chimu and Pachacamac, a "fortress," a "temple," and a "palace" were built on raised ground originally terraced, and each terrace supported by a massive wall of cut stones, the whole surmounted by structures of stone, parts of whose foundations are still to be traced. Some of the stones are very large, and give rise to the old frequently unanswered questions asked also of the Egyptian pyramids and the Palaces of Cuzco, as to the means by which such huge blocks of stone could have been brought to a spot so far from any known quarry. Some of these *monoliths* measured thirteen feet eight inches in length by five feet three inches in breadth, and were two feet six inches thick. On an average the stones are of smaller dimensions than those composing the circle at Stonehenge, but they are much more accurately cut, the front surfaces being perfectly true, and only the backs left in their original rough state, or partially worked. Mr. Squier's opinion is that in no part of the world are stones to be seen cut with such mathematical precision and such admirable skill as in Peru, and in no part of Peru are there any to surpass those which are scattered over the plain of Tiahuanuco.

Among the ruins is also to be seen a monolithic gateway, which, curiously enough, D'Orbigny, who visited Tiahuanuco in 1833, says had then fallen down. It is now upright, but by what agency it was raised is unknown. This block of stone measures thirteen feet in length by seven feet in height, and is eighteen inches thick. A doorway, four feet six inches high and two feet nine inches wide, is cut through its centre. Lines of sculpture are traced above the doorway and a central figure carved in high relief. This figure represents a head, surrounded by rays, each ending in a circle. Each hand grasps a staff of equal length with his body, and they are carved to represent serpents, but with heads like those of a condor and a tiger. An ornamented girdle clasps the waist of the figure, which stands on a base, or series of smaller figures approaching in character the architectural ornament called *grecques*, or zigzags.

Winged human-headed or condor-headed figures are represented on either side in three square divisions, kneeling on one knee with their faces turned towards the great central figure, as if in adoration. Each one holds a staff or sceptre. The relief in their figures is scarcely more than two-tenths of an inch, and the minor features are indicated by very delicate lines slightly incised, which form figures representing heads of condors, tigers, or serpents. This is the principal object among the ruins. Another drawing represented a gateway formed of two cylindrical columns overhung by an arch. The presence of the arch at Tiahuanuco, must be as enigmatical as in Chimu.

Like all other ruins in Peru, those at Tiahuanuco are closely watched by self-appointed guardians, who belong to the Indian village in the neighbourhood. The precise motive for the watch thus kept over objects which apparently have no intrinsic value, at least in the eyes of poor ignorant Indians, is difficult to explain. The Indians are, however, said to entertain the firm conviction (worth noting by future explorers) that all ruins mark the site of *tapadas*, or hidden treasure, so perhaps this belief accounts for the vigilance exhibited in watching the proceedings of any stranger who may be bent on antiquarian research. Mr. Squier relates that no sooner had he begun to explore the ruins, than he became aware of the presence of a very old man, withered and wrinkled and bent with the weight of years, who seemed to be engaged in working a block of stone into the shape of a cross. The old man was on the ground every morning before Mr. Squier himself arrived, and was the last to take his departure.

Among the scanty population which lives on the borders near Lake Titicaca, hardly any language but Aymara is understood. All white men are at once saluted with the words "Tai-tai Viracocha," "Welcome, father of the sea;" for Viracocha, who was reported to have been born of the sea, had blue eyes, fair hair, and a light complexion.

On Lake Titicaca there are eight inhabitable islands, seven of which are known by the names of Amanteme, Tagueli, Soto, Titicaca Coati, Campanario, Toguaré, and Aputo. Titicaca Coati is the sacred island of Peru. Mythology says that it was from thence that Manco Capac and his wife and sister, Mama and Oello, children of the sun, started on their mission to instruct in religion and the arts the savage tribes of the neighbouring coast. On this island, the remains of a temple of the sun, a monastery for priests, a royal palace, and other of the usual vestiges of Inca civilization are still to be seen. The "sacred rock" of Manco Capac is at the northern extremity of the island. Nearly all the old chroniclers, including Calancha and Garcilasso, agree in assigning the date of the erection of these edifices on the island to some time between the years 1425 and 1470, which included the period of Tapac Yupanqui's reign.

On the adjoining peninsula of Sillustriani, Dr. Raimondi, a distinguished Peruvian antiquarian and scientist, has observed many *chulpas*, or burial towers, both round and square in shape. These *chulpas* consist of a solid mass of clay and stones, measuring some sixteen feet in height; they are rectangular in plan, and measure seven and a half feet face by six feet at the sides. Their surface is stuccoed over, and painted white and reddish. They have an opening in front, about eighteen inches square, to admit the corpse. The *chulpas* answer the same purpose as the *kourgans* in Central Asia. There are also a number of figures, formed in the shape of circles and semicircles of varying diameter, resembling very closely the semicircles of Druidical circles in England. One of these measures one hundred and twenty-four feet in diameter, and forms a ring of upright stones, bounded by a platform of flat stones. It has an opening five feet wide on the eastern side, and encloses two large upright stones, placed one-third of the diameter apart.

But notwithstanding all the interesting monuments which are to this day to be seen at Tiahuanuco, Cuzco, and scores of other places in different parts of Peru, the ancient history of the Peruvians remains as yet a disjointed chronicle, a tale where dates and names are continually found wanting. The history is in great part conjecture. Nothing can be less satisfactory than the readings of the *quipus* (or knotted ropes, by means of which events were recorded) performed by the ignorant, and it must be admitted that few facts of any value are to be deduced from the unburied portions of the ruins which are spread broadcast over the country.*

This chapter upon the least known Peruvian antiquities would be incomplete did it not contain some brief description of the pottery ware which is found in great quantities among the ancient *huacas*, which are so numerous throughout the country. As has been previously mentioned, the writer himselt explored no inconsiderable number of these ancient burial mounds in the north of Peru, and made a small collection of the relics which he came across. The apparent use of the pottery dug out was to carry water. These water-jars are made of clay generally identical in quality and either red or black in colour. The clay appears to have been very fine and soft to the touch, and when moistened, susceptible of being

---

* While correcting the proof-sheets of this volume, the author read an identical opinion expressed with respect to the ancient monuments of Mexico by M. A. Dupin de Saint-André in his recently published work entitled, *Le Mexique Augour d'hui.* At page 168 M. de Saint-André writes : " Tous ces monuments ont un grand intérêt archéologique. Ils confirment ce qu'ont dit les auteurs espagnols des idées, de la religion et des connaissances astronomiques des Aztèques ; mais ont ils livré tous leurs secrets ? Ce n'est pas probable. Sans donte les savants de l'avenir arracheront à ces sphinx de pierre des révélations nouvelles sur un passé plein d'obscurités et de mystères, et déchireront peut-être les derniers voiles qui cachent à vos contemporains les origines des peuple des Mexicaines."

moulded in any shape, so as to portray the most delicate lines of the human face. The black ware weighs heavier in proportion than the red, this difference being accounted for by the comparatively greater quantity of mineral substances (sometimes gold) which the former is said to contain. One marked property of the water-jars made out of this particular clay is that water put into them will keep cool, or at least at a low temperature for several hours, even if exposed to the heat of the burning tropical sun. The clay is somewhat porous. The usual form of these jars is melon-shaped ; others have the shape of a pine or an orange. They are often made with a double bowl, connected by a hollow cross-bar, which serves as a handle. The water pours through upright or curved spouts, which in the twin jars are also connected by a narrow square-shaped pipe. The forms and faces of human beings or of beasts are frequently moulded on the outside of these bowls, or a running arabesque pattern ; and the mouths of the spouts are often formed in the shape of a head, either human or that of a beast or bird. Sometimes the moulding is omitted, and the jars are quite smooth and plain. The black clay glazes better than the red, owing no doubt to its being richer in mineral substances. A very little cleaning and brushing makes the surface shine brightly, and reflect images like a looking-glass. In some jars, the mouth of one of the necks is so formed that by blowing into the other musical sounds are produced—some loud and shrill as a railway guard's whistle, others soft and melodious as if coming from a sweet-toned flute.

It is interesting to note the close resemblance which the figures traced on some of the bowls bear to the forms and lineaments of the Indians and half-castes of the present day. As the artist who moulded the jars probably worked from the life, it would seem that the race, though degraded, has survived all revolutions and changes of dynasty, as some of these clay portraits, which have been buried for hundreds of years, might well stand for those of Indians who are now the subject race in the country where probably their ancestors ruled.

The jars are of moderate size, the smaller ones standing six inches in height, and the larger twelve or eighteen. Often the clay is moulded into the form of a man, beast, or bird, with great accuracy of detail. The collection of Peruvian antiquities to be seen at the British Museum contains one especially rare specimen of this class of work in red clay. The figure, which is about nine inches in height, is that of a partly naked Indian, kneeling on his left knee, with the leg under him, and holding in his right hand a mace or mallet, and in his left a round shield. He wears on his head a close fitting cone-shaped turban, in shape something like a Turkish fez, having a wide hood, which envelopes his ears and falls low on his shoulders. The ears thus hidden, appear through the covering to be of extraordinary size, like those of an Egyptian sphinx. The head is small in proportion to the body, and square-shaped, the depth between crown and chin being somewhat shallow. On the other hand, the breadth between the ears is unusually wide, and the cheekbones are strongly marked and protrude very much. The forehead is flat and low, while the jaws are massive and powerful ; the mouth is wide, and the lips thin and sharply cut, while the nose, which in most other faces in this collection is short and flat, in this one is somewhat longer and of the Roman type. The eyes are long-shaped and oval, the lids partly open giving a sleepy, self-complacent expression to the face. A vest, ornamented with a border of mathematically drawn figures, fits close to the body and the upper portions of the arms and legs, while the feet are clothed with sandals. Mr. A. W. Franks, who presides over this department of the British Museum, considers this figure to be of great antiquity, but no one has yet ventured to decide on its origin or date. Another jar, which is thought to be older still than the one just described, is embellished with the figures of two warriors. Its design merits a brief description. The warriors stand in a defiant attitude, holding in the left hand a spear or dart, apparently just lifted to be hurled at an adversary. On the right arm, which is extended as if in self-protection, a broad shield is carried. From the number of straight feathered lines extending beyond the circumference, the shield is apparently meant to carry a large supply of darts. The face of these figures wears a fierce and warlike expression ; the mouth, chin, and nose are like those of an animal. The nose is long, and turns sharply upward at the point, with wide open nostrils ; while the broad mouth exhibits two rows of long, formidable teeth, between which the forked tongue extends far out of the mouth. He wears on his head a close-fitting helmet, surmounted with a sharply pointed crescent. Does this point to the worship of the moon ? That is a question for the antiquarian or comparative mythologist. The dark red lines of the figure are shown well in relief on the body of the bowl, which is much lighter in hue.

Some of the jars are made in very curious shapes. Thus, one represents a whale which has apparently been washed ashore ; the figure of a naked man is seen crawling down his back, as if bent upon catching a snake, which is wriggling away from his reach. Another represents the head of a llama, or Peruvian sheep ; another, which was dug up at Trujillo, that of a woman, with a child under each arm ; while the forms of parrots, ducks, melons, fruits of several sorts, in fact, the forms of all the animal and vegetable world known to these original clay-moulders are called into requisition as models. " It is curious," remarked Mr. Franks to the writer on one occasion, " how closely these Peruvian jars resemble the Etruscan. See this black one, with a human head shown on either side of the bowl ; my *confrère* in the Greek Department sent it to me, thinking it belonged to the Peruvian collection, and I have not myself yet made up my mind as to whether it does so or not, or if I should return it whence it came."

Among Mr. Franks' treasures is a wooden drinking-cup, to which he points with pride. It stands about six inches high, round in shape, the diameter of the brim being much greater than that of the bottom, which makes it almost fan-like in shape. It is carved from a block of black wood, hard in texture and close in grain, which may be either ebony or lignum vitæ. The outside of the cup is ornamented with mastic drawings in red· and blue, representing men in the dress worn by the Spanish invaders, which at all events fixes its date as subsequent to the conquest of Peru. It was found in an Aymara grave near Puno. Besides paddles and javelins about twelve inches long, and pointed with sharp pieces of chalcedony, silver figures, and others made out of pyrites, bronze axes and ploughs, small boxes of red paint, packages of maize, pieces of cloth and yarn, pincers, and hundreds of other curiosities dug out of Peruvian graves, the cases in the British Museum contain a remarkable specimen of stone carving, which, in an age when iron tools were unknown, must have taken an immense time to finish. This is a flat tray, measuring ten inches either way, and having squarely shaped wings projecting at the four corners. It is made of white porphyry, streaked with pink. The hollow of the tray is about one inch and a half deep, and the sides, half an inch thick, have all their edges rounded, as if the tools employed were not capable of cutting sharp edges in this material.

The most valuable portion of the Peruvian antiquities comes from Mr. Henry Christy's private collection, bequeathed by him to the nation. This bequest is supplemented by numerous valuable donations of Mr. Franks, the original collection at the Museum having been but meagre and scanty. But the finest collection known to exist belongs to Dr. Marcedo, a native of Peru. He is said to have brought it to Europe some years ago with the object of selling, and to have offered it to the trustees of the British Museum. The terms asked are not publicly known, but it seems regrettable that so valuable and unique a collection, probably containing in the hieroglyphics engraved on its vases and jars the, as yet, undeciphered history of so interesting an ancient race as the Peruvian, should not be accessible to the inspection of the savants of all nations, who congregate in the galleries of our great national institution.

CHAPTER XII.

JOHN CHINAMAN ABROAD.

The Yellow Stream—" World Servants "—Time Contracts—The Health Committee of Sydney—Mr. Cecil Guinness's Experiences of Chinese in New South Wales—Good Miners—Abstemiousness — Queensland — Dr. Huc's Opinion — A Heavy " Poll-tax "—Commission of the Chinese Government to Cuba—Evidence taken—Kidnapping—Hard Taskmasters — Information withheld—Agreements broken by Employers—A Long Day's Work—The Coolie in Peru—Consul March's Report—" Insubordination "—Conventions between China and Foreign Powers—The Peruvian Convention—Lord Granville's Commissioners in Demerara—The British Pekin Convention—Insufficient Protection for Coolies on Landing—The Price of a " John Chinaman."

SLAVERY is a thing of the past,* and such traces of it as survive are felt to be anomalous and doomed to early extinction. But there is another kind of servitude, partly voluntary and partly enforced, or, as

* Some people, thinking of Turkey, may say otherwise. But the traffic in Circassian women, still carried on in Turkey, is no slave-trade, correctly speaking. The women are not subjected to manual labour, and the traffic is conducted in secret, slavery being prohibited according to Mahomedan law.

some have termed it, "natural and artificial," which has no essential connection with the old form of slavery, but which yet resembles it closely in many respects. The fact of a race of men voluntarily crossing the seas to work out a time-service in a strange country, without any idea of permanently settling, belongs to the present, and constitutes an important factor in the sum of civilization and material development of the globe. By the emigration of Chinese subjects to the West a new phase is opened in the social relationship of one race to another, of the peoples of the civilized and progressive West with those of the primitive East. There can be little doubt that this phase must exercise a stupendous influence on civilization, and the fact that at the present moment there are seventy millions of human beings actually starving in the provinces of North China * is sufficient to account for the impetus which emigration has lately received. In tracing the movement on the map, Chinese emigration appears like a huge stream, which, setting out from China, flows steadily westwards, throwing out here and there tentative branches into countries inhabited by the Frank, the Anglo-Saxon, and their offshoots, introducing on its way new traditions of life, or rather very old theories of an old race which are new to a young one, and setting thoughtful men to speculate as to where its course is likely to end. Will it touch

* As stated by Sir Thomas Wade at Lambeth Palace.

England? In these days, when frequent strikes and wordy meetings among the labouring classes show the unhealthy state of the labour market, who can answer that question? We know there is a party of no inconsiderable weight who have already advocated the employment of Chinese in the coal industry. England is full of industries of various descriptions, and no one knows what the cotton-spinners, lace-weavers, ironmongers, and the thousand and one trades may do when they see a cheap and plentiful supply of intelligent labour placed within their reach. In the meanwhile some knowledge of the character and customs of these " world-servants," taken from the most reliable sources of information, may perhaps be of general interest. The writer having had personal experience among Chinese coolies, has undertaken to contribute his mite of information.

It was for a long time thought that the human family did not contain a more striking contrast in respect both of physique and character than that existing between the white and black races. The appearance of the Chinaman as a competitor with both offered for solution a still more difficult problem, *i.e.* Is the Chinaman inferior or superior to his fellow-men? The varying opinions on this question are evident in the anti-Chinese agitation now raging in California, and in the controversial debates in the Parliaments of our Australian colonies, notably in that of Queensland. In order to arrive at some conclusion we must carefully examine his behaviour, both as a coolie—or labourer by contract—and as a free man. We will begin by describing his condition in Australia. The numbers of Chinese in the different Australian colonies are as follows :—

New South Wales:. In 1861 they numbered 12,988, or 3·71 per cent. of the population ; but at the last census (1871) their number had decreased to 7220, or 1·43 per cent., a diminution of 5768, or 44·41 per cent. In Queensland, at the taking of the census in 1876, there were 10,399 in a population of 188,000, or 5·53 per cent. In Victoria, out of a population of 840,300 (up to December 31, 1876), there were 20,132 Chinese, or 2·39 per cent. In South Australia the number is inconsiderable, probably not exceeding one or two hundred at the present moment. In the colony of New South Wales, in 1875, the Health Board of Sydney appointed a sub-committee to inspect and report on the condition of the Chinese in that town. A single extract from that report (a copy of which has been kindly given to the author by Dr. Read of Sydney) must here suffice to paint the city domestic life of John Chinaman in that part of the world. Dr. Dansey gave evidence on behalf of himself and Mr. Palmer as follows :—

" Met at the Town Hall on Tuesday, December 7, 1875, and went first to Park Street, where we inspected several boarding-houses, all clean and in orderly condition. In the same street is a wooden house, containing eight rooms, occupied by Wah Lu Ong, a Chinaman carpenter, employing a number of men. Seventeen persons sleep in the house, all countrymen of the proprietor. In one room, 14 by 12 feet, were eight beds, the room being partitioned off into bunks, like the steerage of a ship; bedding of a very varied kind. In some bunks were mattresses, in others only rags and clothing; mosquito curtains black with dirt. In another room, over the shop, were five beds of a similar description. We looked into the kitchen downstairs, which was dirty and smoky. The whole place stinks aloud, the horrible and sickening opium smell pervading all through it. Among the workmen were several apprentices. The workmen on wages, we ascertained, earn from 10*s.* to 15*s.* a week and their food. This day's inspection was not performed without serious fatigue and risk to health to Dr. Read and myself. For the next forty-eight hours, the horrible sickly smell of opium-smoking, which pervades all the Chinese quarters, seemed to adhere to us, to say nothing of the fear of infection."

In England, where food and lodging costs considerably more than in New South Wales, there are thousands of unskilled labourers who earn much less than 15*s.* or 20*s.* per week, on which they manage to support themselves and often a large family. But the Chinaman's preference for living in the foul atmosphere of crowded rooms, and on the most meagre fare, is not without explanation. One Chinaman will go to New South Wales actuated by the same motive which takes another to America — the temptation of higher wages. Indeed, England and China have one point of resemblance—both are over-populated. In China, the native finds employment with difficulty, and has to work for wages which afford but the smallest means for supporting life, such as a feed of rice twice a day. With the introduction of steam into navigation, a new vista is opened to his view, new worlds are described, where gold is to be had for the working. Extravagant stories are circulated by the shipping speculators in and about Canton, whence they spread far into the interior—tales of fabulous wages paid for manual labour in California and Peru, in Australia, Cuba, and elsewhere, which encourage the native to seek a way out of his poverty by emigration. The result is obvious. Bands of Chinese eager to acquire wealth are collected by these diligent agents, and shipped off to whatever land it may suit the shipowners to take them. Some provide their passage-money by the sale of all their possessions, and land as free men in search of work ; others, who have nothing to sell, sign a contract to work for eight years on the Peruvian guano and sugar fields, in consideration of which they are allowed a free passage there and back. Thus the emigrant intends only a temporary absence from his native country. His motive is to earn gold, and when that desire is partially satisfied, he turns his thoughts homewards.

He is not an emigrant in the sense in which the early settlers in America were. The Chinaman takes nothing to help him in pushing his fortune; he is strongly attached to his fatherland, and in particular wishes his body to be buried in his native soil. Thus he has but one desire, which becomes a pervading principle of action, that of saving as much money as he can during his absence to take home with him. With this view he spends only just enough to support life under conditions repugnant to every notion of humanity.

The evidence of the Health Committee of Sydney, if not applicable to all classes of Chinese, faithfully describes the privations which a great proportion of them voluntarily endure for the sake of economizing. But it is noticeable that all reports on Chinese dwelling-houses give the same picture of squalor. It is only when brought into some kind of domestic relationship with the white man that John Chinaman learns ideas of order and cleanliness. The writer's object in this paper is to give his own experiences and those of others who have employed Chinese in various parts of the world. Mr. Cecil Guinness has employed Chinese labour for fifteen years in Australia, and it is instructive to contrast his experience (under different circumstances) with that of the Sydney Board of Health. He writes to the author:—

" As to my experience of Chinese as servants in the colonies I have lived in. I have had large sheep-stations in Victoria, New South Wales, and Queensland, in the different places at different times between the years 1862 and 1876. I have employed Chinamen as house-servants, gardeners, shepherds, fencers, and shearers, etc., in fact, in almost every form of employment connected with sheep farming. I have found them most useful and industrious, sober and honest. They all smoke opium, more or less, but you seldom see them affected deleteriously by that indulgence, nor have I ever traced any neglect of their duties to that cause. They are inveterate gamblers, but neither have I ever seen that propensity interfere with their duties. It is chiefly indulged in when they take their holiday, and congregate in the nearest township. They are sticklers for wages, and expect and demand as much as Europeans. As house-servants they are useful and often clean, and a great accession in the up-country homesteads, often capital cooks and bakers, and very careful and economical. As gardeners they are remarkable. Accustomed to keep their own little gardens in their own country under great difficulties, they are invaluable in the arid interior of Australia. At Bourke, on the Darling River, in New South Wales, where I lived for ten years, and where, till the advent of Chinamen, it was thought by the earliest European settlers we should never be able to raise vegetables, we soon were surprised and delighted to find, thanks to the perseverance, energy, and industry of the Chinamen gardeners, that we had all the year round a succession of the finest vegetables I have ever seen in any part of the world. In all other departments of station-labour I may add that they are nearly as useful ; and, in a word, my experience of Chinese labour is most favourable. They are more suited by habit, characteristics, and physique to plodding, fossicking, persevering industry than for heavy work. They are grand stayers and very efficacious light weights. I have not much direct personal experience of Chinese labour on gold fields, but I believe their industry and perseverance have worked wonders in that line, and I believe that some of the greatest gold mines in Victoria and New South Wales, when supposed to be worked out and abandoned by Europeans, have been persevered in by Chinamen till they have taken a fresh start, and, when returned to, have become of vast importance. This is my settled conviction, after many years of personal practical station management, where I had every opportunity of thoroughly knowing my men."

Mr. Guinness's experiences show the original and best side of the Chinaman's character, the great power of endurance, by which he is able to live in the most sterile places. His wants are few, and he shows ready ingenuity in supplying them, in whatever land he may find himself. He looks half-starved, but yet he lives on, and will attain a good old age, as did his father before him. . Some one has compared the Chinaman to the celebrated horse whose owner tried to train him to live on a single straw a day. Nature has been practising the experiment on the " Heathen Chinee " for ages, and he comes nearer this ideal of perfection by several straws than the Anglo-Saxon can hope to do. It cannot be denied that so lithe and easily supported an individual is capable of rendering great service in our colonies, where labour of all kinds is in such great demand. The writer is, moreover, persuaded that his introduction would not find a dissentient voice in the Assemblies of the Colonial governments, should he seek domestic employment. He is by nature well suited for discharging such household duties as washing, cooking, house-cleaning, and is admirable as a nurse. But we know that the Chinaman's views aim higher. The flow of emigration from China to America and Australia is of a steady and irresistible force, and owes its impetus as much to the internal condition of the Chinese Empire as to the facilities afforded by steam navigation.

It is not proposed here to discuss the difference between a military invasion and one purely social, even though the arms of the latter are endurance, abstinence, and ingenuity.* But the habit of looking

* In the July number of the *Fortnightly Review*, in an article entitled " Lancashire," written by the editor, the writer observes this train of thought touched upon in the following lines : " This question (the movement of Chinese to the West) is not a mere question in the air. Nobody with a capacity for taking interest in social possibilities can think without uneasiness of the slow stir which has already begun to make itself felt, like the first still

on the influx of Chinese into Australia with as much apprehension as if it were a martial invasion is widespread, as we may judge from the statements of Mr. Arthur Macalister, agent-general for Queensland. In 1876, the number of Chinese in this colony did not exceed 10,500. Since the opening of the Palmer River Diggings, within eighteen months the influx of Mongolians was considerable, and on his authority they numbered no less than 30,000 in 1878. For some curious particulars concerning the habits and pursuits of these immigrants, the reader is referred to a very interesting paper read by Mr. Macalister before the Royal Colonial Institute in December, 1877, on "Queensland." He objects to the Chinese in unmistakable language, and his descriptions of their mode of life bear a close analogy to those of the Board of Health at Sydney.

"Nowhere," he says, "has the Chinaman settled in any considerable numbers that he has not created a blot on our institutions. Even in cities, among the amenities of city life, the Chinese quarter is viewed with loathing. Nowhere has he blended with the

creeping of matter awakening to the conditions of organization, in the vast empire of China. Of China as a probable source of extreme military danger to English rule in India, this is not the place to speak ; but the economic contest of the *cheap* races over the *dear* is sure to come. The merchants and employers will have themselves to thank. It was the shameless wars waged for the extension of their markets which roused the slumbering leviathan ; it was they who tapped the volcano."

Anglo-Saxon ; the interval between them is so great that it cannot be passed. The progressive ideas of civilization do not harmonize with those dwarfed by age. They are not colonists in our acceptance of the term ; they come alone, and do not bring their babies or families with them. Dr. Huc asserts of them 'that they are sceptical and indifferent to everything that concerns the moral side of man.' And this estimate of them has double force when applied in the exceptional conditions under which they live in Queensland. They regard a good coffin as of more importance than a correct life ; and certainly what we hear of their habits, though unfit for discussion, is sufficient to deter a Government from forcing them on a people unwilling to receive them. They do not speak or understand our language, have no desire for progress, and have no conception of representative or free institutions. They come to Queensland for none of the ordinary mechanical pursuits of life ; their secret is simple enough—to take possession of the gold-fields ; to extract from the earth its auriferous deposits, and to this extent to impoverish the country ; and having done this, to return to China and there spend their days. They invest no capital in our undertakings, and undertake no industries of a permanent character. After they have gone there is no trace of their existence, not even a tombstone. Their very ashes they make an effort to have transplanted to the 'Flowery Land!'"

This may be taken as a fair sample of the colonist's view of Chinese immigration in Queensland, where they perhaps find him a formidable competitor in the most lucrative undertaking there—gold-digging. In Australia, as we have seen, he is welcomed as a servant, and it would seem that in pastoral districts he shows less of his offensive habits than in crowded city life. Some clauses in the Chinese Immigration Act, recently passed in Queensland, provide that vessels bringing Chinese to any of the ports shall only carry them in the proportion of one to every five tons of the vessel's tonnage capacity; thus the number of passengers for a vessel of one thousand tons would be limited to two hundred. The Act also provides that before any Chinese shall be permitted to land, the master of the vessel shall pay to the Collector of Customs the sum of £10 for each, which money will be returned to the passenger at any time within three years, provided his character has been good, and that he has entailed no expense on the public revenue.

Although it would exceed the limits of this chapter to follow John Chinaman to his different places of exile, and to describe the varying treatment he receives at the hand of races widely differing in blood and religion, his experiences in America command special attention, from the influence his presence seems likely to exercise upon the peoples of that continent.

In 1874 the Imperial Chinese government became alarmed at the reports of the bad treatment their countrymen received in Cuba, and resolved to send a commission to that island, to ascertain the condition of the coolies there. The report of this commission, printed for the use of the government at the Imperial Customs Press at Shanghai, in 1876, contains the depositions of some thousands of Chinese as to their position in Cuba. To guide the commission in their work, they were furnished with a set of fifty queries, categorically arranged, on which they were instructed to collect evidence. The depositions and petitions show that eight-tenths of the entire number of Chinese in Cuba declared that they had been kidnapped or decoyed ; that the mortality during the voyage, from wounds caused by blows, suicide, and sickness, exceeded ten per cent. ; that on arrival at Havana they were sold into slavery, a small proportion being disposed of to families and shops, while the large majority became the property of sugar-planters ; that the cruelty displayed even towards those of the former class is great, and that in the latter it assumes proportions which are unendurable. The labour, too, on the plantations is shown to be excessively severe, and the food insufficient. The hours of labour are too long, and the chastisement by rods, whips, chains, stocks, etc., productive of suffering and injury. During past years (prior to 1874) a large number have been killed by blows, or died from the effects of wounds, and have hanged themselves, cut their throats, poisoned themselves with opium, and thrown themselves into wells and sugar caldrons. Personal inspection verified the accounts of wounds inflicted by others, fractured and maimed limbs, blindness, heads covered with sores, teeth knocked out, ears mutilated, and the skin and flesh lacerated, proofs of cruelty patent to all eyes. Thus, in reply to query No. 1, "From what places does Cuba draw coolies?" the petition of Li Chaoch'in and 165 others states:

"We were at various times brought by force to or decoyed into the barracoons of Macao, by certain vicious men of our own nation, suborned by Portuguese."

The petition of Hsien Tso-pang and sixteen others states that:

"The foreigners of Macao sent out vicious Chinese in order to kidnap and decoy men, and to place them in barracoons, and on board of ships, from which they cannot escape, chastising them without restraint, and conveying them against their will to Havana; after removing their queues and changing their clothing, to offer them for sale in the men market."

The petition of Tiao Mu and three others states:

"Vicious men have at various times decoyed here tens and hundreds of thousands of peasants:"

That of P'an T'ai and eighty-nine others states:

"Misled by fair words, or decoyed, we were brought here to be sold as slaves."

Again, it is gathered from the 1176 depositions which have been recorded, that of those who sailed from Macao, Wen Changt'ai and sixty-five others were kidnapped; that Iseng Erhch'i and 689 others were decoyed; that Lai A-gui and fifty others were entrapped into signing contracts in the belief that they were merely doing so in the place of others temporarily absent; that Huang A-mu and ninety-three others were the victims of various snares tendered to them after they had gambled and lost; and that Ch'en and sixty-five others emigrated voluntarily. Of those who sailed from Amoy, Su A-hai and eleven others were kidnapped, Tang-chien and twenty-two others were decoyed, Lindtieng and ten others were the victims of various snares tendered to them after they had gambled and lost, and Huang Shuit'on with five others emigrated voluntarily.

In answer to query No. 7, " During the agreement term, what is his (the coolie's) position ? " Li Chaoch'em and 165 others depose that :

" Ninety per cent. are disposed of to the sugar plantations. There the owners rely on the administrator for the production of a large crop of sugar, and the administrator looks to the overseers to exact the greatest possible amount of labour. They all think only of the profit to be gained, and are indifferent as to our lives. It matters not whether the workmen are miserable or contented, whether they starve or have enough to eat, whether they live or die. The administrator who gives only four unripe bananas as a meal is considered an able servant, and if he gives only three he is regarded as still more efficient. The administrator who forces the Chinese to work twenty hours out of the twenty-four is a man of capacity; if he extorts twenty-one hours, his qualities are of a still higher order; but he may strike, or flog, or chain us as his fancy suggests to him. If we complain of sickness, we are beaten or starved; if we work slowly, dogs are urged after us to bite us. Those of us who are employed on farms or coffee estates, in sugar warehouses and brick kilns, on railways and in bakers', cigar stores, hat and other shops, are in each of these places of service ill-treated, flogged, confined in stocks and in gaol, and tortured in every way as on the plantations."

The writer is taking evidence at haphazard from the report—it is all in the same strain, speaking first of the guile practised in decoying the Chinaman from his home, and then of the cruel treatment dealt out to him in exile. It seems incredible that in this nineteenth century such outrages against humanity should be committed day after day in a civilized land within the dominion of a Christian state. Except unauthenticated rumours, the world at large has heard nothing of what is going on in Cuba. The Chinese Commissioners' Report, it should be remembered, was printed solely for the use of the Chinese government, and it has not been put into public circulation to this day (1884). Possibly the Spanish government has shared this ignorance, seeing that the laws which it has enacted for regulating the immigration are drawn up with the manifest intention of protecting the coolie from the exactions of unscrupulous masters. Unfortunately the troubled state of the island renders the enforcement of these laws a mere farce, and through the corruption of the officials the laws themselves are used as devices for extracting from the coolie his hardly earned savings. Thus, in answer to query No. 9, "If the employers violate the stipulation, what redress has the coolie by law?" Wu A-fa and thirty-nine others state:

"Foreigners in no way consider themselves bound by the provisions of the contracts. After the eight years (the customary duration of the contract, five being the legal limit) are completed, they refuse us the cedulas, and we are forced to remain slaves in perpetuity."

Lo A'voh deposes:

"On the expiration of my contract, I was sent to a depôt where I passed four months. I was then removed by my master, who forced me to labour in chains during three months. He daily beats me, and yesterday beat me with great severity. Five months have now elapsed, during which no wages have been issued to me. On account of this and the other ill-usage, I requested a fellow-workman to, on my behalf, lay a complaint before the officials. He has done so on three occasions, and in each instance it has been rejected, and I have thus to go on labouring, whilst, if I ask for wages, the threat of chaining is made. I, in all earnestness, now meditate suicide."

Ho Assu deposes :

"At the end of the eight years no cedula was supplied to me, and I was forced to work for another term of four years. A few days ago I asked my master for a cedula, and was told by him that I had to serve for other six years. If this be the case, suicide is the best course open to me."

As an example of the work the coolie performs, the petition of Wang A-ching and twenty-two others may be quoted. It states :

"The work is very hard. We get up at three a.m. and labour until noon; at one p.m. we resume work until seven. Then we rest half an hour, and are allowed a ration of maize, after which work is continued up till midnight." Wang A-ching continues :

"We are struck and flogged, and out of our party of more than two hundred men, only about eighty remain."

In addition to enduring all these miseries, the coolie is fleeced of his hard-earned wages by the abominable "truck" system, which prevails throughout these Cuban plantations. Liang A-chao deposes :

"On the plantation is a shop owned by the master,

at which all our purchases have to be effected ; the prices are very high."

T'ang Ming-kwei says :

" Monthly as wages we receive four tickets, which can only be employed in payment of purchases at the plantation shop. Elsewhere they cannot be used, nor is it possible to change them for bank-notes (money)."

These brief extracts may suffice to show the depths of degradation and misery to which poor humanity can be subjected through the avarice and cruelty of a wealthy band of agriculturists.

More to the credit of humanity is the treatment of the coolie in the sugar plantations in Peru, where, though economy is practised, it is not carried to such an excess. There the labourer is allowed two pounds weight of peeled rice per diem and one pound of goat's flesh, which last he sometimes barters for opium. His work hours are from six a.m. to five p.m., with an interval from eleven o'clock till one, when he cooks and eats his food. There is a hospital for the sick, and a doctor to attend them. In consequence his working powers are greater, and his intelligence more alert for his master's interests ; in fact, he has been known to volunteer the extra work of cutting down timber on a clearing instead of burning it, pointing out that the value of the wood thus obtained more than compensates for the time lost in felling it. His neatness in gardening is proverbial, and much may safely be left to his own discretion in working. So though on some haciendas he is roughly treated, as a rule he leads a peaceable, hard-working life, and cases of insubordination are rare in Peru.

Of the 68,825 Chinese who were in Cuba at the time of the commissioners' visit, only three were married to Chinese women, one to a white, and "half a dozen or so" to mulattoes and negresses. The same paucity of marriages is found in Victoria. The number of Chinese males who married in that colony during the eleven years ending in 1876 was 197. Of these 107 married Australians, 43 Englishwomen, 21 Irish, 14 Scotch, and only three united themselves with females of their own race. The number of such marriages in 1876 was 14, less than any year since 1868. For detailed statistics, the reader may consult the *Victorian Year Book* for 1876–77.

Decidedly John Chinaman fares worse in Cuba than in any other country he frequents. The author did not see a single example of such harrowing misery on all the sugar estates, railway, harbour, sanitary, and other works which he visited in Peru, where Chinese are extensively employed for all these purposes. In some places, no doubt, the coolie was indifferently fed and overworked, but these were the exception. He does not wish these observations to be taken as contradicting in any sense the statements made in Consul March's noticeable report to the Foreign Office, dated Callao, February, 1876. In that report Mr. March writes, page 1521 of the *Blue Book* (Nov. 16, 1876) :

"Many of these Chinamen are engaged in the guano deposits, and from personal knowledge I can state that their lot in these dreary spots is a most unhappy one. Besides being worked almost to death, they have neither sufficient food nor passably wholesome water. Their rations consist of two pounds of rice and about half a pound of meat. This is generally served out to them between ten and eleven in the morning, by which time they have got through six hours' work. Each man is compelled to clear from four to five tons of guano a day. During the last quarter of 1875, it is reported that there were 355 Chinamen employed at Pabellon de Pica alone, of whom no less than 98 were in the hospital. The general sickness is swelled legs, caused, it is supposed, by drinking condensed water not sufficiently cooled, and by a lack of vegetable diet. The features of this disease are not unlike those of scurvy or purpura."

Unfortunately, climatic conditions must always render the working of guano beds, at these desert spots of the Peruvian coast, a task of excessive privation and hardship to the workmen employed, of whatever nationality they may be. The absence of one of the chief necessities of life, fresh water, and the pernicious influence of a tropical sun, are obstacles prejudicial to the comfort of the labourers, which the most well-meaning of task-masters often fail to counteract in

Peru as well as elsewhere. The mode of contract is the same as in Cuba, but fortunately the masters are kinder and more considerate, and cases of "insubordination" are rare. The writer remembers but one, and that was at the Hacienda de Pucala, in the province of Lambayeque, when the owner was killed by his Chinese, who rose in revolt against his persecutions. As a rule they are well treated and contented. It is the custom there to put in practice the theory known as the "balance of power;" thus, for every hundred Chinese employed on the estate, they have an equal number of *peones*, and at least fifty negroes or mulattoes. The blacks, who are quarrelsome and hate the "yellows," are physically twice as strong; thus, in a fight, the combatants are balanced, the pacific *peones* being held as a sort of reserve guard to keep the peace and protect the owners' interests.

Once, in travelling through the Andes from Lima (which journey is described in the following chapter), we passed a camp of coolies employed on the railway works a little beyond Matucanas; a little further on were some Chilians engaged in a similar manner, who deeply resented the employment of the Asiatics. A day or so afterwards we heard that a fight had broken out between the rival camps, in which several were killed on both sides. This state of feeling has been going on for years in California, and still continues.

It is noticeable that the only convention which has been ratified between China and a foreign Power relative to the importation of indentured Chinese subjects is one with Peru, dated Tientsin, January, 1875.* The Spanish " Tientsin " Treaty of 1867 contains a clause permitting Chinese subjects to emigrate to Spanish colonies, but does not contain the privileges specified in the Peruvian Convention.

In this treaty Chinese emigrants are placed on an equality as regards legal procedure with the native citizens, and have access to the courts of justice. Their employers must provide them with a return passage on the expiry of their contract ; and in default of such stipulation, the government undertakes to pay their passage money. Further, for their better protection, the Peruvian government is to appoint official interpreters of the Chinese language in the prefectures of those departments of Peru which are the great centres of immigration. So far the convention contains only what is good ; the objection lies in its omissions.

Both the Spanish and British Colonial governments, who receive coolies from India and China, have fixed regulations for the traffic. How far these regulations have been observed is shown by the Report of the Commission sent to Demerara by Lord Granville, in 1870, which has already been critically

---

* " Treaties between the Empire of China and Foreign Powers." Edited by W. F. Mayers (Shanghai, 1877). The British " Pekin Conventions " of 1866 and 1869 relative to coolies have not been ratified by the British government.

analyzed, principally in an able review of the commissioners' labours, entitled "The Coolie, his Rights and Wrongs," written by Mr. Edward Jenkins, M.P.

The Cuban report, to which reference is made in this chapter, shows how far regulations similar to those in British Guiana are observed, or rather neglected, in Spanish colonies. It is to be feared that the coolie benefits very little by laws and regulations contrived for his benefit, in however just and humane a spirit they may be constructed. Carried off to distant plantations, often beyond the reach of the law, he is totally at his master's mercy, and on his humanity, or lack of it, the labourer's fate depends. Too great power often leads to its abuse, and in too many instances the planters and their agents look upon the coolies as beasts of burden from which so much daily toil has to be extracted : on the other hand, we have examples (and many could be cited) where the coolie is kindly and humanely treated, and where conscience forms a better safeguard for the dependants than laws can do. But for the inhuman monsters of the class which certainly exists in Cuba, stringent rules are necessary, and a closer system of inspection, which should hold the *owner* responsible for the good treatment of his servants, and punish with fine or imprisonment any flagrant act of cruelty or neglect to provide the necessaries of life. The subject is one of immense importance, and it is to be hoped that any future convention between China and foreign Powers will contain stringent clauses to this effect, as a simple question of common justice towards her teeming population. New fields are daily opening for the employment of Asiatic labour, and in this age of steam and rapid locomotion fresh difficulties must arise from the social changes operating under our very eyes. But in this chapter the writer has restricted himself to giving in a concise form the most reliable information concerning the habits and condition of the coolie in different parts of the globe. The picture is not a bright one!

One word in conclusion upon the convention negotiated by Sir Rutherford Alcock at Pekin in 1866, which has, however, not yet been ratified by the British government. It contains a set of regulations " to secure for the Chinese emigrants those safeguards which are required for their moral and physical well-being." The term of service, usually extended to eight years, is by this convention fixed at five, after which the emigrant, should he decline to contract for five more years, can claim his passagemoney back to China. Other clauses protect the coolie against deception as to the nature of the contract offered to him, and render it obligatory that the contracts shall specify the wages, rations, and clothing offered, and secure him medical attendance, etc. The hours for work are also restricted. There can be no doubt that the ratification of this convention by the British government would greatly improve the tone of the coolie traffic now carried on between China and certain British colonies. But it is open to emendation. While it shows an intimate acquaintance with the devices and duplicity employed in China to induce natives to leave their homes, and provides for the counteraction of such practices, it takes little account of the coolie after he has left, excepting in Art. XXII., which enacts that in the distribution of labourers the husband shall not be separated from the wife, nor parents from those of their children who are under fifteen years of age; also that no labourer shall be made to change his employer without his own consent, unless in the case of the plantation changing hands. With these exceptions the coolie is left at the mercy of the laws in whatever colony or country he chooses or is sent to —frequently under false pretences. What kind of treatment is sometimes dealt out to him under these local governments, subject as they must be to the all-powerful influence of the "planters," we have seen from the report of the Demerara Commission, and from others to which reference has been made. The Peruvian envoy who negotiated the Tientsin Convention of 1875 between his own country and China had some practical experience of the clemency coolies receive at the hands of their drivers. Article VII. of that convention declares, "The Peruvian government will appoint official interpreters of the Chinese language in the prefectures of all departments of Peru where the great centres of Chinese immigration exist ;" and the subsequent clauses recognize the urgency of an agreement by the high contracting Power receiving the immigrants to protect them from " vicious " masters.

The day may yet be distant when John Chinaman shall be working in our own coal mines and factories, or domesticated in English homes. That many of our countrymen would welcome his introduction there is very sufficient evidence already. It has been calculated that, allowing £100 or £150 as the cost of bringing him to England as a labourer by contract, his five years' labour would amply repay his employer for the outlay ; also that he would supply a growing want in the labour market. However this may be, many of our countrymen in the colonies rely entirely on the Chinaman's assistance for the conduct of their business as well as for domestic comfort. With such good grounds of recommendation, he has strong claims on our notice. Let us hope that his persistence in pushing Westward Ho may excite more welcome than apprehension.*

---

* The writer was much struck at the last Paris Exhibition upon seeing the high prices commanded by the Chinese and Japanese exhibitors for their porcelain and cabinet wares. The originality of design and excellence of workmanship evinced in these exhibits elicited, it may be said, universal praise ; and in these branches of art, the time would seem to be yet a long way off before the " Celestials " are likely to be beaten by their European competitors.

But let our artisans beware, lest, presuming on their power to extort higher and higher wages by placing their employers on the horns of a dilemma, they go just a little too far, and induce a combination among their employers which may result in their work being quietly taken out of their hands by the supple fingers and more easily contented mind of John Chinaman.

CHAPTER XIII.

A RAILROAD ACROSS THE ANDES.

Up the Andes—The River Rimac—Surco—Hill Stations—The Quebrada—Matucanas—Governor's Hospitality—Picturesque Country— Steep Ascent—Zigzagging—Sure-footed Mules—San Mateo—A Stone Staircase—"La Infernilla"— Chilka—Llamas.

In these days of travelling by steam, when every one goes everywhere, and when mountain peaks for ages looked upon as inaccessible, are climbed one after the other by some indefatigable member of the Alpine Club; perhaps some account of a ride across a most difficult and comparatively little known country may be read with interest.

In 1873, the author had an opportunity, through the courtesy of Mr. John Meiggs (brother to the late Mr. Henry Meiggs, railway contractor), of tracing the course of the beautiful river Rimac, in Peru, to its source, and also of ascending to the summit of perhaps the most beautiful chain of mountains in the world.

The Rimac divides the city of Lima into two unequal portions, which have for centuries been connected by a fine stone bridge 530 feet long, having six arches, and resembling in style the "Old Bridge" at Chester. The larger and more important "quartier" lies on the south (or left) bank, reaching as far as the Oroya railroad; the smaller suburb of San Lazaro, north of the river, nestles at the foot of the granitic hills, which, overhanging the city on three sides, may partly account for its close damp climate. In the dry season, the river dwindles to numerous shallow channels, and the huge banks of boulders and sand which are then visible show the varieties of material brought down by it in flood time. Above the old bridge, both banks are fringed with willow trees and shrubbery, which cause no little damage by obstructing the flow, when the stream is swollen by melted snow from the Andes.

In company with an engineer officer belonging to the Peruvian Government, the writer left Lima on Monday, July 21, 1873, at eight a.m., arriving at Surco, the then terminus of the railway, at two p.m. This station is 56 miles from Callao, and 6655 feet above sea level. We had passed the stations of Quiroz, Santa Clara, La Chosica, Boca Chacra, and San Bartolomé, the "reversing station," the formation of the Quebrada * not admitting of the direct prolongation of the line. So far, the road generally follows the left bank of the Rimac, and is "walled in" on both sides by high

* Literally "rent" (in the mountain), the Spanish term for a gorge.

thickets of cane, willow, or reeds, excluding the breeze and adding to the oppressive heat. The level plain behind Lima was however soon traversed, and we entered the Quebrada of Matucanas, where the hillsides are grey and barren, and the low ground covered with sand, or *débris* from the heights. In some places the lower slopes of the hills are seen to be terraced with stone walls, built by the provident Incas, who thus, wherever practicable, increased the area of cultivable ground.

At San Pedro Mama, the two rivers, San Mateo and Santa Olaya, join the Rimac, already swollen to a considerable size by a multitude of rivulets trickling down the sides of the Quebrada. At La Chosica, a grand hotel (brought piecemeal from the United States) was erected in the hope of attracting visitors from Lima to enjoy the delightful climate and lovely scenery at this height, 2800 feet. Leaving the railway at Surco, we transferred ourselves and our baggage to mules, provided ourselves with a guide, and continued our journey, passing along a narrow track on the left slope of the Quebrada ; at one time contouring the hillside at a height of several hundred feet and again descending to the valley, clambering over large boulders and the rough stony bed of a mountain torrent. At six p m., we drew rein at Matucanas, a picturesque mountain village 7788 feet above sea level, consisting of a church and houses built of adobe, or sun-dried bricks, and thatched with straw.

The population is about three hundred. A——, knowing the custom of the country, led the way at once to the governor's house, before he could have time to hear of our arrival and hide, as he probably would, to avoid being called upon for a hospitality frequently ill requited. Luckily we found him standing at his own door, wrapped in a warm poncho, with straw hat closely pressed over his forehead. "Señor Gobernador," said A——, "this gentleman and myself are travelling on a government commission, and beg you to give us *posada* (lodging) for ourselves, and fodder for our mules." This appeal elicited a reply to the effect that "he regretted the inadequacy of his own house, but would do his best to accommodate us elsewhere." We were then conducted to the village school, the tables and forms in which, the governor observed, would serve admirably for couches. Our sleeping quarters being thus settled, if not to our own satisfaction, at least to that of the governor, we dined at an hotel kept by a French cook, lately from California. If he continues to treat the railway workers as well as he regaled us that night, he certainly deserves by this time to have made good progress in that pursuit termed by the Americans "making your pile."

Early next morning we left Matucanas, the Quebrada soon becoming a narrow gorge with steep precipitous sides, rising to one thousand feet or more. Here there is more verdure, and the country is prettier than the sun-burnt slopes round Surco. Many streams pour through fissures in the rock into the river, where clumps of willow and masses of waterweed grow in profusion. Here and there the red thorn-apple clings to the steep declivities, besides a thousand varieties of Alpine plants and flowers. The native Indians make a drink called *tonga* from this apple. It is powerfully narcotic, and they imagine that by its means they are brought into communication with departed spirits.

We reached Tambo de Viso at ten a.m., going at once to the house of the engineer in charge of that section of the railroad, M. Van Brock, well known in the United States for his wide professional experience. From the balcony we observed the grading of the railroad on the opposite side of the river. Here the ascent is made by tracing the line in the form of a Z on the hillside. The grading is commenced on the higher bar and continued along the diagonal, after which the lower bar is formed. In this way, the lower portion of the figure is not buried under the material thrown out of the higher. At each angle a spur of sufficient length enables the driver of the train to reverse its direction, by "backing" along the diagonal, to resume its onward course on the higher bar. Another instance of this zigzagging occurs between Tambo de Viso and San Mateo, which is necessary in order to keep the gradient within the limits of 4 in 100, the maximum considered workable.

In this latitude the summit line of the Cordillera approaches nearer the sea-coast than in any other part of Peru, and from this pass of Antaragua, where the Rimac takes its rise, to Callao, the distance is less than 90 miles. The fall being over 15,500 feet, it follows that the normal slope of the pass corresponds to a rise of 3¼ feet for every 100 feet in length. But nature has broken the incline by deep depressions and sudden risings, which necessarily affect the grading of the railroad, and in places where a deep valley occurs, the line is seen high on the hillside, contouring the slope, here sweeping round a hollow, there tunnelling through projecting ridges. The best grade was obtained by extending the length of the line to 104 miles between Callao and the summit; this on the rough section of the Quebrada allowed an average gradient of 1 in 25, or 4 per cent., but in places this is increased to 5 per cent.* Some portions presented unusual difficulties, both for the survey and location of the road bed. Beyond Tambo de Viso, the abrupt sides of the cliff offered no footing at all for either purpose, and the exact spot which the line should strike could only be reached by lowering men with ropes from above. A foothold being cut in the rock-face, afforded holding for a wire cable, which connected the workings with

* Peru is famous for possessing many steep railways. At places, the Iquique and La Noria Railway (described in the following chapter) has a rise of 5 per cent., or 1 in 20. The " Fairlie " engine has done good service on that line as well as elsewhere.

the bottom of the ravine, where the workmen's huts lay; the men were raised and lowered to their work in a swinging cage, which travelled up and down the suspended wire. The workings are all in granite rock sparingly covered with earth, and much gunpowder is daily consumed in blasting the rock. Porphyry, granite crossed with quartz veins, varieties of marble, slate, and in parts red and yellow sandstone, are packed together in irregular and uneven masses, twisted and distorted by volcanic action, or broken and smoothed by floods. In places, a sheer height of one thousand feet rises from the bottom of the ravine with smooth unscalable sides; at other points the precipice is broken into uneven rock-strewn steps, to climb which endangers both life and limb. These are some of the difficulties in the way of constructing the railway through this broken country.

The mule track between Tambo de Viso and San Mateo, a distance of only nine miles, is on account of these obstacles considered the most dangerous portion of the whole road, the mules having often to scramble over beds of boulders washed down by the stream, or jump from rock to rock at the bottom of the ravine. At places the track is interrupted by immense avalanches of rock blocking the way, and a climb of several hundred feet in zigzag fashion up the hillside must be performed by the persevering surefooted animals. A mere shelf along the side of the precipice next serves as pathway, and frequently, in rounding projecting corners or a spur of the cliff, the rider experiences the unpleasant sensation of finding one leg suspended over a yawning precipice. To the novice in Cordillera travelling these " corners," as they are termed, are startling enough, the road being only visible for one or two feet ahead ; but the mule goes straight on as if he intended walking calmly over the edge, till at the angle he swerves suddenly round, with a *sang-froid* rarely shared by his rider.

At three p.m., we reached San Mateo, the largest village in this " valley," 10,530 feet above the sea. Potatoes, ullucas, maize and lucerne are grown here more or less successfully. It is the last town on this side the Cordillera and lies just below the snow limit. Between San Mateo and Tarma, on the eastern slope, no provision or accommodation of any kind can be obtained at the few intervening Indian villages. We passed the night at the house of the railway superintendent, who lives here with his wife and another American lady. It was pleasant to find an orderly and well-regulated household in the heart of the Andes, and to talk over New York, its Central Park, and the doings of Broadway "in the good old times," with men who knew them well. The household is composed of American engineers and their assistants engaged on the railroad works.

After leaving San Mateo, the track enters a deep

dark ravine, apparently formed by the splitting asunder of the mountain, the sides being as smooth and sharp as if cut with a knife. The black walls draw nearer together as we climb higher, till they end in a fork, up which the pathway rises in steps for some two hundred feet. It is but a rough stone ladder, partly hewn out of the solid rock, partly formed by placing slabs of stone, and up it the mules mount, leaping from step to step like so many goats, first placing their forefeet on the ledge in front, often three feet high, then with a spring bringing their hind feet to the same level, immediately attacking the next step in the like fashion. This "staircase" is called "La Infernilla" (Hell), and from the many accidents occurring, the insecure footing being rendered doubly difficult by a heavy flood of water continually pouring down the pathway, it well merits the name.

On reaching the top of this ladder, the whole character of the scenery changes. The Quebrada, with its smooth walls, is succeeded by the round-shaped undulating hills of the Sierra, clothed with itchu grass. Two leagues beyond San Mateo we reach Chilka, a mere roadside halting-place for the llamas and alpacas which carry wood and minerals from the interior to San Mateo. Here we rested with the "captain" of the station in charge of the mules, etc., belonging to the railroad. The thermometer stood at fifty-five degrees at six p.m., and fell during the night to freezing-point, when we were glad to heap alpaca skins for warmth over the rugs we had brought with us. The only business of the place is housing and feeding the llamas, numbers of which congregated round our sleeping quarters. Always a lovely creature to view, easily managed and tamed, the llama is the stock beast of burden in the interior of Peru, and together with its relations the alpaca, the huanaca, and vicuna, is exceedingly valuable for its wool. In a country so thinly wooded as the Western Cordillera, the llamas are, perhaps, equally valued by the natives for the fuel supplied by their *taquia*, or dung, the habit of these animals being always to deposit that substance in the same place, so that huge mounds of *taquia* are found along their line of march. Mr. A. J. Duffield, the author of an interesting little book entitled " Peru in the Guano Age," tells the writer (what he has not yet told the public) that he made an effort to introduce this animal into Australia. He collected a number at Sucre, in Bolivia, and shipped them at Cobija. But at this stage, misfortune in the shape of bad weather overtook the enterprise, and the ship being delayed on its voyage, great mortality ensued among the llamas. The failure here seems to have been the result of accident, and does not therefore preclude hopes of ultimate success, though it would be well to ascertain whether the animal would thrive deprived of his natural food, the itchu, or native grass, said to be peculiar to the Peruvian Cordillera. Mr. Duffield was engaged for four years in this undertaking, and we may hope he will one day give publicity to his experience, which cannot fail to be of great and general interest, the wool of the vicuna family being of finer texture than that of any other species of sheep on the habitable globe.

We rose early next day, and pricking on our mules, soon reached the Cordillera proper; this name being limited by most writers to the portion of the Andes which is perpetually covered with snow. Two miles beyond Chilka, we passed through a village of Indian huts called Acchahuari, which appeared to be deserted, except for two men sitting by a wall, chewing coca, which they mixed with lime held in small gourds—the rest of the inhabitants were probably working in the fields. This coca-chewing takes the place of the short pipe with our English labourer, and perhaps of the more palatable cigar with ourselves; the Indian, when resting or ruminating, has generally recourse to this narcotic, which is pleasant to the taste and stimulating to the mind and body.

A thin sheet of snow covered the ground, and perfect silence reigned at this elevation, undisturbed even by the bleat of a llama. Some plots of ground near the village were planted with maize and potatoes, and shallow *acequias*, or water-courses, served to irrigate the ground along the hill slopes.

Beyond Acchahuari, the valley spreads out into the shape of a bowl, closing at a distance of some three miles into the topmost ridge of the Cordillera.

We reached the encampment on the top at eleven a.m., where we found a Mr. Toboa, an M.D., and a clerk in charge of the station. Here the height of the railway reached 15,645 feet above sea level ; a tunnel was being pierced through the crown of the mountain, the construction of which was in this wise. First, a drift way was driven for a distance of forty-four metres by hand-tooling, the workmen being experienced miners, receiving as pay 2·50 soles (about 10*s.*) per day. Thirteen hundred feet is to be the total length of the tunnel, which at the time of our visit it was proposed to bore with diamond drills, set in motion by machinery worked by compressed air. The plant had arrived, and it was hoped would soon be in operation.

The view from the Pass of Antaragua is disappointing, the hills around, limiting its extent, being themselves rounder and less picturesque in form than the broken and contorted peaks sometimes seen in a volcanic country. The day was cloudy, and a chilling wind swept over the snow-covered landscape. For some distance the pass is bare of vegetation, and travellers are said to hurry across without looking behind, reluctant to spend more time than necessary in so forbidding and uncongenial a spot. Added to this, most people suffer more or less from *sorroche,* or *veta,* that is, mountain-sickness caused according to some by the rarefaction of the air at such a height, by others attributed to the presence of minerals injurious to health ; an additional reason for hastening to leave the summit. One of our party was seized with *sorroche* immediately on arriving, and only recovered next day, when we had descended several hundred feet on our way to the coast. Within a stone's throw to northward of our position, and a little below, were the eternal glaciers. We could see also the watershed of the country, with streams flowing east and west, the former falling into the Atlantic, the latter into the Pacific Ocean. To the left in a hollow, overhung by the topmost ridge, a small lakelet contributed its waters to the Rimac ; on the right, springs flowed out of the rock and trickled down the hillside, humble tributaries of the mighty Amazon. On the western slope the Rimac is fed by nine lakes at different elevations, varying from 14,065 to 15,968 feet above sea level. Notwithstanding these great heights, the climate is mild, and the lakes are never frozen. The amount of water calculated to be in each is set forth in the following table, also the head of water :—

	Head, in feet.	Cubic feet of water available.
Pirhua	16·4	17,481,000
Manca	34·45	36,022,000
Huachua	13·78	38,600,000
Piuro	34·45	61,167,000
Misa	16·40	21,683,000
Huasca	21·32	190,421,000
Carpa	52·49	737,952,000
Guisha	54·13	350,365,000
Sacra	—	200,233,000

The numerous traces of old channels along the course of the Rimac show clearly that in former times its waters must considerably have exceeded their present amount. Indeed, the large area of cultivable land, which the Incas obtained by terracing both sides of the Quebrada, much in the same way as the banks of the Rhine are terraced, could not have been fertilized by the present scanty supply of water, barely sufficient as it is for the present population of the valley, and for the estates near the capital. But in a volcanic district the whole face of the country may be changed in a day; and shortly after our return to Lima, this was exemplified by a landslip which occurred near the village of Matucanas, damming up the river, and spreading across the Quebrada, thus forming a new lake a mile or so in diameter. It was a striking instance of sudden transformation in the natural features of the country.

The idea of the Oroya railway originated in a bold, if not a very wise mind. It was no easy task to twist a metal thread across the rocky, uneven face of the Andes; indeed, it may be called an unprecedented feat of mountain engineering.

It is not our purpose, however, in this paper to discuss the merits or utility of the Oroya railway. Suffice it to remark that the contract price of the single line was about £5,000,000, and its length being 136 miles gives £36,800 as the rate per mile, a sum considerably higher than was expended on many of the most paying of English railways, which are generally made with two lines of rails. The line goes from Lima to Oroya, which terminus is at present a mere village of Indian huts. Looking at the stupendous works, one cannot help wishing that the days of magic could return, and some fairy transport a flourishing town about the size of London, or even Lima, to this site. The best prospects for the undertaking lie in its use as a means of transport for the silver ores of Cerro de Pasco and other mines along its course. But between Oroya and Cerro de Pasco a great district of rough, mountainous country intervenes, and many miles of railway have yet to be completed before the whistle of the locomotive can be heard at that place. Then an adit must be driven, and the mines will require to be well drained before their undoubted riches can be made available. Thus much work remains to be done before the great scheme can become an accomplished fact. In the meantime, it is to be hoped this railroad across the Andes may at least serve some local purposes.

CHAPTER XIV.

THE SALTPETRE DEPOSITS OF PERU.

Saltpetre—The Seaboard—Pampa de Tamarugal—Currents of air—Algarova Trees—Former Forests—Caliche—Process of Reduction—Nitrate—Results of Boiling by Steam-power —Cost of Working—Transport—The Railway—A New Process—Extent of the Nitrate Fields—Description of the Nitrate Country—Origin of the Deposits.

THE country wherein lies the industry the author proposes to describe in this paper is situated on the West Coast of South America, and belongs to that part known as the Costa Seca or Dry Coast, being the slip of land comprised between the 4th and 40th degrees S. latitude, and which, measured from the River Tumbez, the southern boundary of the republic of Ecuador, to Valdivia in Chile, embraces, within a length of over 2400 miles, the entire seaboard of Peru, Bolivia, and part of Chile. Over this considerable extent of sea coast no rain falls to modify the parched appearance of the soil, and no humidity is obtained from the heavens beyond that acquired from the condensation of the fogs which envelop the coast during the winter months. With the rare exception of a shower of rain occurring once or twice in the year, the cultivator is dependent upon the scanty supply of water afforded by the rivers which derive their origin from the rains and snows which fall but moderately on the western slopes of the lofty Cordilleras. Thus the coast can be briefly described as consisting of a succession of valleys of great fertility, separated by arid wastes of high ground of immense extent.

The section with which we are at present dealing lies at the southern extremity of Peru, and though saltpetre exists in small quantities in Bolivia, up to now it has only been worked in the former country, in the province of Tarapaca, perhaps more familiarly known as the district lying inland of the ports of Patillos, Iquique, Mexillones, and Pisagua. The coast between these ports presents seawards a precipitous front, with its cliffs rising to a height of from one thousand to three thousand feet from the water. These cliffs have but little slope; therefore, all road approaches are traced in a diagonal direction upon their face, or ascended by a series of reversing inclined planes, of exceeding steepness, perilous to the mules performing the transport service.

From the summit of the coast-cliffs the land rises with nearly an uniform ascent, and the construction of the Iquique and La Noria Railway, after deducting for the deviations of the latter, shows that the surface has a general inclination of 50′ until it reaches an elevated plateau known by the name of Pampa de Tamarugal. This pampa, or extensive plain, is situated at an elevation of 3440 feet on its western side, and extending southwards and northwards, measures about three hundred miles in length and from thirty to sixty miles in breadth. The surface is perfectly smooth, and appears level to the eye, but in reality it rises slightly in an easterly direction towards the Cordillera. Its surface is covered in some places by a cap of alluvial soil, but more generally consists of a finely granulated sand, which is raised by the slightest breath, and by a heavy wind is carried over the plains in broad thick clouds which obscure the horizon and blind the traveller with dust. On still days curious conical-shaped clouds, resembling water-spouts, may be seen rising up in all parts of the plain, produced no doubt by the rotary motion which must occur at the meeting of two opposing currents of air. Then a tremulous motion is observed when the eye scans the horizon, and this is caused by the ascent and descent at one and the same time of layers of air at different temperatures—the cool coming down, the warm going up. At different points the horizon is broken by patches of trees ; these trees are algarovas, and, as mentioned in a previous chapter, their wood is hard and brown, not unlike English oak. They seldom grow in this locality to any considerable height. The deposits of roots belonging to this tree, to be found nearly all over the pampa, indicate the existence in former days of an immense forest,

and the traditions of the place explain that formerly
wood was the only fuel used in the reduction of the
saltpetre and other minerals in which the province
abounds. The algarova requires but little moisture,
and subsists on the humidity which it absorbs through
its leaves from the atmosphere.

The mineral containing saltpetre is called *caliche.*
Caliche generally lies at depths of from one to ten
yards below the surface, and sometimes resembles in
appearance loaf sugar, and at other times rock-sulphur;
and again it appears white, crossed with bluish veins.
Its gravity varies from that of common salt to sandstone
(2·41 average), according to the amount and nature
of earthy matters it may be allied with. The nitrate
portion dissolves freely in boiling water, leaving behind
as a residuum the earthy substances. The custom is
to boil it at a temperature of from 220 to 240 degrees
Fahrenheit. This valuable mineral is found beneath
a covering of calcareous earth, generally assuming
the appearance of half-formed sandstone, when it is
serviceable for building purposes. A shaft, or hole,
sufficiently wide to permit of the passage of a man, is
sunk through this cap as far as the under side of the
caliche, at which point the underlying earth is dug out
in a circle for several feet. The chamber thus formed
is charged with gunpowder (manufactured in the district), and on being fired the result is to disengage
and throw up to the surface the subterranean *caliche,*
which is picked out by hand and stacked up in heaps

at some convenient point, whence it is conveyed in carts, capable of holding about a couple of tons, to the *oficina*, or manufactory. Considerable skill is required in selecting the points at which to begin mining operations, and it frequently occurs that large sums of money are paid for lands which on being worked prove to be worthless, either on account of the scarcity of the *caliche*, its bad quality, or its great depth beneath the surface. These losses are sustained on account of the difficulty sometimes experienced of obtaining labour or tools in a country so inhospitable in its resources, and possessing no real indigenous population.

At the manufactory the *caliche* is broken up, either by hand labour or by steam crushers, into cubes capable of passing through a ring of an inch and a half diameter, for which purpose Blake's patent crusher, manufactured by Messrs. Marsden, of Leeds, has of late years been used in several manufactories with marked success.

In the old method of extracting the nitrate from the *caliche*, the broken *caliche* is shovelled into the boiling pan, which is placed over a fire. After from six to eight hours' boiling in a liquid composed of fresh water and the liquid remainder of a former boil —called *agua vieja*, or "old water"—the nitrate of the *caliche* is dissolved and forms part of the solution, which, by means of a ladle, is transferred to a pan, where it deposits its nitrate. In this process the *caliche* is boiled at a low temperature, and the salt is supposed to remain in the refuse. Great waste attends the operation of dissolving at a low temperature, which cannot well be avoided by using the direct fire employed at the *paradas*, and it is estimated that in some cases some thirty per cent. of nitrate is thrown away with the refuse, or, as it is called there, *ripia*. The water is lifted up from wells in buckets attached to ropes working round a drum, which is placed on a vertical shaft and made to revolve by a mule drawing round its circumference. Thus no steam-power is employed in this process. The increasing demand for nitrate caused the introduction of improved plant for its elaboration, and now all the important manufactories are worked by steam-power.

The improved form of *cachucha*, or boiling-tank, is either opened or closed, and the heating agency is steam, introduced at the bottom of the tank by means of a steam-coil. The coil is usually placed beneath a perforated false bottom, thereby allowing the heated vapour to circulate through the *caliche* lying immediately above. Sometimes an additional coil is run directly through the *caliche*.

Great diversity of opinion exists among saltpetre manufacturers upon the most economical form of *cachucha*. Some advocate the closed *cachucha*, which in every respect may be compared to a steam chest, because they maintain that, the steam being enclosed, there is no waste of heat, and consequently an economy is effected in coal. Their opponents assert that the steam in the *cachucha* condenses, and thereby weakens the solution, and that it prevents a most important operation—the stirring-up of the matter during the boiling. On the other hand, the open *cachucha* allows the steam which has passed through the *caliche*, and done its duty, to escape into the air, and enables the attendants, during the entire boiling, to constantly turn over the *caliche*, thereby enabling the heat to penetrate into every crevice of the mass. The result is to extract more nitrate from the *caliche*, and less is thrown away in the *ripia;* hence, by this latter system, an economy is effected in *caliche*, which more than balances the extra consumption of fuel.

In the closed *cachucha* the *caliche* is first placed in boxes made of perforated iron plating, which are mounted on wheels and pushed along a tramway into the *cachucha*. To overcome the difficulty of stirring up the mass, boxes have been made of a circular shape, and capable of revolving on their standards when locked to an axle worked by a wheel on the outside. This plan however proved a failure, on account of the accumulation of insoluble matter at the bottom of the *cachucha*, which completely wedged in the boxes, and the attempt to give the latter a rotary motion could only have been done at the risk of breaking the couplings and damaging the boxes themselves. It is thought that this plan might be carried out by making the plant stronger, and by allowing adequate space for the insoluble matter which escapes from the boxes; but that would be objectionable, on account of the large steam space it would afford in the *cachucha*, and the consequent impoverishment of the solution through the condensation of the steam.

There are other forms, known as egg-shaped *cachuchas*, owing to their similarity in form to an egg placed on its smaller end. These offer great facilities in the operation of charging and discharging the material. The *caliche* is conducted over a road to their upper part, and shot down. After being boiled, the solution is tapped and the refuse allowed to fall into trucks placed beneath, which convey it to the spoil bank. The chief disadvantage of these *cachuchas* consists in the necessity of having at command considerable height for the approach-road, and consequently they are chiefly used at those places where an adjoining hill affords that height, the manufactory being built at its base. Where no hill is available, the trucks may be raised on an inclined plane.

Chemists interested in the trade have of late been engaged in searching for a method of extracting iodine from *caliche*, but as the operation is known but to a few, and where known kept a dead secret, the author does not propose to touch further upon this subject.

The labour required for the different operations attendant on the production of nitrate is chiefly supplied by Bolivians. Great numbers of these people, as we have already seen, annually cross the Cordilleras, taking with them their wives and children, and then offer themselves for hire at the saltpetre establishments. They earn from one to two dollars per day, and perform their work well; and they are much esteemed by the manufacturer for their docile disposition and readiness to obey orders. Their migratory habits never allow them to remain long in one locality; they remain perhaps six or twelve months, then leave in a tribe, to go to some adjacent establishment. Chinese coolies are employed at some places, but the feebleness and lack of *physique* of those who have hitherto visited the district rendered them incapable of performing the hard work of mining and the rough duties attendant upon this manufacture.

Mechanics, bricklayers, carpenters, and skilled artisans of any description command high wages in this district; and the manufacturers can well afford to pay them highly, as they calculate upon at least fifty per cent. of the wages returning to their pockets, by sale of provisions and commodities of every description, of which they are sole purveyors (the truck system).

Below is a copy of the balance-sheet of the working of an *oficina*, which may be taken as showing a fair average of the profits made in prosperous times by careful management :—

March, 1873.

DISBURSEMENTS.

		Soles.
Elaboration...		7680
Coal, 2300 quintals, at 1·5 soles		3450 .
Mules		800
Provisions		3000
House and office		1200
Repairs and loss		600
Gross profit		3670
		20,400

ENTRIES.

	Soles.
Sale of 14,000 quintals of nitrate, at 1·10 soles per quintal	15,400
Item provisions	5000
	20,400

In this case the nitrate was delivered at the manufactory, from whence it had to be conveyed to the
port by the purchaser, either by rail or by mules.

The cost of conveyance by mule service is fixed
according to the distance of the manufactory from
the port. Thus from La Noria to Iquique the price
is from five to six reals (Peruvian); from other *oficinas*
half the distance from the port the price is only half
that amount. A good mule will carry as much as three
quintals, but the usual load is two down to the port, and
one and a half up, loaded with coal or provisions.
Frequently the mules have to perform the journey
there and back, some twenty-eight miles each way,
without touching water, owing to the total absence

of that element in its natural state. For the use of the inhabitants sea-water is condensed, but when the machines fail and there is a scarcity, the price is too high to give drink to the mules; two cents per gallon is the price paid at Iquique for condensed water, and sometimes as much as four is paid.

The construction of the Iquique and La Noria Railway did much to take the transport service away from the mules, but it did not entirely succeed in doing so, owing to its inadequacy to convey the enormous quantity of saltpetre daily brought down. The line starts in a northerly direction from the port, making towards the coast-cliffs, which it reaches at a distance of three miles and at an elevation of some three hundred feet. From that point it reverses its direction to the north, and creeps up the hillside on an incline of three per cent. until it attains the summit of the coast-cliffs at the station called Molle, which is situated at an elevation of 1630 feet above the sea, and at a distance of ten miles from Iquique.

From thence it follows a generally direct course on to La Noria, winding itself round hillsides in curves of from three hundred to five hundred feet radius, sometimes raising itself high above the surrounding country, where the latter dips and assumes the shape of a bowl, over the extreme edge of which the railway must necessarily pass. At other times the line penetrates by deep cuttings through irregular porphyritic rocks, clearly indicating the volcanic agency that must have occurred to have caused their displacement, until it reaches the district known as La Noria. Throughout, the railway is of the 4 ft. 8½ in. gauge. Where there were cuttings near, their *débris* supplied the fillings, and at other places trenches were dug at each side of the line. The chief want experienced was soft earth or sand to pack in the permanent way. This was very scarce, owing to the hard nature of the surface of the ground.

Though it is not proposed to give here a detailed description of the railway, the points bearing on the transport of saltpetre are set down as follows.

The grades between Iquique and La Noria vary from three to five per cent., and the up trains generally consist of the following loads :—

	Eng. tons.
One Fairlie locomotive in running order ...	54
Four American double bogie cars loaded, say 24 tons each	96
One tank holding approximately 2000 gallons of water and its car, say	22
One employé's car	12
Total	184

The inequality of the traffic, the up traffic not amounting to a third of the down, necessitates the hauling up of empty cars. Thus trains of from eight to ten empties are despatched.

On the downward journey, as many as twenty cars loaded with saltpetre have been lowered by these engines, but as the risk attendant upon the train breaking away is so considerable, the number has been reduced to fifteen or twelve, representing a total of some 340 tons. Each car is loaded up to 264 quintals, or nearly twelve English tons, and the bags are laid at each end, immediately over the bogie frames, leaving the middle part of the car empty. The price charged by the late company was one and a half cents per quintal per mile, being the price allowed in the concession from the government; thus, taking the distance of the manufactory from the port, at about thirty-three miles, the cost of conveyance would be five Peruvian reals (equivalent to ten Spanish) per quintal.

From an extract taken from Consul Hutchinson's report on this trade, published in the Foreign Office Blue Book of Consular Reports for 1873, we learn that in eleven months of the year 1872 the total export of nitrate from Iquique was 3,983,798 quintals, or 362,163 per month. Since then it has no doubt increased, but we will take only that amount which would correspond to over 12,000 quintals conveyed daily to the port. For 12,000 quintals some forty-five cars would be required. Supposing the railway worked for a monopoly of both the up traffic (coal and provisions) and the down traffic, it could only approach such a monopoly with the following train service :—

<pre>
Locomotives
  running
  per day.   Cars.
    3 trains of provision and fuel cars, 4 cars loaded
        and one empty   15
    4 trains of 8 empty cars each   32
    2 trains of water tanks to supply the above, 8 tanks
        each.
    ──

                                                               ──
    9   Cars   47
                            Water tanks   16
</pre>

This is only taking the up traffic to be one-fourth of the down ; most probably it would reach as much as one-third if not more. Were the railway to secure a monopoly, then a greater number of trains would be required. It is said that the late company never possessed sufficient rolling-stock to attempt anything of this kind, and, in addition, they had to contend with the water question, which, in the author's opinion, would, were it to remain as at present, entirely prevent their securing a monopoly of the traffic. For working the first section to Molle, the water is obtained from sea-water cleansed at Iquique, and for working the remainder of the line it is brought in tanks from a well in the interior to Molle, at an enormous cost.

To show the large traffic returns which this important railway might, under certain conditions, earn, it is only necessary to refer to the amount of saltpetre shipped from the port of Iquique in 1872, which approached four million quintals. The entries, assuming a monopoly, would then be :—

Soles.

4,000,000 quintals, at 5 reals, taken to port	2,000,000
Up traffic, consisting of coal, corn, hay, provisions, and material of all descriptions, say one-third of above, 1,333,333 at 5 reals	666,666
Total of entries ...	2,666,666

Or equivalent to a sum of over £533,333 pounds sterling, gross receipts.

There were in 1874 some three thousand to four thousand mules competing with the railway.

This line, as well as that from Pisagua to Sal de Obispo, was constructed by a private firm of Peruvians, Messrs. Montero Brothers, who are the owners of the property and by whom it was originally worked.

Whilst dealing with the conveyance of saltpetre to the port, an unsuccessful endeavour, which occasioned much discussion at the time, made by a company to convey down the nitrate in a liquid state through iron piping, should also be mentioned. The company which entertained this project was called "La Compania Salitrera Barrenechea," since, it is understood, put into liquidation. The objects of the promoters were, firstly, to avoid as much as possible the use of steam in the reduction of the mineral and thereby secure an economy in coal; secondly, to save the freight of conveyance by rail or mule to port. The first was sought by dissolving the *caliche* in vertical pans by passing cold water through it—a process resembling filtration. The solution drawn from the bottom of the pan was pumped up to high ground (for the mines lay in a hollow), whence it ran down by gravitation through piping to the works at the port. At the latter place the solution was boiled in large circular pans, heated by a fire placed so as to spread over the entire bottom of the pan. The result of the first experiment may be easily anticipated. The solution, impregnated with the salts it held in suspension, soon began to precipitate them, and a thick cake of nitrate and salt shortly collected at the bottom of the boilers, which were in consequence burnt, and rendered useless. Notwithstanding the wrong principles upon which the plant was designed, which the directors recognized, and which could have been remedied by an additional expenditure, the company apparently took no steps to modify these evils, and the real cause of their suspending their operations at last was, it is understood, the fear they entertained regarding the quality of their lands. With *caliche* containing a large percentage of common salt no profit is to be made by working it either with this or another system, though, it must be understood, the writer does not give any opinion upon the nature of the mines in question.

As regards the extent of land supposed to contain saltpetre, no formal measurement or survey has been made, for frequently land is supposed to contain nitrate, but, on being opened, proves to be barren of that mineral.

The lands round about La Noria were those first worked, and there remains very little "virgin land" left in that quarter. There are large spaces, however, left untouched on the Pampa de Tamarugal, and nitrate is supposed to exist all along the southern border of the pampa, between the points known as Pozo de Almonte and Sal de Obispo, which have been referred to before.

Numerous deposits are reported to exist in the south, where some *oficinas* have been opened and a railway made to them from the port of Patillos; but for the reasons before stated, namely, for the want of a geological survey, it would be impossible to give any definite opinion as to the area of land containing saltpetre or its quality. On the other hand, large portions of land in the south are said to contain nothing but beds of common salt.

The author observes that Mr. Markham says, in his "Travels in Peru and India:" "It is calculated that the nitrate grounds in this district (Tarapaca) cover fifty square leagues, and allowing one hundred pounds weight of nitrate for each square yard, this will give sixty-three million tons, which at the present rate of consumption will last 1393 years." He cannot agree with Mr. Markham that the deposits cover so large an area as four hundred and fifty square miles, but the space covered might amount to one hundred, though that can only be a supposition, and no opinion can be formed in reference to the quality of the nitrate. The estimate of one quintal to the square yard is too low in his opinion. On making an analysis of two specimens of *caliche*, they were found to contain the following substances :—

1ST SPECIMEN (WHITE).

	Per cent.
Nitrate of soda	48
Common salt	40
Insoluble matters	12
	100

2ND SPECIMEN (YELLOW).

Nitrate of soda	55
Salt	35
Insoluble matters (containing sulphur)	10
	100

The mineral is found in layers of from a few inches to three yards in thickness, and it is thought that three quintals per yard of surface is a fair average for land containing nitrate in sufficient quantities to repay its working. Provided these lands in the south prove to be good, we may in that case assume a total area of one hundred square miles; but otherwise, excluding these, it would not be safe to count upon more than one-third of that area. One hundred square miles at three quintals per square yard would give 42,240,000 tons, which at a consumption of three million quintals per annum would last over three centuries. All these grounds were originally claimed under the mining laws of the country by private individuals, but have been subsequently purchased by the Peruvian government.

The writer will now describe the physical features of the country, upon which are based his suppositions as to the origin of these deposits. Ascending from the sea-board, the cuttings in the railway bring to view rocks of porphyritic formation. Granite is seen in a state of decomposition, crossed with veins of quartz, and in other places are beds of coal and sandstone. At the summit the railway cuts through a bed of white limestone, resembling marble as to the polish it will take, and for which rock it has been mistaken by many. To this coast range succeeds the vast plain of Tamarugal, with its alluvial coating, which extends some thirty miles to the foot of the second range of mountains, chiefly composed of sandstone, and among which extinct volcanoes have been recognized. Another level plain intervenes between these latter and the range of mountains known as the Cordillera proper, among which is situated the famous volcano Isluga.

Returning to the Pampa of Tamarugal, a group of hills, ranging from two hundred to five hundred feet above its level, borders its western extremity. On the slope of these hills lie the deposits of saltpetre, and in no case has that mineral been found on the pampa itself. On its eastern side stands the second range of mountains already mentioned. These mountains are pierced at frequent intervals by deep ravines, at the bottom of which small streams find their bed, but the uniform layers of boulders packed up on each side of the ravines leads the imagination to picture the large rivers, which at one time, no doubt, travelled down these channels on their way to water the wooded plains of the pampa. In the journey already described it will be remembered that upon entering the ravine of Tarapacá, two leagues of ground covered with boulders had to be traversed, and a deep gully could still be traced in the neighbourhood, which points out the course taken by a pre-historic river.

By one of those revolutions in Nature, the occurrences of which are proved by the researches of the geologist, the rains ceased to fall with their accustomed abundance, and have left, where formerly were forests and grassy plains, nothing but an immense arid desert. But though the rains are now insufficient to form themselves into rivers, they fall with regularity on the slopes of the distant Cordillera, and, being absorbed by the earth, they percolate through porous strata, to empty themselves into the natural reservoir beneath the surface of the pampa. Thus water may be seen jetting out in springs at the foot of the eastern range of mountains, where it is obtained in large quantities by the natives, by driving tunnels into the yellow sandstone which forms the foundation

of the slope. The crust at this point is chiefly sand
and a limestone having a very washed appearance,
from which water is also obtained ; but it does not
repay the working, as it is soon dried out.

At Pica, as we have noticed, there are two basins
supplied with water in this manner, the one placed
some fifteen feet above the other. The top one
receives from its tunnel supplies of cold water, whilst
the bottom receives warm water (ninety degrees Fahr.).
At a point a quarter of a mile up the hill, and at an
elevation of about one hundred feet, another basin
receives warm water ; thus the anomaly is presented
of a cold stream running between two hot streams.

Following the section of the pampa westwards for
about ten miles, water is found beneath the surface at
a depth of three yards. In this latitude that novel
kind of cultivation already described is practised, the
capillary attraction which some plants possess to an
inordinate degree being utilized by making them suck
up the water through several feet of earth. Alfafa,
vegetables, and different cereals thrive well in these
pits, and the cultivation proved so successful that the
government, who in that country must have a finger
in every pie, established an agency to collect rents
and to plant a farm on their own account, with the
object of supplying the soldiery with vegetables.

Resuming a westerly course at the termination of
another eight miles, water is found at a lower
depth, namely, at about six or eight yards below the

surface. It is still sweet to the taste. Another eight miles in the same direction and the western hills are arrived at, where the water is reached only at depths of from forty to one hundred yards, and with only a few notable exceptions, so strongly impregnated with saliferous matter that it is unfit for the use of animals. Thus the pampa may be compared to a cup, slightly tilted up at one end and filled with a fluid, the surface of which is depressed from the natural level by the weight of a covering whose depth increases in proportion to its distance from its raised end. This subterranean reservoir is supplied directly from the rainy district, and as a proof of the free connection which exists between itself and its sources, it is only necessary to refer to the fact of the simultaneous rising of the water in the wells almost immediately after the commencement of the rainy season.

Now, taking into consideration the facts above enumerated, the position of the deposits beneath the surface of a "lee-shore," the proximity of numerous volcanoes probably uniting with their lava large quantities of salts, sodas, sulphurs, and other substances, and lastly, the direct communication maintained by the rivers between the volcanoes and the nitrate grounds, would it not be reasonable to suppose that these deposits derive their origin from volcanic discharge? Is it not probable that the lava discharged during eruptions, falling into the ravines, was snatched up by the rivers in the latter, and whilst its heavier particles were deposited in the neighbourhood, the lighter, consisting of the salts, might have been conveyed across the desert and thrown upon the opposing shore, which thus, on the withdrawing of the waters in the dry season, became coated with the deposits ?

With the arrival of the fogs in winter, this coating of soda would experience rapid liquefaction through the condensation of the fogs, and the product would be absorbed by the porous soil of the formation.

Apparently no suitable place offered itself for the accumulation of the deposits on the eastern side of the pampa, where they would have been rapidly dissolved and washed off by the rains, and, indeed, where the hardness of the formation would not have permitted of their percolation.

Bolleart, in his " Antiquities of Peru," etc., whilst opposing Darwin's opinion, that the pampa was formerly an inland sea and obtained its salt thereby, says, " As to iodic salts, we need not look for them to the sea, as iodine and bromine exist in the minerals of the regions ; " and in another part he hints at the probability of their being derived from volcanic sources.

If Darwin was right, would not the greater part of the pampa be covered with salt on the evaporation of the sea-water ? But it is not so, as no beds of salt on the pampa have been discovered after boring for a considerable depth. It lies only on the slopes of the western shore.

The heavy fogs of which mention has been made appear between the months of March and October, and on condensing leave a thin coating of chloride of sodium on projecting rocks and stones, or on any impediment which seems to arrest their course.

To bring back to memory the origin of these sea fogs, it may be useful to quote what Captain Maury says about those of Newfoundland, in his "Physical Geology of the Sea," article 166: "The fogs of Newfoundland, which so much endanger navigation in the spring and summer, doubtless owe their existence to the presence in that cold sea of immense volumes of warm water, brought by the Gulf Stream." The distinguished Peruvian scientist, Señor Raimondi, in his "Apuntes sobre la Provincia litoral de Loreto," says at p. 7: "The immense extent of sand stretching along the coast of Peru, in some places from fifteen to twenty leagues in breadth, has likewise to do with the absence of rain, because, being a good conductor of caloric, the sand, acted upon by the sun, evaporates a current of warm air, which prevents the watery vapours already spoken of from being condensed. In winter time, the atmosphere being of course colder, and the sand being a better conductor of heat than the water of the sea, becomes colder than the latter, so that its low temperature causes the condensation from which we have the fogs so general in winter-time on the coast of Peru."

It appears to the writer that, in addition to this last

reason given by Señor Raimondi, the fogs are caused just in the same manner as those off Newfoundland, with the difference that, in lieu of warm water pouring itself upon cold, the cold water of Humboldt's current, coming from the south polar regions, mingles with the comparatively warm waters of the Pacific coast, thus producing the same effect. These fogs appear at night-time, when frequently the thermometer descends below freezing point, to rise again at ten a.m. to sixty degrees Fahr., and at noon to eighty degrees Fahr. in the shade.

To strengthen the supposition of these deposits having been created through volcanic agency, Humboldt may be again quoted ; at p. 397 in vol. iii. of his "Travels in South America," he says : "The enormous masses of muriate of soda recently thrown up by Vesuvius ; the small veins of that salt which I have often seen traverse the most recently ejected lavas, and of which the origin (by sublimation) appears similar to that of ologist-iron deposited in the same vents ; the layers of gem salt and saliferous clay of the trachyte soil of the plains of Peru, and around the volcanoes of the Andes of Quito, are well worthy the attention of geologists who would discuss the origin of formations."

It must be mentioned that the grounds are nearly everywhere covered with flat pieces of clinkstone or phonolite, varying in size from a few inches to a square foot. A strong opinion is entertained by the natives that, these blocks of stone are aerolites. As they belong to the trachytic family, it is reasonable to suppose that they have been washed down from the volcanic mountains, and to account for their being found on the top of hills of moderate height, an upheaval might have occurred subsequently to their being deposited.

If we admit Humboldt's view as regards the sometime disposal of materials discharged from volcanoes, the origin of the saltpetre deposits will have been almost proved to demonstration, for the volcanoes would supply the materials, and these would be conveyed by the hydraulic agency which it has been attempted to describe, to the site they now occupy, where, after being dissolved by the fogs—naturally converted into liquid—and absorbed by the earth, in union with nitrogen derived from the atmosphere, they would be dug out as nitrate of soda, for the use and to promote the prosperity of man.

CHAPTER XV.

CONCLUSION.

Dangerous Coasts—The Balsas—Humboldt's Current—The Littoral—Tame Scenery—Types of Nationality—Mismanagement of Loans—Characteristics of the Peruvians—Indians on the Coast—Degraded Races—Resemblances of Races—The Lost Ten Tribes—Indians of the Sierra—Coca-chewing—Various Races—Character of the Peruvians—Literature of Peru—Poets of Peru—Peruvian Poetry—Traces of African Blood—Mixed, very Mixed Races—Pride of Caste—The Zambo-Pariahs—Native Intelligence—Missionary Work—Beauty of the Chacra—Produce grown in the Chacras—Vegetables of Peru—Fruits of Peru—Riches of Peru—Mines, Ancient and Modern—Antiquarian Researches—Hidden Treasures—Death of Atahualpa—Conclusion.

In taking leave of Peru, perhaps some remarks may be made on the formation of the land, and also as to the great ocean whose waters bathe its shores. The dangers of navigating along Peruvian shores are but too well known, for unhappily this coast has been the scene of numerous shipwrecks.

The Cordillera, or western chain of mountains, intersecting Peru from S.S.W. to N.N.E., and running parallel with the Andes, has a precipitous slope, terminating sometimes on the sea-coast, sometimes as far as one hundred and fifty miles inland. At Lima, a toe or offshoot of the great mountain is washed by the waters of the Pacific; at Concepcion in Chili, the foot-line recedes to its extreme distance from the sea. The intervening space forms the littoral of Peru and Chili. In the south of Peru the two mountain chains stand at a wider distance from each other, and the Cordillera, which at that point is considerably lower than the Andes, throws out many *spurs*, which often extend as far as the sea, and form short promontories.

In northern and central Peru, where the ranges draw nearer together, and where the Cordillera is higher than the Andes, the littoral is in consequence broader and the slope seawards at a more gentle inclination, leaving a wide belt of shallow water along the coast. Thus the depth of water along shore is much less north of the seventeenth degree south latitude than it is south of that line, and the navigation along that part is performed at a distance of about three miles from the shore. The so-called "anchorage ground" for steamers at the ports of San José, Eten, Salaverry, and other places, is from one to two miles off shore.

In the south, where the cliffs end more abruptly, there are some good and fairly safe harbours. Those of Callao, Arica, and Iquique, are naturally formed bays, all of which afford a tolerably secure refuge for ships. On the other hand, in the open roadsteads to the north, the surf is generally heavy, and the embarkation of passengers and goods is only safely performed by means of *balsas*, or huge rafts.

These *balsas* are formed by lashing together a number of trunks of the cabbage or cork tree, and stretching a piece of tarpaulin or matting over them. Frequently, at the smaller ports, the round rough logs have no covering of any kind. This primitive craft is propelled by means of a large mainsail, and often considerable skill is shown by the sailors who steer the vessel across the high foaming breakers.

To assist the explanation of certain phenomena, it should be noted that the prevailing current, sometimes known as the "Humboldt," and so-called after the great naturalist who studied its influence on the climate of the country, runs parallel with the coast from south to north. The prevalent wind, which increases in force towards the afternoon, blows also from the south or south-west. The difficulties of navigation on this coast are greatly increased by the dense fogs which appear regularly between the months of March and October along the whole of the Peruvian coast. These fogs are said to arise much in the same way as those which occur off the Newfoundland coast; that is to say, they result from the commingling of waters different in temperature. Instead, however, of warm water pouring itself into cold, as when the Gulf Stream mingles with the cold water of the North Atlantic, here the cold water of " Humboldt's current," flowing from the south polar regions, mixes with the warm water of the Pacific and causes condensation, which produces fogs.

The higher temperature of the Pacific is easily accounted for by the degrees of latitude, and by the immense expanse of sand in Peru, which must absorb the heat of the sun, and warm both sea and atmosphere. The absence of rain, which never falls on the western slope of the Cordillera, may perhaps also be partly due to these long sandy stretches. Sand being a good conductor of heat causes a current of warm air to rise from its surface when heated by the sun, which prevents the condensation of vapour.

The littoral thus described is the most thickly populated and the best known portion of Peruvian territory. As has been related, the greater portion of it is divided into a succession of valleys by intervening spaces of elevated ground. The remaining part, not counting the Pampa de Tamarugal in the south, consists of the "Altos," or mountainous slopes of the Cordilleras and Andes.

In addition, there is an immense stretch of country between the Andes and the Brazilian frontier, which is bordered on the north side by the tributaries of the Amazon. But as this country is little known, and is supposed to be peopled by mere savage Indians, its possession hitherto has been of little advantage to Peru. The district is however worth exploring, as it is reported to be thickly covered with forests containing trees and plants of the most valuable description.

To give the reader a general impression of the " Altos " of Peru, it is perhaps unnecessary to relate a number of distinct journeys ; in fact, one journey through this region very closely resembles another.

In many ways the scenery of the Peruvian Cordillera is decidedly disappointing, especially to any one who (like the writer) has had the opportunity of seeing the majestic beauties of the Caucasian Mountains, or who has travelled through Switzerland.

The heights of the Cordillera are always approached through a narrow valley, whose steep precipitous sides generally shut out the view of whatever picturesque peaks or cones may be beyond. The view is restricted to the opposite side of the valley. Neither does the Peruvian Cordillera contain any remarkable peaks, the view from which is likely to repay the climber for his trouble. The outlook from the summit of the several " passes " which the writer has crossed would be described by the Alpine Club as "tame." The summits are smooth and rounded, something like a beehive in shape. There are no high peaks rising above the low hills in the immediate vicinity.

Some reference to the character of the Peruvians may not be out of place in this concluding chapter. In describing national character, the mistake to be feared is that very common one of taking a single individual, or a limited number of individuals, as the representative type of the whole nation. Like the well-known traveller in Alsace, who being one day afflicted with a drunken landlord and his red-haired wife, wrote in his diary, " All Alsatian landlords drunkards ; all the women red-haired." As an illustration of this, it is said that many people on the Continent take the portrait of " John Bull," which *Punch* has reproduced for so many years, as a faithful representation of the modern Britisher. It would, perhaps, be difficult to name the particular class of Englishmen, among the many classes composing the population, who would adopt the heavy and somewhat stupid-looking person dressed in hunting costume as the type of their order. If we are to believe Mr. Max O'Rell, there is also a tendency abroad to take the bourgeois as the type of the modern English gentleman.

So in delineating the Peruvian character, it is obviously incorrect to take one class of individuals, probably the best known, as typical of the inhabitants of Peru. The writer has often regretted to hear epithets expressing the utmost disdain and contempt applied to the whole Peruvian race, in consequence of losses sustained in Peruvian loans, by persons who certainly should have been better informed.

Let us briefly consider the injustice of these remarks. The proceeds of loans raised under the Presidency of the late Colonel Balta were admittedly misapplied and wasted in making railroads which under no circumstances could pay even the cost of working, instead of being laid out as they should have been in productive works such as irrigation, which would have considerably added to the prosperity of the country. Persuaded by advice which was not entirely disinterested, a serious error of judgment was made by Colonel Balta, who in the end paid with his life for his want of judgment and knowledge, for he was assassinated during a revolution caused by the anarchy into which his mismanagement of affairs had thrown the capital, but not the country. It is quite consistent with the facts to say that none of the Peruvians, except the paid official classes and the richer merchants, knew anything, or had a voice in the raising of these loans in Europe, or in directing the manner in which the money was spent in Peru.

In a country like this one, where there are few railways and telegraphs, news travels slowly, and besides, under the traditional habits of its inhabitants, engendered by centuries of submission to Spanish authorities, the interests of the Peruvian are provincial and he rarely interferes in politics. It must be borne in mind that it is not very long since a viceroy of Spain ruled supreme at Lima. The effect which privation and hardship continued for generations had upon native character is not yet entirely worn off.

In describing therefore the character of the Peruvians, it must be distinctly understood that the writer does not take any individual, be he politician, merchant, or even agriculturist, as his type, but that he simply recounts in a general sense his opinion of the race and of their natural characteristics, as they came under his observation during a two years' residence in the country.

As to the race, subdivision is necessary, the population of the coast naturally differing in character and appearance from the inhabitants of the Highlands. The climate is different also, but that is not sufficient to account for the widely varying characteristics; the fact is, the races have different blood in their veins. On the coast, the population consists of three distinct types: the whites, chiefly of Spanish extraction; the blacks, from Ethiopia; and the native Indian. These by their intermarriages have produced numerous and varied mixed races.

The Indian of the coast is in better circumstances than his brother who inhabits the interior, and has become more affiliated to the character and disposition of the creole. In the Sierra, the Indian is characterized by reserve, obstinacy, and suspicion; he is little inclined to give information, and is entirely bereft of any public spirit.

The hand of the conqueror, which fell so heavily on the ancient monuments, proved no lighter when framing rules for the government of the half-conquered races; and as is often said, the subject races are what the dominant ones make them—centuries of oppression and injustice have produced their natural result in these vices.

Accustomed to be robbed systematically and treated as beasts of burden by the commissioners or emissaries of the viceroy at Lima, the poor Indian of the Sierra soon sinks to the level of a slave, and finds that the only means of retaining in his possession anything of value is to observe absolute secrecy regarding its existence. In appearance, the Indian is short of stature; the chest broad and deep; the limbs round and strong; the features, as has been remarked, closely resembling those of the Inca race preserved on the clay pots. In the writer's opinion, their character indicates a Tartar origin; but this is a moot point among antiquarians and historians.

Some of the theories broached on the subject are worthy of mention. The great army of Roman Catholic priests, and many who follow them, reject the notion of any Adam and Eve being created except those mentioned in Holy Writ; ethnologists, from their study of the human race, are of a different opinion. Those who hold that the eastern and western hemispheres were peopled by the same races, are of opinion that the two continents were at one time joined, Behring's Straits being the most probable point of junction. On the authority of Captain Behring we are told that he saw the straits at one time frozen over, forming a safe bridge for the passage of human beings.

Assuming that this physical connection was a fact, it is endeavoured to prove that Chinese Tartary was the birthplace of the first emigrants to America. In support of this theory, a number of remarkable facts are brought forward, such as the calendars in Mexico and Chinese Tartary being the same, the two languages having many words with identical terminations ; the numerous names of Hebrew origin, such as Jonas, David, Samson, Solomon, being heard among the Calchaquies in the provinces of Tucuman, Chaco, etc. Noticeable in this connection are the terminations of the names of magnates in both countries, which invariably end with the reverential participle "Trin."

Captain Behring also stated that he met a Jesuit priest who informed him that he knew an Indian woman belonging to the Arona nation, whom he had baptized in Canada, and who, in answer to his inquiry as to how she came there, assured him that she had come *overland* as a slave.

The peopling of Assyria and Media, eventually spreading to Russia and Chinese Tartary, is said by the same chroniclers to be due to Teglatfalasar and his son Salmanasar, kings of Assyria, who carried away captive numbers of the tribes of Gilead, Reuben, Gad, Zabulon, and Naphtali, as also of the other five tribes composing the Israelitish nation. This latter is the final link in the chain of evidence which connects the modern Peruvian with the lost tribes of Israel.

Be his origin what it may, there is little to find

fault with in the life led by the Serraño.   Provided that the cultivation of the small plot of arable land usually to be found reclaimable in the *quevradas*, or mountain valleys, produces sufficient to maintain himself and family, he is content, especially if he can supplement it by keeping a small flock of llamas.   As a rule he is sober and industrious, and his ambition is limited to the being allowed to be happy in his own way, and live as he likes, without being impoverished by the exactions of the authorities, often onerous and difficult to satisfy.

Like most mountaineers, he is fond of his home and imbued with a reverence for the traditions of his race, and he prefers to live quietly where his ancestors lived before him rather than to court wealth in the more prosperous towns and coast settlements, where he would be despised by his fellow-townsmen, the white men.   " Liberty and thistles " is his motto, and as thistles go, his share is a succulent species.

If the Indians of the Sierra may be accused of any kind of hurtful self-indulgence, it must be that of chewing coca leaves.   The coca tree (*Erythroxylon coca*) is a low shrub with bright green leaves and white blossoms, which blossoms are succeeded by small scarlet berries.   The Indians masticate this coca. Each individual carries a small leathern pouch called the *huallqui*, or the *chuspa*, and a small flask gourd called *ishcupuru*.   The flask contains a supply of coca leaves, and the gourd is filled with pulverized unslaked lime.   Usually four times, but never less than three times a day does the Indian stop his work for the purpose of chewing this coca. The operation (which is termed *chucchar*, or *acullicar*) is thus performed. Some of the coca leaves, the stalk having been carefully removed, are chewed till they form a small ball, or, as it is called, an *acullico*. A thin strip of damp wood is then thrust into the lime gourd ; when drawn out with some portion of lime adhering, it is thrust again and again into the ball of coca leaves which still remains in the mouth, until the lime is sufficiently mixed with it to give a proper relish. The abundant flow of saliva thus generated is partly expectorated and partly swallowed. When the ball ceases to emit juice it is thrown away, and a new one made by the mastication of a fresh mouthful of coca leaves. The application of the unslaked lime requires some precaution, for should it come into direct contact with the lips or gums, it would cause a very painful burning.

The effect of coca is similar to that of narcotics administered in small doses, and it is a well-known fact that Indians who regularly masticate it require but little food, and nevertheless can go through excessive labour with apparent ease. The incredible fatigue endured by the Peruvian infantry on very spare diet, but with the regular use of coca, the laborious toil of the Indian miner under similar circumstances throughout a long series of years, certainly afford sufficient ground for attributing to these coca leaves the quality, not only of a temporary stimulant, but also of a strong nutritive principle.

It is interesting to note that at a recent meeting of the Royal Botanic Society in Regent's Park, Professor Bentley mentioned a note made by the secretary as to the fruiting of the coca plant in one of the society's greenhouses, for the first time in this country. He mentioned that the generic name of *Theobroma* was given to this plant by Linnæus, and signified "food for the gods." Speaking of the consumption of coca, he said the amount imported in 1820 was only one hundred and twenty-five thousand pounds, in 1866 it had reached four million pounds, in 1873 eight million, and at the present time probably the consumption is not less than twelve million pounds per annum.

, To return to the population on the coast. The middle class is composed of the *mélange*, more or less white-complexioned, which results from the crossing of the indigenous with the pure Spanish and African races. Notwithstanding that Peru is the most republican of all the South American States, in certain respects its aristocracy is composed of the more or less direct descendants of the Spanish colonists, and of the richer classes of creoles.

Speaking generally, the Peruvian is more gay than serious in disposition, more talkative than profound in conversation, not the least addicted to criticising, or joking, or parrying words with his neighbour. He is fond of the society of the fair sex, addicted to games and other amusing pursuits rather than to applying his energies to any serious work. Thus he is often unjustly accused of being an indolent *farceur*. But is not the extent of a man's industry too often measured by the pressure of the necessities which compel him to work? In Peru, the actual necessaries of life are easily obtained, and there is absolutely no comparison to be drawn between the difficulties of earning a living there, and those which are known, alas, to so many in the over-populated countries of Europe.

Fairly to estimate the character of the Peruvian, if we enter on the one side his lack of seriousness and his indolence, we must on the other hand give him credit for a good-natured disposition and a kind heart. He generally makes an affectionate husband, and is devotedly attached to his children. His good nature and willingness to oblige even perfect strangers is remarkable, and by these qualities the writer benefited largely during his travels through all parts of the country. Of the courage and bravery of the race there can be no question. The long and sanguinary war in which they engaged, in order to throw off the hated Spanish yoke; the very acts of personal bravery so often performed in the troubled times of revolution, which, alas, occur so frequently; and the recent four years' war with Chili, in which an old rivalry between kindred races revived ancient blood feuds, and caused one of the most remorseless and blood-thirsty conflicts known in history ;—these place beyond a doubt the natural bravery of the race.

It is generally stated that none of the South American peoples have a literature of their own ; that tied to Spain during nearly three centuries of subjection, by habits, identity of language and beliefs, there are no distinct features in the compositions of the native poets in any of the freed colonies. With respect to Peru, it is urged that the poems, romances, and dramas of Peruvian authors are the exact reflex of that class of inspiration which is wont to animate the Castilian mind. There is much truth in these remarks. The early poets and writers, among whom are reckoned Peralta, Valdez, Cabiedes, Olavidey, Larriva, all natives of Lima, are stamped in a less brilliant degree with the poetic sentiment and inspiration of the land which produced Lope de Vega and Quevedo.

The civil wars which, after the emancipation, followed each other in rapid succession until 1845, were the real obstacles to the progress of literature. But a new literary era for the country began with the publication of the works of Felipe Pardoy Aliaga who is the pride of American literature, and was the cause of many youths applying themselves to the study of *les belles lettres.* Since the days of Felipe Pardo, Peru can boast of a fair list of poets.

The names of Manuel Castillo, Arnaldo Marquez, Adolfo Garcia, Carlos Augusto Salaverry, Manuel A. Segura, are the most distinguished. Salaverry, the dramatic poet, is one of the most popular among his countrymen. Born in 1831, Carlos Salaverry evinced considerable poetic talent even at an early age. It is related that, at the age of fifteen, when he held the rank of cadet in the army, he employed the greater part of his leisure in translating into his own language the works of Shakspeare, Byron, Dante, and Tasso, and in making comments on the "Lusiad." *Arturo*, a drama belonging to the classic and romantic school, was one of his earliest productions, and was acted at the theatre of Lima, where it was much applauded by the audience. *Abel el Pescador* followed *Arturo*. The argument of this play is based upon an ancient tradition of the Incas, and the story abounds with interesting episodes of that time, as likewise *Atahualpa*, in which the author endeavoured to reproduce the most striking scenes of the conquest. Besides his more serious productions, he wrote numerous sonnets, such as the "Kiss in the Glass," of which the concluding stanza will give some idea of the natural beauty of his versification.

> " Mi corazon es tu espejo,
> Y si lo rompe tu amor
> Cadra fibra de dolor
> Tendra entero tu reflejo."

Which may be freely translated thus—

> " Mine heart is thy mirror rare,
> Which, if thy love does break,
> Each pang of grief and care
> The reflection of thyself will take."

The muse of Adolfo Garcia produced many poems which, both as regards language and ideas, must place him in the first rank of Peruvian bards. His poem on "Christopher Columbus," and more especially that on "Bolivar," in which he lauds the great South American liberator in heroic strains, and records his exploits among the majestic scenery of the Cordilleras, is well worth perusal by lovers of Peruvian literature.

As is well known, African blood is widely diffused among the races of the Peruvian littoral, notwithstanding that the negro is so despised by the descendants of the old colonists, who have more or less preserved the whiteness of their complexion ; one can often find traces of the "tar-brush" among the "best" families of the land. The crisp, curly hair, large expressive black eye, full, not to say thick, lips, are some of these evidences which tend to beauty rather than the reverse, as the discolouration of the finger-nails, etc., tends the other way.

The proper designation of the children resulting from the intermarriage of negroes with creoles and others of mixed blood, or with the indigenous population, gives rise to many mistakes, and, as may be expected, occasions much gossip among the relatives of bride and bridegroom. It is said that to "get a rise out of" a white man in these regions, it is only necessary to mix a glass of port wine with another of water, then a glass of the mixture with another of water, till the process being five times repeated, the glass appears to hold water alone. The application of this to his own descent is too much for his equanimity.

The subjoined list of permutations may not be without interest to the ethnologist.

Father.		Mother.		Children.
White	+	Negro	=	Mulatto.
White	+	Indian	=	Mestizo.
White	+	Mulatto	=	Cuarteron. / Quadroon.
White	+	Mestiza	=	Creole (only to be distinguished from a white by a pale brownish complexion).
White	+	China	=	Chino-blanco.
White	+	Quadroon	=	Quintero.
White	+	Quintera	=	White.
Indian	+	Negro	=	Chino.
Indian	+	Mulatto	=	Chino-oscuro.
Indian	+	Mestiza	=	Mestizo-claro (frequently beautiful).
Indian	+	China	=	Chino-cholo.
Indian	+	Zamba	=	Zambo-claro.
Indian	+	China-cholo	=	Indian (with rather short frizzy hair).
Indian	+	Cuarterona or Quintera	=	Mestizo (rather brown).
Negro	+	Mulatta	=	Zambo-negro.
Negro	+	Mestiza	=	Mulatto-oscuro.
Negro	+	China	=	Zambo-chino.
Negro	+	Zamba	=	Zambo-negro.
Negro	+	Cuarterona or Quintera	=	Mulatto (rather dark).
Mulatto	+	Zamba	=	Zambo (miserable race).
Mulatto	+	Mestiza	=	Chino (complexion rather clear).
Mulatto	+	China	=	Chino (rather dark).

This list does not include *all* the half-castes, which, as will be observed, may be multiplied by crossing and recrossing to an extent that would baffle description. As it is, few persons can distinguish other than the most marked types of half-castes in the above list. The colour of the skin is sometimes quite at variance with the characteristic features of the race. The best criterion is the hair, far less deceptive than the complexion.

Despite its republican institution, there prevails throughout Peru a strong pride of caste, which shows itself at every opportunity. In quarrels, for example, the fairer antagonist always taunts the darker one about *descent.* The Indian looks with abhorrence on the negro, the latter returns the compliment, and so on among all the half-castes and mixed races who differ in shades of colour. The taunts are only less bitter as the shades approach each other.

Zambos are the really troublesome members of this strangely mixed population. In them the hereditary vices of each race seem to have attained their utmost degree of development. Their colour is black, sometimes tinged with olive brown; their figures are athletic and powerfully built, the nose less flat than the negro's, but the very prominent lips denote the extreme sensuality of their nature. They commit the most hideous crimes with the utmost indifference, and their lawless propensities are continually bringing them into collision with the constituted authorities. The outlaws, who in troublous times disturb the peace of the haciendados in the large sugar estates of the north, by making a raid on their horses or by robbing travellers in the open country, are chiefly recruited from this class.

The conduct of the negroes and half-castes in Peru, who are mainly descendants of slaves originally brought from Africa, must be interesting to watch by those who hope for the amelioration of the black race. It is notorious that most of the oldest observers of the negro totally disbelieve in the possibility of his passing a certain stage in the path of Christian civilization.

At the present moment, when the English Government is asked to follow the example of the United States, and recognize the flag of the society which the King of the Belgians has formed on the Upper Congo, with the object of " assisting towards the civilization of Central Africa," it is curious to note the opinion of an old English resident on the West Coast of Africa. Writing from Punta de Lenho, in a letter to the *Pall Mall Gazette* of March 25, 1884, Mr. G. C. Phillips begs to remind his readers " that while the coast line is perfectly open, the natives are altogether uncivilized." " Take the three places," he continues, " Goboon under the French rule, Loanda under the Portuguese, and Banana under the natives, places perfectly ' free ' to the influences of civilization, and you will find that the mere planting of ' stations ' has not the slightest effect upon the native character. If any imparter of civilization desires scope for his labours, he can go to either of these places ; he will find an ample field for exertion. Why should he expect that 'stations' in the interior will be more effective than on the coast ?"

This, if not an exaggerated picture, is not encouraging to the great numbers who have in a most praiseworthy manner assisted the work of African missionaries, under the belief that the negro possesses, equally with the white man, a mind which for its expansion only needs to hear His words and gospel, and to have a good example set him. Perhaps if there were also taken into account the centuries of barbarism through which the race has struggled, we should better realize the fact that many years and much patience must needs be spent on them before they can be "educated up to" the pitch of civilization which surrounds us from our cradles, and insensibly becomes part of our very being.

It has been the author's object in these pages to set before his readers as exact a description as words will convey of what he saw in Peru with his own eyes, to draw, so to speak, verbal pictures of its valleys, deserts, and mountains, and of the interesting races composing its population. He was himself strongly impressed with the beauty and novelty of nearly everything he encountered in his wanderings. If any interest attend the tale of his wanderings, it must be due to the marvellous forms and peculiar characteristics of nature and humanity in this corner of our busy world, rather than to his own power of description.

As to lovely scenes, perhaps few in Peru are more to be admired than a native *chacra*, or farm, at harvest-time. Who among those who have seen it can forget the rows of thickly leaved orange trees, laden with bright golden fruit, dotted amidst the dark green foliage; the plots of fresh young lucerne and the larger plantations of sugar-cane, from which a peculiar sighing music proceeds as the long leaves are swayed to and fro in the afternoon breeze; the sudden screech overhead which denotes the flight of bright-coloured parrots making a raid on the adjoining field of maize, whose golden "cobs" are ripe for plucking; the sparkling water of the irrigation canals as it trickles on, giving life and nourishment to all this beautiful vegetation; the brown hairless faces of the cholos, dressed in white, bending over their separate tasks, or grouped together at their afternoon meal in the shade of a clump of bananas;—the whole scene illuminated by the bright Western sun, which warms the atmosphere and one's self? Could the Garden of Eden have been lovelier than this?

But the *chacra* is not only beautiful to view, it is also very productive when skilfully managed; for skill and a sufficiency of water are the only things needed for success in farming on a rich virgin soil such as this, and in a land where there are no extremes of climatic variation. Besides sugar-cane and

Indian corn, which are the principal crops, rice is extensively planted in the valleys where water is plentiful. The seeds of the rice grown in Peru are much larger, heavier, and whiter than that brought from India. Native rice is therefore in greater demand, and, in consequence, fetches the highest price in the market.

Among the root crops of the *chacra* figure *camotes* (*Convolvulus batatas*), which are sometimes called sweet potatoes. There are two kinds of *camotes*, the yellow and the violet; both are much liked for their excellent flavour. The *Aracacha* (*Conium moschatum*) is a very agreeable and nutritious kind of tuberous vegetable, in flavour not unlike celery. It is cooked by being simply boiled in water, or made into a kind of soup.

The *Yucca* (*Jatropha manihot*) is one of the finest vegetables of Peru; the roots, which are the edible part of the plant, grow from one to two feet long, and are somewhat of a turnip form. They are very agreeable in taste and easy of digestion, and from them sometimes a fine flour is prepared, which is used for making certain kinds of bread and biscuits.

Among the pulse there are different kinds of peas (*garbanzos*) on the coast, and beans (*frijoles*) on the higher grounds. The climate suits all vegetables of the cabbage and salad kinds which are so largely cultivated in Europe. The tomato (or love apple) and the *Aji* (Spanish pepper) are some of the edibles which serve for spicery. The olive is cultivated chiefly in the southern provinces, and its fruit approximates in flavour to the Spanish olive. The castor-oil plant (*Ricinus communis*) grows wild, and, in districts where the ground is marshy, in great profusion. The oil which is pressed out of the seeds is used for lighting purposes, and for greasing the machines employed at the sugar-mill.

The fruits of Southern Europe thrive luxuriantly in the warm climate of Peru. Lemons, oranges, pomegranates, limes and water-melons, and figs are seen nearly everywhere in great abundance.

Among the tropical fruits ranks first the *chirimoya* (*Anona tripetala*), which has already been described. The *palta* (*Persea gatissima*) is a fruit of the pear form, and dark brown or green in colour. The edible substance is soft and green, and is sometimes called "Peruvian butter." It dissolves in the mouth as easily as butter; and when quite ripe is scooped out with a teaspoon, and eaten like cream. *Platanos* (bananas) thrive well nearly everywhere; the favourite way to eat them is fried with meat, like broccoli at home. The *granadilla* (*Passiflora quadrangularis*) is about the size of an apple, but oblong in shape; the skin is reddish yellow, hard and rather thick. The edible part is grey and gelatinous, and contains a quantity of black seeds, which are embedded in the fruit. The fruit tastes like gooseberry, and is very pleasant and cooling. The *granadilla* is a climbing shrub, and twines itself round the trunks of trees or climbs up the walls of houses.

The *pacay* is the fruit of a large-sized tree (*Prosopis dulcis*), with a rather low and broad top. It consists of a pod from twenty to thirty inches long, enclosing black seeds buried in a white, soft, flaky substance. This coating, which is as white as snow, is the eatable part of the fruit ; its taste is sweet and somewhat insipid. *Tunas* are fruits of different species of cactus. The husk, which is covered with sharp prickles, is green or yellow, or red in colour, and is easily separated from the pulp, which is of the consistency of cream cheese, with a pleasant sweet taste.

The *guayava* (*Psidium pomiferum*) grows on a low shrub, and the fruit is in form and size like a large orange. The rind is bright yellow, and thin ; the pulp is either white or red, and is full of little' egg-shaped granulations. The fruit dissolves in the mouth ; its flavour is somewhat acid when not quite ripe.

The *Pepino* (a *cucurbitacea*) is grown in great abundance in the fields. The plant is only about eighteen inches high, and it creeps along the ground. The fruit is from four to five inches long, cylindrical and pointed at both ends, something like a cucumber ; the husk is of a yellowish green colour, with long rose-coloured stripes, and the pulp or edible part is solid, juicy, and well flavoured.

The *Mani*, or earth almond (*Arachis hypogæa*), is grown in the northern provinces. The plant is from eighteen inches to two feet high, and very leafy ; the kernels have a grey, shrivelled husk ; they are white and contain much oil. Often they are eaten with sugar, after being roasted or crushed.

The *capulies* (*Prunus capulin*) grows in the open fields ; the fruit, which is of a deep yellow colour, and has an acid taste, is a little bigger than a cherry. On account of their very pleasant odour, they are frequently used in making *Pucheros de flores* (China bowls filled with dried flowers), or with other sweet-smelling flowers are besprinkled with *agua rica*, and laid in drawers to perfume linen. Peruvian ladies often wear these fruits.

The *Palillos* (*Campomanesia lineatifolia*) grows in trees from twenty to thirty feet in height. The fruit is bright yellow in colour, and about the size of a moderate-sized apple, sweet and pleasant to the taste ; and its scent is delicious. It is used for making per-fumed water. When rubbed between the fingers, the leaves smell like those of myrtle.

Owing to her great natural resources, Peru has been often and justly described as one of the richest countries of the globe. But the possession of un-limited wealth does not always bring with it pros-perity and power. The position of England as certainly the wealthiest and perhaps the most power-ful nation in the world is not alone due to the immense stores of coal and iron contained in her soil, important as the possession of those minerals has been to her advancement. Had not Englishmen shown energy in digging out and utilizing these valuable deposits, our coal and iron would probably have become mortgaged, like the guano of Peru, as security for loans of money from some more energetic race than our own. In such a case, the load of debt and obligation might have had the usual result of crippling action and preventing progress in whatever direction we might have tried to expand our natural growth.

The stories of the immense quantities of gold and silver which the Peruvian mines yielded in former days have not, it is thought, been unduly exaggerated. It is generally admitted by mineralogists who have visited the mining districts of the Cerro de Pasco and Huancalvelica and Janja, that the disused workings probably yielded in full the fabulous wealth accredited to them in the old Spanish records. Indeed, at the present time, there are many silver mines worked which repay their cost handsomely to the owners, and fresh veins of silver ore are constantly being discovered. The principal things necessary to success in Peruvian mining are good roads to provide cheap means of transit for the ores, and the provisions and requirements of the miners. It is to be hoped that some of the railways, the construction of which has caused so large an outlay, may contribute largely to the development of the mining industry.

In addition to minerals and sugar, the long list of miscellaneous exports from Peru testify to the fecundity of its soil, which, influenced by varying conditions of climate, is capable of producing nearly all the numerous articles of consumption used by man. The productions of the Sierra are not in importance behind those of the sea-coast. Skins of the llama, alpaca, huanuca, and of the vicuña, bundles of Peruvian bark, packages of feathers of all hues and sizes, coffee, and cocoa, tobacco, the dried flesh of sheep, roe-deer, and oxen, are only a few of the products of the Cordillera, to which reference has been made in this volume.

To the antiquarian Peru is, comparatively speaking, a new field ready to hand for his researches, and it is worthy of Dr. Schliemann's best attention whenever he shall quite have finished exploring the ruins of Tiryns.

The author must confess that he can gather but little reliable information about the ancient inhabitants of Peru, notwithstanding all the researches that have been made since the Spanish conquest. Clearly this may be attributed to the fact that antiquarian research undertaken seriously and on a large scale, with a definite object in view, is practically a modern pursuit.

In Peru, the early explorers and those that followed in their footsteps were content with probing some of the most prominent and easily reached *huacas*, or burial-mounds, to see if they contained anything worth carrying away. If their first efforts were unsuccessful, they speedily packed up their tools and sought "fresh fields and pastures new."

Perhaps there is no field which, apart from its historical interest, offers so great a temptation to the explorer as Peru. Here there is at least the *chance* of recouping one's self for all the labour and expense by the discovery of treasures which, as all ancient records tend to show, were concealed by the Incas. The tradition of the treasures amassed at Cajamarca for the payment of Atahualpa's ransom to Pizarro, is firmly believed to this day by both Peruvian and Spanish chroniclers.

The price offered by the king for his liberty was the undertaking to fill the cell in which he was confined with gold, up to a certain line on the wall, which Pizarro marked with his sword. The cell measured twenty-two feet by seventeen, and the height to which it was to be filled with gold is stated at about four feet from the ground.

Atahualpa ordered all the gold available in Cajamarca and its vicinity to be collected ; but when piled up on the floor of the cell, it did not reach above half-way up to the mark. Messengers were dispatched to obtain the gold required for completing the deficiency from the royal treasures at Cuzco, and it is said that eleven thousand llamas, each laden with one hundred pounds weight of gold, were started on the road to Cajamarca. But before the treasure reached its destination the unfortunate Atahualpa was hanged by his impatient conqueror, and the news spreading swiftly across the Cordillera, reached the train of gold-bearers. The tradition ends by saying that the dismayed Indians concealed all this treasure, and then dispersed.

In taking leave of his readers, the author would express a hope that the account of his experiences and travels in Peru may prove a slight means of diffusing some additional knowledge respecting that interesting country and its inhabitants, who, though misguided in some respects, possess many praiseworthy and encouraging qualities. With the spread of education, it is to be hoped that public opinion may become more hopeful, and that the government of the country, like our own, may daily realize more and more the responsibility placed in their hands. If Peru will but be " true to herself" and recognize the great fact that prosperity is largely dependent upon good faith and credit before the eyes of the civilized world, she has yet a future before her, and may fill her natural place, an honourable one among the independent nations of South America. That *should* be hers if she takes for her motto the safe one put into clear words by one who knew human nature perhaps as thoroughly as any of our great writers, and more than most.

> " This above all, to thine own self be true,
> And it shall follow as the night the day,
> Thou canst not then be false to any man."
>
> SHAKSPEARE.

FINIS.

PRINTED BY WILLIAM CLOWES AND SONS, LIMITED,
LONDON AND BECCLES.

PRINTED BY WILLIAM CLOWES AND SONS, LIMITED,
LONDON AND BECCLES.

A LIST OF

KEGAN PAUL, TRENCH & CO.'S

PUBLICATIONS.

1, Paternoster Square,
London.

A LIST OF
KEGAN PAUL, TRENCH & CO.'S
PUBLICATIONS.

CONTENTS.

GENERAL LITERATURE.

ADAMSON, H. T., B.D.—The Truth as it is in Jesus. Crown 8vo, 8s. 6d.

The Three Sevens. Crown 8vo, 5s. 6d.

The Millennium; or, The Mystery of God Finished. Crown 8vo, 6s.

A. K. H. B.—From a Quiet Place. A Volume of Sermons. Crown 8vo, 5s.

ALLEN, Rev. R., M.A.—Abraham: his Life, Times, and Travels, 3800 years ago. With Map. Second Edition. Post 8vo, 6s.

ALLIES, T. W., M.A.—Per Crucem ad Lucem. The Result of a Life. 2 vols. Demy 8vo, 25s.

A Life's Decision. Crown 8vo, 7s. 6d.

AMOS, Professor Sheldon.—The History and Principles of the Civil Law of Rome. An aid to the Study of Scientific and Comparative Jurisprudence. Demy 8vo. 16s.

ANDERDON, Rev. W. H.—Fasti Apostolici; a Chronology of the Years between the Ascension of our Lord and the Martyrdom of SS. Peter and Paul. Second Edition. Enlarged. Square 8vo, 5s.

Evenings with the Saints. Crown 8vo, 5s.

ANDERSON, David.—"Scenes" in the Commons. Crown 8vo, 5*s*.

ARMSTRONG, Richard A., B.A.—Latter-Day Teachers. Six Lectures. Small crown 8vo, 2*s*. 6*d*.

AUBERTIN, J. J.—A Flight to Mexico. With Seven full-page Illustrations and a Railway Map of Mexico. Crown 8vo, 7*s*. 6*d*.

BADGER, George Percy, D.C.L.—An English-Arabic Lexicon. In which the equivalent for English Words and Idiomatic Sentences are rendered into literary and colloquial Arabic. Royal 4to, 80*s*.

BAGEHOT, Walter.—The English Constitution. New and Revised Edition. Crown 8vo, 7*s*. 6*d*.

    Lombard Street. A Description of the Money Market. Eighth Edition. Crown 8vo, 7*s*. 6*d*.

    Essays on Parliamentary Reform. Crown 8vo, 5*s*.

    Some Articles on the Depreciation of Silver, and Topics connected with it. Demy 8vo, 5*s*.

BAGENAL, Philip H.—The American-Irish and their Influence on Irish Politics. Crown 8vo, 5*s*.

BAGOT, Alan, C.E.—Accidents in Mines: their Causes and Prevention. Crown 8vo, 6*s*.

    The Principles of Colliery Ventilation. Second Edition, greatly enlarged. Crown 8vo, 5*s*.

BAKER, Sir Sherston, Bart.—The Laws relating to Quarantine. Crown 8vo, 12*s*. 6*d*.

BALDWIN, Capt. J. H.—The Large and Small Game of Bengal and the North-Western Provinces of India. With 20 Illustrations. New and Cheaper Edition. Small 4to, 10*s*. 6*d*.

BALLIN, Ada S. and F. L.—A Hebrew Grammar. With Exercises selected from the Bible. Crown 8vo, 7*s*. 6*d*.

BARCLAY, Edgar.—Mountain Life in Algeria. With numerous Illustrations by Photogravure. Crown 4to, 16*s*.

BARLOW, James H.—The Ultimatum of Pessimism. An Ethical Study. Demy 8vo, 6*s*.

BARNES, William.—Outlines of Redecraft (Logic). With English Wording. Crown 8vo, 3*s*.

BAUR, Ferdinand, Dr. Ph.—A Philological Introduction to Greek and Latin for Students. Translated and adapted from the German, by C. KEGAN PAUL, M.A., and E. D. STONE, M.A. Third Edition. Crown 8vo, 6*s*.

BELLARS, Rev. W.—The Testimony of Conscience to the Truth and Divine Origin of the Christian Revelation. Burney Prize Essay. Small crown 8vo, 3*s*. 6*d*.

BELLINGHAM, Henry, M.P.—Social Aspects of Catholicism and Protestantism in their Civil Bearing upon Nations. Translated and adapted from the French of M. le BARON DE HAULLEVILLE. With a preface by His Eminence CARDINAL MANNING. Second and Cheaper Edition. Crown 8vo, 3*s.* 6*d.*

BELLINGHAM, H. Belsches Graham.—Ups and Downs of Spanish Travel. Second Edition. Crown 8vo, 5*s.*

BENN, Alfred W.—The Greek Philosophers. 2 vols. Demy 8vo, 28*s.*

BENT, J. Theodore.—Genoa: How the Republic Rose and Fell. With 18 Illustrations. Demy 8vo, 18*s.*

BLACKLEY, Rev. W. S.—Essays on Pauperism. 16mo. Cloth, 1*s.* 6*d.* ; sewed, 1*s.*

BLECKLEY, Henry. — Socrates and the Athenians: An Apology. Crown 8vo, 2*s.* 6*d.*

BLOOMFIELD, The Lady.—Reminiscences of Court and Diplomatic Life. With 3 Portraits and 6 Illustrations. Sixth Edition. 2 vols., 8vo, cloth, 28*s.*

*** New and Cheaper Edition. With Frontispiece. Crown 8vo, 6*s.*

BLUNT, The Ven. Archdeacon.—The Divine Patriot, and other Sermons. Preached in Scarborough and in Cannes. New and Cheaper Edition. Crown 8vo, 4*s.* 6*d.*

BLUNT, Wilfred S.—The Future of Islam. Crown 8vo, 6*s.*

BOOLE, Mary.—Symbolical Methods of Study. Crown 8vo, 5*s.*

BOUVERIE-PUSEY, S. E. B.—Permanence and Evolution. An Inquiry into the Supposed Mutability of Animal Types. Crown 8vo, 5*s.*

BOWEN, H. C., M.A.—Studies in English. For the use of Modern Schools. Seventh Thousand. Small crown 8vo, 1*s.* 6*d.*

English Grammar for Beginners. Fcap. 8vo, 1*s.*

BRADLEY, F. H.—The Principles of Logic. Demy 8vo, 16*s.*

BRIDGETT, Rev. T. E.—History of the Holy Eucharist in Great Britain. 2 vols. Demy 8vo, 18*s.*

BRODRICK, the Hon. G. C.—Political Studies. Demy 8vo, 14*s.*

BROOKE, Rev. S. A.—Life and Letters of the Late Rev. F. W. Robertson, M.A. Edited by.

    I. Uniform with Robertson's Sermons. 2 vols. With Steel Portrait. 7*s.* 6*d.*
    II. Library Edition. With Portrait. 8vo, 12*s.*
    III. A Popular Edition. In 1 vol., 8vo, 6*s.*

BROOKE, *Rev. S. A.—Continued.*

> **The Fight of Faith.** Sermons preached on various occasions. Fifth Edition. Crown 8vo, 7s. 6d.

> **The Spirit of the Christian Life.** New and Cheaper Edition. Crown 8vo, 5s.

> **Theology in the English Poets.**—Cowper, Coleridge, Wordsworth, and Burns. Fifth and Cheaper Edition. Post 8vo, 5s.

> **Christ in Modern Life.** Sixteenth and Cheaper Edition. Crown 8vo, 5s.

> **Sermons.** First Series. Thirteenth and Cheaper Edition. Crown 8vo, 5s.

> **Sermons.** Second Series. Sixth and Cheaper Edition. Crown 8vo, 5s.

BROWN, *Rev. J. Baldwin, B.A.*—**The Higher Life.** Its Reality, Experience, and Destiny. Sixth Edition. Crown 8vo, 5s.

> **Doctrine of Annihilation in the Light of the Gospel of Love.** Five Discourses. Fourth Edition. Crown 8vo, 2s. 6d.

> **The Christian Policy of Life.** A Book for Young Men of Business. Third Edition. Crown 8vo, 3s. 6d.

BROWN, *S. Borton, B.A.*—**The Fire Baptism of all Flesh;** or, The Coming Spiritual Crisis of the Dispensation. Crown 8vo, 6s.

BROWN, *Horatio F.*—**Life on the Lagoons.** With two Illustrations and Map. Crown 8vo, 6s.

BROWNBILL, *John.*—**Principles of English Canon Law.** Part I. General Introduction. Crown 8vo, 6s.

BROWNE, *W. R.*—**The Inspiration of the New Testament.** With a Preface by the Rev. J. P. NORRIS, D.D. Fcap. 8vo, 2s. 6d.

BURDETT, *Henry C.*—**Hints in Sickness—Where to Go and What to Do.** Crown 8vo, 1s. 6d.

BURTON, *Mrs. Richard.*—**The Inner Life of Syria, Palestine, and the Holy Land.** Cheaper Edition in one volume. Large post 8vo. 7s. 6d.

BUSBECQ, *Ogier Ghiselin de.*—**His Life and Letters.** By CHARLES THORNTON FORSTER, M.A., and F. H. BLACKBURNE DANIELL, M.A. 2 vols. With Frontispieces. Demy 8vo, 24s.

CARPENTER, *W. B., LL.D., M.D., F.R.S., etc.*—**The Principles of Mental Physiology.** With their Applications to the Training and Discipline of the Mind, and the Study of its Morbid Conditions. Illustrated. Sixth Edition. 8vo, 12s.

Catholic Dictionary. Containing some account of the Doctrine, Discipline, Rites, Ceremonies, Councils, and Religious Orders of the Catholic Church. By WILLIAM E. ADDIS and THOMAS ARNOLD, M.A. Second Edition. Demy 8vo, 21s.

CERVANTES.—Journey to Parnassus. Spanish Text, with Translation into English Tercets, Preface, and Illustrative Notes, by JAMES Y. GIBSON. Crown 8vo, 12*s.*

CHEYNE, Rev. T. K.—The Prophecies of Isaiah. Translated with Critical Notes and Dissertations. 2 vols. Third Edition. Demy 8vo, 25*s.*

CLAIRAUT.—Elements of Geometry. Translated by Dr. KAINES. With 145 Figures. Crown 8vo, 4*s.* 6*d.*

CLAYDEN, P. W.—England under Lord Beaconsfield. The Political History of the Last Six Years, from the end of 1873 to the beginning of 1880. Second Edition, with Index and continuation to March, 1880. Demy 8vo, 16*s.*

Samuel Sharpe. Egyptologist and Translator of the Bible. Crown 8vo, 6*s.*

CLIFFORD, Samuel.—What Think Ye of the Christ? Crown 8vo, 6*s.*

CLODD, Edward, F.R.A.S.—The Childhood of the World : a Simple Account of Man in Early Times. Seventh Edition. Crown 8vo, 3*s.*
A Special Edition for Schools. 1*s.*

The Childhood of Religions. Including a Simple Account of the Birth and Growth of Myths and Legends. Eighth Thousand. Crown 8vo, 5*s.*
A Special Edition for Schools. 1*s.* 6*d.*

Jesus of Nazareth. With a brief sketch of Jewish History to the Time of His Birth. Small crown 8vo, 6*s.*

COGHLAN, J. Cole, D.D.—The Modern Pharisee and other Sermons. Edited by the Very Rev. H. H. DICKINSON, D.D., Dean of Chapel Royal, Dublin. New and Cheaper Edition. Crown 8vo, 7*s.* 6*d.*

COLERIDGE, Sara.—Memoir and Letters of Sara Coleridge. Edited by her Daughter. With Index. Cheap Edition. With Portrait. 7*s.* 6*d.*

Collects Exemplified. Being Illustrations from the Old and New Testaments of the Collects for the Sundays after Trinity. By the Author of " A Commentary on the Epistles and Gospels." Edited by the Rev. JOSEPH JACKSON. Crown 8vo, 5*s.*

CONNELL, A. K.—Discontent and Danger in India. Small crown 8vo, 3*s.* 6*d.*

The Economic Revolution of India. Crown 8vo, 4*s.* 6*d.*

CORY, William.—A Guide to Modern English History. Part I.—MDCCCXV.-MDCCCXXX. Demy 8vo, 9*s.* Part II.—MDCCCXXX.-MDCCCXXXV., 15*s.*.

COTTERILL, H. B.—An Introduction to the Study of Poetry. Crown 8vo, 7*s.* 6*d.*

COX, Rev. Sir George W., M.A., Bart.—A History of Greece from the Earliest Period to the end of the Persian War. New Edition. 2 vols. Demy 8vo, 36*s.*

The Mythology of the Aryan Nations. New Edition. Demy 8vo, 16*s.*

Tales of Ancient Greece. New Edition. Small crown 8vo, 6*s.*

A Manual of Mythology in the form of Question and Answer. New Edition. Fcap. 8vo, 3*s.*

An Introduction to the Science of Comparative Mythology and Folk-Lore. Second Edition. Crown 8vo. 7*s.* 6*d.*

COX, Rev. Sir G. W., M.A., Bart., and JONES, Eustace Hinton.—Popular Romances of the Middle Ages. Third Edition, in 1 vol. Crown 8vo, 6*s.*

COX, Rev. Samuel, D.D.—Salvator Mundi ; or, Is Christ the Saviour of all Men? Eighth Edition. Crown 8vo, 5*s.*

The Genesis of Evil, and other Sermons, mainly expository. Third Edition. Crown 8vo, 6*s.*

A Commentary on the Book of Job. With a Translation. Demy 8vo, 15*s.*

The Larger Hope. A Sequel to "Salvator Mundi." 16mo, 1*s.*

CRAVEN, Mrs.—A Year's Meditations. Crown 8vo, 6*s.*

CRAWFURD, Oswald.—Portugal, Old and New. With Illustrations and Maps. New and Cheaper Edition. Crown 8vo, 6*s.*

CROZIER, John Beattie, M.B.—The Religion of the Future. Crown 8vo, 6*s.*

DANIELL, Clarmont.—The Gold Treasure of India. An Inquiry into its Amount, the Cause of its Accumulation, and the Proper Means of using it as Money. Crown 8vo, 5*s.*

Darkness and Dawn : the Peaceful Birth of a New Age. Small crown 8vo, 2*s.* 6*d.*

DAVIDSON, Rev. Samuel, D.D., LL.D.—Canon of the Bible : Its Formation, History, and Fluctuations. Third and Revised Edition. Small crown 8vo, 5*s.*

The Doctrine of Last Things contained in the New Testament compared with the Notions of the Jews and the Statements of Church Creeds. Small crown 8vo, 3*s.* 6*d.*

DAVIDSON, Thomas.—The Parthenon Frieze, and other Essays. Crown 8vo, 6*s.*

DAWSON, Geo., M.A. Prayers, with a Discourse on Prayer. Edited by his Wife. First Series. Eighth Edition. Crown 8vo, 6*s.*

Prayers, with a Discourse on Prayer. Edited by GEORGE St. CLAIR. Second Series. Crown 8vo, 6*s.*

DAWSON, Geo., M.A.—continued.

Sermons on Disputed Points and Special Occasions. Edited by his Wife. Fourth Edition. Crown 8vo, 6s.

Sermons on Daily Life and Duty. Edited by his Wife. Fourth Edition. Crown 8vo, 6s.

The Authentic Gospel, and other Sermons. Edited by GEORGE ST. CLAIR. Third Edition. Crown 8vo, 6s.

Three Books of God: Nature, History, and Scripture. Sermons edited by GEORGE ST. CLAIR. Crown 8vo, 6s.

DE JONCOURT, Madame Marie.—Wholesome Cookery. Second Edition. Crown 8vo, 3s. 6d.

DE LONG, Lieut. Com. G. W.—The Voyage of the Jeannette. The Ship and Ice Journals of. Edited by his Wife, EMMA DE LONG. With Portraits, Maps, and many Illustrations on wood and stone. 2 vols. Demy 8vo, 36s.

DESPREZ, Philip S., B.D.—Daniel and John ; or, The Apocalypse of the Old and that of the New Testament. Demy 8vo, 12s.

DEVEREUX, W. Cope, R.N., F.R.G.S.—Fair Italy, the Riviera, and Monte Carlo. Comprising a Tour through North and South Italy and Sicily, with a short account of Malta. Crown 8vo, 6s.

DOWDEN, Edward, LL.D.—Shakspere: a Critical Study of his Mind and Art. Seventh Edition. Post 8vo, 12s.

Studies in Literature, 1789–1877. Third Edition. Large post 8vo, 6s.

DUFFIELD, A. J.—Don Quixote: his Critics and Commentators. With a brief account of the minor works of MIGUEL DE CERVANTES SAAVEDRA, and a statement of the aim and end of the greatest of them all. A handy book for general readers. Crown 8vo, 3s. 6d.

DU MONCEL, Count.—The Telephone, the Microphone, and the Phonograph. With 74 Illustrations. Second Edition. Small crown 8vo, 5s.

DURUY, Victor.—History of Rome and the Roman People. Edited by Prof. MAHAFFY. With nearly 3000 Illustrations. 4to. Vol. I. in 2 parts, 30s.

EDGEWORTH, F. Y.—Mathematical Psychics. An Essay on the Application of Mathematics to Social Science. Demy 8vo, 7s. 6d.

Educational Code of the Prussian Nation, in its Present Form. In accordance with the Decisions of the Common Provincial Law, and with those of Recent Legislation. Crown 8vo, 2s. 6d.

Education Library. Edited by PHILIP MAGNUS :—

> An Introduction to the History of Educational Theories. By OSCAR BROWNING, M.A. Second Edition. 3*s.* 6*d.*

> Old Greek Education. By the Rev. Prof. MAHAFFY, M.A. Second Edition. 3*s.* 6*d.*

> School Management. Including a general view of the work of Education, Organization and Discipline. By JOSEPH LANDON. Third Edition. 6*s.*

Eighteenth Century Essays. Selected and Edited by AUSTIN DOBSON. With a Miniature Frontispiece by R. Caldecott. Parchment Library Edition, 6*s.* ; vellum, 7*s.* 6*d.*

ELSDALE, Henry.—Studies in Tennyson's Idylls. Crown 8vo, 5*s.*

ELYOT, Sir Thomas.—The Boke named the Gouernour. Edited from the First Edition of 1531 by HENRY HERBERT STEPHEN CROFT, M.A., Barrister-at-Law. With Portraits of Sir Thomas and Lady Elyot, copied by permission of her Majesty from Holbein's Original Drawings at Windsor Castle. 2 vols. Fcap. 4to, 50*s.*

Enoch the Prophet. The Book of. Archbishop LAURENCE's Translation, with an Introduction by the Author of " The Evolution of Christianity." Crown 8vo, 5*s.*

Eranus. A Collection of Exercises in the Alcaic and Sapphic Metres. Edited by F. W. CORNISH, Assistant Master at Eton. Second Edition. Crown 8vo, 2*s.*

EVANS, Mark.—The Story of Our Father's Love, told to Children. Sixth and Cheaper Edition. With Four Illustrations. Fcap. 8vo, 1*s.* 6*d.*

> A Book of Common Prayer and Worship for Household Use, compiled exclusively from the Holy Scriptures. Second Edition. Fcap. 8vo, 1*s.*

> The Gospel of Home Life. Crown 8vo, 4*s.* 6*d.*

> The King's Story-Book. In Three Parts. Fcap. 8vo, 1*s.* 6*d.* each.

> *** Parts I. and II. with Eight Illustrations and Two Picture Maps, now ready.

"Fan Kwae" at Canton before Treaty Days 1825–1844. By an old Resident. With Frontispiece. Crown 8vo, 5*s.*

FLECKER, Rev. Eliezer.—Scripture Onomatology. Being Critical Notes on the Septuagint and other Versions. Second Edition. Crown 8vo, 3*s.* 6*d.*

FLOREDICE, W. H.—A Month among the Mere Irish. Small crown 8vo, 5*s.*

FOWLE, Rev. T. W.—The Divine Legation of Christ. Crown 8vo, 7s.

FULLER, Rev. Morris.—The Lord's Day ; or, Christian Sunday. Its Unity, History, Philosophy, and Perpetual Obligation. Sermons. Demy 8vo, 10s. 6d.

GARDINER, Samuel R., and J. BASS MULLINGER, M.A.—Introduction to the Study of English History. Second Edition. Large crown 8vo, 9s.

GARDNER, Dorsey.—Quatre Bras, Ligny, and Waterloo. A Narrative of the Campaign in Belgium, 1815. With Maps and Plans. Demy 8vo, 16s.

.Genesis in Advance of Present Science. A Critical Investigation of Chapters I.–IX. By a Septuagenarian Beneficed Presbyter. Demy 8vo. 10s. 6d.

GENNA, E.—Irresponsible Philanthropists. Being some Chapters on the Employment of Gentlewomen. Small crown 8vo, 2s. 6d.

GEORGE, Henry.—Progress and Poverty : An Inquiry into the Causes of Industrial Depressions, and of Increase of Want with Increase of Wealth. The Remedy. Fifth Library Edition. Post 8vo, 7s. 6d. Cabinet Edition. Crown 8vo, 2s. 6d. Also a Cheap Edition. Limp cloth, 1s. 6d. Paper covers, 1s.

   Social Problems. Fourth Thousand. Crown 8vo, 5s. Cheap Edition. Sewed, 1s.

GIBSON, James Y.—Journey to Parnassus. Composed by MIGUEL DE CERVANTES SAAVEDRA. Spanish Text, with Translation into English Tercets, Preface, and Illustrative Notes, by. Crown 8vo, 12s.

Glossary of Terms and Phrases. Edited by the Rev. H. PERCY SMITH and others. Medium 8vo, 12s.

GLOVER, F., M.A.—Exempla Latina. A First Construing Book, with Short Notes, Lexicon, and an Introduction to the Analysis of Sentences. Second Edition. Fcap. 8vo, 2s.

GOLDSMID, Sir Francis Henry, Bart., Q.C., M.P.—Memoir of. With Portrait. Second Edition, Revised. Crown 8vo, 6s.

GOODENOUGH, Commodore J. G.—Memoir of, with Extracts from his Letters and Journals. Edited by his Widow. With Steel Engraved Portrait. Third Edition. Crown 8vo, 5s.

GOSSE, Edmund W.—Studies in the Literature of Northern Europe. With a Frontispiece designed and etched by Alma Tadema. New and Cheaper Edition. Large crown 8vo, 6s.

   Seventeenth Century Studies. A Contribution to the History of English Poetry. Demy 8vo, 10s. 6d.

GOULD, Rev. S. Baring, M.A.—Germany, Present and Past. New and Cheaper Edition. Large crown 8vo, 7s. 6d.

GOWAN, Major Walter E.—A. Ivanoff's Russian Grammar. (16th Edition.) Translated, enlarged, and arranged for use of Students of the Russian Language. Demy 8vo, 6s.

GOWER, Lord Ronald. My Reminiscences. Second Edition. 2 vols. With Frontispieces. Demy 8vo, 30s.

***** Also a Cheap Edition. With Portraits. Large crown 8vo, 7s. 6d.

GRAHAM, William, M.A.—The Creed of Science, Religious, Moral, and Social. Second Edition, Revised. Crown 8vo, 6s.

GRIFFITH, Thomas, A.M.—The Gospel of the Divine Life: a Study of the Fourth Evangelist. Demy 8vo, 14s.

GRIMLEY, Rev. H. N., M.A.—Tremadoc Sermons, chiefly on the Spiritual Body, the Unseen World, and the Divine Humanity. Fourth Edition. Crown 8vo, 6s.

G. S. B.—A Study of the Prologue and Epilogue in English Literature from Shakespeare to Dryden. Crown 8vo, 5s.

GUSTAFSON, A.—The Foundation of Death. Crown 8vo.

HAECKEL, Prof. Ernst.—The History of Creation. Translation revised by Professor E. RAY LANKESTER, M.A., F.R.S. With Coloured Plates and Genealogical Trees of the various groups of both Plants and Animals. 2 vols. Third Edition. Post 8vo, 32s.

The History of the Evolution of Man. With numerous Illustrations. 2 vols. Post 8vo, 32s.

A Visit to Ceylon. Post 8vo, 7s. 6d.

Freedom in Science and Teaching. With a Prefatory Note by T. H. HUXLEY, F.R.S. Crown 8vo, 5s.

HALF-CROWN SERIES :—

A Lost Love. By ANNA C. OGLE [Ashford Owen].

Sister Dora : a Biography. By MARGARET LONSDALE.

True Words for Brave Men : a Book for Soldiers and Sailors. By the late CHARLES KINGSLEY.

Notes of Travel : being Extracts from the Journals of Count VON MOLTKE.

English Sonnets. Collected and Arranged by J. DENNIS.

London Lyrics. By F. LOCKER.

Home Songs for Quiet Hours. By the Rev. Canon R. H. BAYNES.

HARROP, Robert.—Bolingbroke. A Political Study and Criticism. Demy 8vo, 14s.

HART, Rev. J. W. T.—The Autobiography of Judas Iscariot. A Character Study. Crown 8vo, 3s. 6d.

HAWEIS, Rev. H. R., M.A.—Current Coin. Materialism—The Devil—Crime—Drunkenness—Pauperism—Emotion—Recreation —The Sabbath. Fifth and Cheaper Edition. Crown 8vo, 5*s.*

Arrows in the Air. Fifth and Cheaper Edition. Crown 8vo, 5*s.*

Speech in Season. Fifth and Cheaper Edition. Crown 8vo, 5*s.*

Thoughts for the Times. Thirteenth and Cheaper Edition. Crown 8vo, 5*s.*

Unsectarian Family Prayers. New and Cheaper Edition. Fcap. 8vo, 1*s.* 6*d.*

HAWKINS, Edwards Comerford.—Spirit and Form. Sermons preached in the Parish Church of Leatherhead. Crown 8vo, 6*s.*

HAWTHORNE, Nathaniel.—Works. Complete in Twelve Volumes. Large post 8vo, 7*s.* 6*d.* each volume.

VOL. I. TWICE-TOLD TALES.
II. MOSSES FROM AN OLD MANSE.
III. THE HOUSE OF THE SEVEN GABLES, AND THE SNOW IMAGE.
IV. THE WONDERBOOK, TANGLEWOOD TALES, AND GRAND-FATHER'S CHAIR.
V. THE SCARLET LETTER, AND THE BLITHEDALE ROMANCE.
VI. THE MARBLE FAUN. [Transformation.]
VII. }
VIII. } OUR OLD HOME, AND ENGLISH NOTE-BOOKS.
IX. AMERICAN NOTE-BOOKS.
X. FRENCH AND ITALIAN NOTE-BOOKS.
XI. SEPTIMIUS FELTON, THE DOLLIVER ROMANCE, FANSHAWE, AND, IN AN APPENDIX, THE ANCESTRAL FOOTSTEP.
XII. TALES AND ESSAYS, AND OTHER PAPERS, WITH A BIO-GRAPHICAL SKETCH OF HAWTHORNE.

HAYES, A. A., Junr.—New Colorado, and the Santa Fé Trail. With Map and 60 Illustrations. Square 8vo, 9*s.*

HENNESSY, Sir John Pope.—Ralegh in Ireland. With his Letters on Irish Affairs and some Contemporary Documents. Large crown 8vo, printed on hand-made paper, parchment, 10*s.* 6*d.*

HENRY, Philip.—Diaries and Letters of. Edited by MATTHEW HENRY LEE, M.A. Large crown 8vo, 7*s.* 6*d.*

HIDE, Albert.—The Age to Come. Small crown 8vo, 2*s.* 6*d.*

HIME, Major H. W. L., R.A.—Wagnerism : A Protest. Crown 8vo, 2*s.* 6*d.*

HINTON, J.—Life and Letters. Edited by ELLICE HOPKINS, with an Introduction by Sir W. W. GULL, Bart., and Portrait engraved on Steel by C. H. Jeens. Fourth Edition. Crown 8vo, 8*s.* 6*d.*

Philosophy and Religion. Second Edition. Crown 8vo, 5*s.*

The Law Breaker. Crown 8vo.

HINTON, J.—continued.

The Mystery of Pain. New Edition. Fcap. 8vo, 1*s.*

Hodson of Hodson's Horse ; or, Twelve Years of a Soldier's Life in India. Being extracts from the Letters of the late Major W. S. R. Hodson. With a Vindication from the Attack of Mr. Bosworth Smith. Edited by his brother, G. H. HODSON, M.A. Fourth Edition. Large crown 8vo, 5*s.*

HOLTHAM, E. G.—Eight Years in Japan, 1873–1881. Work, Travel, and Recreation. With three Maps. Large crown 8vo, 9*s.*

HOOPER, Mary.—Little Dinners : How to Serve them with Elegance and Economy. Eighteenth Edition. Crown 8vo, 2*s.* 6*d.*

Cookery for Invalids, Persons of Delicate Digestion, and Children. Third Edition. Crown 8vo, 2*s.* 6*d.*

Every-Day Meals. Being Economical and Wholesome Recipes for Breakfast, Luncheon, and Supper. Fifth Edition. Crown 8vo, 2*s.* 6*d.*

HOPKINS, Ellice.—Life and Letters of James Hinton, with an Introduction by Sir W. W. GULL, Bart., and Portrait engraved on Steel by C. H. Jeens. Fourth Edition. Crown 8vo, 8*s.* 6*d.*

Work amongst Working Men. Fifth Edition. Crown 8vo, 3*s.* 6*d.*

HOSPITALIER, E.—The Modern Applications of Electricity. Translated and Enlarged by JULIUS MAIER, Ph.D. 2 vols. Second Edition, Revised, with many additions and numerous Illustrations. Demy 8vo, 12*s.* 6*d.* each volume.
VOL. I.—Electric Generators, Electric Light.
VOL. II.—Telephone : Various Applications : Electrical Transmission of Energy.

Household Readings on Prophecy. By a Layman. Small crown 8vo, 3*s.* 6*d.*

HUGHES, Henry.—The Redemption of the World. Crown 8vo, 3*s.* 6*d.*

HUNTINGFORD, Rev. E., D.C.L.—The Apocalypse. With a Commentary and Introductory Essay. Demy 8vo, 5*s.*

HUTTON, Arthur, M.A.—The Anglican Ministry : Its Nature and Value in relation to the Catholic Priesthood. With a Preface by His Eminence CARDINAL NEWMAN. Demy 8vo, 14*s.*

HUTTON, Rev. C. F.—Unconscious Testimony ; or, The Silent Witness of the Hebrew to the Truth of the Historical Scriptures. Crown 8vo, 2*s.* 6*d.*

HYNDMAN, H. M.—The Historical Basis of Socialism in England. Large crown 8vo, 8*s.* 6*d.*

IM THURN, Everard F.—**Among the Indians of Guiana.** Being Sketches, chiefly anthropologic, from the Interior of British Guiana. With 53 Illustrations and a Map. Demy 8vo, 18*s.*

Jaunt in a Junk: A Ten Days' Cruise in Indian Seas. Large crown 8vo, 7*s.* 6*d.*

JENKINS, E., and RAYMOND, J.—**The Architect's Legal Handbook.** Third Edition, Revised. Crown 8vo, 6*s.*

JENNINGS, Mrs. Vaughan.—**Rahel:** Her Life and Letters. Large post 8vo, 7*s.* 6*d.*

JERVIS, Rev. W. Henley.— **The Gallican Church and the Revolution.** A Sequel to the History of the Church of France, from the Concordat of Bologna to the Revolution. Demy 8vo, 18*s.*

JOEL, L.—**A Consul's Manual and Shipowner's and Shipmaster's Practical Guide in their Transactions Abroad.** With Definitions of Nautical, Mercantile, and Legal Terms; a Glossary of Mercantile Terms in English, French, German, Italian, and Spanish; Tables of the Money, Weights, and Measures of the Principal Commercial Nations and their Equivalents in British Standards; and Forms of Consular and Notarial Acts. Demy 8vo, 12*s.*

JOHNSTONE, C. F., M.A.—**Historical Abstracts:** being Outlines of the History of some of the less known States of Europe. Crown 8vo, 7*s.* 6*d.*

JOLLY, William, F.R.S.E., etc.—**The Life of John Duncan, Scotch Weaver and Botanist.** With Sketches of his Friends and Notices of his Times. Second Edition. Large crown 8vo, with etched portrait, 9*s.*

JONES, C. A.—**The Foreign Freaks of Five Friends.** With 30 Illustrations. Crown 8vo, 6*s.*

JOYCE, P. W., LL.D., etc.—**Old Celtic Romances.** Translated from the Gaelic. Crown 8vo, 7*s.* 6*d.*

JOYNES, J. L.—**The Adventures of a Tourist in Ireland.** Second edition. Small crown 8vo, 2*s.* 6*d.*

KAUFMANN, Rev. M., B.A.—**Socialism:** its Nature, its Dangers, and its Remedies considered. Crown 8vo, 7*s.* 6*d.*

Utopias; or, Schemes of Social Improvement, from Sir Thomas More to Karl Marx. Crown 8vo, 5*s.*

KAY, David, F.R.G.S.—**Education and Educators.** Crown 8vo, 7*s.* 6*d.*

KAY, Joseph.—**Free Trade in Land.** Edited by his Widow. With Preface by the Right Hon. JOHN BRIGHT, M.P. Seventh Edition. Crown 8vo, 5*s.*

KEMPIS, Thomas à.—Of the Imitation of Christ. Parchment Library Edition.—Parchment or cloth, 6s. ; vellum, 7s. 6d. The Red Line Edition, fcap. 8vo, red edges, 2s. 6d. The Cabinet Edition, small 8vo, cloth limp, 1s. ; cloth boards, red edges, 1s. 6d. The Miniature Edition, red edges, 32mo, 1s.

   *** All the above Editions may be had in various extra bindings.

KENT, C.—Corona Catholica ad Petri successoris Pedes Oblata: De Summi Pontificis Leonis XIII. Assumptione Epigramma. In Quinquaginta Linguis. Fcap. 4to, 15s.

KETTLEWELL, Rev. S.—Thomas à Kempis and the Brothers of Common Life. 2 vols. With Frontispieces. Demy 8vo, 30s.

KIDD, Joseph, M.D.—The Laws of Therapeutics ; or, the Science and Art of Medicine. Second Edition. Crown 8vo, 6s.

KINGSFORD, Anna, M.D.—The Perfect Way in Diet. A Treatise advocating a Return to the Natural and Ancient Food of our Race. Small crown 8vo, 2s.

KINGSLEY, Charles, M.A.—Letters and Memories of his Life. Edited by his Wife. With two Steel Engraved Portraits, and Vignettes on Wood. Fourteenth Cabinet Edition. 2 vols. Crown 8vo, 12s.

   *** Also a People's Edition, in one volume. With Portrait. Crown 8vo, 6s.

All Saints' Day, and other Sermons. Edited by the Rev. W. HARRISON. Third Edition. Crown 8vo, 7s. 6d.

True Words for Brave Men. A Book for Soldiers' and Sailors' Libraries. Tenth Edition. Crown 8vo, 2s. 6d.

KNOX, Alexander A.—The New Playground ; or, Wanderings in Algeria. New and cheaper edition. Large crown 8vo, 6s.

LANDON, Joseph.—School Management ; Including a General View of the Work of Education, Organization, and Discipline. Third Edition. Crown 8vo, 6s.

LAURIE, S. S.—The Training of Teachers, and other Educational Papers. Crown 8vo, 7s. 6d.

LEE, Rev. F. G., D.C.L.—The Other World ; or, Glimpses of the Supernatural. 2 vols. A New Edition. Crown 8vo, 15s.

Letters from a Young Emigrant in Manitoba. Second Edition. Small crown 8vo, 3s. 6d.

LEWIS, Edward Dillon.—A Draft Code of Criminal Law and Procedure. Demy 8vo, 21s.

LILLIE, Arthur, M.R.A.S.—The Popular Life of Buddha. Containing an Answer to the Hibbert Lectures of 1881. With Illustrations. Crown 8vo, 6s.

LLOYD, Walter.—The Hope of the World : An Essay on Universal Redemption.   Crown 8vo, 5s.

LONSDALE, Margaret.—Sister Dora : a Biography.   With Portrait. Twenty-seventh Edition.   Crown 8vo, 2s. 6d.

LOUNSBURY, Thomas R.—James Fenimore Cooper.   Crown 8vo, 5s.

LOWDER, Charles.—A Biography.   By the Author of " St. Teresa." New and Cheaper Edition.   Crown 8vo.   With Portrait.   3s. 6d.

LYTTON, Edward Bulwer, Lord.—Life, Letters and Literary Remains.   By his Son, the EARL OF LYTTON.   With Portraits, Illustrations and Facsimiles.   Demy 8vo.   Vols. I. and II., 32s.

MACAULAY, G. C.—Francis Beaumont : A Critical Study.   Crown 8vo, 5s.

MAC CALLUM, M. W.—Studies in Low German and High German Literature.   Crown 8vo, 6s.

MACDONALD, George. —Donal Grant.   A New Novel.   3 vols. Crown 8vo, 31s. 6d.

MACHIAVELLI, Niccolò. — Life and Times.   By Prof. Villari. Translated by Linda Villari.   4 vols.   Large post, 8vo, 48s.

MACHIAVELLI, Niccolò.—Discourses on the First Decade of Titus Livius.   Translated from the Italian by NINIAN HILL THOMSON, M.A.   Large crown 8vo, 12s.

The Prince.   Translated from the Italian by N. H. T.   Small crown 8vo, printed on hand-made paper, bevelled boards, 6s.

MACKENZIE, Alexander.—How India is Governed.   Being an Account of England's Work in India.   Small crown 8vo, 2s.

MACNAUGHT, Rev. John.—Cœna Domini : An Essay on the Lord's Supper, its Primitive Institution, Apostolic Uses, and Subsequent History.   Demy 8vo, 14s.

MACWALTER, Rev. G. S.—Life of Antonio Rosmini Serbati (Founder of the Institute of Charity).   2 vols.   Demy 8vo.
[Vol. I. now ready, price 12s.

MAGNUS, Mrs.—About the Jews since Bible Times.   From the Babylonian Exile till the English Exodus.   Small crown 8vo, 6s.

MAIR, R. S., M.D., F.R.C.S.E.—The Medical Guide for Anglo-Indians.   Being a Compendium of Advice to Europeans in India, relating to the Preservation and Regulation of Health. With a Supplement on the Management of Children in India. Second Edition.   Crown 8vo, limp cloth, 3s. 6d.

MALDEN, Henry Elliot.—Vienna, 1683.   The History and Consequences of the Defeat of the Turks before Vienna, September 12th, 1683, by John Sobieski, King of Poland, and Charles Leopold, Duke of Lorraine.   Crown 8vo, 4s. 6d.

Many Voices.   A volume of Extracts from the Religious Writers of Christendom from the First to the Sixteenth Century.   With Biographical Sketches.   Crown 8vo, cloth extra, red edges, 6s.

MARKHAM, Capt. Albert Hastings, R.N.—The Great Frozen Sea: A Personal Narrative of the Voyage of the *Alert* during the Arctic Expedition of 1875-6. With 6 Full-page Illustrations, 2 Maps, and 27 Woodcuts. Sixth and Cheaper Edition. Crown 8vo, 6s.

A Polar Reconnaissance: being the Voyage of the *Isbjörn* to Novaya Zemlya in 1879. With 10 Illustrations. Demy 8vo, 16s.

Marriage and Maternity; or, Scripture Wives and Mothers. Small crown 8vo, 4s. 6d.

MARTINEAU, Gertrude.—Outline Lessons on Morals. Small crown 8vo, 3s. 6d.

MAUDSLEY, H., M.D.—Body and Will. Being an Essay concerning Will, in its Metaphysical, Physiological, and Pathological Aspects. 8vo, 12s.

McGRATH, Terence.—Pictures from Ireland. New and Cheaper Edition. Crown 8vo, 2s.

MEREDITH, M.A.—Theotokos, the Example for Woman. Dedicated, by permission, to Lady Agnes Wood. Revised by the Venerable Archdeacon DENISON. 32mo, limp cloth, 1s. 6d.

MILLER, Edward.—The History and Doctrines of Irvingism; or, The so-called Catholic and Apostolic Church. 2 vols. Large post 8vo, 25s.

The Church in Relation to the State. Large crown 8vo, 7s. 6d.

MINCHIN, J. G.—Bulgaria since the War: Notes of a Tour in the Autumn of 1879. Small crown 8vo, 3s. 6d.

MITCHELL, Lucy M.—A History of Ancient Sculpture. With numerous Illustrations, including 6 Plates in Phototype. Super royal 8vo, 42s.

Selections from Ancient Sculpture. Being a Portfolio containing Reproductions in Phototype of 36 Masterpieces of Ancient Art to illustrate Mrs. Mitchell's "History of Ancient Sculpture." 18s.

MITFORD, Bertram.—Through the Zulu Country. Its Battlefields and its People. With five Illustrations. Demy 8vo, 14s.

MOCKLER, E.—A Grammar of the Baloochee Language, as it is spoken in Makran (Ancient Gedrosia), in the Persia-Arabic and Roman characters. Fcap. 8vo, 5s.

MOLESWORTH, Rev. W. Nassau, M.A.—History of the Church of England from 1660. Large crown 8vo, 7s. 6d.

MORELL, J. R.—Euclid Simplified in Method and Language. Being a Manual of Geometry. Compiled from the most important French Works, approved by the University of Paris and the Minister of Public Instruction. Fcap. 8vo, 2s. 6d.

MORRIS, George.—The Duality of all Divine Truth in our Lord Jesus Christ. For God's Self-manifestation in the Impartation of the Divine Nature to Man. Large crown 8vo, 7s. 6d.

MORSE, E. S., Ph.D.—First Book of Zoology. With numerous Illustrations. New and Cheaper Edition. Crown 8vo, 2s. 6d.

MURPHY, John Nicholas.—The Chair of Peter; or, The Papacy considered in its Institution, Development, and Organization, and in the Benefits which for over Eighteen Centuries it has conferred on Mankind. Demy 8vo, 18s.

My Ducats and My Daughter. A New Novel. 3 vols. Crown 8vo, 31s. 6d.

NELSON, J. H., M.A.—A Prospectus of the Scientific Study of the Hindû Law. Demy 8vo, 9s.

NEWMAN, Cardinal.—Characteristics from .the Writings of. Being Selections from his various Works. Arranged with the Author's personal Approval. Sixth Edition. With Portrait. Crown 8vo, 6s.

  *** A Portrait of Cardinal Newman, mounted for framing, can . be had, 2s. 6d.

NEWMAN, Francis William.—Essays on Diet. Small crown 8vo, cloth limp, 2s.

New Truth and the Old Faith: Are they Incompatible? By a Scientific Layman. Demy 8vo, 10s. 6d.

New Werther. By LOKI. Small crown 8vo, 2s. 6d.

NICHOLSON, Edward Byron.—The Gospel according to the Hebrews. Its Fragments Translated and Annotated, with a Critical Analysis of the External and Internal Evidence relating to it. Demy 8vo, 9s. 6d.

  A New Commentary on the Gospel according to Matthew. Demy 8vo, 12s.

NICOLS, Arthur, F.G.S., F.R.G.S.—Chapters from the Physical History of the Earth: an Introduction to Geology and Palæontology. With numerous Illustrations. Crown 8vo, 5s.

NOPS, Marianne.—Class Lessons on Euclid. Part I. containing the First Two Books of the Elements. Crown 8vo, 2s. 6d.

Notes on St. Paul's Epistle to the Galatians. For Readers of the Authorized Version or the Original Greek. Demy 8vo, 2s. 6d.

Nuces: EXERCISES ON THE SYNTAX OF THE PUBLIC SCHOOL LATIN PRIMER. New Edition in Three Parts. Crown 8vo, each 1s.
  *** The Three Parts can also be had bound together, 3s.

OATES, Frank, F.R.G.S.—Matabele Land and the Victoria Falls. A Naturalist's Wanderings in the Interior of South Africa. Edited by C. G. OATES, B.A. With numerous Illustrations and 4 Maps. Demy 8vo, 21s.

OGLE, W., M.D., F.R.C.P.—**Aristotle on the Parts of Animals.** Translated, with Introduction and Notes. Royal 8vo, 12s. 6d.

O'HAGAN, Lord, K.P.—**Occasional Papers and Addresses.** Large crown 8vo, 7s. 6d.

OKEN, Lorenz, **Life of.** By ALEXANDER ECKER. With Explanatory Notes, Selections from Oken's Correspondence, and Portrait of the Professor. From the German by ALFRED TULK. Crown 8vo, 6s.

O'MEARA, Kathleen.—**Frederic Ozanam,** Professor of the Sorbonne : His Life and Work. Second Edition. Crown 8vo, 7s. 6d.

Henri Perreyve and his Counsels to the Sick. Small crown 8vo, 5s.

OSBORNE, Rev. W. A.—**The Revised Version of the New Testament.** A Critical Commentary, with Notes upon the Text. Crown 8vo, 5s.

OTTLEY, H. Bickersteth.—**The Great Dilemma.** Christ His Own Witness or His Own Accuser. Six Lectures. Second Edition. Crown 8vo, 3s. 6d.

Our Public Schools—Eton, Harrow, Winchester, Rugby, Westminster, Marlborough, The Charterhouse. Crown 8vo, 6s.

OWEN, F. M.—**John Keats :** a Study. Crown 8vo, 6s.

Across the Hills. Small crown 8vo, 1s. 6d.

OWEN, Rev. Robert, B.D.—**Sanctorale Catholicum ;** or, Book of Saints. With Notes, Critical, Exegetical, and Historical. Demy 8vo, 18s.

OXENHAM, Rev. F. Nutcombe.—**What is the Truth as to Everlasting Punishment.** Part II. Being an Historical Inquiry into the Witness and Weight of certain Anti-Origenist Councils. Crown 8vo, 2s. 6d.

OXONIENSIS.—**Romanism, Protestantism, Anglicanism.** Being a Layman's View of some questions of the Day. Together with Remarks on Dr. Littledale's "Plain Reasons against joining the Church of Rome." Crown 8vo, 3s. 6d.

PALMER, the late William.—**Notes of a Visit to Russia in 1840–1841.** Selected and arranged by JOHN H. CARDINAL NEWMAN, with portrait. Crown 8vo, 8s. 6d.

Early Christian Symbolism. A Series of Compositions from Fresco Paintings, Glasses, and Sculptured Sarcophagi. Edited by the Rev. Provost NORTHCOTE, D.D., and the Rev. Canon BROWNLOW, M.A. In 8 Parts, each with 4 Plates. Folio, 5s. coloured ; 3s. plain.

Parchment Library. Choicely Printed on hand-made paper, limp parchment antique or cloth, 6s. ; vellum, 7s. 6d. each volume.

The Book of Psalms. Translated by the Rev. T. K. CHEYNE, M.A.

Parchment Library—*continued.*

The Vicar of Wakefield. With Preface and Notes by AUSTIN DOBSON.

English Comic Dramatists. Edited by OSWALD CRAWFURD.

English Lyrics.

The Sonnets of John Milton. Edited by MARK PATTISON. With Portrait after Vertue.

Poems by Alfred Tennyson. 2 vols. With miniature frontispieces by W. B. Richmond.

French Lyrics. Selected and Annotated by GEORGE SAINTSBURY. With a miniature frontispiece designed and etched by H. G. Glindoni.

Fables by Mr. John Gay. With Memoir by AUSTIN DOBSON, and an etched portrait from an unfinished Oil Sketch by Sir Godfrey Kneller.

Select Letters of Percy Bysshe Shelley. Edited, with an Introduction, by RICHARD GARNETT.

The Christian Year. Thoughts in Verse for the Sundays and Holy Days throughout the Year. With Miniature Portrait of the Rev. J. Keble, after a Drawing by G. Richmond, R.A.

Shakspere's Works. Complete in Twelve Volumes.

Eighteenth Century Essays. Selected and Edited by AUSTIN DOBSON. With a Miniature Frontispiece by R. Caldecott.

Q. Horati Flacci Opera. Edited by F. A. CORNISH, Assistant Master at Eton. With a Frontispiece after a design by L. Alma Tadema, etched by Leopold Lowenstam.

Edgar Allan Poe's Poems. With an Essay on his Poetry by ANDREW LANG, and a Frontispiece by Linley Sambourne.

Shakspere's Sonnets. Edited by EDWARD DOWDEN. With a Frontispiece etched by Leopold Lowenstam, after the Death Mask.

English Odes. Selected by EDMUND W. GOSSE. With Frontispiece on India paper by Hamo Thornycroft, A.R.A.

Of the Imitation of Christ. By THOMAS à KEMPIS. A revised Translation. With Frontispiece on India paper, from a Design by W. B. Richmond.

Tennyson's The Princess: a Medley. With a Miniature Frontispiece by H. M. Paget, and a Tailpiece in Outline by Gordon Browne.

Poems: Selected from PERCY BYSSHE SHELLEY. Dedicated to Lady Shelley. With a Preface by RICHARD GARNETT and a Miniature Frontispiece.

Tennyson's In Memoriam. With a Miniature Portrait in *eau-forte* by Le Rat, after a Photograph by the late Mrs. Cameron.

*** The above volumes may also be had in a variety of leather bindings.

PARSLOE, Joseph.—**Our Railways.** Sketches, Historical and Descriptive. With Practical Information as to Fares and Rates, etc., and a Chapter on Railway Reform. Crown 8vo, 6s.

PAUL, Alexander.—**Short Parliaments.** A History of the National Demand for frequent General Elections. Small crown 8vo, 3s. 6d.

PAUL, C. Kegan.—**Biographical Sketches.** Printed on hand-made paper, bound in buckram. Second Edition. Crown 8vo, 7s. 6d.

PEARSON, Rev. S.—**Week-day Living.** A Book for Young Men and Women. Second Edition. Crown 8vo, 5s.

PESCHEL, Dr. Oscar.—**The Races of Man and their Geographical Distribution.** Second Edition. Large crown 8vo, 9s.

PETERS, F. H.—**The Nicomachean Ethics of Aristotle.** Translated by. Crown 8vo, 6s.

PHIPSON, E.—**The Animal Lore of Shakspeare's Time.** Including Quadrupeds, Birds, Reptiles, Fish and Insects. Large post 8vo, 9s.

PIDGEON, D.—**An Engineer's Holiday;** or, Notes of a Round Trip from Long. o° to o°. New and Cheaper Edition. Large crown 8vo, 7s. 6d.

POPE, J. Buckingham. — **Railway Rates and Radical Rule.** Trade Questions as Election Tests. Crown 8vo, 2s. 6d.

PRICE, Prof. Bonamy. — **Chapters on Practical Political Economy.** Being the Substance of Lectures delivered before the University of Oxford. New and Cheaper Edition. Large post 8vo, 5s.

Pulpit Commentary, The. (Old Testament Series.) Edited by the Rev. J. S. EXELL, M.A., and the Rev. Canon H. D. M. SPENCE.

    Genesis. By the Rev. T. WHITELAW, M.A. With Homilies by the Very Rev. J. F. MONTGOMERY, D.D., Rev. Prof. R. A. REDFORD, M.A., LL.B., Rev. F. HASTINGS, Rev. W. ROBERTS, M.A. An Introduction to the Study of the Old Testament by the Venerable Archdeacon FARRAR, D.D., F.R.S.; and Introductions to the Pentateuch by the Right Rev. H. COTTERILL, D.D., and Rev. T. WHITELAW, M.A. Eighth Edition. 1 vol., 15s.

    Exodus. By the Rev. Canon RAWLINSON. With Homilies by Rev. J. ORR, Rev. D. YOUNG, B.A., Rev. C. A. GOODHART, Rev. J. URQUHART, and the Rev. H. T. ROBJOHNS. Fourth Edition. 2 vols., 18s.

    Leviticus. By the Rev. Prebendary MEYRICK, M.A. With Introductions by the Rev. R. COLLINS, Rev. Professor A. CAVE, and Homilies by Rev. Prof. REDFORD, LL.B., Rev. J. A. MACDONALD, Rev. W. CLARKSON, B.A., Rev. S. R. ALDRIDGE, LL.B., and Rev. MCCHEYNE EDGAR. Fourth Edition. 15s.

Pulpit Commentary, The—*continued.*

> **Numbers.** By the Rev. R. WINTERBOTHAM, LL.B. With
> ·Homilies by the ·Rev. Professor W. BINNIE, D.D., Rev. E. S.
> PROUT, M.A., Rev. D. YOUNG, Rev. J. WAITE, and an Intro-
> duction by the Rev. THOMAS WHITELAW, M.A. Fourth
> Edition. 15*s.*

> **Deuteronomy.** By the Rev. W. L. ALEXANDER, D.D. With
> Homilies by Rev. C. CLEMANCE, D.D., Rev. J. ORR, B.D.,
> Rev. R. M. EDGAR, M.A., Rev. D. DAVIES, M.A. Third
> edition. 15*s.*

> **Joshua.** By Rev. J. J. LIAS, M.A. With Homilies by Rev.
> S. R. ALDRIDGE, LL.B., Rev. R. GLOVER, REV. E. DE
> PRESSÉNSÉ, D.D., Rev. J. WAITE, B.A., Rev. W. F. ADENEY,
> M.A.; and an Introduction by the Rev. A. PLUMMER, M.A.
> Fifth Edition. 12*s.* 6*d.*

> **Judges and Ruth.** By the Bishop of Bath and Wells, and
> Rev. J. MORRISON, D.D. With Homilies by Rev. A. F. MUIR,
> M.A., Rev. W. F. ADENEY, M.A., Rev. W. M. STATHAM, and
> Rev. Professor J. THOMSON, M.A. Fourth Edition. 10*s.* 6*d.*

> **1 Samuel.** By the Very Rev. R. P. SMITH, D.D. With Homilies
> by Rev. DONALD FRASER, D.D., Rev. Prof. CHAPMAN, and
> Rev. B. DALE. Sixth Edition. 15*s.*

> **1 Kings.** By the Rev. JOSEPH HAMMOND, LL.B. With Homilies
> by the Rev. E. DE PRESSENSÉ, D.D., Rev. J. WAITE, B.A.,
> Rev. A. ROWLAND, LL.B., Rev. J. A. MACDONALD, and Rev.
> J. URQUHART. Fourth Edition. 15*s.*

> **Ezra, Nehemiah, and Esther.** By Rev. Canon G. RAWLINSON,
> M.A. With Homilies by Rev. Prof. J. R. THOMSON, M.A., Rev.
> Prof. R. A. REDFORD, LL.B., M.A., Rev. W. S. LEWIS, M.A.,
> Rev. J. A. MACDONALD, Rev. A. MACKENNAL, B.A., Rev. W.
> CLARKSON, B.A., Rev. F. HASTINGS, Rev. W. DINWIDDIE,
> LL.B., Rev. Prof. ROWLANDS, B.A., Rev. G. WOOD, B.A.,
> Rev. Prof. P. C. BARKER, M.A., LL.B., and the Rev. J. S.
> EXELL, M.A. Sixth Edition. 1 vol., 12*s.* 6*d.*

> **Jeremiah.** By the Rev. T. K. CHEYNE, M.A. With Homilies
> by the Rev. W. F. ADENEY, M.A., Rev. A. F. MUIR, M.A.,
> Rev. S. CONWAY, B.A., Rev. J. WAITE, B.A., and Rev. D.
> YOUNG, B.A. Vol. I., 15s.

Pulpit Commentary, The. (New Testament Series.)

> **St. Mark.** By Very Rev. E. BICKERSTETH, D.D., Dean of Lich-
> field. With Homilies by Rev. Prof. THOMSON, M.A., Rev. Prof.
> GIVEN, M.A., Rev. Prof. JOHNSON, M.A., Rev. A. ROWLAND,
> B.A., LL.B., Rev. A. MUIR, and Rev. R. GREEN. 2 vols.
> Fourth Edition. 21*s.*

> **The Acts of the Apostles.** By the Bishop of Bath and Wells.
> With Homilies by Rev. Prof. P. C. BARKER, M.A., LL.B., Rev.
> Prof. E. JOHNSON, M.A., Rev. Prof. R. A. REDFORD, M.A.,
> Rev. R. TUCK, B.A., Rev. W. CLARKSON, B.A. 2 vols., 21*s.*

Pulpit Commentary, The—*continued.*

    1 Corinthians. By the Ven. Archdeacon FARRAR, D.D. With Homilies by Rev. Ex-Chancellor LIPSCOMB, LL.D., Rev. DAVID THOMAS, D.D., Rev. D. FRASER, D.D., Rev. Prof. J. R. THOMSON, M.A., Rev. J. WAITE, B.A., Rev. R. TUCK, B.A., Rev. E. HURNDALL, M.A., and Rev. H. BREMNER, B.D. Price 15*s.*

PUSEY, Dr.—Sermons for the Church's Seasons from Advent to Trinity. Selected from the Published Sermons of the late EDWARD BOUVERIE PUSEY, D.D. Crown 8vo, 5*s.*

QUILTER, Harry.—"The Academy," 1872–1882. 1*s.*

RADCLIFFE, Frank R. Y.—The New Politicus. Small crown 8vo, 2*s. 6d.*

RANKE, Leopold von.—Universal History. The oldest Historical Group of Nations and the Greeks. Edited by G. W. PROTHERO. Demy 8vo, 16*s.*

Realities of the Future Life. Small crown 8vo, 1*s. 6d.*

RENDELL, J. M.—Concise Handbook of the Island of Madeira. With Plan of Funchal and Map of the Island. Fcap. 8vo, 1*s. 6d.*

REYNOLDS, Rev. J. W.—The Supernatural in Nature. A Verification by Free Use of Science. Third Edition, Revised and Enlarged. Demy 8vo, 14*s.*

    The Mystery of Miracles. Third and Enlarged Edition. Crown 8vo, 6*s.*

    The Mystery of the Universe; Our Common Faith. Demy 8vo, 14*s.*

RIBOT, Prof. Th.—Heredity: A Psychological Study on its Phenomena, its Laws, its Causes, and its Consequences. Second Edition. Large crown 8vo, 9*s.*

ROBERTSON, The late Rev. F. W., M.A.—Life and Letters of. Edited by the Rev. STOPFORD BROOKE, M.A.

    I. Two vols., uniform with the Sermons. With Steel Portrait. Crown 8vo, 7*s. 6d.*

    II. Library Edition, in Demy 8vo, with Portrait. 12*s.*

    III. A Popular Edition, in 1 vol. Crown 8vo, 6*s.*

    Sermons. Four Series. Small crown 8vo, 3*s. 6d.* each.

    The Human Race, and other Sermons. Preached at Cheltenham, Oxford, and Brighton. New and Cheaper Edition. Small crown 8vo, 3*s. 6d.*

    Notes on Genesis. New and Cheaper Edition. Small crown 8vo, 3*s. 6d.*

    Expository Lectures on St. Paul's Epistles to the Corinthians. A New Edition. Small crown 8vo, 5*s.*

    Lectures and Addresses, with other Literary Remains. A New Edition. Small crown 8vo, 5*s.*

ROBERTSON, The late Rev. F. W., M.A.—continued.
> **An Analysis of Mr. Tennyson's "In Memoriam."** (Dedicated by Permission to the Poet-Laureate.) Fcap. 8vo, 2s.
> **The Education of the Human Race.** Translated from the German of GOTTHOLD EPHRAIM LESSING. Fcap. 8vo, 2s. 6d.
> The above Works can also be had, bound in half morocco.

*** A Portrait of the late Rev. F. W. Robertson, mounted for framing, can be had, 2s. 6d.

ROMANES, G. J.—**Mental Evolution in Animals.** With a Posthumous Essay on Instinct by CHARLES DARWIN, F.R.S. Demy 8vo, 12s.

ROSMINI SERBATI, A., Founder of the Institute of Charity. **Life.** By G. STUART MACWALTER. 2 vols. 8vo.
> [Vol. I. now ready, 12s.

Rosmini's Origin of Ideas. Translated from the Fifth Italian Edition of the Nuovo Saggio *Sull' origine delle idee.* 3 vols. Demy 8vo, cloth. [Vols. I. and II. now ready, 16s. each.

Rosmini's Philosophical System. Translated, with a Sketch of the Author's Life, Bibliography, Introduction, and Notes by THOMAS DAVIDSON. Demy 8vo, 16s.

RULE, Martin, M.A.—**The Life and Times of St. Anselm, Archbishop of Canterbury and Primate of the Britains.** 2 vols. Demy 8vo, 32s.

SALVATOR, Archduke Ludwig.—**Levkosia, the Capital of Cyprus.** Crown 4to, 10s. 6d.

SAMUEL, Sydney M.—**Jewish Life in the East.** Small crown 8vo, 3s. 6d.

SAYCE, Rev. Archibald Henry.—**Introduction to the Science of Language.** 2 vols. Second Edition. Large post 8vo, 21s.

Scientific Layman. The New Truth and the Old Faith : are they Incompatible ? Demy 8vo, 10s. 6d.

SCOONES, W. Baptiste.—**Four Centuries of English Letters :** A Selection of 350 Letters by 150 Writers, from the Period of the Paston Letters to the Present Time. Third Edition. Large crown 8vo, 6s.

SHILLITO, Rev. Joseph.—**Womanhood :** its Duties, Temptations, and Privileges. A Book for Young Women. Third Edition. Crown 8vo, 3s. 6d.

SHIPLEY, Rev. Orby, M.A.—**Principles of the Faith in Relation to Sin.** Topics for Thought in Times of Retreat. Eleven Addresses delivered during a Retreat of Three Days to Persons living in the World. Demy 8vo, 12s.

Sister Augustine, Superior of the Sisters of Charity at the St. Johannis Hospital at Bonn. Authorised Translation by HANS THARAU, from the German "Memorials of AMALIE VON LASAULX." Cheap Edition. Large crown 8vo, 4s. 6d.

SKINNER, James.—A Memoir. By the Author of "Charles Lowder." With a Preface by the Rev. Canon CARTER, and Portrait. Large crown, 7s. 6d.

SMITH, Edward, M.D., LL.B., F.R.S.—Tubercular Consumption in its Early and Remediable Stages. Second Edition. Crown 8vo, 6s.

SPEDDING, James.—Reviews and Discussions, Literary, Political, and Historical not relating to Bacon. Demy 8vo, 12s. 6d.

Evenings with a Reviewer; or, Bacon and Macaulay. With a Prefatory Notice by G. S. VENABLES, Q.C. 2 vols. Demy 8vo, 18s.

STAPFER, Paul.—Shakspeare and Classical Antiquity: Greek and Latin Antiquity as presented in Shakspeare's Plays. Translated by EMILY J. CAREY. Large post 8vo, 12s.

STEVENSON, Rev. W. F.—Hymns for the Church and Home. Selected and Edited by the Rev. W. FLEMING STEVENSON. The Hymn Book consists of Three Parts :—I. For Public Worship.—II. For Family and Private Worship.—III. For Children.

*** Published in various forms and prices, the latter ranging from 8d. to 6s.

Stray Papers on Education, and Scenes from School Life. By B. H. Second Edition. Small crown 8vo, 3s. 6d.

STREATFEILD, Rev. G. S., M.A.—Lincolnshire and the Danes. Large crown 8vo, 7s. 6d.

STRECKER-WISLICENUS.—Organic Chemistry. Translated and Edited, with Extensive Additions, by W. R. HODGKINSON, Ph.D., and A. J. GREENAWAY, F.I.C. Demy 8vo, 21s.

Study of the Prologue and Epilogue in English Literature. From Shakespeare to Dryden. By G. S. B. Crown 8vo, 5s.

SULLY, James, M.A.—Pessimism : a History and a Criticism. Second Edition. Demy 8vo, 14s.

SWEDENBORG, Eman.—De Cultu et Amore Dei ubi Agitur de Telluris ortu, Paradiso et Vivario, tum de Primogeniti Seu Adami Nativitate Infantia, et Amore. Crown 8vo, 6s.

SYME, David.—Representative Government in England. Its Faults and Failures. Second Edition. Large crown 8vo, 6s.

TAYLOR, Rev. Isaac.—The Alphabet. An Account of the Origin and Development of Letters. With numerous Tables and Facsimiles. 2 vols. Demy 8vo, 36s.

TAYLOR, Sedley.—Profit Sharing between Capital and Labour. To which is added a Memorandum on the Industrial Partnership at the Whitwood Collieries, by Archibald and Henry Briggs, with remarks by Sedley Taylor. Crown 8vo, 2s. 6d.

Thirty Thousand Thoughts. Edited by the Rev. Canon Spence, Rev. J. S. Exell, Rev. Charles Neil, and Rev. Jacob Stephenson. 6 vols. Super royal 8vo.
[Vols. I. and II. now ready, 16s. each.

THOM, J. Hamilton.—Laws of Life after the Mind of Christ. Second Edition. Crown 8vo, 7s. 6d.

THOMSON, J. Turnbull.—Social Problems; or, An Inquiry into the Laws of Influence. With Diagrams. Demy 8vo, 10s. 6d.

TIDMAN, Paul F.—Gold and Silver Money. Part I.—A Plain Statement. Part II.—Objections Answered. Third Edition. Crown 8vo, 1s.

TIPPLE, Rev. S. A.—Sunday Mornings at Norwood. Prayers and Sermons. Crown 8vo, 6s.

TODHUNTER, Dr. J.—A Study of Shelley. Crown 8vo, 7s.

TREMENHEERE, Hugh Seymour, C.B.—A Manual of the Principles of Government, as set forth by the Authorities of Ancient and Modern Times. New and Enlarged Edition. Crown 8vo, 3s. 6d.

TUKE, Daniel Hack, M.D., F.R.C.P.—Chapters in the History of the Insane in the British Isles. With 4 Illustrations. Large crown 8vo, 12s.

TWINING, Louisa.—Workhouse Visiting and Management during Twenty-Five Years. Small crown 8vo, 2s.

TYLER, J.—The Mystery of Being: or, What Do We Know? Small crown 8vo, 3s. 6d.

UPTON, Major R. D.—Gleanings from the Desert of Arabia. Large post 8vo, 10s. 6d.

VACUUS VIATOR.—Flying South. Recollections of France and its Littoral. Small crown 8vo, 3s. 6d.

VAUGHAN, H. Halford.—New Readings and Renderings of Shakespeare's Tragedies. 2 vols. Demy 8vo, 25s.

VILLARI, Professor.—Niccolò Machiavelli and his Times. Translated by Linda Villari. 4 vols. Large post 8vo, 48s.

VILLIERS, The Right Hon. C. P.—Free Trade Speeches of. With Political Memoir. Edited by a Member of the Cobden Club. 2 vols. With Portrait. Demy 8vo, 25s.
⁎ People's Edition. 1 vol. Crown 8vo, limp cloth, 2s. 6d.

VOGT, Lieut.-Col. Hermann.—The Egyptian War of 1882. A translation. With Map and Plans. Large crown 8vo, 6s.

VOLCKXSOM, E. W. v.—Catechism of Elementary Modern Chemistry. Small crown 8vo, 3*s.*

VYNER, Lady Mary.—Every Day a Portion. Adapted from the Bible and the Prayer Book, for the Private Devotion of those living in Widowhood. Collected and Edited by Lady Mary Vyner. Square crown 8vo, 5*s.*

WALDSTEIN, Charles, Ph.D.—The Balance of Emotion and Intellect; an Introductory Essay to the Study of Philosophy. Crown 8vo, 6*s.*

WALLER, Rev. C. B.—The Apocalypse, reviewed under the Light of the Doctrine of the Unfolding Ages, and the Restitution of All Things. Demy 8vo, 12*s.*

WALPOLE, Chas. George.—History of Ireland from the Earliest Times to the Union with Great Britain. With 5 Maps and Appendices. Crown 8vo, 10*s.* 6*d.*

WALSHE, Walter Hayle, M.D.—Dramatic Singing Physiologically Estimated. Crown 8vo, 3*s.* 6*d.*

WARD, William George, Ph.D.—Essays on the Philosophy of Theism. Edited, with an Introduction, by WILFRID WARD. 2 vols. Demy 8vo, 21*s.*

WEDDERBURN, Sir David, Bart., M.P.—Life of. Compiled from his Journals and Writings by his sister, Mrs. E. H. PERCIVAL. With etched Portrait, and facsimiles of Pencil Sketches. Demy 8vo, 14*s.*

WEDMORE, Frederick.—The Masters of Genre Painting. With Sixteen Illustrations. Post 8vo, 7*s.* 6*d.*

WHEWELL, William, D.D.—His Life and Selections from his Correspondence. By Mrs. STAIR DOUGLAS. With a Portrait from a Painting by Samuel Laurence. Demy 8vo, 21*s.*

WHITNEY, Prof. William Dwight.—Essentials of English Grammar, for the Use of Schools. Second Edition. Crown 8vo, 3*s.* 6*d.*

WILLIAMS, Rowland, D.D.—Psalms, Litanies, Counsels, and Collects for Devout Persons. Edited by his Widow. New and Popular Edition. Crown 8vo, 3*s.* 6*d.*

Stray Thoughts Collected from the Writings of the late Rowland Williams, D.D. Edited by his Widow. Crown 8vo, 3*s.* 6*d.*

WILSON, Sir Erasmus.—The Recent Archaic Discovery of Egyptian Mummies at Thebes. A Lecture. Crown 8vo, 1*s.* 6*d.*

WILSON, Lieut.-Col. C. T.—The Duke of Berwick, Marshal of France, 1702-1734. Demy 8vo, 15*s.*

WILSON, Mrs. R. F.—The Christian Brothers. Their Origin and Work. With a Sketch of the Life of their Founder, the Ven. JEAN BAPTISTE, de la Salle. Crown 8vo, 6*s.*

WOLTMANN, Dr. Alfred, and WOERMANN, Dr. Karl.—**History of Painting.** Edited by SIDNEY COLVIN. Vol. I. Painting in Antiquity and the Middle Ages. With numerous Illustrations. Medium 8vo, 28*s*. ; bevelled boards, gilt leaves, 30*s*.

Word was Made Flesh. Short Family Readings on the Epistles for each Sunday of the Christian Year. Demy 8vo, 10*s*. 6*d*.

WREN, Sir Christopher.—**His Family and His Times.** With Original Letters, and a Discourse on Architecture hitherto unpublished. By LUCY PHILLIMORE. Demy 8vo, 10*s*. 6*d*.

YOUMANS, Eliza A.—**First Book of Botany.** Designed to Cultivate the Observing Powers of Children. With 300 Engravings. New and Cheaper Edition. Crown 8vo, 2*s*. 6*d*.

YOUMANS, Edward L., M.D.—**A Class Book of Chemistry,** on the Basis of the New System. With 200 Illustrations. Crown 8vo, 5*s*.

THE INTERNATIONAL SCIENTIFIC SERIES.

I. **Forms of Water:** a Familiar Exposition of the Origin and Phenomena of Glaciers. By J. Tyndall, LL.D., F.R.S. With 25 Illustrations. Eighth Edition. Crown 8vo, 5*s*.

II. **Physics and Politics;** or, Thoughts on the Application of the Principles of "Natural Selection" and "Inheritance" to Political Society. By Walter Bagehot. Sixth Edition. Crown 8vo, 4*s*.

III. **Foods.** By Edward Smith, M.D., LL.B., F.R.S. With numerous Illustrations. Eighth Edition. Crown 8vo, 5*s*.

IV. **Mind and Body:** the Theories of their Relation. By Alexander Bain, LL.D. With Four Illustrations. Seventh Edition. Crown 8vo, 4*s*.

V. **The Study of Sociology.** By Herbert Spencer. Eleventh Edition. Crown 8vo, 5*s*.

VI. **On the Conservation of Energy.** By Balfour Stewart, M.A., LL.D., F.R.S. With 14 Illustrations. Sixth Edition. Crown 8vo, 5*s*.

VII. **Animal Locomotion;** or Walking, Swimming, and Flying. By J. B. Pettigrew, M.D., F.R.S., etc. With 130 Illustrations. Third Edition. Crown 8vo, 5*s*.

VIII. **Responsibility in Mental Disease.** By Henry Maudsley, M.D. Fourth Edition. Crown 8vo, 5*s*.

IX. **The New Chemistry.** By Professor J. P. Cooke. With 31 Illustrations. Seventh Edition. Crown 8vo, 5*s*.

X. **The Science of Law.** By Professor Sheldon Amos. Fifth Edition. Crown 8vo, 5*s.*

XI. **Animal Mechanism :** a Treatise on Terrestrial and Aerial Loco-motion. By Professor E. J. Marey. With 117 Illustrations. Third Edition. Crown 8vo, 5*s.*

XII. **The Doctrine of Descent and Darwinism.** By Professor Oscar Schmidt. With 26 Illustrations. Fifth Edition. Crown 8vo, 5*s.*

XIII. **The History of the Conflict between Religion and Science.** By J. W. Draper, M.D., LL.D. Eighteenth Edition. Crown 8vo, 5*s.*

XIV. **Fungi :** their Nature, Influences, Uses, etc. By M. C. Cooke, M.D., LL.D. Edited by the Rev. M. J. Berkeley, M.A., F.L.S. With numerous Illustrations. Third Edition. Crown 8vo, 5*s.*

XV. **The Chemical Effects of Light and Photography.** By Dr. Hermann Vogel. Translation thoroughly Revised. With 100 Illustrations. Fourth Edition. Crown 8vo, 5*s.*

XVI. **The Life and Growth of Language.** By Professor William Dwight Whitney. Fourth Edition. Crown 8vo, 5*s.*

XVII. **Money and the Mechanism of Exchange.** By W. Stanley Jevons, M.A., F.R.S. Sixth Edition. Crown 8vo, 5*s.*

XVIII. **The Nature of Light.** With a General Account of Physical Optics. By Dr. Eugene Lommel. With 188 Illustrations and a Table of Spectra in Chromo-lithography. Third Edition. Crown 8vo, 5*s.*

XIX. **Animal Parasites and Messmates.** By Monsieur Van Beneden. With 83 Illustrations. Third Edition. Crown 8vo, 5*s.*

XX. **Fermentation.** By Professor Schützenberger. With 28 Illus-trations. Fourth Edition. Crown 8vo, 5*s.*

XXI. **The Five Senses of Man.** By Professor Bernstein. With 91 Illustrations. Fourth Edition. Crown 8vo, 5*s.*

XXII. **The Theory of Sound in its Relation to Music.** By Pro-fessor Pietro Blaserna. With numerous Illustrations. Third Edition. Crown 8vo, 5*s.*

XXIII. **Studies in Spectrum Analysis.** By J. Norman Lockyer, F.R.S. With six photographic Illustrations of Spectra, and numerous engravings on Wood. Third Edition. Crown 8vo, 6*s.* 6*d.*

XXIV. **A History of the Growth of the Steam Engine.** By Professor R. H. Thurston. With numerous Illustrations. Third Edition. Crown 8vo, 6*s.* 6*d.*

XXV. **Education as a Science.** By Alexander Bain, LL.D. Fourth Edition. Crown 8vo, 5*s.*

XXVI. **The Human Species.** By Professor A. de Quatrefages. Third Edition. Crown 8vo, 5*s*.

XXVII. **Modern Chromatics.** With Applications to Art and Industry. By Ogden N. Rood. With 130 original Illustrations. Second Edition. Crown 8vo, 5*s*.

XXVIII. **The Crayfish :** an Introduction to the Study of Zoology. By Professor T. H. Huxley. With 82 Illustrations. Third Edition. Crown 8vo, 5*s*.

XXIX. **The Brain as an Organ of Mind.** By H. Charlton Bastian, M.D. With numerous Illustrations. Third Edition. Crown 8vo, 5*s*.

XXX. **The Atomic Theory.** By Prof. Wurtz. Translated by G. Cleminshaw, F.C.S. Third Edition. Crown 8vo, 5*s*.

XXXI. **The Natural Conditions of Existence as they affect Animal Life.** By Karl Semper. With 2 Maps and 106 Woodcuts. Third Edition. Crown 8vo, 5*s*.

XXXII. **General Physiology of Muscles and Nerves.** By Prof. J. Rosenthal. Third Edition. With Illustrations. Crown 8vo, 5*s*.

XXXIII. **Sight :** an Exposition of the Principles of Monocular and Binocular Vision. By Joseph le Conte, LL.D. Second Edition. With 132 Illustrations. Crown 8vo, 5*s*.

XXXIV. **Illusions :** a Psychological Study. By James Sully. Second Edition. Crown 8vo, 5*s*.

XXXV. **Volcanoes : what they are and what they teach.** By Professor J. W. Judd, F.R.S. With 92 Illustrations on Wood. Second Edition. Crown 8vo, 5*s*.

XXXVI. **Suicide :** an Essay in Comparative Moral Statistics. By Prof. E. Morselli. Second Edition. With Diagrams. Crown 8vo, 5*s*.

XXXVII. **The Brain and its Functions.** By J. Luys. With Illustrations. Second Edition. Crown 8vo, 5*s*.

XXXVIII. **Myth and Science :** an Essay. By Tito Vignoli. Second Edition. Crown 8vo, 5*s*.

XXXIX. **The Sun.** By Professor Young. With Illustrations. Second Edition. Crown 8vo, 5*s*.

XL. **Ants, Bees, and Wasps :** a Record of Observations on the Habits of the Social Hymenoptera. By Sir John Lubbock, Bart., M.P. With 5 Chromo-lithographic Illustrations. Sixth Edition. Crown 8vo, 5*s*.

XLI. **Animal Intelligence.** By G. J. Romanes, LL.D., F.R.S. Third Edition. Crown 8vo, 5*s*.

XLII. **The Concepts and Theories of Modern Physics.** By J. B. Stallo. Second Edition. Crown 8vo, 5*s.*

XLIII. **Diseases of the Memory**; An Essay in the Positive Psychology. By Prof. Th. Ribot. Second Edition. Crown 8vo, 5*s.*

XLIV. **Man before Metals.** By N. Joly, with 148 Illustrations. Third Edition. Crown 8vo, 5*s.*

XLV. **The Science of Politics.** By Prof. Sheldon Amos. Second Edition. Crown 8vo, 5*s.*

XLVI. **Elementary Meteorology.** By Robert H. Scott. Second Edition. With Numerous Illustrations. Crown 8vo, 5*s.*

XLVII. **The Organs of Speech and their Application in the Formation of Articulate Sounds.** By Georg Hermann Von Meyer. With 47 Woodcuts. Crown 8vo, 5*s.*

XLVIII. **Fallacies.** A View of Logic from the Practical Side. By Alfred Sidgwick. Crown 8vo, 5*s.*

MILITARY WORKS.

BARRINGTON, Capt. J. T.—**England on the Defensive**; or, the Problem of Invasion Critically Examined. Large crown 8vo, with Map, 7*s. 6d.*

BRACKENBURY, Col. C. B., R.A.—**Military Handbooks for Regimental Officers.**

    I. **Military Sketching and Reconnaissance.** By Col. F. J. Hutchison and Major H. G. MacGregor. Fourth Edition. With 15 Plates. Small crown 8vo, 4*s.*

    II. **The Elements of Modern Tactics Practically applied to English Formations.** By Lieut.-Col. Wilkinson Shaw. Fourth Edition. With 25 Plates and Maps. Small crown 8vo, 9*s.*

    III. **Field Artillery.** Its Equipment, Organization and Tactics. By Major Sisson C. Pratt, R.A. With 12 Plates. Second Edition. Small crown 8vo, 6*s.*

    IV. **The Elements of Military Administration.** First Part: Permanent System of Administration. By Major J. W. Buxton. Small crown 8vo. 7*s. 6d.*

    V. **Military Law:** Its Procedure and Practice. By Major Sisson C. Pratt, R.A. Second Edition. Small crown 8vo, 4*s. 6d.*

BROOKE, Major, C. K.—**A System of Field Training.** Small crown 8vo, cloth limp, 2*s.*

CLERY, C., Lieut.-Col.—**Minor Tactics.** With 26 Maps and Plans. Sixth and Cheaper Edition, Revised. Crown 8vo, 9*s.*

COLVILE, Lieut.-Col. C. F.—**Military Tribunals.** Sewed, 2*s.* 6*d.*

CRAUFURD, Lieut. H.J.—**Suggestions for the Military Training of a Company of Infantry.** Crown 8vo, 1*s.* 6*d.*

HARRISON, Lieut.-Col. R.—**The Officer's Memorandum Book for Peace and War.** Third Edition. Oblong 32mo, roan, with pencil, 3*s.* 6*d.*

Notes on Cavalry Tactics, Organisation, etc. By a Cavalry Officer. With Diagrams. Demy 8vo, 12*s.*

PARR, Capt. H. Hallam, C.M.G.—**The Dress, Horses, and Equipment of Infantry and Staff Officers.** Crown 8vo, 1*s.*

SCHAW, Col. H.—**The Defence and Attack of Positions and Localities.** Second Edition, Revised and Corrected. Crown 8vo, 3*s.* 6*d.*

SHADWELL, Maj.-Gen., C.B.—**Mountain Warfare.** Illustrated by the Campaign of 1799 in Switzerland. Being a Translation of the Swiss Narrative compiled from the Works of the Archduke Charles, Jomini, and others. Also of Notes by General H. Dufour on the Campaign of the Valtelline in 1635. With Appendix, Maps, and Introductory Remarks. Demy 8vo, 16*s.*

WILKINSON, H. Spenser, Capt. 20th Lancashire R.V.—**Citizen Soldiers.** Essays towards the Improvement of the Volunteer Force. Crown 8vo, 2*s.* 6*d.*

POETRY.

ADAM OF ST. VICTOR.—**The Liturgical Poetry of Adam of St. Victor.** From the text of GAUTIER. With Translations into English in the Original Metres, and Short Explanatory Notes, by DIGBY S. WRANGHAM, M.A. 3 vols. Crown 8vo, printed on hand-made paper, boards, 21*s.*

AUCHMUTY, A. C.—**Poems of English Heroism :** From Brunanburh to Lucknow; from Athelstan to Albert. Small crown 8vo, 1*s.* 6*d.*

AVIA.—**The Odyssey of Homer.** Done into English Verse by. Fcap. 4to, 15*s.*

BANKS, Mrs. G. L.—**Ripples and Breakers :** Poems. Square 8vo, 5*s.*

BARING, T. C., M.A., M.P.—**The Scheme of Epicurus.** A Rendering into English Verse of the Unfinished Poem of Lucretius, entitled "De Rerum Naturâ" ("The Nature of Things"). Fcap. 4to.

BARNES, *William.*—Poems of Rural Life, in the Dorset Dialect. New Edition, complete in one vol. Crown 8vo, 8s. 6d.

BAYNES, *Rev. Canon H. R.*—Home Songs for Quiet Hours. Fourth and Cheaper Edition. Fcap. 8vo, cloth, 2s. 6d.
*** This may also be had handsomely bound in morocco with gilt edges.

BENDALL, *Gerard.*—Musa Silvestris. 16mo, 1s. 6d.

BEVINGTON, *L. S.*—Key Notes. Small crown 8vo, 5s.

BILLSON, *C. J.*—The Acharnians of Aristophanes. Crown 8vo, 3s. 6d.

BLUNT, *Wilfrid Scawen.* — The Wind and the Whirlwind. Demy 8vo, 1s. 6d.

BOWEN, *H. C., M.A.*—Simple English Poems. English Literature for Junior Classes. In Four Parts. Parts I., II., and III., 6d. each, and Part IV., 1s. Complete, 3s.

BRASHER, *Alfred.*—Sophia ; or, the Viceroy of Valencia. A Comedy in Five Acts, founded on a Story in Scarron. Small crown 8vo, 2s. 6d.

BRYANT, *W. C.*—Poems. Cheap Edition, with Frontispiece. Small crown 8vo, 3s. 6d.

BYRNNE, *E. Fairfax.*—Milicent : a Poem. Small crown 8vo, 6s.

CAILLARD, *Emma Marie.*—Charlotte Corday, and other Poems. Small crown 8vo, 3s. 6d.

Calderon's Dramas : the Wonder-Working Magician — Life is a Dream—the Purgatory of St. Patrick. Translated by DENIS FLORENCE MACCARTHY. Post 8vo, 10s.

Camoens Lusiads. — Portuguese Text, with Translation by J. J. AUBERTIN. Second Edition. 2 vols. Crown 8vo, 12s.

CAMPBELL, *Lewis.*—Sophocles. The Seven Plays in English Verse. Crown 8vo, 7s. 6d.

Castilian Brothers (The), Chateaubriant, Waldemar : Three Tragedies ; and The Rose of Sicily : a Drama. By the Author of " Ginevra," etc. Crown 8vo, 6s.

Chronicles of Christopher Columbus. A Poem in 12 Cantos. By M. D. C. Crown 8vo, 7s. 6d.

CLARKE, *Mary Cowden.*—Honey from the Weed. Verses. Crown 8vo, 7s.

Cosmo de Medici ; The False One ; Agramont and Beaumont : Three Tragedies ; and The Deformed : a Dramatic Sketch. By the Author of " Ginevra," etc., etc. Crown 8vo, 5s.

COXHEAD, *Ethel.*—Birds and Babies. Imp. 16mo. With 33 Illustrations. Gilt, 2*s.* 6*d.*

David Rizzio, Bothwell, and the Witch Lady: Three Tragedies. By the author of " Ginevra," etc. Crown 8vo, 6*s.*

DAVIE, *G. S., M.D.*—The Garden of Fragrance. Being a complete translation of the Bostán of Sádi from the original Persian into English Verse. Crown 8vo, 7*s.* 6*d.*

DAVIES, *T. Hart.*—Catullus. Translated into English Verse. Crown 8vo, 6*s.*

DENNIS, *J.*—English Sonnets. Collected and Arranged by. Small crown 8vo, 2*s.* 6*d.*

DE VERE, *Aubrey.*—Poetical Works.

 I. THE SEARCH AFTER PROSERPINE, etc. 6*s.*
 II. THE LEGENDS OF ST. PATRICK, etc. 6*s.*
 III. ALEXANDER THE GREAT, etc. 6*s.*

 The Foray of Queen Meave, and other Legends of Ireland's Heroic Age. Small crown 8vo, 5*s.*

 Legends of the Saxon Saints. Small crown 8vo, 6*s.*

DILLON, *Arthur.*—River Songs and other Poems. With 13 autotype Illustrations from designs by Margery May. Fcap. 4to, cloth extra, gilt leaves, 10*s.* 6*d.*

DOBELL, *Mrs. Horace.*—Ethelstone, Eveline, and other Poems. Crown 8vo, 6*s.*

DOBSON, *Austin.*—Old World Idylls and other Poems. Third Edition. 18mo, cloth extra, gilt tops, 6*s.*

DOMET, *Alfred.*—Ranolf and Amohia. A Dream of Two Lives. New Edition, Revised. 2 vols. Crown 8vo, 12*s.*

Dorothy: a Country Story in Elegiac Verse. With Preface. Demy 8vo, 5*s.*

DOWDEN, *Edward, LL.D.*—Shakspere's Sonnets. With Introduction and Notes. Large post 8vo, 7*s.* 6*d.*

DUTT, *Toru.*—A Sheaf Gleaned in French Fields. New Edition. Demy 8vo, 10*s.* 6*d.*

EDMONDS, *E. W.*—Hesperas. Rhythm and Rhyme. Crown 8vo, 4*s.*

ELDRYTH, *Maud.*—Margaret, and other Poems. Small crown 8vo, 3*s.* 6*d.*

 All Soul's Eve, " No God," and other Poems. Fcap. 8vo, 3*s.* 6*d.*

ELLIOTT, *Ebenezer, The Corn Law Rhymer.*—Poems. Edited by his son, the Rev. EDWIN ELLIOTT, of St. John's, Antigua. 2 vols. Crown 8vo, 18*s.*

English Odes. Selected, with a Critical Introduction by EDMUND W. GOSSE, and a miniature frontispiece by Hamo Thornycroft, A.R.A. Elzevir 8vo, limp parchment antique, or cloth, 6*s.* ; vellum, 7*s.* 6*d.*

English Verse. Edited by W. J. LINTON and R. H. STODDARD.
5 vols. Crown 8vo, cloth, 5*s.* each.
I. CHAUCER TO BURNS.
II. TRANSLATIONS.
III. LYRICS OF THE NINETEENTH CENTURY.
IV. DRAMATIC SCENES AND CHARACTERS.
V. BALLADS AND ROMANCES.

EVANS, Anne.—**Poems and Music.** With Memorial Preface by
ANN THACKERAY RITCHIE. Large crown 8vo, 7*s.*

GOSSE, Edmund W.—**New Poems.** Crown 8vo, 7*s.* 6*d.*

GRAHAM, William. **Two Fancies,** and other Poems. Crown 8vo, 5*s.*

GRINDROD, Charles. **Plays from English History.** Crown
8vo, 7*s.* 6*d.*

The Stranger's Story, and his Poem, The Lament of Love: An
Episode of the Malvern Hills. Small crown 8vo, 2*s.* 6*d.*

GURNEY, Rev. Alfred.—**The Vision of the Eucharist,** and other
Poems. Crown 8vo, 5*s.*

HELLON, H. G.—**Daphnis:** a Pastoral Poem. Small crown 8vo,
3*s.* 6*d.*

HENRY, Daniel, Junr.—**Under a Fool's Cap.** Songs. Crown 8vo,
cloth, bevelled boards, 5*s.*

Herman Waldgrave: a Life's Drama. By the Author of "Ginevra,"
etc. Crown 8vo, 6*s.*

HICKEY, E. H.—**A Sculptor,** and other Poems. Small crown
8vo, 5*s.*

HONEYWOOD, Patty.—**Poems.** Dedicated (by permission) to Lord
Wolseley, G.C.B., etc. Small crown 8vo, 2*s.* 6*d.*

INGHAM, Sarson, C. J.—**Cædmon's Vision,** and other Poems.
Small crown 8vo, 5*s.*

JENKINS, Rev. Canon.—**Alfonso Petrucci,** Cardinal and Con-
spirator: an Historical Tragedy in Five Acts. Small crown 8vo,
3*s.* 6*d.*

JOHNSON, Ernle S. W.—**Ilaria,** and other Poems. Small crown 8vo,
3*s.* 6*d.*

KEATS, John.—**Poetical Works.** Edited by W. T. ARNOLD. Large
crown 8vo, choicely printed on hand-made paper, with Portrait
in *eau-forte.* Parchment, 12*s.*; vellum, 15*s.*

KING, Edward.—**Echoes from the Orient.** With Miscellaneous
Poems. Small crown 8vo, 3*s.* 6*d.*

KING, Mrs. Hamilton.—**The Disciples.** Sixth Edition, with Portrait
and Notes. Crown 8vo, 5*s.*

A Book of Dreams. Crown 8vo, 3*s.* 6*d.*

KNOX, The Hon. Mrs. O. N.—**Four Pictures from a Life,** and
other Poems. Small crown 8vo, 3*s.* 6*d.*

LANG, A.—XXXII Ballades in Blue China. Elzevir 8vo, parchment, 5*s*.

LAWSON, Right Hon. Mr. Justice.—Hymni Usitati Latine Redditi : with other Verses. Small 8vo, parchment, 5*s*.

Lessings Nathan the Wise. Translated by EUSTACE K. CORBETT. Crown 8vo, 6*s*.

Life Thoughts. Small crown 8vo, 2*s*. 6*d*.

Living English Poets MDCCCLXXXII. With Frontispiece by Walter Crane. Second Edition. Large crown 8vo. Printed on hand-made paper. Parchment, 12*s*. ; vellum, 15*s*.

LOCKER, F.—London Lyrics. A New and Cheaper Edition. Small crown 8vo, 2*s*. 6*d*.

Love in Idleness. A Volume of Poems. With an etching by W. B. Scott. Small crown 8vo, 5*s*.

Love Sonnets of Proteus. With Frontispiece by the Author. Elzevir 8vo, 5*s*.

LUMSDEN, Lieut.-Col. H. W.—Beowulf : an Old English Poem. Translated into Modern Rhymes. Second and Revised Edition. Small crown 8vo, 5*s*.

Lyre and Star. Poems by the Author of " Ginevra," etc. Crown 8vo, 5*s*.

MAGNUSSON, Eirikr, M.A., and PALMER, E. H., M.A.—Johan Ludvig Runeberg's Lyrical Songs, Idylls, and Epigrams. Fcap. 8vo, 5*s*.

M.D.C.—Chronicles of Christopher Columbus. A Poem in Twelve Cantos. Crown 8vo, 7*s*. 6*d*.

MEREDITH, Owen [The Earl of Lytton].—Lucile. New Edition. With 32 Illustrations. 16mo, 3*s*. 6*d*. Cloth extra, gilt edges, 4*s*. 6*d*.

MORRIS, Lewis.—Poetical Works of. New and Cheaper Editions, with Portrait. Complete in 3 vols., 5*s*. each.

> Vol. I. contains " Songs of Two Worlds." Ninth Edition. Vol. II. contains " The Epic of Hades." Seventeenth Edition. Vol. III. contains " Gwen " and " The Ode of Life." Fifth Edition.

> The Epic of Hades. With 16 Autotype Illustrations, after the Drawings of the late George R. Chapman. 4to, cloth extra, gilt leaves, 21*s*.

> The Epic of Hades. Presentation Edition. 4to, cloth extra, gilt leaves, 10*s*. 6*d*.

> Songs Unsung. Fourth Edition. Fcap. 8vo, 6*s*.

MORSHEAD, E. D. A. — The House of Atreus. Being the Agamemnon, Libation-Bearers, and Furies of Æschylus. Translated into English Verse. Crown 8vo, 7*s*.

> The Suppliant Maidens of Æschylus. Crown 8vo, 3*s*. 6*d*.

NADEN, Constance W.—Songs and Sonnets of Spring Time. Small crown 8vo, 5*s.*

NEWELL, E. J.—The Sorrows of Simona and Lyrical Verses. Small crown 8vo, 3*s. 6d.*

NOEL, The Hon. Roden.—A Little Child's Monument. Third Edition. Small crown 8vo, 3*s. 6d.*

The Red Flag, and other Poems. New Edition. Small crown 8vo, 6*s.*

O'HAGAN, John.—The Song of Roland. Translated into English Verse. New and Cheaper Edition. Crown 8vo, 5*s.*

PFEIFFER, Emily.—The Rhyme of the Lady of the Lock, and How it Grew. Small crown 8vo, 3*s. 6d.*

Gerard's Monument, and other Poems. Second Edition. Crown 8vo, 6*s.*

Under the Aspens; Lyrical and Dramatic. With Portrait. Crown 8vo, 6*s.*

PIATT, J. J.—Idyls and Lyrics of the Ohio Valley. Crown 8vo, 5*s.*

POE, Edgar Allan.—Poems. With an Essay on his Poetry by ANDREW LANG, and a Frontispiece by Linley Sambourne. Parchment Library Edition.—Parchment or cloth, 6*s.* ; vellum, 7*s. 6d.*

RAFFALOVICH, Mark André. — Cyril and Lionel, and other Poems. A volume of Sentimental Studies. Small crown 8vo, 3*s. 6d.*

Rare Poems of the 16th and 17th Centuries. Edited W. J. LINTON. Crown 8vo, 5*s.*

RHOADES, James.—The Georgics of Virgil. Translated into English Verse. Small crown 8vo, 5*s.*

ROBINSON, A. Mary F.—A Handful of Honeysuckle. Fcap. 8vo, 3*s. 6d.*

The Crowned Hippolytus. Translated from Euripides. With New Poems. Small crown 8vo, 5*s.*

Schiller's Mary Stuart. German Text, with English Translation on opposite page by LEEDHAM WHITE. Crown 8vo, 6*s.*

SCOTT, George F. E.—Theodora and other Poems. Small crown 8vo, 3*s. 6d.*

SEAL, W. H.—Ione, and other Poems. Crown 8vo, gilt tops, 5*s.*

SELKIRK, J. B.—Poems. Crown 8vo, 7*s. 6d.*

Shakspere's Sonnets. Edited by EDWARD DOWDEN. With a Frontispiece etched by Leopold Lowenstam, after the Death Mask. Parchment Library Edition.—Parchment or cloth, 6*s.* ; vellum, 7*s. 6d.*

Shakspere's Works. Complete in 12 Volumes. Parchment Library Edition.—Parchment or cloth, 6s. each; vellum, 7s. 6d. each.

SHAW, W. F., M.A.—**Juvenal, Persius, Martial, and Catullus.** An Experiment in Translation. Crown 8vo, 5s.

SHELLEY, Percy Bysshe.—**Poems Selected from.** Dedicated to Lady Shelley. With Preface by RICHARD GARNETT. Parchment Library Edition.—Parchment or cloth, 6s.; vellum, 7s. 6d.

Six Ballads about King Arthur. Crown 8vo, cloth extra, gilt edges, 3s. 6d.

SKINNER, H. J.—**The Lily of the Lyn,** and other Poems. Small crown 8vo, 3s. 6d.

SLADEN, Douglas B.—**Frithjof and Ingebjorg,** and other Poems. Small crown 8vo, 5s.

SMITH, J. W. Gilbart.—**The Loves of Vandyck.** A Tale of Genoa. Small crown 8vo, 2s. 6d.

Sophocles: The Seven Plays in English Verse. Translated by LEWIS CAMPBELL. Crown 8vo, 7s. 6d.

SPICER, Henry.—**Haska:** a Drama in Three Acts (as represented at the Theatre Royal, Drury Lane, March 10th, 1877). Third Edition. Crown 8vo, 3s. 6d.

TAYLOR, Sir H.—**Works.** Complete in Five Volumes. Crown 8vo, 30s.

Philip Van Artevelde. Fcap. 8vo, 3s. 6d.

The Virgin Widow, etc. Fcap. 8vo, 3s. 6d.

The Statesman. Fcap. 8vo, 3s. 6d.

TAYLOR, Augustus.—**Poems.** Fcap. 8vo, 5s.

Tennyson Birthday Book, The. Edited by EMILY SHAKESPEAR. 32mo, limp, 2s.; cloth extra, 3s.

*** A superior Edition, printed in red and black, on antique paper, specially prepared. Small crown 8vo, extra, gilt leaves, 5s.; and in various calf and morocco bindings.

THORNTON, L. M.—**The Son of Shelomith.** Small crown 8vo, 3s. 6d.

TODHUNTER, Dr. J.—**Laurella,** and other Poems. Crown 8vo, 6s. 6d.

Forest Songs. Small crown 8vo, 3s. 6d.

The True Tragedy of Rienzi: a Drama. 3s. 6d.

Alcestis: a Dramatic Poem. Extra fcap. 8vo, 5s.

WALTERS, Sophia Lydia.—**A Dreamer's Sketch Book.** With 21 Illustrations by Percival Skelton, R. P. Leitch, W. H. J. Boot, and T. R. Pritchett. Engraved by J. D. Cooper. Fcap. 4to, 12s. 6d.

WATTS, Alaric Alfred and Anna Mary Howitt.—**Aurora.** A Medley of Verse. Fcap. 8vo, bevelled boards, 5s.

WEBSTER, Augusta.—In a Day : a Drama. Small crown 8vo, 2*s.* 6*d.*
>   Disguises : a Drama. Small crown 8vo, 5*s.*

Wet Days. By a Farmer. Small crown 8vo, 6*s.*

WILLIAMS, J.—A Story of Three Years, and other Poems. Small crown 8vo, 3*s.* 6*d.*

Wordsworth Birthday Book, The. Edited by ADELAIDE and VIOLET WORDSWORTH. 32mo, limp cloth, 1*s.* 6*d.* ; cloth extra, 2*s.*

YOUNGS, Ella Sharpe.—Paphus, and other Poems. Small crown 8vo, 3*s.* 6*d.*

WORKS OF FICTION IN ONE VOLUME.

BANKS, Mrs. G. L.—God's Providence House. New Edition. Crown 8vo, 3*s.* 6*d.*

INGELOW, Jean.—Off the Skelligs : a Novel. With Frontispiece. Second Edition. Crown 8vo, 6*s.*

MACDONALD, G.—Castle Warlock. A Novel. New and Cheaper Edition. Crown 8vo, 6*s.*

>   Malcolm. With Portrait of the Author engraved on Steel. Sixth Edition. Crown 8vo, 6*s.*

>   The Marquis of Lossie. Fifth Edition. With Frontispiece. Crown 8vo, 6*s.*

>   St. George and St. Michael. Fourth Edition. With Frontispiece. Crown 8vo, 6*s.*

PALGRAVE, W. Gifford.—Hermann Agha : an Eastern Narrative. Third Edition. Crown 8vo, 6*s.*

SHAW, Flora L.—Castle Blair ; a Story of Youthful Days. New and Cheaper Edition. Crown 8vo, 3*s.* 6*d.*

STRETTON, Hesba.—Through a Needle's Eye : a Story. New and Cheaper Edition, with Frontispiece. Crown 8vo, 6*s.*

TAYLOR, Col. Meadows, C.S.I., M.R.I.A.—Seeta : a Novel. New and Cheaper Edition. With Frontispiece. Crown 8vo, 6*s.*

>   Tippoo Sultaun : a Tale of the Mysore War. New Edition, with Frontispiece. Crown 8vo, 6*s.*

>   Ralph Darnell. New and Cheaper Edition. With Frontispiece. Crown 8vo, 6*s.*

>   A Noble Queen. New and Cheaper Edition. With Frontispiece. Crown 8vo, 6*s.*

>   The Confessions of a Thug. Crown 8vo, 6*s.*

>   Tara : a Mahratta Tale. Crown 8vo, 6*s.*

Within Sound of the Sea. New and Cheaper Edition, with Frontispiece. Crown 8vo, 6*s.*

BOOKS FOR THE YOUNG.

Brave Men's Footsteps. A Book of Example and Anecdote for Young People. By the Editor of "Men who have Risen." With 4 Illustrations by C. Doyle. Eighth Edition. Crown 8vo, 3s. 6d.

COXHEAD, Ethel.—**Birds and Babies.** Imp. 16mo. With 33 Illustrations. Cloth gilt, 2s. 6d.

DAVIES, G. Christopher.—**Rambles and Adventures of our School Field Club.** With 4 Illustrations. New and Cheaper Edition. Crown 8vo, 3s. 6d.

EDMONDS, Herbert.—**Well Spent Lives ;** a Series of Modern Biographies. New and Cheaper Edition. Crown 8vo, 3s. 6d.

EVANS, Mark.—**The Story of our Father's Love,** told to Children. Sixth and Cheaper Edition of Theology for Children. With 4 Illustrations. Fcap. 8vo, 1s. 6d.

JOHNSON, Virginia W.—**The Catskill Fairies.** Illustrated by Alfred Fredericks. 5s.

MAC KENNA, S. J.—**Plucky Fellows.** A Book for Boys. With 6 Illustrations. Fifth Edition. Crown 8vo, 3s. 6d.

REANEY, Mrs. G. S.—**Waking and Working ;** or, From Girlhood to Womanhood. New and Cheaper Edition. With a Frontispiece. Crown 8vo, 3s. 6d.

Blessing and Blessed : a Sketch of Girl Life. New and Cheaper Edition. Crown 8vo, 3s. 6d.

Rose Gurney's Discovery. A Book for Girls. Dedicated to their Mothers. Crown 8vo, 3s. 6d.

English Girls : Their Place and Power. With Preface by the Rev. R. W. Dale. Fourth Edition. Fcap. 8vo, 2s. 6d.

Just Anyone, and other Stories. Three Illustrations. Royal 16mo, 1s. 6d.

Sunbeam Willie, and other Stories. Three Illustrations. Royal 16mo, 1s. 6d.

Sunshine Jenny, and other Stories. Three Illustrations. Royal 16mo, 1s. 6d.

STOCKTON, Frank R.—**A Jolly Fellowship.** With 20 Illustrations. Crown 8vo, 5s.

STORR, Francis, and TURNER, Hawes.—**Canterbury Chimes ;** or, Chaucer Tales re-told to Children. With 6 Illustrations from the Ellesmere MS. Third Edition. Fcap. 8vo, 3s. 6d.

STRETTON, Hesba.—**David Lloyd's Last Will.** With 4 Illustrations. New Edition. Royal 16mo, 2s. 6d.

Tales from Ariosto Re-told for Children. By a Lady. With 3 Illustrations. Crown 8vo, 4s. 6d.

WHITAKER, Florence.—**Christy's Inheritance.** A London Story. Illustrated. Royal 16mo, 1s. 6d.

www.ingramcontent.com/pod-product-compliance
Lightning Source LLC
Chambersburg PA
CBHW031147120726
47905CB00006B/1844